Dark Prospects 2

Into the Abyss

Author: Xu Lei
Translator: Gaines Post
Editor: Kim Fout, Verbena C.W., Judy Ye

CONTENTS

1 THE VIEW FROM THE PLANE

No one who lived through the bitter winter of 1962 could ever forget those stormbound months. They were the postscript to the three years of natural disasters that had just wracked the nation. But now the so-called Great Leap Forward was quietly concluding; the border war between China and India was dying down and many believed that the country's chaotic early stages were behind it. They hoped calmer days lay ahead. While everyone's attention was captured by these great events, my comrades and I were deep beneath China's northern borderlands, facing a critical decision.

We—Wang Sichuan, Ma Zaihai and me, Wu—were at the end of an underground river, 3,600 feet underground, in a base constructed more than 20 years ago by the Japanese. Their sole reason for building it: the limitless abyss into which the river fell. They wanted to fly a plane into the void we had found, and they had done so. Now we had in our hands the secret recording of that flight, but once we delivered it to our superiors our involvement in the affair would be over. We could kiss goodbye any hope of ever discovering what the Japanese had seen. It was at least 10 hours of hard trek to the nearest sunlight. On the other hand, there was a film projector only a short distance behind us on the lower level of the dam we had been crawling around beneath for days. If we headed there now, our journey would only be delayed a couple of hours and at long last we would find out what the Japanese had been after. We might even learn what secrets were hidden inside the abyss.

To stay or to go?

For us, the children of rural peasants who had never before been given an opportunity like this – and likely never would again – the decision was easy.

Thinking back on it now, I realize what a big risk we were taking. There was an enemy spy lurking down there, lying in wait. The longer we lingered, the more likely he would reappear and cause us trouble. Unfortunately, at the time we didn't give the matter much thought. Who could have known that this single oversight would be the turning point of the whole affair?

***

Once the decision to stay was made, we headed back towards the dam, keeping one eye over our shoulders the whole time. We were soon back inside. We knew the way by now and before long we'd reached the projection room. We inspected the place much more thoroughly than we had the last time. The room was considerably larger than I had thought. It seemed small only because it was crammed with long tables and chairs. A thick layer of dust coated everything. I worried the projector might no longer work.

The projector was about the size of a box of ammunition. Two revolving wheels, used for spooling the film, were attached to its side. Fearing a sneak attack from the spy who had followed us, Wang Sichuan hefted an iron club and went to guard the door. I began nervously looking the projector over. Having never operated one before, I feared one wrong move and I might break it. Really, all I needed to do was thread the film into the dual wheels. Perhaps it was nerves, perhaps something else, but my hands were slick with sweat. I fiddled with the projector for some time and made not the slightest bit of progress. At last Ma Zaihai came over to help. As an engineering soldier, he knew his way around all sorts of machines. After taking one look at it, he loaded the film and started the thing up.

A flickering black pattern appeared on the dust-covered cloth screen before us. Aerial recording technology was still very basic in the 1940s and the image was too shaky to be made out. Ma Zaihai then cranked the lever attached to the side of the projector. I leaned forward in anticipation as the image on the screen began to move.

Why had the Japanese built this dam? What had they seen in the abyss? The answers to these questions were only moments away. The image changed. Black spots now covered the white screen. This was merely waste film, deliberately unused, much as the beginning of a roll of photographic film is always black. The black spots started to move, but after about a minute the image remained nearly unchanged. I began to feel nervous. Why didn't Ma Zaihai go faster? Or was the projector simply broken? Just as I was starting to fear the worst, a line of text suddenly flashed across the screen. Ma Zaihai stopped the film and rewound until the text was centered.

The words were Japanese, but scribbled so hastily that they barely qualified as such. Although I couldn't be sure what the message was saying, I could tell it was a warning of the sternest kind.

2 THE SECRET FOOTAGE

At the bottom of the screen, scrawled in black ink, were the words: "Extra-Normal Event 07—Classified Fortification Engineering Corps."

Seeing the words "Engineering Corps" gave me a queer feeling, as if our own military had been behind this but, of course, Japanese and Chinese writing shared many characters. In Chinese, we generally referred to ourselves as the "Construction Corps" or the "Inner Mongolian Engineering Corps." "Fortification Engineering Corps" sounded extremely odd. This title screen was obviously handwritten. It was as if it had been hastily jotted down right after filming was completed. I suspected it said something like, "This film is classified. Only those with the very highest security clearance are permitted to watch," though it probably said something more specific than that. Otherwise, why would they have felt the need to write it with such urgency? As I read the word "classified" the breath caught in my throat. I thought of the oath we had sworn before descending into the cave. The text appeared onscreen for only a few seconds, just long enough to warn away anyone lacking the necessary credentials. I signaled to Ma Zaihai.

He nodded and began once more cranking the lever. An image appeared. We held our breaths.

The film totaled no more than an hour and was divided into a number of scenes. It could be roughly split into two. The first 10 minutes consisted of several loosely connected scenes leading to the second portion, the flight into the abyss. The quality of the footage was poor. Prior to the Liberation, most aerial reconnaissance was conducted using photography rather than film. The footage obtained from airborne film recordings was extremely shaky—just think of the black-and-white clip of the destruction of Nagasaki and you'll know what I mean. Luckily the film reel was still in good enough condition to tell what was going on. The biggest strike against it was that it had no sound. Perhaps it had always been silent or perhaps the projection room simply lacked a speaker system. Quiet, disconnected, jumpy scenes skittered along, one to the next. In one sense you could say it contained little new information, but in another it was absolutely mind-blowing. The Japanese had seemingly made no attempt to capture everything that happened, but rather focused on recording a few pieces of pertinent information. Almost all of the scenes were very short, and though some seemed superfluous, they each contained particular telling details. When it ended, none of us moved. The screen was blank and the projector remained on, but we did nothing about either. We just sat there in silence, our hearts seized by an indescribable fear.

The movie opened with a black and white airfield filmed from ground level. It was daytime, the sky clear and bright. We'd spent the last several days in the recesses of a pitch-black river cave. When we raised our heads we saw only rugged cliff rock. The moment I glimpsed this pale gray sky on the screen, I was filled with a longing for the surface.

Several planes were parked on the airfield. Pilots and various other Jap devils hurried from all directions, each of them hefting supplies for transport. Suddenly the camera turned to focus on a man wearing an officer's uniform, but before I could get a good look at him, the film jumped to the next scene. Two Japanese pilots now stood talking beneath the wing of a plane. They patted the landing gear as they spoke, appearing to roar with laughter. I could only imagine what these scenes were supposed to mean. A moment later, the image changed once more. Now the camera was being aimed through the side window of a plane, filming the ground below. I saw villages, forests, rivers. The plane was obviously flying through the sky—not down here, above the underground river. This had to be in the early stages of their journey. The camera turned to the plane's interior. It was a cargo plane. Inside were row upon row of squatting Jap soldiers and neatly stacked supplies. The devils were all silent, their heads lowered, rocking with the movement of the plane. They looked exhausted, much as we had when we'd bounced through the forests of Inner Mongolia in the back of that truck.

These scenes might sound rather insignificant, but they conveyed two important pieces of information. First, I could tell the situation must have been extremely urgent, because during the War of Resistance troops were transported by plane in only the most time-pressed of operations. And second, from the fact that the cameraman had filmed these several rather aimless scenes, I suspected he hadn't yet been informed of the true nature of his mission; otherwise I doubt he would have felt so carefree.

A moment later they were deep in the forest. Wooden barracks appeared amid the trees. They'd already rotted through by the time I'd gotten to them, but in the film they appeared brand new. The Japanese officer appeared once more. The black and white film made his skin look pale white as he gazed over the bustling camp, his face emotionless. This time the camera stopped long enough for me to get a good look at him. I felt a kind of nervous curiosity as I studied his features. Japanese soldiers were always depicted as buffoons in our movies. Onstage only the most clownish actors were chosen to play them. But these soldiers were the real thing and there was nothing funny about them. I looked closer. A strange energy seemed concealed beneath his face. No fictional villain could ever have been this frightening. Although I was alive during only the final decade or so of the War of Resistance, I nonetheless heard countless stories about the horrors committed by the Japanese. The region where I grew up saw no combat, so I never actually encountered one in real life, but in my imagination they were the most ferocious of monsters. As I grew older, my concept of the Japanese was formed entirely from our movies, the stories from my elders, and the performances put on by the propaganda teams. Only now, in this decades-old dam beneath the earth, did I learn what they really looked like. It was not what I expected. They were neither ugly nor monstrous. They looked just like us, but for some reason this only made things worse.

The camera remained on the officer for a long time. At first I assumed this was a sign of respect, but then a woman entered the frame. She strode over to the officer and the two began to converse. The camera now focused on the woman. Realizing that she was being filmed, she turned and looked at the cameraman. She didn't seem to mind, though. A moment later she turned back to the officer and continued to speak. Her body was long and spindly and clothed in military attire. She was far from beautiful. The camera zoomed in on her face. Seeing her features up-close—her expression, the look in her eyes—I suddenly felt as if I'd seen her before, but just as I was trying to remember where, the woman and the officer disappeared. Several shots of the wooden barracks flashed before my eyes, then the entire screen went black.

I was about to tell Ma Zaihai to rewind the film when the screen lit up and something very strange appeared. At once my curiosity about the woman was gone. Onscreen was a ball of light, about the size of a washbasin. Something seemed to be churning inside of it. What is that? I wondered. The moon?

But that was impossible; the light was much too round. Even the mid-autumn moon wasn't this round. Had they already reached the abyss? If so, then what was this thing? My heart shivered. How could there be a ball of light like a little moon in the midst of an underground abyss?

3 FILMING THE VOID

What was going on here? Why had the film jumped right to this footage? There should at least have been a scene of the plane taking off into the void.

Then the ball of light began to move. It flew from the screen's center to its very top, paused for a moment, then zoomed back down to the center. After pausing again, it shot to the bottom. A few seconds later it vanished and the screen went black. But only a moment later the ball quickly reappeared and began to move once more, repeating the same pattern over and over again. The movements were jerky and abrupt. There was something distinctly abnormal about it, but what was really strange was that the longer I watched, the more familiar the light began to seem. I racked my brain for where I'd seen it. Suddenly, it occurred to me: the searchlight! I remembered how it had looked as it strafed the ceiling of the cave. This must be the illuminated circle of the searchlight beam. Still I was baffled. Why was the cameraman recording the searchlight? Had he noticed something odd about it? I looked closer but could find nothing amiss.

"What the hell is that?" asked Wang Sichuan.

I told him.

Ma Zaihai nodded. "Engineer Wu is correct. That's the searchlight. They must be adjusting the beam."

"Adjusting the beam?" I asked. "Adjusting it for what?"

"I would imagine they're synchronizing the movements of the searchlight with the focal point of the camera," he said. "Once, while watching an anti-aircraft exercise, I saw the cannon and searchlight operators coordinate their aim in much the same way. When setting up broadcasting stations, we perform similar adjustments—sending out a few transmissions, receiving a few, then checking the results." Ma Zaihai took care in how he worded this. He knew that us two engineers were completely ignorant about such matters and was afraid of making us lose face by saying too much.

Looking back at the light, I realized the churning at its center was the quickly flowing underground river. The plane must already have been parked atop the iron railway on the inner side of the dam with the camera fixed to its exterior and aiming downward. The searchlight was thus aimed at the river and the camera was aimed at the searchlight. Ma Zaihai sped up the film. The scene changed once more and the screen went black. Ever so slightly, I felt my body begin to shake. At last we had reached the heart of the matter.

The screen lit up once more, albeit dimly. A single tiny light glimmered within the darkness. It had to be the searchlight glimpsed from far away. From the shakiness of the footage I knew the plane had already taken off and was now cruising through the abyss. Holding my breath, I stared straight ahead. A dark gray mist floated somewhere far below. Its appearance was odd, heavy yet indistinct, as if it were somewhere between a solid and a gas. But the light was too low and the film quality too poor for me to get more than the barest sense of it. The plane began to descend, but before reaching the mist, it stopped and began flying levelly once more. For the next twenty-some minutes there was not the slightest change. The plane cruised just above the uppermost reaches of the mist, which neither rose nor shifted at all. The abyss was beyond vast; the plane had been speeding across it this whole time and still there was no end in sight. Just how big was it?

As the minutes passed, there was practically no change in the footage, but for fear we might miss something, none of us dared look away. Suddenly the screen went white and we all jumped in surprise. Another line of text appeared and then vanished. Ma Zaihai quickly stopped the film and rewound until the text reappeared. It was a string of numbers, written as illegibly as before, but these I at least recognized. They pertained to the height, time, and general position of the plane. These were the first coordinates on the film. The Japanese must have found something here. As soon as the numbers disappeared, the void reappeared onscreen. My heart skipped a beat. The plane was no longer flying smoothly and the camera was shaking violently. The entire screen juddered. I was dizzy enough to vomit, but I forced myself to keep watching.

Despite the choppy images, I could tell that the plane was diving steeply and banking sharply to the right. Towering out of the dense, gray cloud ahead was a giant black shape, its visible portion already six or seven stories tall. I held my breath as the plane broke through the mist and the thing was revealed in full. My jaw dropped open. It was far bigger than I had imagined. Its lower half was sunk deep into the mist. More astonishing than its size, though, was its appearance. It looked just like a man.

Stunned, I told Ma Zaihai to proceed at half-speed. Appearing out of the darkness was a great human-shaped thing, its "skull" enormous, its body slumped strangely over, as if in mourning. Both arms hung at its sides, disappearing into the lower reaches of the mist. Amid that thick cloud, the thing was far from distinct, yet it was clear enough to be identifiable. I couldn't believe my eyes. The hairs on my back all stood up. What could it be? Some eerily anthropomorphic mass of cave rock? A great stone statue carved by a god? Or was it a living organism, enormous, and shaped like a man?

Though I might not want to acknowledge what I was seeing, there was no point in deceiving myself. I had glimpsed enough of its dark shape to know that whatever it was, it hadn't formed naturally. This thing was definitely manmade. But what was it doing down here? The dark structure filled the screen as the plane sped towards it. Veering in close, the pilot lapped it once, then cut a steep ascent. A moment later we were out of the mist. Just as I was hoping that the plane would fly back down and give us a closer look, the footage abruptly froze.

We all flinched. Cold sweat covered my hands. Wang Sichuan ran to check the film reel. We'd reached the final frame. The movie was over. Silence descended on the room. We just sat there, staring at the frozen image onscreen. I don't remember who was first to speak or what he said. It couldn't have been important. My own mind was blank. As if moving automatically, my right hand reached into my pocket for a cigarette, but I was shaking too much to pull one free.

4 THE FIGURE IN THE MIST

Only after Ma Zaihai shut off the projector, returning the screen to its original tattered, white appearance, did I begin to regain my composure. I was the first to ask the question on all of our minds. "What was that thing?"

No one replied. I forced myself to calm down. Gradually my shaking stopped. I took out a cigarette, lit it and inhaled deeply. I looked over at Wang Sichuan. His normally dark face was somehow even paler than Ma Zaihai's.

We'd both graduated from university and, while educational standards back then were nowhere near what they are today, China's schools of higher learning were hardly as abysmal as you might imagine, especially in technical fields like ours. We'd been taught exclusively by venerable scholars who had studied in the United States and the Soviet Union. We fancied ourselves pretty worldly, smart, and wise. Our teachers were all staunch materialists; it was the prevailing mindset of the academic environment in which we had grown up. For unswerving atheists like us to come upon so unexplainable a circumstance was terrifying. It jarred our well-ordered worldview much more severely than it would have the average person. I couldn't even begin to guess what we'd seen. With only a vague, mist-shrouded form to go on, the wheels of my mind refused to turn. All the same, I knew it wasn't an illusion. This great abyss, 3,600 feet underground, was already a kind of geological miracle. Now that we'd found some enormous, apparently artificial thing rising out of its center, one had to wonder: Just whose masterpiece was this? It had to be manmade, but who could have built something so huge in a place like this? My materialistic worldview began to waver. My mind was filled with questions, but I knew there was no one who could begin to answer them.

Taking a deep breath, Wang Sichuan walked over and asked me for a cigarette. His hands were shaking. After handing one over, I passed him my lighter as well. I held one out for Ma Zaihai, but the poor kid was so stunned that it took him several seconds to respond. Turning back to Wang Sichuan, I saw that rather than smoke his cigarette, he'd lit it and placed it on the table in front of him. As I watched, he performed some strange ceremonial rite. Several sentences of Mongolian flowed solemnly from his lips. This behavior only increased the strangeness of our situation. Once he'd finished, he turned to me and said this was a prayer to Ehegazhar, the Earth Mother, asking for her protection. Lamps and sticks of incense were ordinarily placed burning on an altar for this ceremony, but now all he had was a lit cigarette and a wooden table. He had never before given any credence to his parents' faith in Ehegazhar, believing it was all just superstition. Even now he remained filled with doubt, but all the same he said it was wise to at least cover his bases by paying the appropriate respects. I wanted to tell him that this was nonsense, a relic of blind faith from the time of feudalism, but when I looked back at the image frozen onscreen, the words refused to come. Ma Zaihai asked Wang Sichuan how the prayer was performed, but he replied that only Mongolians could receive the Earth Mother's blessing.

The film was definitively over and we had no desire to watch it again. Nor did we want to discuss its content. What could we say? This affair had already far exceeded the scope of our understanding. After Ma Zaihai said a few sentences asking Buddha for his protection, we all went silent.

After a few minutes, Wang Sichuan got up, placed the film back in its canister and turned to us. "It's time we made a little pact," he said. We looked at him. The color had returned to his face. He seemed to have regained his composure. "There's no use in considering the matter any further," he said. "The three of us haven't got the barest chance of figuring out what that thing was, and in any case, its existence is simply not something that the world needs to know about. Once we deliver this to our superiors, it's going to be sealed away forever. So there's no reason for any of us to ever mention we watched it. Agreed?"

I understood him completely. This clip was much too subversive. If we let on that we'd seen it, we were sure to be in for trouble. I nodded.

"I've never been good at lying," said Ma Zaihai. "As soon as the Company Commander takes one look at me, I won't be able to hide it."

"Don't be so goddamned soft!" snapped Wang Sichuan. "Keep your mouth shut and you'll be promoted to squad leader when we get out of here. You can count on it."

Ma Zaihai's face lit up immediately. He turned to Wang Sichuan and gave a smart salute. "Thank you, Engineer Wang," he said. "I swear I won't say a thing."

Truth be told, we had no authority over who rose and fell in rank, but so long as we made it to the surface with the film intact, all three of us were sure to be rewarded. Even if Ma Zaihai didn't make it to squad leader, he'd at least be promoted to deputy squad leader.

"It's time to get going," said Wang Sichuan. "The longer we stay here the more likely it is that something bad will happen."

Ever since retrieving the film canister from the spy, I'd wanted to return to the surface as soon as possible. Watching the footage only increased my fear of this place. My desire to leave was stronger than ever, but for some reason I found myself momentarily unable to move. Still, spurred by Wang Sichuan's repeated urgings, we managed to rouse ourselves. With effort we gathered our things and strapped on our packs. I couldn't help but regret our decision to watch the film. What we'd seen weighed on my mind like a bad dream. Nothing good would come from it. Any sense of calm felt miles away.

Wang Sichuan strode over to the door and pulled free the iron club he'd wedged behind the handle. He yelled back to us to hurry up, saying we'd already delayed two hours and couldn't afford to waste any more time. We gathered beside the door. He cautiously pressed against it, as if afraid someone might be waiting in ambush.

"We have to be careful," he said. "It could swing open at any time."

He gave it a little push. The door didn't budge. Surprise flashed across his face. He pushed harder. The door shifted a smidgen, but would go no farther. Wang Sichuan looked back at me, his expression worried. Grabbing hold of the door handle, he yanked it with all his might. Nothing. Something was wrong. The door was not simply stuck. Again he tried to heave it backwards. Sheets of dust fell softly to the floor, but the door did not move.

Turning around, Wang Sichuan took a few steps back. "Goddamnit," he said, a trace of astonishment in his voice. "That son of a bitch locked the door."

5 TRAPPED

This was a military base. Everything within it was military-grade, the doors all triple-proofed, iron-sheeted and lined with cotton, the walls thick of concrete. Once a door like this was locked, even dynamite might not blast it open. Not that we had any, of course.

I gave the door a push. It was sealed tight. Someone must have snuck up while we were watching the movie and trapped us inside. My mind was filled with unease. Wang Sichuan was right. This had to be the work of the enemy agent. Could he have followed us all the way back here? How had we not noticed?

In a rage, Wang Sichuan violently smashed his bearish frame against the door. I tried to help, but it was like ramming into a cement wall. Wang Sichuan's anger seemed to reach its peak. With a terrible look on his face, he slammed into the door again and again—to no effect. Undaunted, he tried to kick it open, but this made even less of an impact. Still, he gave it several more kicks before, huffing and puffing, he finally stopped and sat down heavily.

"You underhanded mother-fucker," he panted. "Get out of the goddamn shadows and face me like a man."

From beyond the door there came only silence. This was a projection room. Its soundproofing had to be excellent. That was how the spy who had chased us all this way had locked the door without Wang Sichuan and the rest of us realizing. He'd pulled this same trick on us back in the warehouse. My blood boiled. After getting the drop on him and retrieving the film, how could we have fallen for this again? But I knew that anger would achieve nothing. "See how fast he followed us?" I said to them. "It's obvious he'll stop at nothing to get the film back. Trapped like this we're at a severe disadvantage. He's definitely planning something. We have to get out of here before we find out what it is."

"Not so fast," said Wang Sichuan. "We need to stop and think for a second. If we start behaving rashly, we're bound to spring his trap. And anyway, with the door locked there's nothing else he can do."

But the moment the words left his mouth, all the lights in the room abruptly flickered and died. Once more our surroundings were bathed in darkness. The power had been cut. We switched on our flashlights.

"Fucking cunt!" yelled Wang Sichuan. He angrily kicked the door.

Suddenly, from all around us there came a strange sound. It was a kind of low hum. Feeling along the walls, I discovered they were softly vibrating, as if some nearby machine had been switched on. Fear crept up my spine. This sequence of events had occurred extremely fast—it must have been planned out in advance. While I didn't know what was going on, it was obviously nothing good.

"Come on," I said. "We need to find another exit—now."

At once the three of us split up and began turning the room upside-down. The space was not large and soon we had covered nearly every inch of it, but all we found was an air vent hidden behind the projection screen. The opening was circular, covered by an iron grate and about the size of a large foot basin. Just inside was a small fan covered in thick dust like wads of dirty cotton. Clearly it could no longer turn. This vent was much cruder than the one we'd seen earlier in the caisson. The Japanese had probably decided that air filtration wasn't necessary here. I knelt down beside the opening. A breeze blew softly from it and a flurry of noise was emanating from somewhere deep within. The strange sounds I'd heard moments before must have been a machine starting up inside the ventilation system. Wang Sichuan attempted to remove the grate, but the edges were tightly sealed with cement as thick as a finger. He could pull all he wanted, it wasn't going anywhere.

"Goddamn, the Japs were thorough," said Wang Sichuan. He turned to Ma Zaihai. "You're an engineering corpsman. What do you think we should do?"

Ma Zaihai took a long look at the grate, then rubbed his fingers across the cement. He shook his head. "This stuff is much too thick. We'd need a geological hammer or a blowtorch, maybe even dynamite."

None of which we had.

Suddenly Wang Sichuan leapt to his feet and hurried off. A moment later he was back, carrying the iron club. Kneeling down, he smashed it again and again into the hardened cement. The skin between his thumb and forefinger was soon cracked and raw, but only the smallest fragments of cement skittered to the ground. This place might have been crudely built, but it was sturdy. We'd have to try something else. Wang Sichuan struck the cement a few more times before stopping. Then without pausing for a moment, he stuck the club into one of the big spaces in the crisscrossing bars of the grate and attempted to pry it open. The opening widened slightly. Encouraged, he kept at it, but the wider the space got, the less leverage Wang Sichuan could get. Eventually, the hole was too big for the bar, but not nearly big enough for us. Wang Sichuan hurled the club into the darkness, bent over and began panting heavily. His expression would've been funny if the situation weren't so serious.

I returned to the center of the room and swept my flashlight across the cement walls, searching for another opening. Suddenly, I realized something wasn't right. A queer odor filled the air. I turned in the direction of the iron door. It was open, though only slightly. When had this happened? Snapping my fingers to draw my companions' attention, I pointed towards the door. Then I hurried over, the smell growing stronger with each step. Soon enough I realized what it was. Smoke.

As if by instinct, I pushed against the door as soon as I reached it. It moved and my heart skipped a beat. Was the door unlocked? Leaning heavily into it, I watched the opening widen slightly, but at the same moment a thick cloud of smoke rushed into the room, burning my eyes until tears streamed forth. As I rubbed my eyes, I called out for Wang Sichuan to come quick and give me a hand. He sprinted over. Together we tried to force the door open, but it held fast. There seemed to be something attached to its apex, fixing it in place. Though we rammed into it again and again, the opening grew no wider. All the while smoke continued to fill the room.

So this was his plan—he meant to suffocate us. I shouted for Ma Zaihai to come as well. All three of us tried pulling it closed. It wouldn't budge. We pulled harder. Still nothing. I cursed under my breath. A thick rope or something had probably been hooked to the door and tied tightly to the frame overhead. We could push or pull all we wanted—it wasn't going to move.

Soon the smoke was so thick we could barely breathe or open our eyes. Coughing hard, Wang Sichuan began tearing off his clothes. "Help me!" he shouted between coughs. "Seal the door!"

Shutting our eyes, we rushed forward, undressed, and stuffed our clothing into the gap, but the opening was much too large. We would never fill it. By now Wang Sichuan's clothing was already flame-licked. He pulled it free, stamped it out, and put it back on. Ma Zaihai and I quickly followed suit.

Exploding with rage, Wang Sichuan picked up the iron club, swore violently, and shoved it through the crack in the door. He roared with effort as he tried to force it open, but it was no use. The club bent from the strain and he had to give up. Then I noticed something—other pry marks had been scraped all along the door. Had others been trapped in here as well? But I had no time to consider these questions. The billowing smoke had already spread throughout the room. Even at some distance from the door our throats constricted and breathing was difficult. If this kept up, we'd be done for.

After bellowing a final string of curses, Wang Sichuan went silent. We retreated to the back of the room where we tore dust-covered strips from the projection screen, wetted them from our canteens and placed them over our mouths. Amid the chaos, I somehow caught sight of the air vent. Plumes of smoke were billowing out of it. I thought of the noise I'd heard humming from within. That son of a bitch must have used some machine to redirect the smoke through the vent. Wang Sichuan was howling in blind fury—he had completely lost control. I was just afraid. There were only two ways out of here and both were belching smoke. Everything else was seamless concrete. We were screwed. I looked back at Wang Sichuan. There was no time to calmly consider the situation. His eyes blazed like hot coals through the smoke as he yelled for us to make way.

Brandishing the twisted club, he charged at the vent. With the door impassable, this was our only chance for survival. Sparks flew and the club shook as Wang Sichuan smashed it wildly against the iron bars. At last he could persist no longer. The club slipped from his hands. Shining my light on the grate, I despaired. It had barely been dented. Ma Zaihai was starting to panic as well. No longer worrying about rank or seniority, he grabbed the club from Wang Sichuan's hand and began striking it against the grate. His force appeared even greater than Wang Sichuan's, his movements more precise. He must have perfected his skill while leveling mountains with the Engineering Corps. Still, he could do no more than dent the bars. With his final swing the club flew from his hand and smashed into the grate. His efforts had all been in vain—the vent remained closed and by now the smoke was so thick we could barely breathe. Covering my mouth, I watched as it flooded the room. My mind was nearly empty, only one miserable thought endlessly repeating: This is how I'm going to die.

It was at this point that something suddenly drew Wang Sichuan's attention. He swung his flashlight around and aimed it at a spot beneath one of the long wooden tables. Ma Zaihai and I followed suit. Under the concentrated light of our three beams I saw it.

Something was drawing the smoke down into the floor.

21

6 THE WAY OUT

The three of us rushed over and pulled the table out of the way. Underneath it was another air vent, much smaller than the last. A little fan was concealed behind an identical iron grate, each bar as thick as a finger, but this time there was no cement. It had been merely screwed on. Still, I wondered, could we fit inside? The space was tiny. But there was no time for such worries.

Wang Sichuan immediately wedged the iron club between the bars and began to pry. The screws had already been loosened. Had people already been through here? And if so, why had they replaced the grate?

By now Wang Sichuan had already pulled it free and was attempting to tear apart the fan, blade by blade. The Japanese military bases constructed towards the beginning of the war often used an excess of materials, ensuring each part – even the most inconsequential – was impressively sturdy. Thus the fan's iron blades and its central axis were astonishingly thick and solidly welded together. Wang Sichuan tore at it until his hands were covered in dust and grease, but the thing wouldn't move. At last, Ma Zaihai asked Wang Sichuan to let him try.

On the side of the fan was a large bolt attaching it to the wall of the shaft. Using the diagonal openings of the grating as a makeshift wrench, Ma Zaihai managed to twist the bolt free. Wang Sichuan grabbed the fan with both hands and tossed it away. It hit the floor with a deep clang. It had to weigh at least 20 pounds. The thing must have been built in the early days of the war. By its end, the Japanese would never have been willing to waste so much metal on a little part like this.

The projection room was now hidden behind a haze of smoke. Even with our flashlights on, we could barely see anything. I squinted down the air shaft. A mass of electrical cables, each as thick as an arm, ran through the tunnel at its bottom. The ventilation system was connected to the electrical canal.

Skinny Ma Zaihai went first. As I watched him squeeze himself inside, my heart sank. I wasn't worried about myself – if Ma Zaihai could make it, then aside from a few cuts and scrapes I should be fine – but what about Wang Sichuan? At the bottom of the airshaft the space widened. After dropping all the way down, Ma Zaihai signaled to us that it was safe. Wang Sichuan and I looked at one another.

He laughed. "You go first. I need a moment to limber up."

I shook my head. This guy didn't have a chance of making it by himself. "No," I said. "You'd better go first. I'll stay up here and help push. We're getting you to the bottom, even if it means breaking a few bones along the way."

What could he say? He didn't want to die. He tried different contortions. None worked. Finally, and without preamble, he stripped off his clothes and climbed in headfirst. Then sure enough, after having wriggled only halfway in, he became utterly stuck. Without a second thought I jumped on him. As he wailed in pain, I used my full body weight to force him down the tunnel, little by little. Both his shoulders were scraped raw, leaving a pair of bloody trails on the walls of the shaft, but he made it through.

I gathered Wang Sichuan's clothes and climbed in headfirst. It was a tight fit, but with the two of them pulling me along I was soon out the other end. To our left the tunnel ran below the corridor outside the projection room, where the spy was hiding. Air vents lined the ceiling and a faint light streamed through. I crawled toward them. Smoke continued to pour into the tunnel, filling it with an acrid odor. Once I judged myself somewhere beneath the outer corridor, I squeezed up under one of the vents and stood up. My head was just below the iron grate. I peeked through the bars. Smoke swirled down the dark corridor above me. I could see the flickering beam of that son of a bitch's flashlight, but everything else was obscured. Had I a pistol, I could easily have shot him dead from this range. His brains would already be splattered across the wall. But I didn't even have a rock to throw. My only consolation was that he, too, was weaponless. After sliding back down to the electrical canal, I gauged the topside locations of the other vents. I wanted to sneak up on the bastard and slit his throat—let him know I was not one to be messed with.

The wide halls and corridors of the dam were bathed in silence. If we chose an air vent too close to him, he'd hear us when we broke through the grate. No reason to disturb a snake in the grass. It would be wisest to continue down the tunnel until we were a safe distance away. He'd wait awhile for us to suffocate before checking, so we should still have some time before our escape was discovered.

With my two comrades close behind, I crawled cautiously forward, following the electrical cables. More ventilation shafts opened overhead, each containing a motionless iron-bladed fan. The tunnel system was cramped and intricate. I guessed we were passing beneath various rooms and hallways, though not a single light was on. Darkness surrounded us and the air smelled of mildew. Shining my flashlight through the openings, I could see only the dim outline of objects strewn chaotically about. A thick layer of dust and grime covered every inch of the tunnel. Soon it was all over me. The stuff was disgusting, a sort of gray, gelatinous grease that wouldn't wipe off. After passing six ventilation shafts I decided we'd gone far enough. It was time to ascend. But when I tried to lift the grate atop the seventh shaft, I found it had been tightly screwed in place. We had nothing to wrench it off with and time was running out.

We stared at the grate for several minutes before Wang Sichuan cried, "This is no time to sit back and wait! Let's just kick the damn thing out! Do you want to suffocate down here before the spy even finds us?"

He was right. At this point we had no other choice. Ma Zaihai lay on his back, threaded his legs between the blades of the fan, and gave the grate several vicious kicks. It didn't flex an inch. The grate was too solid, had been attached too securely. I knew this would never work. Wang Sichuan and I tried as well, both with no effect. We checked the next grate, but it was just as immovable. My spirits fell. Would this tunnel be our grave?

We continued on, attempting to force our way through every opening we passed. The grates were all equally, immovably sturdy. I had no idea how long we crawled through that dank hole in the earth.

Just when I was about to give up hope, Ma Zaihai called out, "Hey! This one is loose!"

I hurried over. Sure enough, the grate moved slightly outward from the force of his kicks. Ma Zaihai looked over at us, grinning gleefully, then gave it several more strong blows, loosening it even further. I shined my flashlight on the grate. Unlike the others, this one was secured only from the top. Ma Zaihai gave the grate a final, savage kick. It flew into the air, clattering down a few feet away. He rolled over, reached up and began to remove the bolt holding the fan in place. It was already loose.

Strange, I thought. Had someone already come this way? It seemed rather unlikely. The opening was clear. Like a baby escaping his mother's womb, Wang Sichuan desperately wriggled through. Ma Zaihai and I followed shortly after. We found ourselves in a great gloomy tunnel, three-stories tall and wide enough for two trucks to drive comfortably side by side. Every inch was covered in bare concrete. It was a desolate expanse. My heart sank. Now where were we?

This appeared to be the inner dam's main transport road. We were already some distance away from the projection room and its surrounding maze of offices and living quarters. We'd left the once-populated part of the dam behind. The tunnel was a dreadful place, in every aspect eerie and unfamiliar. I was sure that strange, terrible things had happened here. We needed to keep our wits about us.

I swept my flashlight beam across the immense tunnel. Rows of tracks, assumedly for transport, ran along the floor, joining and diverging as they extended into the black distance. Looking at them, I was reminded of a brick and tile factory in my hometown. My flashlight beam passed across an iron sign hanging on one of the walls. I strode over and wiped off the dust. Just as I was attempting to parse a meaning, I heard Wang Sichuan call for me to hurry up. I jogged toward the sound of his voice, passing boarded-up rooms and passageways on both sides. The tunnel showed no sign of stopping. My curiosity rose. This place was even stranger than the rest of the dam—more obviously abandoned, sunk deeper into bleak ruination. And all the exits were sealed. What had happened here? Were the entryways blocked to protect whatever was inside? This would hardly be an effective deterrent. When leaving a base, the Japanese usually showed no hesitation in destroying what they were unable to transport. So what had been different here? At last I caught up with my companions.

Wang Sichuan was looking at the thick wooden boards nailed to the outside of a doorway. "Did they use these to seal the Chinese laborers inside?" he muttered to himself.

I shook my head. The Japanese method for dealing with laborers was never this complex. Once a project was completed they simply massacred them.

Wang Sichuan shined his flashlight through the cracks in the boards. The space inside seemed to be arranged similarly to the projection room, though much was obscured. We kept going and soon we'd reached the end of the tunnel. Every room and corridor along the way had been tightly sealed. The Japanese hadn't missed a single one.

"This whole area is closed off," said Wang Sichuan. "Seems like we'll have to head back down the ventilation shaft."

"I don't think so," I said. "After sealing this place up the devils would have needed a way out themselves. There must be an exit somewhere around here."

We headed back down the tunnel, weaving from one entryway to the next. I watched the left side, Wang Sichuan looked right, and Ma Zaihai watched the ceiling, but all rooms and corridors were blocked-off. At the far end of the tunnel, however, we discovered something else—a pair of giant iron doors, cut into the concrete. They were magnificently rusted and tightly welded from within. How were we supposed to get them open?

Not wanting to give up, I took a closer look, but they were sealed seamlessly shut. A feeling of deep gloom set in.

We gathered beside the door and talked it over. This didn't make a lick of sense. If every exit was closed, then whoever had done the job must have remained inside, but then where were their corpses? Except for a few empty wooden boxes, the tunnel was entirely bare. Wang Sichuan didn't say much. He, too, was clearly at a loss. The three of us looked at one another hopelessly. Suddenly, Wang Sichuan turned and marched toward one of the boarded-up rooms.

"Come on!" he called over his shoulder. "Let's pry this thing open and see what's inside. Maybe we'll be able to figure out what's going on!"

Wang Sichuan was holding the iron club, by now our trustiest tool. The boards across the door nailed across the door were poplar, a common tree in this region. They likely had been cut from the forest. The wood had softened over the years and Wang Sichuan was able to pry the boards apart. The opening was soon wide enough for us to pass through. I shined my flashlight ahead. Inside, numerous beds were arrayed in the darkness. As I swept the beam across them, I felt a sudden stab of terror.

Something was lying on each of the beds.

7 THE SEALED ROOM

I shined the dim beam of my flashlight through the opening. Dark shapes were lying on every bed, absolutely motionless. My hair stood on end. Was this a mortuary? I looked back at the great span of the outer tunnel and thought of all the boarded-up rooms we had passed. If it was, then how many corpses were sealed inside?

Wang Sichuan was pressing me to hurry up. I turned around and explained the situation. His expression didn't change at all.

Stepping in front of me, he peered into the gloom. "What are you so scared of?" he asked. "They're already dead, aren't they?" And with that he climbed through the opening and into the room.

Forcing myself to be calm, I told Ma Zaihai to stand guard, then cautiously followed Wang Sichuan. I scanned my surroundings. Things were not entirely as I had expected. Crude, sleeping bag-like sacks were arranged atop rows of wide, three-story bunk beds. The canvas sacks were greenish-yellow, just like the devils' military attire, and stuffed full so that the room appeared filled with fat cocoons. Each was filthy, covered in dark red stains that seemed to have seeped from within. They could be only one thing—body bags.

I felt a wave of nausea. Wang Sichuan was not at all squeamish. "Get ready," he said. He used the iron club to flip over one of the sacks. It was filled to the point of bursting. As he pried it open, out lolled a rigid black hand. After all the dark days we'd spent down here and all the horrors we'd encountered, a sight like this made barely an impact on me. Wang Sichuan continued to lift away the canvas covering. Soon the upper body of a desiccated corpse was revealed.

"He's dead all right," said Wang Sichuan.

Ma Zaihai had never seen anything like this before. He was so scared that he cowered behind us a step or two.

Patting him on the back, I told him to toughen up. How was he going to make it to squad leader if he couldn't handle a little blood and guts?

Wang Sichuan shined his flashlight beam across the body. From the tattered military uniform we could tell it was a Japanese soldier. His clothing was covered in coagulated bodily fluids and had gone completely stiff. His skin was black and unevenly rotted down to the bone in parts, in others not at all. Riddled with hollows, it looked like a dark honeycomb, just like the pilot's corpse I'd found in the Shinzan, the first plane we had discovered. We opened another canvas bag. The corpse inside looked the same.

"These two were both poisoned," said Wang Sichuan in a quiet voice. "Probably victims of the toxic mist. Where the poison builds up, everything rots away. And I'd bet that where the skin looks untouched, the toxins have killed everything, even the germs. That's why they look so messed up. But what's with the color?"

He had a point. The corpse was much too black. Hefting the iron club, Wang Sichuan dipped it into a hole rotted in the torso. He stirred it around for a moment, then pulled it back out. Stuck to the end were what appeared to be pieces of cotton batting. Lifting the club to his nose, he gave it a sniff. Ma Zaihai looked as if he were about to vomit. I shook my head. This kid wasn't as promising as I'd thought. Wang Sichuan held the club up for me. The smell was indescribable, but not disgusting—or at least not as disgusting as I'd imagined.

"The mist must be extremely poisonous if it caused a change in skin color this severe," said Wang Sichuan. "When toxins are simply inhaled this doesn't happen. This stuff must also seep in through touch. If we encounter it again, we need to be extremely careful."

I nodded. We'd learned all this in Attack Preparation class, but I'd never imagined it would actually come in handy. After wiping the club on the side of the canvas bag, Wang Sichuan turned and walked farther into the room.

I looked down at the filthy bag surrounding the corpse. Suddenly it occurred to me. "Wait a second," I said. "These soldiers look like they're part of the Japs' forward unit. I bet they were the first ones down here."

"How can you tell?" asked Wang Sichuan. He had climbed atop one of the beds and was surveying the room.

"This kind of simple canvas sleeping bag is standard equipment for troops in the field," I replied. "If these devils were garrisoned here fulltime they would surely have been given regular bedding. After all, it's freezing down

here. I'm sure this whole area can't just be filled with corpses. Think of all
the boarded-up rooms we passed. Even if everyone working on the project
died, there still wouldn't be enough people to fill the place. The Japs'
forward unit wouldn't have known the mist was poisonous when they first
arrived and began construction on the dam. A heavy rain must have fallen,
filling the underground river. Then, when the mist rose up, it massacred
the Japanese soldiers and Chinese laborers who were down here."

"Then why weren't these corpses disposed of?" asked Ma Zaihai.
"Couldn't they have just cremated them?"

For a moment I ignored his question and stared at the too-perfect
arrangement of the corpses. Suddenly, an idea occurred to me. I turned to
Ma Zaihai. "They must have been forced into leaving the bodies like this.
Otherwise, why arrange the bodies one to a bed? It's an awfully inefficient
arrangement. Were this room really a mortuary, only a third of the space
could have been used to store all these corpses. Even when the Japanese
were at the height of their military power, they still would never have been
so wasteful as to wrap each of their dead in an individual sleeping bag."

Still, why were there so many corpses here and all of them arrayed as if in
the middle of a deep sleep? Because, I realized, that's exactly what they
were doing when they died. These were barracks, I guessed, and late one
night, when most of the soldiers were already asleep, the toxic mist must
have seeped in through the ventilation system. Only the lucky few would
have escaped. Once the mist receded they would have returned to find that
the barracks had become a tomb; all was quiet and everyone was dead.
Faced with this terrible scene, the survivors must have panicked. With
their ranks severely thinned, they would have been unable to properly
dispose of the corpses until reinforcements arrived. But the sight of their
comrades' faces, pockmarked and ravaged by poison, must have haunted
them. They surely worried about what would happen as the bodies
decomposed. So, to prevent the spread of disease, they'd boarded up every

opening, including the air vents, and abandoned the area.

All of them soundlessly dying in a single night—I trembled just to think about it. Sure, it was a peaceful death, but I hated it all the same. When it was my time to go, I wanted to be aware enough to say goodbye.

Suddenly, Wang Sichuan cried out. I looked up. He was beckoning me over. I walked to the bed where he stood and climbed up. He'd opened another canvas sleeping bag. As he shined his flashlight on the corpse inside, he motioned for me to look closer. There was a bullet hole through the corpse's brow.

Giving me a look, he said, "This guy was executed. Now take a look at this." He pointed at the body of the corpse. Bullet holes riddled its chest. "First they shot him in the lungs," said Wang Sichuan, "and then they put one in the brain. Probably just wanted to help the guy die a little easier."

He jumped down from the bed and opened a number of sleeping bags in quick succession. Sure enough, several of the men inside had been shot to death. Some had a single bullet wound through the front of the skull. Others were riddled with them. Very strange.

"The poison may have killed some of them," said Wang Sichuan, "but just as many were executed by their comrades. This situation is a lot more complex than you said."

It didn't make any sense. After executing these men, the Japanese had wrapped them in sleeping bags and then placed them neatly upon the beds. For some unfathomable reason, they'd made this room a mortuary, and although the corpses must surely have stunk, they didn't incinerate them. Why? I could think of only one possible explanation.

"What if something happened to these corpses?" I asked. "Perhaps they changed somehow—terribly—and the others boarded up the openings because they were too frightened to come close."

Wang Sichuan shook his head. "That's too big a leap," he said. "Boarding up the openings could just as easily be to keep something out as to keep something in."

"This isn't some desolate wilderness where wild beasts lurk in the shadows," I said. "What would they need to protect the corpses from?"

Wang Sichuan's face lit up as if something had just occurred to him. "Why leave so many corpses to rot instead of just cremating them?" he asked. "I'd say it's somehow connected to the devils' abrupt departure. Think about it. If all these soldiers died shortly before the Japs had to abandon the base, then there was probably no time left to deal with the bodies."

Wang Sichuan had raised the most unsettling part of the whole affair. Why had the Japanese left as they did? Their secret installations had remained perfectly intact. We'd found troves of data, codebooks and potentially revealing files, all unburned. Their departure had been much too casual. It was as if they'd simply vanished. As for the dam itself, too much of it defied explanation—the immense icehouse and the frozen warheads we had found, the Wurzburg Giant we had seen. What had the devils been planning? There seemed no logic to their activities, no clear motive to the structures they'd built. Thinking about it, I was overcome by a feeling of deep unease.

We tabled our discussion for the moment and continued searching the room. There wasn't a single air vent in its walls or floor. No other clues were found. Wang Sichuan then suggested we tear the boards from the other entryways and look inside.

Not all the rooms looked like this. We could see that others led to dark passageways, and who knew where these ran? One had to be a way out. Better to return to the ventilation shaft and continue on from there, I thought. Although cramped and tough to negotiate, it was still preferable to searching the countless rooms and tunnels sealed inside this giant tomb.

We debated it back and forth, but couldn't come to a decision. Suddenly Ma Zaihai, who had been silent, motioned for us to stop talking. He was standing by the door, his ears pricked. With a finger to his lips, he beckoned us over. Quietly we approached. Then I heard it. The sound was very low, emerging from somewhere out in the vast tunnel. I listened closer. It was a noise, like creaking wood, like something was pushing up against one of the sealed entryways. What was out there?

We looked at one another, then quickly climbed through the door opening. The tunnel was empty. Sweeping our flashlights across the black expanse, we followed the sound. It was coming from somewhere far ahead. As the baleful creaking continued, I thought of the rotting tomb we'd just left. Goosebumps ran down my arms. I looked over at Wang Sichuan. He strode into the darkness gripping the club so tightly his hand trembled.

8 SOUNDS OF THE TOMB

We stood in the dark tunnel and listened. Near silence. For a time none of us even breathed. All the while the low creaking continued, without pattern, incessantly. It sounded almost as if someone were repairing one of the boarded-up entryways. Wang Sichuan was about to say something, but I stopped him.

"We need to keep quiet," I whispered.

Dozens of rooms and passageways extended from both sides of the tunnel. It was a vast and complex place. I could gauge the sound's approximate direction, but who knew how long it would take to find the source?

What was causing the sound? I could think of a few possibilities. If we were especially unlucky, it might be the spy, still hunting us. Maybe he'd checked the projection room and discovered our escape. Maybe he was trying to enter the tunnel through another of the blocked-off passageways. No, not nearly enough time had passed, I decided. He couldn't have already realized we were gone, figured out where we'd fled, and arrived here himself. A second possibility seemed a little more probable. What if it were Old Cat, Old Tang, and the rest of our group? Perhaps they'd gotten lost and ended up here. But Old Cat and Old Tang were each leading groups of soldiers. And they were armed. They wouldn't be making such cautious, little noises. As for the third possibility, well, I couldn't help but think of the rotting corpses back in that silent room. Cold sweat dripped down my back. Was there something wrong with these men? Was that why the devils sealed off this place?

The three of us spread out and began to search. As we continued down the tunnel the sound became clearer, but after I went a little farther it abruptly became harder to distinguish. Echoes emerged from every direction. No matter where I moved they all sounded more or less the same. One by one I pressed my ear to the wooden boards nailed to each entryway. At some there was merely a dull echo while at others the creaking was almost perfectly clear. Then I found one entryway where I could literally hear the sound rolling down the passageway. I beckoned Wang Sichuan over.

Raising the iron club to his shoulder, he stepped quietly in front of the entrance. He squatted down and softly rapped his fist against the boards at the bottom. He carefully pulled one off. This board had merely been set in place with no nails fixing it to the entryway. Shining my flashlight across the other boards, I could see they were riddled with cracks—pry-marks— and they'd had been made a long time ago. Wang Sichuan looked up at me, his expression saying, Now isn't that interesting?

He continued to lift the boards away. A hole big enough for a man appeared, clearly many years old. Whoever had made it was careful to close it up behind him, so that this looked no different than the other entryways. Was this really the exit taken by the Japanese? I wondered. Why had they decided to conceal it?

With the boards pulled away the sound was much clearer. We cautiously climbed through. Inside the temperature sharply dropped. We had to be getting closer to the icehouse. We found ourselves in a long, narrow hallway. A number of doorways appeared on both sides, though most were boarded shut. We approached one of the open few, only to find another pitch-black corridor. We'd entered a maze, passageways weaving in and out of one another. Taking great care, we followed the sound into the darkness. With each step it seemed to grow clearer. When at last we arrived at the entrance to a second black-mouthed corridor, we stopped. The sound was less than a hundred feet ahead. Wang Sichuan raised his club in readiness. Ma Zaihai and I shined our flashlights inside. The moment the beams pierced the darkness, the sound vanished. An abrupt silence fell all around us. The passageway was sunk into the shadows, but I could tell something was moving inside. It looked like a person.

"Who's there?" cried Wang Sichuan.

At once the shape darted to the side and was gone, disappearing into some adjoining corridor or room.

"You think it's that spying son of a bitch?" Wang Sichuan asked me, rolling up his sleeves in anticipation.

I quickly shook my head. "No way could he have found us this fast. He's probably still back at the projection room." I waved my hand, dismissing the idea. "It doesn't matter who it is. Either way we have to catch him. Come on."

We hurried into the dark passageway and soon we'd reached its end. A doorway, also boarded over, appeared on the left. Several of the boards had been ripped away, creating a large opening. Inside all was blackness. I was about to climb in when Wang Sichuan pulled me back.

"Careful," he said. "It might be an ambush."

He leaned up against the boards and shined his flashlight through. Suddenly someone appeared on the other side of the entryway. A hand shot through the opening and grabbed Wang Sichuan's flashlight. Before he could react it was gone. He reached for it, but grasped only air as he fell. The beam of the flashlight flew back deep into the room. With a roar, Wang Sichuan leapt to his feet and dove through the opening. Ma Zaihai and I immediately clambered in after him.

By the time I was inside, I heard Wang Sichuan yell out, "We've been tricked! Quick, block the entrance!"

I heard a commotion to my right. Turning just in time, I saw one of the beds falling towards me and a black shape leaping from the top bunk. I dodged backwards and the bed crashed down. Out of the corner of my eye, I glimpsed the fleeing shape. It was already halfway through the hole in the doorway. A millisecond slower and he would have been gone, but I pounced on him and pulled him back inside the room. My flashlight swung wildly and the beam momentarily illuminated his face. I was stunned. The face was filthy and ghostly white, but I recognized it immediately. This was no man. It was Yuan Xile.

I managed only to blurt out two words. "Engineer Yuan!"

She had disappeared earlier and we had no idea what happened to her. She did not return my greeting. Instead, she reared back and struck me hard in the face, knocking my teeth into my lip, drawing blood. Without hesitating for a second, she threw me off, grabbed my flashlight and sprinted for the door. I dove after her, but she was already gone.

Wang Sichuan, still without flashlight, came hurtling out of the darkness. "It's me!" I cried, but it was too late and his head smacked straight into mine. I fell back, seeing stars.

He swore incomprehensibly—Mongolian, most likely—then asked if I'd seen who it was.

"It's Yuan Xile!" I yelled. "After her!"

Wiping the blood gushing from my lip, I leapt to my feet and struggled through the opening. The darkness was overwhelming. Yuan Xile's flashlight beam was already far down the corridor and moving fast. Without another thought I took off after her, running like a madman. The network of narrow corridors and abandoned rooms spider-webbed out, but luckily most of the entrances were blocked off. Stumbling through the pitch-black passageways at high speed, I followed the distant flashlight beam, smacking into objects unseen and turning one corner after the next until the light suddenly disappeared. Yuan Xile must have switched it off. I paused for a moment to let my eyes adjust. Twenty steps on I hit an intersection. The sound of footsteps came from all directions. I couldn't tell which was the source and which the echo. I looked back. Wang Sichuan and Ma Zaihai were nowhere to be seen. I started to feel a little nervous.

"Guys?" I called.

"I'm here!" cried Wang Sichuan from somewhere behind me.

"You two wait right there!" I called back. "Her light is gone and I can't tell where her footsteps are coming from, but I think she's somewhere up ahead. Once I have her we'll regroup!"

Turning back toward the intersection, I listened hard for the footsteps. They seemed to have vanished. I listened again. Then I heard it—directly ahead of me, the faint sound of someone walking. She sounded some distance away, but fortunately she still seemed to be in the same passageway. I hurried on. By now my eyes had adjusted to the darkness. I picked up my pace, crushing all manner of things underfoot as I chased the sound. After following it for some time, the sound abruptly disappeared. I continued a few steps farther before realizing I was in a dead-end. A great deal of shadowy objects were piled all about, but Yuan Xile was nowhere to be seen.

I crept forward. "Engineer Yuan, I'm a fellow prospector!" I called out. "Please don't run. I'm on your side."

She didn't answer. Not that I had expected her to. I took a few more steps forward. In front of me was a huge box of ammunition. I walked closer. There was Yuan Xile. She was huddled tightly against the side of the box, trembling uncontrollably.

Breathing a deep sigh of relief, I let down my guard. "Engineer Yuan," I said, "there's no reason to be afraid. You and I are on the same team."

But something was wrong. Her trembling grew even more severe and every few seconds she would glance off to one side. Suddenly I realized: Yuan Xile wasn't hiding from me; she was hiding from something on the other side of the ammo box. Something I couldn't see. What was at the end of this corridor? An ominous feeling fell over me like a black cloak. I took a few steps forward. Something was waiting in the darkness. I looked closer.

It was a man, standing absolutely still.

9 THE MADMAN

Before I could register my surprise, the man dove forward, knocking me to the ground. The stink of piss and shit filled my nostrils. Recoiling in fear and disgust, I swung my fist hard into his face and threw him off of me. I struggled to my feet, but he was on me again and we tumbled back to the floor. His smell was nauseating. I retched, my mind reeling as I swung wildly for him. This time I didn't connect. Panicking, I reached forward and tried to throttle him.

A sudden stabbing pain shot up my arm and I saw red. Howling with rage, I smashed my forehead into his nose and rolled to my feet. My mind buzzed from the impact and my arm throbbed like hell. Blood soaked through my shirtsleeve and I pulled it back. My forearm was torn open, belching blood. Eyes narrowing, I looked at the shadowy figure crouching in the darkness and holding his face. Anger pulsed through my veins. I rushed forward and kicked him viciously in the gut. As he doubled over, I grabbed my flashlight back from Yuan Xile, switched it on, and swung it back towards him. He dodged out of the way, but not before I saw a cold, metallic light glint off something in his hand. He staggered heavily against the back wall. I raised the beam and shined it directly into his eyes. Immediately he turned away and raised his hands to protect his eyes, but I'd already gotten a good look at his face. I couldn't believe it. This son of a bitch was Chen Luohu. His face was as pale as a corpse, covered in blood, mucus, and filth. A crazed, furious look was in his eyes. He'd gone absolutely mad.

"Luohu!" I cried.

He made no response, only turned his mangled face back towards me. He rushed forward, a long, sharp blade in his hand. He thrust it at me, once, twice and then again, but I dodged each time. The beam of my flashlight swung with my movements, illuminating his glinting blade, then his murderous visage. The tunnel was so narrow that there was barely room to maneuver, but I managed to grab his hands and force him up against the wall. I dropped my flashlight and it rolled out of reach. For several interminable minutes I struggled blindly against him. Then a pair of flashlight beams cut through the darkness, moving fast. A moment later Wang Sichuan and Ma Zaihai appeared. At once they rushed over to help and together we immobilized him.

For the past who-knows-how-long I had been running on nothing but fear and adrenaline. Now it was finally over. A feeling of immeasurable relief washed over me. For a moment I relaxed my grip.

That was a mistake. Chen Luohu had risen to prospector from the lowest level of the engineering corps and in this instant he proved himself worthy. The guy was as strong as a bull and didn't lack for reflexes either. The moment I loosened my hold he twisted wildly around, freeing himself. Then he picked up the blade and ran at us, swinging it in long, gleaming arcs. Instinctively we made way, dodging to the sides of the narrow corridor. With his mad eyes fixed on the darkness beyond, Chen Luohu sprinted past and was soon out of sight. Ma Zaihai turned to give chase, but Wang Sichuan quickly stopped him.

"It's too dangerous to go after him right now," he said. "And anyway, we already have Yuan Xile."

Breathing hard, I slumped to the ground, my limbs so weary that they felt paralyzed. The pain radiating from my arm flooded my body. I leaned over and scooped up my flashlight. Its exterior was cracked from the fall. I switched it on and found that my entire arm was red, as if it had been dyed. Blood dripped from my shirtsleeve, but I rolled it up. The wound was deep and star-shaped and utterly nasty-looking. I guessed it was the work of some ancient military dagger or bayonet—amazing that after so many years it was still this sharp. After tearing off a piece of his shirt, Ma Zaihai squatted down beside me and tied it around my arm. The bleeding soon slowed and then stopped altogether.

Wang Sichuan remained standing, his eyes fixed in the direction Chen Luohu had fled. "What the hell is going on here?" he said quietly. "Everyone is losing their goddamn minds."

I looked over at Yuan Xile. She was huddled in a corner, her head between her knees and her entire body shaking with fear. It was a terrible sight. She was one of our generation's "Iron Women." She had studied in the Soviet Union and commanded her own team of prospectors. And now look at her.

I turned to Wang Sichuan. "Chen Luohu was always weak-hearted," I said. "This cursed place must have been too much for him. And who wouldn't have gone mad, all alone in the dark like that? But the real question is, how did the two of them end up here?"

He shook his head. "If one of us went mad, we wouldn't grab a knife and go for the heart. You saw the way he acted—that wasn't fear-induced madness. The man nearly sliced my hands off. And if we hadn't showed up when we did, you'd be sitting here with a blade in your belly."

He was right, and as I thought back on what had just occurred, I shivered—whether from fear or relief I don't know.

"This goddamn place," said Wang Sichuan, his eyes darting back and forth. "Something terrible must have happened here. Tengri protect us, we need to leave as soon as possible."

Ma Zaihai's head was drooped wearily between his legs as he squatted. Suddenly he looked up. "What if he was possessed?" he asked in a still tone. "After all, this place is full of dead devils..."

Wang Sichuan and I stared at him.

"That kind of thing doesn't exist," I said. "We live in the real world. Forget those supernatural beliefs."

"No wonder you never made squad leader," said Wang Sichuan sharply.

Ma Zaihai said nothing. We may have scolded him, but inside I was scared, too. Yuan Xile, Chen Luohu, the special emissary Su Zhenhua—everyone was losing their minds and it made me extremely uneasy. Whether it was ghosts or some resident evil lurking in the dark, it didn't matter; something was definitely wrong here, and I feared that the worst was yet to come. We had to get out of here soon. If not, we would surely go mad ourselves.

Kneeling down before Yuan Xile, Wang Sichuan tried to pacify her. It was no use. She refused to meet his eyes. And as soon as he stood up and walked off, her shaking became even more severe, no different than when we had first found her. It was obvious she wouldn't be able to tell us what had happened here.

Staring off into the darkness, Wang Sichuan asked me what I planned to do. I thought about it. For the moment it was hard to say. Should we go after Chen Luohu? I doubted that he would persist in this violent state for much longer, and if we abandoned him I knew he had almost no chance of finding his way back to the surface. Although I had forgotten about him for a while, he remained my comrade. We'd spent more than a month together on the surface. I had called him brother. His fate was not to be casually decided. In those days, abandoning a comrade was considered a terrible offense. In the movies characters that did this were always played by the vilest-looking actors, so that viewers would instantly despise them. Now I was considering doing that very thing. I felt deeply conflicted. But I had to be realistic. Even if we found Chen Luohu, bringing him with us—mad as he was—would be a great encumbrance. There was no way around it. We would have to leave him behind, at least temporarily. Once we reached a point where Wang Sichuan or I could travel safely back to headquarters with the film canister we could reassess, but for now we had no other choice.

I looked at Yuan Xile. What was she doing here? I wondered. Surely she hadn't crawled through the same ventilation shaft as us. This meant that we were on the right track. There had to be another way out, and it was most likely somewhere within these corridors. I thought again of Yuan Xile and Chen Luohu's silent disappearance from the caisson. They really had snuck out through the darkness. By then Yuan Xile had already gone mad, so who knows what she was thinking, but why had Chen Luohu followed her?

Having been part of the earlier prospecting team, Yuan Xile knew this place well. When the toxic mist first rose earlier, she had led Ma Zaihai and Chen Luohu into the caisson. Somewhere in her addled mind she must have remembered that it was safe. And after the caisson was dropped to the bottom of the dam, she'd immediately fled all the way here. I was sure there was a reason behind this as well. But what was it? I thought of all the mysterious rooms and equipment we'd seen, of the devils' abrupt and unexplained disappearance, and of my comrades who had gone mad down here in the darkness.

A terrible feeling crept up my spine. Something bad had happened here—was still happening here—and the sooner we left the better.

10 THE UNKNOWN THREAT

Not wanting Yuan Xile to run away again, we had no choice but to tie a leash to her. Ma Zaihai pulled a rope from his pack and we fastened it around her waist. Curious as I was to find out what had happened here, I didn't want to end up like Chen Luohu. We started back down the corridor immediately. Wang Sichuan led the way, cautiously sweeping his flashlight beam through the darkness. Chen Luohu could reappear and attack at any time, so we proceeded with great care. I watched Yuan Xile as we walked, hoping she might give us some sign we were heading in the right direction.

The system of tunnels and passageways here was immensely complex, filled with boarded-up rooms and intersecting corridors. By now we were paying very close attention to our surroundings. This part of the dam was different than any we'd previously explored. In other places the cement walls had yellowed with age, but here they were almost entirely covered in splotches of some unknown black substance. The stuff wasn't blood and it wasn't paint. It almost seemed to have seeped out of the walls. Under the beam of my flashlight, the cement appeared dressed in a patchwork of decay. Had the base of the dam begun to corrode? We continued on, the darkness around us so quiet my hair stood on end. Eventually, we reached a fork in the road. Yuan Xile abruptly stopped. I gave her a little push, but she refused to move, her eyes remaining fixed on one of the passageways. It was black as the mouth of a cave.

"This way?" asked Wang Sichuan, but Yuan Xile made no response.

I glanced over at him. He nodded. I led her towards the opening. She didn't resist. I allowed myself a satisfied smile—it was working. I motioned to Wang Sichuan and we stepped into the darkness. Before long we were splashing through a puddle of black water. The tunnel floor was covered in it. One step might be shallow, but the next would be deep and it was growing deeper still. The water was turbid, filthy, and our every movement only made it worse. Mold bloomed across the walls, its scent overpowering, and unseen objects rubbed against the bottoms of our feet. After taking several more turns, we reached the source of the water. A hole had been smashed in the cement wall, revealing a complex skeleton of rusted pipes. Water dripped from a crack in the lowest pipe. To be sure, only a small amount of water was seeping out, but after this many years, it was bound to accumulate. A boarded-up entryway stood at the end of the passageway. The water had seeped into the wood and much of it had rotted away, leaving a ragged, person-sized hole. We climbed through.

A small flooded room lay beyond. Three iron beds, piled with things indiscernible in the dark, stood amid the stagnant water. We waded over. The beds were covered in equipment bearing the marks of the Chinese engineering corps. We investigated and inside one canvas bag I discovered Yuan Xile's work diary and a book in Russian. On one of the other beds Ma Zaihai discovered a pistol. It appeared to be Yuan Xile's.

"Look for the exit!" cried Wang Sichuan.

We immediately searched the room. Yuan Xile had clearly been through here—the place was still covered in her stuff, after all—and so we assumed this was just one stop on her way out of the dam, but the place was sealed tight. The only exit was the way we'd come in. There wasn't even an air vent.

Wang Sichuan sat down on the centermost bed, his face sunk in disappointment. "Dammit!" he said, looking over at Yuan Xile. "Why the hell did you bring us here?"

She didn't respond, but neither did she look as scared as before. She climbed onto the bed Wang Sichuan was sitting on, crawled to the far end and curled into a ball, her eyes staring dazedly off to the side.

And with that our hopes vanished. Frustrated, I took several deep breaths, trying to calm myself down. It would be good to rest for a moment, I told myself.

That's when Ma Zaihai abruptly yelled out, "Food!"

Turning around, I saw he'd located several cans of food in one of the canvas rucksacks. He handed me one. I was familiar with the stuff. It was certainly a lot tastier than the condensed grain rations we'd been given. Yuan Xile and the rest of her team had been treated well. I hadn't realized how hungry I was until that moment. Without a second thought, the three of us sliced open several cans and tore into the food. After untying Yuan Xile's rope, Wang Sichuan placed a can in front of her. She didn't touch it.

I looked at the water below my feet as I ate. Several vague shapes bobbed in the watery darkness. I scooped one out. It was a can, identical to those we were eating from but empty. Reaching back down, I grabbed several more and began to count them up.

"What are you doing?" asked Wang Sichuan.

"Look how many cans there are," I said. "She must have stayed here for a long time." I paused for a moment to think about my discovery. "You see how she behaved when we first arrived? I think she sees this place as some kind of safe room, somewhere to hide out."

Ripples formed in the filthy water as I continued to dredge up the cans. By now I had piled at least 30 on the bed, forming a little mountain. They were significantly heavier than our rations. No more than five were generally assigned per person. Carry too many and your strength would drain away. It would have taken seven or eight people to carry this many. It seemed Yuan Xile hadn't been alone. The place was damp and stinking and flooded with dirty water. If they'd needed somewhere to hide out, why hadn't they chosen one of the many rooms that lined the corridor outside? I thought again of Yuan Xile's sudden disappearance from the caisson. She had fled through the darkness, probably hoping to once more hide herself here. Clearly she believed it was the safest place to be. I racked my brain but could find no explanation for her behavior. Still, mad as she was, Yuan Xile knew the dam much better than us. If she felt this room was safe, then it probably was. With that thought in mind, I finally relaxed.

The bedposts were all sunk in the water and rotted, the beds themselves tilting unsteadily and wobbling with our movements, but the place was not awful. The moist stench in the air was bearable, the temperature not overly cold. Still, this was no time to rest. After quickly finishing our meals, we smoked cigarettes and got ready to set out. By now the spy had surely discovered our escape, and there was no way to know what his next move would be. Now it would simply be a matter of who was cleverest—us or him.

Ma Zaihai grabbed several more cans of food from Yuan Xile's bag and placed them in our own. Then we refastened the rope around Yuan Xile and tried to pull her towards the door. This time she wouldn't cooperate.

Pulling herself free, she scurried back to the bed and curled up. Wang Sichuan was right behind her. He picked her up like an eagle plucking a baby bird. Immediately she let out an ear-piercing scream and raked her nails against his flesh. As soon as he let go, she crawled back to the corner of the bed and began to shake. Looking at the scratch marks she'd left on his arm, Wang Sichuan grimaced in pain. His eyes flashing in anger, he grabbed her rope and was about to yank her along when I stopped him.

"Let me try," I said.

He shrugged as if he couldn't care less. Wearing my friendliest expression, I sat down beside Yuan Xile. "Engineer Yuan," I said in a soft voice, "it's time for us to leave. We are your friends and will protect you. There's nothing to fear." Yuan Xile's trembling had only grown more severe after I sat down. Now she stared at me, her face twisted into a horrible mask of terror. "It's okay," I said, "don't be afraid."

Remembering the leadership training classes I'd taken while studying in Xinjiang, I very slowly moved closer to her, then grasped her hand in mine. She had been down here for weeks, crawling through the caves, sweating in these same clothes, not bathing—she did not smell good—but her hand was still soft, smooth, and unmistakably feminine. When I held it my heart began to quiver. When one spends one's days exploring misty mountains and bushwhacking through dark forests, the mere sight of a woman is a rare treat. Relationships? Love? These things were near impossibilities. We were just happy to be around someone with two X chromosomes, even if for only a moment. And so, for these few seconds, I could barely help myself. I felt my pulse speed up and, although it was too dark for anyone to see, I'm sure I was blushing bright red. Luckily my back was to the others. Regaining my composure, I dispelled several distracting thoughts from my mind, and gently lifted Yuan Xile to her feet. Maybe it was my calm tone, I don't know, but Yuan Xile became placid, even docile. Her breathing steadied and she regarded me blankly.

Meeting her eyes, I nodded. "Trust me."

At last her shoulders relaxed, and after exchanging a glance with Wang Sichuan, I led her towards the door. Wang Sichuan and Ma Zaihai hefted their packs—all of us silent by tacit agreement—and one by one we climbed through the rotted opening and into the outer corridor. Yuan Xile made no resistance, but I didn't dare lose focus. As we stepped outside I felt her hand begin to tremble. Tightening my grip on her arm, I softly urged her along the pitch-black corridor. Suddenly, a blue-green light blinked on ahead of us, dimly illuminating our surroundings. The power appeared to be back on. The spy must have realized we were gone.

One after another, the lights that remained intact flickered to life. There were not many of them and were widely scattered. Every short, lonely stretch of light was followed by a length of utter darkness, as if the corridor were moving from day to night and back again. What a stroke of luck, I thought. Now we no longer needed to grope blindly through the blackness. We each switched off our flashlights. It was then I realized Yuan Xile's hand was shaking far more than before. I held firm, hoping to reassure her, but in a flash she threw me off, climbed back through the opening and retreated to the exact same spot on the bed as before.

This was beginning to get annoying. Wang Sichuan and I exchanged a glance. The rope was in his hands and from the look in his eyes I could tell he didn't give a damn anymore. He was going to tie her tight and drag her the whole way back if he had to. Seeing no alternative, I followed him over. That's when I heard it. Yuan Xile was speaking. At first I thought she was reciting a prayer, but, drawing closer, I realized she was repeating the same two sentences over and over again.

"Turn off the lights," she murmured. "Ghosts live in the shadows. Turn off the lights. Ghosts live in the shadows. Turn off the lights..."

11 GHOSTS IN THE SHADOWS

I stared at Yuan Xile. Then I looked back at the dimly lit hallway. A shiver ran down my spine. It wasn't her words that scared me. It was her expression as she said them.

Clearly she was terrified of the lights in the hallway. Given how well she knew this place, I didn't doubt that some new danger was going to appear now that they'd been switched back on.

"Ghosts live in the shadows."

The special emissary Su Zhenhua had said almost the same thing back in the abandoned warehouse. What did it mean? What ghosts lived in the shadows? Hearing Yuan Xile's plea for us to turn off the lights, I suddenly remembered where we'd first found her. She'd been wandering through the pitch-black caverns for who knows how long, all without a flashlight or any other kind of light source to shine the way. I didn't believe in ghosts, but two people had said this same thing to us, and both had gone crazy. We'd be fools not to take it seriously.

I grabbed Wang Sichuan and stopped him from binding Yuan Xile. Though he might deny it, he was a religious man and therefore much more sensitive to this kind of talk. I feared that if he was unable to control his emotions, he might use too much force. Again I looked back at the silent hallway, split into sections of light and dark, and I felt myself hesitate. But we couldn't wait here forever, and who knew when the lights would go out again? Passively holing up had never been my style anyway. Not to mention that we'd been using flashlights to shine our way this entire time, and not once had we lit upon anything like a ghost.

"Engineer Wu," said Ma Zaihai, "why don't I go first? If something's not right I'll holler."

I shook my head. Yuan Xile was going to be a big hassle and we had only three people. With one person minding her, the other two would be barely enough to watch the front and rear. And with all the stuff we were now carrying it would be unwise to split up. Better to stick together, thinking and moving quickly as a team. By now I'd decided that rather than continue our search for the exit here, we should first return to the ventilation shaft in the main tunnel and then decide on our next move. If the lights were merely a benign stroke of luck, then there was nothing to fear.

And if there was? Well, then we had nowhere to hide. This was how I calmed myself. At this time we were driven by a kind of fatalistic passion. There were few cowards in our ranks, kind of like knowing that a tiger lurked in the mountains ahead, yet marching resolutely onwards. That was our principal, though such thinking must appear almost incomprehensible to some people. These were extraordinary times and dedication to heroism was often the only thing that got us through. At the very least, it kept us from backing down.

By now there was no longer any hope of placating Yuan Xile. Without waiting another moment, Wang Sichuan grabbed her, sealed her mouth, roped her up, and lifted her over his shoulder. Grabbing the iron club, I led the way out of the room. Wang Sichuan was a few steps behind me and Ma Zaihai brought up the rear. We climbed through the opening, waded through the stagnant water and soon enough were back on dry cement. Although the origins of life—and therefore of man—emerged from the primordial seas, one couldn't help but feel a much deeper affection for solid ground. After shaking the water from my boots, my mind felt much more at ease. Had it not been for Yuan Xile's ominous words, I would have felt only great happiness upon leaving that wretched chamber.

Up ahead was the first of the emergency lights. Amid all this darkness, there was something decidedly inauspicious about it, but without hesitating, I turned and beckoned everyone onward. Once we were all standing beneath the light, I took a closer look at it. It was encased in an iron shell and appeared entirely ordinary. I rapped the casement several times with the club. It sounded much too thick to be simply cracked open. Why had these lights been so heavily reinforced? My first thought upon being told to "Turn off the lights" was to do just that, but now I could see this wasn't going to be possible.

With Yuan Xile's words echoing in the back of my mind, I found myself watching my shadow in the lamplight. It was thinly stretched out across the blackened cement. We looked at one another, my shadow and I, and at first I noticed nothing amiss. Then I saw it—something wasn't right here at all. Cold beads of sweat dripped down my back. Something very strange had happened to my shadow.

12 STRANGE SHADOWS

Everyone knows that even if one's shadow becomes elongated, it is still easily recognizable as one's own. But these shadows were not simply elongated. Something was wrong with them, but I found it very difficult to determine exactly what. If pressed, though, I would have said this: These shadows were not our own.

They clearly extended from our feet up onto the wall, but in no way did they resemble us. Each was bent-backed and severely stooped at the waist, as if they belonged to someone 60- or 70-years-old. My hair stood on end. Had Yuan Xile not spoken those words, I would surely have assumed my eyes were playing tricks on me, but now I couldn't ignore them. Ma Zaihai waved his hand. His crooked shadow did the same. Somehow they were ours.

"What the hell?" I said beneath my breath. I looked up at the light. "Maybe it's got something to do with the angle."

Ma Zaihai shook his head.

Wang Sichuan waved his hand, then made a complex series of movements. His shadow followed along, but there was something off and sluggish about the way it moved. A chill ran down my spine as I watched. Yuan Xile was right; there were ghosts in the goddamn shadows. This was bad. We all knew it. Was this what had caused the others to go mad? Such a reaction seemed more than a little extreme. Scary as these bent forms were, the shadows couldn't actually do anything to us. I knew the situation couldn't be so simple.

Yuan Xile and Chen Luohu had both gone crazy. Now they were each scared of the shadows and scared of the lights. I had no idea what was going on, but I was sure the mere sight of the shadows had not made them this way. I looked at Yuan Xile, slung over Wang Sichuan's shoulder. Her face was twisted away from the wall, absolutely unwilling to even look. She was so scared her entire body was shaking. A single thought stuck in my mind. We need to get out of here. Whatever was going on was already way past anything we could understand. There was no sense in sticking around trying to figure it out. We could rack our brains all we wanted once we were back in the main tunnel, but the sooner we got there the better. Giving Wang Sichuan and Ma Zaihai a forceful nudge, I told them not to worry about it, and we ran on.

Increasing our pace, we hurried down the passageway. At the very first intersection we realized our mistake. We'd followed Yuan Xile here, stumbling through the darkness. Not once had we given any thought on to how to get back. Every route looked the same, all of them lined with identical boarded-up rooms and corridors. None of us had any idea what to do. We were all twitchy and shaken. The shadows never ceased in their pursuit. At each pool of light I would turn and look back and there they would be, misshapen as ever and floating along the wall just behind us. Proving his worth once more, Ma Zaihai managed to lead us back to the main tunnel, although by a different route. We kicked out the boards sealing the final doorway and stepped through into the wide tunnel. The lights were all on.

They were gas lamps, set high on the walls, and they bathed the entire tunnel in a pale yellow light. Everything was illuminated. Combined with the great width of the tunnel, this put me into an easier mood. We hurried out into the light. Here the light was too strong and coming from too many angles to create much of a shadow. As I looked down I couldn't tell whether mine had returned to normal. We all breathed a sigh of relief. Wang Sichuan turned to look for the ventilation shaft. Finding it would be no easy task, but it was still much preferable to searching the tortuous, half-light/half-dark corridors we'd been stuck in. This tunnel just ran in a long, straight line. It was only a matter of time.

We split up and began to search. Although I was still terribly uneasy, I told myself that even if there really were ghosts, this place was bright enough that we should be safe. As I thought this, I turned and looked back at the darkened corridor. Something was standing just beyond the entryway. Several somethings. They were bent-backed and curved at the waists, half their bodies hidden in the darkness. Squeezed into the narrow opening, they stood still as statues. I squinted into the dark. There were four. My body went cold. Had our shadows climbed off the walls of the passageway and followed us here?

13 LAST BREATH

Wang Sichuan's eyes went wide. Whispering a prayer in Mongolian, he tightened his grip on the iron club. Looking down, though, I realized something wasn't right. I could still make out the faint outline of our shadows on the floor. They were still with us, not bent-backed and lurking in the dark entryway. If those weren't our shadows, then why were they nearly identical to how ours had bent in the half-lit corridor?

As long as they weren't ghosts we'd be fine, I thought. I'd encountered my share of savage beasts and seen some strange things while exploring China's wildest territories, but I'd never come across anything supernatural. We glanced at one another and started toward the waiting shadows. Wang Sichuan switched on his flashlight and shined it ahead. As soon as the light crossed the entryway, we froze. The space was empty. The shadows had vanished. Wang Sichuan moved the light away. Immediately the shadows reappeared. When he shined it back at the entryway, it was once more utterly empty. We exchanged a worried glance.

"They really are ghosts," said Ma Zaihai, his voice quaking.

Yuan Xile was still slung over Wang Sichuan's shoulder, her face twisted away from the shadows. She stared straight at the blinding lights overhead. Her whole body was shaking. Cold sweat dripped down my back. If it weren't so bright, I would have already taken off running in the opposite direction.

I turned to Wang Sichuan. "Why don't you go take a look?" I said. "Tengri's protecting you."

"Yeah and Marx is protecting you," he replied. "Tenggri and I haven't spoken in a while."

I looked at him. This wasn't good. I recalled my education in materialism, repeated several famous lines to bolster my courage, then turned back to Wang Sichuan. "Keep your flashlight on," I said. "I'm going to take a look." I hefted the club and walked straight for the entryway. I was convinced that the shadows weren't ghosts, but just what they were, I had no idea.

Wang Sichuan kept the entryway illuminated and it stayed empty. When I was standing just outside of it, I signaled to him and got ready. He moved the light away. Immediately the "shadows" reappeared, but now that I was close I could see they weren't shadows at all. Inside the dark entryway were slightly lighter and slightly darker patches of darkness. It was as if the light from the main tunnel became somehow distorted as it flowed through the entryway. This phenomenon was difficult to describe, but it didn't appear dangerous. I waved for Wang Sichuan and Ma Zaihai to come closer. Shining our flashlights into the entryway, we could see that this distortion happened all the way down the corridor.

"There's something in the air," I said. The wheels in my mind began to turn. I looked back at Wang Sichuan. "Do you remember much of physics class?" I asked.

"Which part?" he replied.

"Light refraction."

"Umm… When light rays pass through gases—or liquids or solids—of different densities, the amount of refraction differs. This means the light appears to change. Like a rainbow—that's just light passing through suspended water droplets. Are you talking about that?"

I nodded and shined my flashlight along the ceiling of the corridor. Sure enough, the level of refraction was even more severe. This explained our shadows' stooped appearances. There was a large difference in density as the air rose up in the passage, but what was causing it? Rather than ease them, my worries increased. Yuan Xile was a brilliant woman. Anything I could think of would already have occurred to her. The shadows would never have frightened her into madness.

She had spoken two sentences to us, but only one of them was a command. It was explicit: "Turn off the lights." I remembered that when we traveled down the tunnel she hadn't once looked at the shadows, but rather stared at the lights the whole time. By now I was back inside the corridor. The first of the lamps was just ahead. I walked quickly over, my crooked shadow following closely behind. The light here was heavily distorted. When I waved my hand the air seemed to ripple, as if from desert heat. The closer I got to the lamp, the more pronounced the phenomenon became. I felt the wall. It was burning hot. The heat from the lamp must have begun to melt the wall, releasing some substance into the air and causing this distortion. I thought of the black streaks that had formed along the corridor walls and of Yuan Xile and Chen Luohu cowering madly in the darkness. At once I covered my mouth. A wave of dizziness rushed over me. Telling myself it was all in my head, I took several deep breaths, but this made me feel even worse. With my heart pounding in my chest, I turned and sprinted back out of the passageway. Only once I reached Wang Sichuan did I dare take another breath.

"It's the air!" I yelled at them, pointing at the lamps overhead. "The air here is toxic!" As I looked up, the words caught in my throat. The air wavered overhead. The light twisted and bowed.

Wang Sichuan's eyes went wide. "What the hell is that?" he asked.

Shaking my head, I looked over at Yuan Xile. She was still staring at the lights and shaking worse than ever. I swept my hand through the air. It must already be full of the toxin. My skull felt like it was cracking open. Ma Zaihai began to grab at his throat.

"What the hell is this place," yelled Wang Sichuan, "a goddamn gas chamber?" His hand was over his mouth, but he didn't seem to be affected yet.

"What do we do now?" I asked. I thought of Chen Luohu. I didn't want to turn into that. "This stuff does something to your brain," I continued. "If we stay here too long we'll all go crazy or just die on the spot."

We all looked at Yuan Xile. She was staring down the black corridor from which we'd come.

"The safe room!" yelled Wang Sichuan. "This is why she hid out there—why she refused to leave. We'll be safe inside."

At once he set her down, untied her ropes and took a step back. In the blink of an eye she was sprinting for the mouth of the corridor. Yuan Xile knew this place well. She was sure to lead us back to the safe room via the fastest route possible. Without a second thought, we took off after her.

14 DEAD MAN'S WALK

Some of the corridor lights were on, but most weren't. We were running like mad and, even with our flashlights shining the way, it was difficult to see. We tried our best to follow Yuan Xile, but the path kept branching and she kept turning. Eventually we were just following the sound of her footsteps. After taking several turns, I realized Yuan Xile's route was far from the most direct. Instead, it was the darkest, the one with the fewest lamps. She was trying to keep from inhaling any more of the poison than she had to. This was obviously a fixed route, one she or someone else had figured out long ago. Unfortunately, this made it impossible for anyone who didn't know the way to keep up. Soon Wang Sichuan, Ma Zaihai and I had all taken separate turns. I could no longer see them. Footsteps echoed all around me and I couldn't tell one pair from the next. The lightest and nearest had to be Yuan Xile's. They never stopped moving.

I quickly reached a long, pitch-black corridor, at least 500 feet from the nearest lamp. Someone was stumbling blindly about inside. I'd found her. She had slowed greatly. Something was in her way. Watching her stagger along in the dark, I knew it wouldn't be any easier for me. If I could catch up to her now, I'd be saved, but if I was too slow getting through this stretch, she'd leave me in the dust the moment she was out. Unlike her, though, I had a flashlight. With the beam cutting through the darkness, I took off down the corridor. Not 10 steps later I toppled to my knees. I looked to see why I'd fallen. The floor was covered with bodies.

They all lay crosswise down the length of the corridor, each man dressed in the uniform of the Chinese engineering corps. I recognized several faces—these were Old Tang's men. Crouching beside one soldier, I felt his pulse. Then I tried the next man, and the next. They were all dead. I stood and shined my flashlight across the bodies. The dim beam revealed face after familiar face. I couldn't determine how they had died. My mind went blank. In a place like this there was safety in numbers and I had never lost hope that we would soon run into the other groups. Now, as I took in the scene before me, this hope was finally dashed.

Then I saw Old Tang. He was stretched out on the floor, same as the rest of the men. His nose and mouth were covered in dried blood and mucus. My heart pounded as I knelt down and felt his pulse. He'd been dead a long time. I didn't know Old Tang well, but over the last few days we'd often spoke. His death hit me hard. Cursing under my breath, I was about to continue after Yuan Xile when I saw something in Old Cat's hand. It was a small bag. Remembering the map Old Tang had carried, I tried to pull the bag from his clenched fingers. It wouldn't budge. His corpse was locked in rigor mortis. His hand was tight as a steel vise. One by one, I peeled his fingers back and pulled the bag free. Then I remembered his gun. I checked his hip holster. It was empty. I searched the rest of the men. Their guns and grenades were all gone. There was no time to think about it. I looked up. Yuan Xile was nearing the end of the passageway. I had to get moving.

I hurried along, stepping over the sprawled corpses. They soon thinned out. Most were packed in the middle of the corridor. Had they come here to escape the poison, then fallen victim to someone's plot? The more I thought about it, the more convinced I became that this was no accident. Their bodies had been searched, their weapons removed. My heart filled with fear. It had to be the spy. He was sure to know all about this place, about the lights and the poison and the winding, pitch-black corridors. And that the ventilation shaft in the projection room ran straight here. Had it all been a ploy? Had he smoked out the projection room only to lead us here?

Yuan Xile herself knew these corridors well. I couldn't help wondering how she'd first found this place. Had the spy managed to lead not only us but the majority of our team—and Yuan Xile's before us—into these poisoned passageways so he could do away with us en masse? If so, then he definitely didn't come with our team. He must have arrived with Yuan Xile. After finishing off her comrades, he'd laid low and waited for the next contingent. Then he'd done it all over again.

Thinking about this filled me with regret. The spy, this unseen enemy, had toyed with us from the moment we entered the cave. He knew this place like the back of his hand and he was deadly smart. I had vastly underestimated him. I'd believed our greatest threat came from the cave itself. The spy had been merely a concept—something we had to be cautious about, nothing more—but I was wrong. He was far and away the most dangerous thing down here.

Soon I was once more beneath the lamps. My shadow was even more distorted than before and I was overcome with dizziness. A strange ringing sounded in my ears. I didn't know if it was the toxins or if I was already starting to lose my mind. The tunnel before me began to twist and elongate. I could barely keep my balance as I ran. Up ahead, Yuan Xile tumbled to the floor again and again, but each time she crawled to her feet and carried on. My entire being was focused on keeping up with her. Forcing myself to stay upright, I pinballed off the walls and sprinted wildly down the corridor. Two or three more minutes later we reached a familiar turn. She rounded it and I followed. The flooded hallway was before us, the safe room at its end.

As soon as I stepped into the water, my head began to clear. The walls were ice-cold and the water was deep. As we waded in, our shadows quickly returned to normal. Somehow the water here counteracted the poison in the air. I forced myself to take several deep breaths. The air smelled as foul as before, but now I could see straight. I looked up. Yuan Xile was gone. I hurriedly followed her into the safe room. My eyes went wide. Yuan Xile stood in the center of safe room removing her clothes.

15 SAFE ROOM

I watched as Yuan Xile dunked her head into the filthy water, then vigorously washed her eyes, ears, nose, and mouth. I did the same. My pounding headache and the ringing in my ears soon went away. Without hesitation, she then began peeling off her clothes, piece by piece, and throwing them into the water. My mouth dropped open. I had never seen a naked woman before. All at once my eyes were filled with her snow-white body. She dunked her clothes in the water and used them to wipe herself down. I stood there in a daze, watching her. My whole body had gone stiff.

It's difficult to do justice to what I saw. Yuan Xile was slender yet well-endowed, her body rich in feminine charms. Her skin was white as lambswool, her shape soft and full. I probably could have stood there forever, but she pushed me under. As the freezing water rushed into my nose, I was shocked back to consciousness. As soon as I climbed to my feet she began tearing off my clothes. I could tell she knew what she was doing and was trying to help me. Following her example, I rubbed myself down with my soaked clothes. They felt extremely smooth, almost satiny. After a few scrapes, my skin felt the same. Whatever was in the water was working. I didn't stop until my skin had gone bright red. Yuan Xile was already curled up on the bed, her wet clothes draped over her. She was hugging them to herself. Her body was mostly covered, but her bare shoulders and voluptuous curves were still enough to set my mind ablaze.

After standing there awkward and naked for several moments, I also wrapped my clothes around me. They were freezing, of course, but gradually my shivering slowed. This was when I began to react to the poison. Every part of me felt as if it were breaking down. With my last bit of strength I climbed onto the bed. And then I moved no more.

The ringing in my ears and the pain in my skull brought me back to consciousness. I writhed and squirmed and was out again. This continued over and over. My life was in Heaven's hands. I had inhaled much more gas than Yuan Xile. I didn't know if I would make it. I thought again of her body. The full peaks of her breasts and her slender waist were like a joke God was playing on me. In my final moments of consciousness, He'd decided to show me the most beautiful thing in the world.

I had no idea how long I was out. When I finally came to my clothes were already dry. Vomit caked the sides of my mouth and my pants stunk of urine. I must have pissed myself in my sleep. Who knew when I had thrown up? I forced myself to get up. Switching on my flashlight, I scanned the room. Yuan Xile was now lying on a different bed. I walked over. Her face was white as a ghost and the blood had drained from her lips. She couldn't stop shaking. Much of the clothing covering her body had slipped off. As I placed my hand against her forehead, my heart sank. It was burning hot. She was sick.

For a time I despaired. There was no medicine for her take and no one to ask for help. I knew she was too frail to last much longer. That she had survived until now was pretty damn impressive. Then I remembered Old Tang's bag. I found it and searched through it. There was no medicine, but I did find several boxes of matches. Yuan Xile needed warmth and hot water to drink. I needed them, too. I stacked the empty food cans into a pyramid and placed pieces of relatively dry wood into the cans at the top. I then tore off strips of my clothing, lit them on fire, and dropped them inside. Finally, I filled a can with the water that dripped from the pipe outside and placed it atop the structure. Before long the water was hot. I helped Yuan Xile drink some, then placed several of the cans, now filled with hot coals, around her body, hoping to warm her up. Slowly the color returned to her face.

Seeing Yuan Xile take a turn for the better, I allowed myself to relax and think back on what had happened. I was overcome with guilt. Yuan Xile had given us ample warning—and we had known this place was dangerous—yet I had still behaved so rashly. It was obvious that Wang Sichuan and Ma Zaihai had never found the safe room. I walked to the entryway and shouted their names again and again, but I didn't dare go out. There was no response. My heart went cold. The corridors were almost silent. If my comrades were still conscious, they would definitely have heard my voice. Had they fainted, I wondered, or were they already dead? I thought of Old Tang and his dead men. Things didn't look good for my two friends. At last I had led them to their deaths.

The weight of what I'd done bore down on me. The lamps outside remained on and the poison continued to fill the air. Yuan Xile and I would be trapped inside for as long as this kept up. I wanted to smash my head into the wall, but I had to think of a way out. Pawing through Old Tang's bag, I came upon several pieces of hardtack. I broke off a small chunk and chewed it mechanically. Tucked away at the very bottom of the bag were the blueprints of the dam and cave system we had earlier found. I deduced our general location. We were in a huge area at the very heart of the dam, next to a space labeled "Level 4." The icehouse was on the opposite side of Level 4. Then I realized: Level 4 was the abandoned warehouse we had investigated. The sealed iron door at the end of the main tunnel led directly there. We'd made a huge loop since being trapped in the electrical canal beneath the warehouse. We were almost back where we began. Now I was certain the tunnel had been built for transporting supplies. The pieces began to fit together. The icehouse connected to the warehouse, the warehouse to the transport tunnel. Yuan Xile and Chen Luohu had vanished from the icehouse, only to reappear here, and we'd found the special emissary Su Zhenhua in the warehouse. He, too, had lost his mind. I was sure that he had been through here as well. This meant I was right—there was a route that led to the warehouse from here.

Unfortunately, I'd never been particularly skilled at reading blueprints. The area in the prints was crisscrossed with countless passageways to form a kind of chessboard. Each passageway was lined with rooms on both sides. At first I was unable to determine which was ours, but because I knew this room, unlike most others, was located at a dead-end, I was able to narrow it down. But where were all the exits? There didn't seem to be any marked except for the iron door at the end of the main tunnel. There must be some other way to reach the warehouse. I searched my memory until my brain hurt. Even if I found a way out, how the hell were we supposed to get there? I looked at the lamps glowing in the corridor. What would happen to us if they never went off?

I lay down and closed my eyes. Suddenly, I thought of where I'd first seen Yuan Xile. I sat back up at once. Something didn't make sense. The first prospecting team had most likely been tricked by the spy into exploring these corridors, after which he'd turned on the lights and released the poison. Out of sheer, desperate luck, Yuan Xile and some others had found this room and hidden inside. Afterwards, Yuan Xile and Su Zhenhua had each escaped this part of the dam. Yuan Xile had even made it all the way back to the rocky shoal. The poison was too deadly for them to have fled while it still filled the air. The lights must have turned off. Why?

I could think of two possibilities. The first was that the spy had inexplicably cut the power. The second was that so little rain had fallen that there was not enough water in the dam to keep the electricity on. As Yuan Xile waited in this flooded room, something had caused the dam to go dark. Seeing her chance, she had escaped, but then, wandering through the pitch-black caverns, she'd completely lost her mind. Eventually she ran into us. Knowing no better, we'd brought her back here. I looked over at her. At last I understood the extent to which we'd betrayed her trust. If she hadn't gone mad, I'm sure she would have hacked me to pieces by now.

Soft sounds escaped her lips as she slept. I covered her back up and felt her forehead. Her fever had not abated, so I dunked a strip of clothing in the cold water and placed it on her forehead. Then I forced myself to use the time I had to study the blueprint.

I couldn't help wishing Ma Zaihai were here. I was sure that with one glance he'd have the whole thing figured out. I rifled through my memories, trying to recall times we'd discussed the blueprints. The only thing I could remember was Old Tang talking about the difference between the solid and dotted indicator lines. The solid black lines represented electrical wires, he'd said, while the dotted line represented the antenna. Scanning the many solid indicator lines, I gasped. Was this how Yuan Xile and company had turned off the lights? Had they cut the power? One by one, I charted the course of every electrical wire. At last I found the one I was looking for, the primary wire. It led to a room from which nearly all the other wires originated. I could tell this room was nearby and a master switch appeared to be inside, but then my heart sank. Even if I was able to make it there, I'd never survive. The poison wasn't going to vanish as soon as the lights went out and I didn't have a chance of quickly finding my way back here in the dark.

I folded up the map. The damn thing was useless to me. The mission was incomplete, we had run out of options, and we were going to starve to death down here. The mission? The film canister!

I felt my back. It wasn't there. Wang Sichuan must still have it, I thought. Shit. I swallowed hard and wrapped my hands against my skull. The film canister was still our last chance out of here.

And we weren't the only one who wanted it.

16 CLOSE QUARTERS

As far as I knew, the spy's only remaining objective was to retrieve the film canister. Wang Sichuan might have it now, but sooner or later the spy would be coming for it. I needed to get ready. Thus far the spy had executed his plans with remarkable precision, but the network of rooms and passageways here was intricate and sprawling. It would be impossible for him to know exactly where the film canister had ended up. And I was sure he was unaware of the safe room. Otherwise Yuan Xile would have long since been done away with. Once the spy assumed us dead or crazy, he would make his way down here and begin a slow and systematic search. First, he would either turn off the lights or put on a gas mask, with the latter being more likely. This would be easy, I told myself. A man's greatest desire is also his greatest weakness, so long as the spy didn't immediately locate Wang Sichuan, I could set a trap for him. One good ambush deserved another. I would have my revenge.

I knew the bastard wouldn't be arriving anytime soon. As I thought about it, the outline of a plan began to take shape. My limbs ached as I moved about the room. I had no chance of subduing the spy in my present condition. For now, my best bet was to rest. First, though, I had to deal with Yuan Xile. I carried her toward the bed farthest from the entryway. Her limbs hung limply and her skin was feverishly hot. The smell of her body made my heart pound. As soon as I lifted her up, the clothes covering her fell away. Holding them with my mouth, I did my best not to look, but my face still turned bright red. After gently laying her down, I sat for a moment and composed myself, and then once more arranged the hot cans around her body. Here the faint light they emitted was hidden from the entryway.

Although the hole in the boards blocking the entryway made me uneasy, sealing it up would be too obvious. The spy would get suspicious if he saw it. That's when I remembered the deep water filling the corridor outside. If anyone approached I'd definitely hear them. I covered myself with my clothing and lay back down. As soon as my eyes closed I was asleep.

I slept fitfully, dreaming many dreams, none of them peaceful. Suddenly, in the hazy borderland between dreams and reality, I felt myself come to. Something wasn't right. As I struggled back to consciousness, a faint, pleasant scent invaded my nostrils. My body felt unusually warm. I forced myself awake. Someone was lying on top of me. I gave a start, but when my hand touched the smooth, hot skin of a naked back, I knew exactly what had happened. It was Yuan Xile.

I froze. All at once I felt her spellbinding curves and soft skin pressed against every part of my body, her face buried against my neck, her hands clinging tightly to my torso. For a moment my whole being went stiff, but I soon calmed down, pulled my clothing out from between us and laid it over her. Then I held her.

I don't understand women, don't know why something like this would happen, but now that it was happening, I had no complaints. Even if she suddenly came to and slapped me across the face, I would regret nothing. Even if she reported me for crimes of indecency, it would still have been worth it. She rocked slightly on my chest, as if to tell me that it was okay, that she felt the same as me. Then she held me tighter and I felt tears drip down my stomach. As I nuzzled her hair with my chin, a strange feeling suddenly rushed forth from deep inside me. It wasn't desire; I know it wasn't desire. I'm just that simple. For no reason in particular, I suddenly felt that I loved this woman, and that I had to protect her—no matter what.

Young love is always like this. It requires only the tiniest spark to set aflame, but once burning it is unconditional and undying—even to the point of complete irrationality. Holding Yuan Xile in my arms, I wondered if it really was love I was feeling. I knew such thoughts were far from her mind. She had been in a state of absolute terror for the past several weeks. She'd experienced horror after horror, had been driven mad. Yuan Xile wanted only to hold someone and to be held, to press close against someone else's body. Had Wang Sichuan been here in my place, I'm sure the same thing would have happened. But there was nothing coincidental or random about the way I felt. My feelings were directed at Yuan Xile and at her alone. As we held one another, they grew inside of me until they were more beautiful than any I had ever known. I dared not move. Nor did I want to. I merely lay there, contentedly stroking her hair.

Having perhaps drawn some of my body heat, Yuan Xile began to sweat. As drops of it fell from her forehead onto my chest, her breathing relaxed and her temperature dropped. Our sweat-soaked bodies were soon stuck together. After a while, I gently lifted her off and went to add wood to the hot cans. The corridor lights remained on. I took a deep breath, trying to wake myself up, and splashed my face with dirty water. I heard Yuan Xile roll over on the bed, searching for a more comfortable position. Then I began to plan. First of all, this place was too quiet to hunt the spy through the corridors. I needed to lure him close, then attack. But if I set the trap in here and it failed, Yuan Xile would suffer the consequences. It would also be foolish to reveal the safe room's location—it was much too important to us. I needed to find somewhere else to ambush him.

I soaked myself with water, cautiously stepped outside the room and shined my flashlight down the corridor. Nothing glinted in the half-lit darkness. No one was there. Several entryways yawned blackly on either side. A second corridor crossed this one at the far end of the stagnant water approximately 60 feet from the safe room and far enough away to ensure Yuan Xile would remain hidden. Rooms lined the corridor. This was where I would spring my trap.

Now I needed to think of a way to stay out there as long as possible without getting sick. The water was the key. Somehow it counteracted the poison. I thought of turning my undershorts into a face-mask, wetting them with the clean water that dripped from the pipe and using them to cover my mouth, but too much of my body would still be exposed. I remembered the blackened corpses in the silent barracks. The poison could surely be absorbed through one's skin as well. Just as I was considering whether it would be best to simply wet all of my clothes, I heard a noise from inside the room. Something had fallen over. Yuan Xile must have woken up. I hurried back. She was standing in the center of the room, still unclothed, shaking with fear. The hot cans I'd placed beside her had fallen to the ground.

I stepped close. "Xile."

Seeing me, she rushed over and threw her arms around me. I could feel her entire body tremble. She must have thought I'd abandoned her. This realization made me cringe. Any man, let alone a woman, left here stranded and solitary was bound to fall apart

"It's okay," I whispered. "I'm here." I took a deep breath and embraced her, hoping she'd calm down and let go, but she only held me tighter. So I picked her up and laid her down on the bed. "I won't leave you," I said to her, squeezing her hand. "I'm just thinking of a way to get us out of here. Don't be afraid."

She continued to stare at me, no less agitated than before. Tears ran down her cheeks. She reached out and embraced me again. I sighed. What could I do? The look on her face would have softened the hardest heart. I couldn't bear to push her away again, so I hugged her close and together we slowly relaxed together.

I don't know how long I held her before she began to calm down. Pointing at the cans, I indicated that I needed to fetch more wood to relight them. She reluctantly let me go. Taking a deep breath, I stood up and gathered all the cans she'd knocked over. I filled each with firewood and relit them. While doing so, I realized that this wasn't going to work. There was no way I'd be able to persuade her to calmly wait here while I ambushed the spy. She'd been alone in the darkness for too long. Watching me leave would terrify her and I didn't want to torment her any further. She couldn't speak and probably couldn't understand me when I did. I had to think of some other method to let her know I would always return.

I walked back to the bed and felt Yuan Xile's forehead. Her fever remained, but she was used to braving the elements and was in excellent shape. If not, she would have already been long dead. Standing over her now, I saw her body and face were filthy. I felt her hands and feet. They were frigid. Her feet were covered in blisters, yet despite it all they remained slender and fine. She must come from a good family, I thought. Still, after all the miles she'd walked as a prospector, the cramped confines of her PLA boots had left their mark.

I heated up a can of water. When it was warm, I tore off a piece of my clothing, wetted it, and wiped her feet clean. Then I used the prong from my belt buckle to pop her blisters one by one. The warm water had already softened them and she seemed to feel no pain. She just kept staring up at me, not saying a word. I squeezed her blisters dry, then once more wiped her feet with warm water. This had to hurt. Several times her whole body clenched up, but she continued to watch me calmly, doing her utmost to endure the pain. And then she smiled. My heart melted. Back when she was known as the "Soviet Witch," her smile had been extremely hard to come by, but now she looked just like a young girl again, incomparably gentle and sweet. What a pity all this had to happen under these circumstances; if she ever regained her sanity, none of this would mean anything to her. Our relationship would be just as it had been before. Yet somehow, my heart was content. In a place like this, to see her perfect smile was all I could ask for.

When I was done, I laid her slender feet on the bed, then washed her socks and placed them aside. Even with several recent-looking holes, they were still in much better shape than mine, which had long since begun to resemble a pair of dirty nets.

"Tomorrow you can get up," I said, looking at her, "but right now it would be best to stay in bed. How about it?"

She nodded and motioned for me to lie down with her, but I shook my head. Suddenly I understood how to get her to let me leave the room.

Over the next three days, I never stopped listening for noise from the corridor beyond, but all was silent. The spy's patience was remarkable. Unfortunately, there was also no word from Wang Sichuan or Ma Zaihai. Twice a day I washed Yuan Xile's feet. Gradually, her blisters disappeared. Given how dirty the place was, it set my heart at ease to see no sign of infection. Once her feet were washed clean, I'd walk outside the room, dump out the dirty water and fill a can with clean water from the exposed pipe in the wall. I did this every time, and each time I made sure to stay away longer than the last. At first this worried her, but when she saw I always returned she began to trust me. Soon she was no longer so anxious.

As for the other part of my plan, I shaped one of the can lids into a triangular, three-pointed blade. Cans in those days were sturdy and sharp-edged. With only a little work, one could be turned into a vicious weapon. I also experimented with soaking my clothing in water and venturing out into the poisoned air. I discovered that if I wrapped three layers of wet cloth over my nose and mouth, I could last for five or six minutes before beginning to feel the ill effects. This might not be long, but it was long enough. Next I attached the prong from my belt buckle to the inside of one of the empty cans, forming a makeshift bell. Then I took apart Old Tang's bag and tied a length of its thick cotton thread to the end of the prong, allowing me to ring the bell at a distance. Finally, I hung the bell in the room that was to be my trap.

Each night we retired to our separate beds, but, when I opened my eyes the next morning, there she was, soundly asleep on my chest. At the time I believed this was the most intimate two people could be with one another. I'm no saint, though, and feverish urges gripped me, but I could see no alternative. In the quietest hours of the night, as she slept peacefully on me, a single hope would appear in my mind.

I hoped the spy would never come, that Yuan Xile and I would remain alone in this quiet forever. But what must come will come. It always does.

17 THE SPY

Four days passed before it happened. I was sitting by the entryway, silently listening for sounds from the corridor, when I heard the soft echo of footsteps. I'd become so accustomed to quietly passing each day that at first I thought I must have been mistaken, but there was no mistaking it. The echo continued. Someone else was down here. My heart sprinted. Grabbing my blade, I tried to gauge where the footsteps were coming from, but all I could tell was they weren't yet close by.

I hurriedly washed Yuan Xile's feet and signaled to her that I was going out. My face must have betrayed my agitation. She seemed reluctant to let me go, but I gave her no time to react. Grabbing the empty water can, I quickly stood and left. Out in the corridor, I felt around for the end of the thread I'd prepared. I pulled it and the makeshift bell rang out, breaking the silence. The clang of metal striking metal ricocheted through the passageways. The footsteps stopped.

Not wanting him to become overly suspicious, I waited a minute before ringing again. I held my breath and listened. His footsteps, softer now, their direction impossible to discern, creaked through the quiet that followed. He was being more cautious.

Taking a deep breath, I waited, ringing the bell only once every two or three minutes. Curious of the sound's pattern, he gradually drew closer.

Gripping the blade between my teeth, I sunk underwater and floated towards the bell room.

I didn't know which direction he'd be coming from. If he appeared somewhere ahead of me along the corridor, I could probably the jump on him, but I hoped this wouldn't be the case. Yuan Xile was directly behind me, waiting in the darkened safe room. Ideally, the spy would come from the far end of the bisecting corridor and as soon as he was inside the bell room, I'd make my move.

Now that I was soaked to the bone, I'd be able to stay out here for at least five minutes before worrying about the poison. All the time in the world. The footsteps were soon very close by. He was moving much more slowly now, pausing a few seconds between each step. There was a lonely stand of light some distance ahead of me. No shadow appeared. He must be coming from another direction. Indeed, the more I listened, the more the footsteps seemed to be sounding from somewhere off to my right. Just as I had hoped; he was coming from the far end of the bisecting corridor.

I crept up to the intersection of the two corridors and peered to the right. No lights in that direction, a sheet of total darkness. Crouched just beyond the water, hiding behind the corner of the intersection, I started to feel sick. I had to dunk my head in the water every few minutes to stay lucid. I'd never been gone this long before. Yuan Xile was like a ticking time bomb, just waiting to go off.

I didn't ring the bell again. I didn't want to risk him hearing the thread rub against the side of the entryway. Gritting my teeth, I endured the nausea and focused all my attention on what I was hearing. The footsteps drew closer and closer. At last I could hear the rustle of his clothing. He was somewhere just outside the bell room. I didn't dare move. I heard the boards being lifted away. I had placed those boards there. He was so close, but still I waited. Come on, little one, I thought toward him. There's nothing in there, nothing to be afraid of. It's perfectly safe. Go inside now.

I heard a loud grunt and then a crash. He must have tossed a board down the corridor. My heart skipped a beat. All was silent. Was he already inside the room? Impossible. The entryway was tiny and the boards weren't the only things I'd left there. No way could he have made it through without making a sound. He was still waiting just outside the opening. Waiting for whoever was inside to come out. I swore to myself. What was I supposed to do now? How long would this standoff last? But I knew my only choice was to just keep waiting. This was a test of patience. Sweat dripped down my forehead and I realized that I'd erred in believing everything would go perfectly. My target was a master strategist, not some reckless, wild sparrow. I waited.

Nearly 15 minutes passed before I heard another sound. This time I knew he was climbing inside. At last. A crash sounded from within. The objects I'd placed must have toppled over. Wild with excitement, I dashed towards the entryway, hoping the clatter would muffle my footsteps. Feeling my way along the wall, I readied the blade. I came to the entryway, told myself to be calm and rounded the corner. A light shined into my eyes, blurred my vision, and some unseen object smashed into the side of my head. Seeing stars, I lurched backwards. Something slammed into my knee, crushing the cartilage. My opposite knee dropped to the floor. In an instant I felt the cold blade of a knife pressed against my throat.

I almost jumped out of my skin.

A voice emerged from behind me. "Move and I slit your throat."

I froze. My arm was yanked back and I was forced up against the wall. I wanted to speak, but the knife was pressed so close to my throat, the slightest movement and I feared it would slice right through me. I'd never been in a situation like this before. I had no idea what to do. On each exhale the blade pierced my skin. It was some time before I fully comprehended what was going on.

"Where is it?" the voice continued. "Where is the film?"

The voice was deep and hoarse, its accent indescribable. I searched my memory, but it didn't belong to anyone I knew. Who was he? My mind was full of questions, but this wasn't the time to pursue them.

Pressing the blade tighter against my throat, he spoke again. "Answer the question."

I tried to compose myself. I needed to think of a way to escape. I could figure out his identity later. But my body was too weak to think. I could only stammer out a few unintelligible words.

He grabbed my chin and wrenched it upwards. "Speak. Or I'll split you open right here." The voice had grown deeper.

What was I supposed to say? I didn't know where Wang Sichuan and the film canister were. And even if I told him everything I did know, I was still going to die. I knew I should just keep my mouth shut. "Let me go so I can take a few breaths, and then I'll talk," I said.

"Cut the bullshit." His voice was emotionless. "You haven't seen my face yet, which means I don't have to kill you, but I will if you don't tell me what I want to hear. It's up to you."

Fear grew as I listened to him. If I were in his place, I could never have remained so composed. This was clearly nothing new to him. Behaving recklessly would only get me killed. I decided to tell the truth. "I know you're not going to believe me," I said, "but I don't know where the film is either. I do know how to find it though."

As soon as I stopped speaking he slid the knife lightly up my throat. My heart skipped a beat. I was sure he didn't believe me and was going to kill me right then and there. Instead he slid it all the way up my face until its point was inches away from my eye. "Don't lie to me," he said, "and don't try to think your way out of this. If you even attempt to escape, I'll dig out your eyeball and slit the tendons in your hands and then make you lead the way. You'll wish you were dead. I don't intend to kill you if you tell me the truth, but you're not giving me an alternative. For the last time, where is it? Do not lie to me again."

At last I could see it was hopeless. Movie protagonists are always given endless opportunities to escape from such situations, but this was real life and I was out of options. "Wang Sichuan has it," I said, "not me."

"Who is that? And where is he?"

"He's dead," I lied.

"Dead?" The voice was surprised. "Then where is his corpse? Why didn't you take the film?"

"There was no time. The air here is toxic and the woman I were both sick. We were lucky to make it this far."

"Lucky?" He laughed coldly. "No one sent to this place could be called lucky." Pulling my hair, he yanked my head back. "Let's go take a look. If you're tricking me, prepare to lose an eye."

My head was spinning. The poison had spread throughout my body. "I'll be dead before we get there."

He laughed again, and was about to respond when something heavy suddenly struck him from behind. He groaned and toppled forward. His dagger cut a bloody arc down the side of my face. Before I knew what was happening, he was struck again. His head smashed into mine. His flashlight flew from his grip and knocked against the wall, switching back on.

As it dropped to the ground, the twirling beam illuminated Yuan Xile. A triangular blade in her hand, she was stabbing him again and again. The two twisted together in a flurry of blood and flailing limbs.

18 DEATH BOUND

I grabbed the fallen flashlight and ran over to help. The spy's hazmat suit was already pockmarked with holes from Yuan Xile's blade, but her strength was no match for his. In a moment he'd thrown her off and was wildly brandishing his dagger. Pulling Yuan Xile away, I shone the flashlight beam on him. He stumbled backwards, holding his wounds. Then he turned and fled into the darkness.

Looking around, I swore to myself. The floor was covered in blood. Yuan Xile must have taken the spy completely by surprise. I was sure his wounds were deep. Even his gas mask had been riddled with holes. I should have grabbed him while I had the chance.

Dropping the blade, Yuan Xile grabbed hold of my arm. Her hands were covered in blood and she was shaking terribly. Holding her close, I illuminated the bloody blade. Where had it come from? I wondered. There was no time to think about it. My chest was already aching with poison. We returned to the safe room and washed and scraped our bodies clean. This time I knew what I was doing, but when I looked over at Yuan Xile, I still couldn't help but feel a little embarrassed.

I didn't know what to say to her. I'd never imagined she'd come to my rescue, but if she hadn't I would probably be dead by now. Still, she'd taken too great of a risk. I almost wished she'd just stayed put. Later, when

I washed her hands I saw her palm was split open, though the blood had already dried. She must have crafted a weapon in the style of my own when I was out of the room, but she'd left the edges of the handle sharp and they'd sliced through her skin. I was moved as I thought of the danger she'd faced for my sake. I looked her in the eye.

"Thank you," I said. I took her hand in mine and smiled at her.

Previously when we'd worked together, she'd always been stern and untouchable. I'd never imagined we could be so close. Now she was almost acting like my girlfriend. She stared silently at me with tears in her eyes. Her mouth opened as if she were about to speak. Biting my lip, I waited for a long time, but in the end she said nothing. I sighed and patted her hand. We have to get out of here, I told myself. The sooner I turned off the lights the better. But as I tried to stand, she grabbed my arm and pulled me back down. My heart ached. I knew I'd lost her trust. I was thinking about how to explain things when she suddenly leaned forward and kissed me. For an instant, the most wonderful fragrance flooded my senses. My mind emptied of all thought. Our lips parted. She took my hand and led me behind the bed.

A single sentence was carved inconspicuously into the wall. What will be will be. The words were nearly illegible. Although I didn't know what they meant, they must have been carved by one of those trapped here, probably by Yuan Xile herself.

"Did you write this?" I asked.

Shaking her head, she pointed to my heart.

91

The sentence was baffling, but it was a good sign that she wanted me to read it. I could tell she was recovering. Then, from the corner of my eye, I saw something move. All the lights in the corridor had gone out. Total darkness descended once more. Had the power shorted? Or had someone flipped the master switch? Could it be Wang Sichuan and Ma Zaihai? I knew this was unlikely. Even if they were somehow still alive, they wouldn't be doing well. Their chance to cut the power had long since passed. It had to be the spy. With his gas mask full of holes, he was as helpless against the poison as we were. If he wanted to make it out of here alive, his only choice was to turn off the lights. He'd done me no small favor. Now Yuan Xile and I could leave right away.

When I thought about it, however, I realized the situation wasn't so simple. Although the lights were off, I didn't know how long the poison would remain in the air. And while the spy's wounds might be serious, but they weren't immediately fatal. Yuan Xile just wasn't strong enough. Not enough time had passed. They spy was sure to be somewhere nearby. But wherever he was, he had to be hurting. Still, if he wasn't dying, then Yuan Xile and I were in extreme danger. We'd defeated him last time only by catching him off-guard. Now the tables had turned. Now it was he who was crouched somewhere in the darkness, waiting for us. We were flirting with disaster no matter what we did. With my flashlight off, we'd be lost in the dark. With it on, we'd be asking him to come and slit our throats. I could only hope the bastard was dead.

Worse than all this, I had no idea where to go. Even with the flashlight on, we might never find the exit. Previously, the spy had had an objective, and that objective had become his weakness. Now our roles were reversed. It occurred to me that as long as a person desires something, he becomes weak. I shivered involuntarily. I suddenly understood that the three of us had begun a deadly game of hide-and-seek, and there was no telling how long it would last.

Taking a step back, I appraised our situation. I have never been a strategist or a schemer—designing that ambush had already taxed my intellect to the limit. The joy I'd felt only moments before was gone. I sunk into a deep gloom. With my head in my hands, I tried to suppress my frustration. We'd been so close to succeeding, but I had failed. Now we were right back where we'd started. How could I have been so stupid? If I had just grabbed the son of a bitch, everything would have been fine. So close. We had been so close!

But that single screw-up made all the difference. All the while Yuan Xile never let go of me. She was sitting next to me on the bed, her arms wrapped around me. Taking a deep breath, I slowly began to relax. Staying in this stinking, soaking, pitch-black room was no picnic. I was lucky not to be alone. So lucky. Once the poison outside had dispersed, we could probably find somewhere drier to stay.

We waited there one more night, though I barely slept. I just lay there staring at the black entryway, unable to shake the feeling that, as soon as I closed my eyes, something bad would happen. Of course I knew that with all of the lights off it would be close to impossible for the spy to find us. He might know these corridors, but he didn't know everything. Yuan Xile was lying on my chest as usual. It had become the only way she could fall asleep, but tonight she too was having trouble staying under. I watched as she moved restlessly about. Perhaps she was afraid that I would steal off sometime in the night.

I knew that searching aimlessly in the dark for a way out was no kind of plan, but if I wanted to switch the lights back on, I'd have to leave Yuan Xile here by herself. And, to be honest, I was scared of the poison. At least the darkness was safe. Anyway, I told myself, the spy had probably destroyed the master switch after using it. Thankfully I still had the map. Once I figured out where we were, we could begin hunting for an exit. I smiled to myself. Things weren't so bad. We just had to watch out for the spy, that was all. As I pictured us wandering through the dark corridors, I suddenly remembered when we'd found Yuan Xile down here. She'd been climbing into one of the boarded-up rooms. Wait a second, I thought. She knew the way in here. Had she been on her way out? Excitement lit up in me. The more I thought about it, the more convinced I became. I might not know how to get there, but at least I knew what I was looking for. And once we were close enough, Yuan Xile would probably be able to show me the way.

I suddenly felt light and carefree and I nearly roused Yuan Xile at once, but I controlled myself. She was asleep, if only lightly. I could feel her hair fluttering against my chin in time with my breath. Shifting to a more comfortable position, I inhaled the scent of her body. I rested my cheek on her forehead and closed my eyes. As I did so, I felt her move. I sensed she was looking up at me. Her nose brushed against my chin. I felt her moist lips and the warmth of her breath on my face. I went stiff and a hot feeling spread throughout my body. My heart began to beat faster. Pulling her closer, I suppressed the strange excitement building inside of me. She moaned softly. Her chin traced a slow, intimate line down my cheek. I was overcome with the scent of her breath and her body. My mind emptied out. Unable to help myself, I kissed her. For a moment I forgot we were in a stinking, flooded room 3,600 feet below the surface, forgot that some unknown poison filled the corridors just beyond, forgot everything that wasn't perfect and divine.

All that was left was Yuan Xile, her lips and mine, her hot skin pressed against my body. In the whole world, nothing could compare to her.

19 RISKING IT

Most nights you never remember. Some you never forget, like they were written onto your bones. Often you might think a situation has changed, when in fact, it only looks different. And sometimes you might think nothing has changed at all when you have been transformed.

From then on, that's how it was for me. I woke the next morning to see Yuan Xile lying on top of me, still fast asleep. Images from the night before flashed through my mind. I'd never been with a woman before, never even seen one naked. As I thought about what had happened, I was filled with both embarrassment and crackling desire. Maybe it had all been a dream? But when she awoke there was something a little awkward about her expression. The look in her eyes was profoundly complex. It gave me a marvelous feeling, as if this were to be a secret known only to us.

After taking a moment to compose myself, I packed up our belongings and led Yuan Xile out of the room. Before long we'd left the flooded corridor far behind. Although the air seemed superficially unchanged, I no longer felt any of the debilitating effects of the poison. We proceeded with the utmost caution, her hand held tightly in mine. This is not just any hand you're holding, I told myself. This is the hand you must protect at all costs. That might sound a little ridiculous, but I knew I would sacrifice anything for the owner of that hand and never feel even a hint of regret.

Little by little we advanced, sticking close to the walls and guided by nothing but my intuition. Every so often I would stop and listen for sounds of movement, but our surroundings were utterly silent. Where was the spy? Already dead? Perhaps, but perhaps he was just lying low. We reached a fork. As I hesitated, Yuan Xile grabbed my hand and placed it against the wall to my right. Three deep notches were cut where the wall rounded the bend. Suddenly it all made sense. These marks were deep enough that even someone groping along blindly could find them. No wonder Yuan Xile had been able to essentially sprint to the safe room through total darkness, making no wrong turns along the way. I took her hand and we continued in the direction indicated by the scratches. Soon we reached another fork. Sure enough, three deep notches had been cut into the corner to my left. I smiled to myself. We were on the right track. Without Yuan Xile pointing out the marks, I never would have noticed them.

We finally reached a boarded-up room. Even with my flashlight off, I could tell this was where we'd found Yuan Xile. We removed some of the boards and revealed a black crawlspace. Although seemingly fit for a dog, it was big enough for a man. I relaxed, though only slightly. I hadn't expected everything to go this smoothly. At the same time I couldn't help but feel suspicious. Why had nothing happened? I stopped and listened. We were surrounded by silence. The spy must have heard us fumbling along in the dark, and yet he'd done nothing to stop us. It made no sense. What was he waiting for? Was he really dead? Fear gripped my heart. There was another possibility. Perhaps he was doing just what I'd done: lying in wait in the one place he knew we'd have to go.

Yuan Xile was about to climb into the room when I stopped her, led her back a few steps and crouched down. At last the way out was right in front of us, yet I hung back. Was this where the spy had set his trap? He had to know about this exit. So why aimlessly hunt us all over the map when he could wait right here? For a moment I was stunned. If the situation weren't so serious, I might even have applauded. I had pulled this very trick on the spy yesterday; now it was I who was facing probable ambush, but unable to turn back. Still, there was no other way out.

The rest of the wooden boards were nailed securely across the entryway. Without Wang Sichuan's iron club, it would be impossible to enlarge the opening. My only choice was to crawl inside, though that was like handing anyone waiting on me my life on a silver platter. The world went gray as I prepared to die.

I strapped my pack across my chest, then scurried through the opening, triangular blade in hand. Once inside, I sprang to my feet, arms out in front for protection. I could almost see him flying at me from out of the darkness. But no one was there. I swung around, blade at the ready. All was silent. I couldn't believe it.

I cautiously switched on my flashlight and shined it around the room. The place was empty. Then I saw something. High on the wall, above one of the beds, was a ventilation shaft, its cover already removed. I scanned the room once more. All at once I wanted to laugh. Goddamn, it had all been in my head.

I called for Yuan Xile to come inside. Then I watched as, with practiced ease, she climbed up the bed and shimmied into the vent. I followed after her. The shaft was similar to the one we'd crawled through earlier, though I doubted they were connected. An opening soon appeared before us and out we went. We emerged in an unfamiliar place, so I shined our surroundings. A gigantic pool of water was just below our feet. Rust-covered iron walls and a ceiling rose 20 feet overhead. Stagnant, rust-brown water filled the pool. It was impossible to tell its depth. The openings to countless ventilation shafts pockmarked the walls just above the water. An elevated walkway encircled the room, level with the openings. It appeared to be the dam's atmospheric purification room. All of the air in the ventilation system would be piped in here, cleaned, then re-circulated throughout the base. My flashlight beam lit upon a door. It was just off the walkway on the opposite side of the room.

Yuan Xile smiled. She ran over and tried to pull the door open. It wouldn't budge. Her expression fell. She clearly couldn't believe it could be locked. We tried pulling together, but it was no use. I banged on it with all my might. This had to be the work of the spy. What else had the bastard arranged for us?

I looked at the other ventilation shafts, wondering where they led. Then I remembered: the blueprints! I plucked them from my bag and began searching for the room we were in. I found it, but there was no sign of what I was really after: the ventilation system. I should have expected this. These shafts ran throughout the base and they could easily be used for infiltration and sabotage. Their locations would be a closely guarded secret. Within the stagnant pool, however, was a tunnel that connected to the underground river beyond. The swim couldn't be more than 150 feet, but at the end of the tunnel was a sluice gate for letting in fresh water from the river. If the gate was closed there would be no way out. I remembered having seen its control switch back in the command center. No way were we returning all the way there.

Lucky for us, I knew my way around an electrical system. Electrical cables emerged from all of the air vents, crowding the room, but it was easy to locate what I was after. Only a single cable ran underwater. I took off my coat and wrapped it around my hands, then used my blade to slice open the cable's rubber sheath. I looked around and found an electrified cable of approximately the same thickness. After cutting it open, I brought the two cables together. Sparks flew in all directions. A spiraling vortex formed in the center of the pool; the sluice gate had opened. As the dirty water drained out, fresh river water rushed in to replace it. Soon it was clean enough to see through. Yuan Xile and I exchanged a glance. Then I hugged her and we leapt into the water.

My flashlight died moments after we went under, but I had already spotted the entrance to the tunnel. We swam toward it through the blackness. To some, 150 feet underwater would be a hard swim, to others a piece of cake. I didn't know how skilled a swimmer Yuan Xile was, nor did I wish to test her limits. I pressed on as fast as I could, keeping one eye on her and one hand overhead, feeling for the opening at the top of the tunnel. Before long I was out of breath. No opening had appeared. Should I go back and look at the map? I wondered. I knew that if I was wrong, both of us were going to drown. I hesitated. My hands and feet slowed. All the air seemed to evacuate my lungs and my chest began to burn. I wanted to breathe so badly. I knew that if I didn't turn around right away, I would soon be choking on water. Just as I turned to head back, Yuan Xile pushed me onwards. With no air left, I began to panic, but she grabbed my hand and squeezed it tight. I could feel her determination. I swam after her, barely aware of what I was doing. Several long seconds passed, then the tunnel ceiling was suddenly gone and we began to float upwards. Countless lights appeared from above, blinding me. How strange, I thought.

Then someone grabbed hold of me. I was lifted out of the water and onto a raft.

20 CHANGE OF PLANS

I watched as Yuan Xile was hauled dripping from the water. A cold wind blew across the underground river, chilling me to my bones and bringing me back to reality. I was surrounded by soldiers from the Chinese engineering corps. There were at least a hundred of them, their rafts packed full of supplies. Large, bright gas lamps flickered above the water nearby, illuminating a barebones encampment. We paddled over to a sprawling network of iron platforms built atop the river. Yuan Xile and I were helped from the rafts as a crowd formed around us. I was barely able to stand. Several soldiers rushed forward to give us a hand.

"What's going on?" I asked, but the men supporting me made no response.

The crowd parted and an officer stepped to the fore. He gave a crisp salute and motioned for us to follow him. Two soldiers helped me stumble behind the officer as he threaded his way through the camp. All around us a legion of engineers was busy fixing up the place. Arrayed among the tents were the pieces of high-tech Russian equipment we'd seen on the surface. At last we reached an open-air supply depot where a second officer stood waiting for us. I recognized this man. To everyone he was simply Commander Cheng, leader of West China's famous Twenty-Fourth Battalion. Although he wasn't part of the engineering corps, his battalion was responsible for accompanying all geological teams operating in the Northwest. All security and secrecy measures relating to those teams fell under his purview. I had met him during my time in Karamay. Anyone traveling near Xinjiang in those years would have heard of the Twenty-Fourth, but that was on the opposite side of the country. I couldn't imagine what he was doing here. In Karamay he'd shown my team great courtesy, but I knew he was a taciturn and serious man—the consummate professional soldier.

He strode over at once. Seeing we had no energy to speak, he turned to the soldiers supporting us and said, "Bring them to the medical camp. I'll be there soon."

With that we were off. I recognized the head doctor when we got there. He'd been at headquarters on the surface. As soon as he and the other doctors and nurses saw us, they rushed over to help. I was still holding Yuan Xile's hand. When they tried to separate us, she gripped me tighter and refused to let go. I looked into her eyes, no less unwilling, but as I saw all the people swarming around us, I hesitated and relaxed my grip. In an instant they'd pulled her away. She didn't resist, just watched me. I waved at her, wanting to tell her not to be afraid, that I would be right here, but she was already gone, swallowed by the mass of people ferrying her into the next tent. It suddenly felt as if a black divide had opened between us. I could almost see it, an ill omen, but then the sensation vanished, and I was rushed inside another tent.

I asked one of the doctors what was going on and why had the whole operation suddenly been moved down here. At first he didn't reply, just regarded me with an inscrutable look. Then he told me not to ask so many questions. I would soon know everything I needed to know. The most important thing now was to rest.

After removing my clothes, they began my examination. As I watched the stone-faced doctors and nurses, I became increasingly uneasy. What could have happened to justify a move like this of so many?

Such questions soon fled from my mind. When I lay down, my forgotten exhaustion swept over me like the ocean tide. A nurse hooked me up to the intravenous drip, and I gradually fell into a bottomless sleep. Lost to the world, I dreamed not a single dream.

***

When I awoke, two days had passed. My body must have gone through some bone-rattling torment. I ached all over. Even my toenails hurt. When I tried to get out of bed, the doctor made me stay put. He instructed the nurses to give me some liquid food and told me to keep resting.

When I asked how Yuan Xile was doing, he smiled ambiguously and said, "About the same as you."

I didn't know what this meant and his smile made me extremely uneasy. Although I tried time and time again to slip away and see her, I was still too weak. The moment I left the bed, I'd fall to the floor. Eventually one of the nurses scolded me, saying she was yelled at each time I fell. If I did it again she'd be written up. After that I stayed in bed.

I had no idea what was wrong with me. I wondered if I was experiencing the aftereffects of the poison. The doctor told me I was indeed experiencing aftereffects—but from the antidote, not the poison. This variety of poison affected the nervous system. For the last several days my IV bags had been filled with its antidote. This struck me as strange. How did they already know what kind of poison it was?

But the doctor would reveal nothing further. He told me the poison was
extremely complex and I'd have to wait until I was better for him explain
it. In those years, the warnings of one's superiors were taken very seriously.
The line between what one did and did not need to know was always clear.
The doctor was obviously under orders. I didn't press him. Instead I asked
him when I'd be able to get out of bed and move around again.

"At least another three days," he said. "After that it depends on the results
of your urine sample." He told me that even though I hadn't inhaled too
much poison, it still might have done permanent damage to my body. Its
effects wouldn't necessarily appear while I was young, but as I aged they
could become a real problem. The most important factor was how
successfully the poison was treated now.

I thought of Yuan Xile. She must be feeling as sick as I was; probably even
worse. For the moment there was nothing I could do, though. I was still
too weak to get out of bed.

Sure enough, three days later I was allowed to leave the tent. Some of the
nurses helped me to sit on a stool placed just outside. I remained too weak
to go any farther. Looking around, I couldn't believe what I saw. The
whole camp was ablaze with lights. In only the past few days this little
encampment had become an underground city, filled with tents and
burning lanterns. I stared wide-eyed. Something very strange was going on.
With this much equipment and this many people, it was obvious we were
going to be here for a long time. Rather than wait for us to return, our
superiors had gone ahead and relocated the base.

Plans had changed. It was almost as if we were preparing for war.

21 ONLY THE BEGINNING

The doctors and nurses would tell me nothing, but from eavesdropping on their conversations I figured out that none of them really understood why we were here either. They were just doing what they were told. One thing, however, was certain: the order to move camp was given two days after Old Cat had entered the cave. At that point, Old Cat and the rest of us were still trapped in the tunnels beneath the warehouse. I looked again at the Japanese maps of the river system. The tributary our team had navigated wasn't the only one leading to significant areas of the cave. Other teams could have reached them as well. Perhaps one of these teams had already returned to the surface carrying some important object and it was this that sparked our full-scale relocation. But what could this object be? Even the film we'd found wouldn't have convinced our superiors to dispatch men and machines in these numbers. I knew from past experience that it was not the object itself but what it signified that mattered. The frozen warheads we found in the icehouse were one possibility. Depending on what they contained, they could easily have aroused the interest of our superiors.

All this occurred to me while I was lying alone in the hospital tent. I would probably spend my whole life ignorant of the true motivation behind the military's sudden change of plans. Not that it really mattered. At the time there were so many unknowns, it was hard to really care about one more mystery. Anyway, I had nothing to complain about. The arrival of the troops saved my life. Now I had a comfortable bed to sleep on, three hot meals a day and people taking care of me. Still, I slept poorly, awakening each night from restless dreams. Each time it would take me several seconds to understand that I was alone in the hospital tent, not back in the flooded safe room with Yuan Xile. My desire to see her was never stronger than in these silent hours. That wasn't the only thing that kept me up at night. I felt uneasy there. I couldn't forget the room full of Jap corpses. I saw them whenever the lights went out. Shadowy fears haunted me in the dark. I couldn't shake the feeling that something bad was coming for us— something we didn't know anything about.

Another week recuperating in the tent and I'd mostly recovered, though I still had to walk with a cane. One week after that I was finally given permission to walk freely around the medical camp. The first thing I did was look for Yuan Xile. I soon located hers, but the guard refused to let me inside. I stood there for a long time as people streamed by. They gave me all manner of curious looks, as if they already knew who I was. Slowly my desire to see her shriveled. I didn't even call her name, just imagined how she must look lying inside. Then I turned and left, ashamed of my cowardice.

I walked aimlessly through the medical camp, feeling sad and distracted, watching people bustle about in every direction. I suddenly felt as if I'd been transported back in time. This must have been just how the place looked 20 years ago, when the Japanese were still there. The devils could never have guessed that two decades later their base would be replaced by ours, and that someone like me would be strolling through it with these thoughts on my mind and these feelings in my heart. I smiled bitterly. I never used to be so sentimental. Now look at me. I was practically depressed.

Wanting to clear my head, I was about to go look for a cigarette when I saw a big, sturdy fellow emerge from the tent to my right. He was holding a bowl of porridge and eating from it as he greeted the people who passed. I stared, unable to believe my eyes.

"Wang Sichuan!" I yelled.

He turned his head and his eyes went wide. For a moment we stood there looking at each other. A hundred feelings welled inside me. I couldn't believe he was all right. I peppered him with questions. "What happened? Why did you go silent? How did you escape from the poisoned passageways?"

He was about to respond, but held his tongue and checked if anyone was watching. Then he pulled me inside his tent and closed the flap. This was odd. If our superiors didn't want us to meet, they would have kept me on a tighter leash. His tent was almost identical to my own, even down to the IV bags. He must have been given the same antidote.

Only when we were in the back of the tent did he finally began to speak. "Damn lucky running into you like this. I've been worried about how I was going to find you. We need to get out of here as soon as possible."

I was stunned. "What are you talking about?"

He leaned in close and spoke in almost a whisper. "When I heard you'd been rescued I started searching for you, but they wouldn't let me inside a number of the tents. I couldn't find you anywhere. That's when I started to worry."

"Worry about what? What the hell is going on?"

"I can't say for sure myself, but I'm telling you we're in danger here, and we need to think of a way out." He glanced back at the entrance, then continued. "All right, I'll tell it to you from the beginning."

He and Ma Zaihai had searched for us after we split up, but they soon realized Yuan Xile and I were long gone. By then they knew they didn't have a chance of finding the safe room fast enough to escape the poison. Their only hope was to return to the ventilation shaft in the main tunnel and crawl back to the projection room. They didn't even stop to discuss it—they were immediately off and running. I remembered after chasing Yuan Xile halfway to the safe room that I'd listened for them, but heard nothing. By then they were already back inside the ventilation shaft. They crawled back to the projection room, but the smoke was too thick. Afraid that if the room was still sealed they'd suffocate, they crawled on. Eventually they reached a section where the cement walls had partially caved in, filling the shaft. They hid on the other side of the rubble, using their bags to fill the gaps and block the toxins. They covered their faces with wet clothing and waited.

With no lights in the shaft, whatever toxins drifted inside were not volatilized. They waited a long time. Eventually, the smoke thinned out and they climbed back into the projection room. Just as they'd feared, the door was still sealed. Although they devised countless ways to escape, none of them worked. Two days after Yuan Xile and I were rescued, the search party discovered Wang Sichuan and Ma Zaihai still trapped inside the projection room. They had been exposed to much less of the poison than us and were in far better health. Wang Sichuan's recovery was quick. Upon being rescued, the two of them were immediately assigned to the tent we were in and treated for the poison. Although Wang Sichuan had already learned of my rescue, he was initially barred from going to look for me. Still, he thought the worst was over. Then, without warning, Ma Zaihai developed a host of strange new symptoms. Three hours later he was dead.

"Dead?" My heart skipped a beat.

"I watched him die," said Wang Sichuan, a dark look on his face. "I held his hand as they tried to save him. He was in incredible pain."

"How can that be?" I asked. "You said you two had barely been poisoned."

Wang Sichuan shook his head. "The doctor said he was allergic to the antidote." His eyes were filled with more than just sadness.

"You think it wasn't the antidote?" I asked.

After glancing back at the entrance to the tent, he removed something from beneath his bedding and handed it to me. "Ma Zaihai slipped this to me right before he died. Read what it says."

22 THE PLOT THICKENS

Baffled, I looked at what he'd given me. It was a small medicine bottle. "What's this supposed to mean?"

Wang Sichuan rotated the bottle. A short sentence was scrawled beneath the label: Watch out. They've poisoned me.

I froze. "What's going on here?"

"He didn't have time to explain," Wang Sichuan replied. "And I don't know when he wrote it or why he waited until then to tell me. But so far he's the only one to have reported our findings to command."

This was all too strange. Why would someone have poisoned Ma Zaihai? And why had he been so secretive about letting us know? Could this be the work of the spy?

"His warning was no joke," said Wang Sichuan. "Ever since I've refused the IV."

"What does command think?"

"They think his death was suspicious, I know that, but I think they're suspicious of me. After all, we were in the same tent."

I thought of the guard posted outside Yuan Xile's tent. Was this measure taken in response to Ma Zaihai's death?

"I guarantee you, enemy agents have infiltrated the mission," said Wang Sichuan. "Now they're trying to get rid of us. As long as we stay here we're in danger."

I knew he was serious, but a spy would be taking a huge risk trying to assassinate us here. And our job was done already. "Even if there were spies here," I asked, "what would they care about us for?"

"How would I know? I'm not a spy. But I'm telling you, if we stay here, sooner or later one of them is going to get us. There are too many people around. No way can we guard against all of them." He sighed. "I barely even sleep anymore."

"You think that sneaky bastard is still alive? You think it's him?" He'd followed us like a shadow. I sincerely hoped he was gone, but ever since being rescued we'd been kept completely in the dark. Who knew what was happening now?

"No way," said Wang Sichuan. "He's not that good. Not on his own at least. He'd need powerful friends to pull this off. Smells like there's a rat at the top."

I frowned. "We're not going to be able to handle this thing ourselves. We should just relay our suspicions to command and let them take care of the investigation."

Wang Sichuan shook his head. "Neither of us has a goddamn clue who's in charge here or who's dirty. If we say something to the wrong person, we're both dead. The best thing would be to get ourselves sent topside as soon as possible. Once we're at surface headquarters, we can tell them what we know." He peeled the label from the medicine bottle, tore it up and threw it in the trash. "So what do you think? You with me?"

"Has command requested your report yet?" I asked. He shook his head. "Ma Zaihai was just a soldier," I continued. "No way would his report alone be sufficient. I'd bet someone has already given a geological report. That's why command isn't anxious to speak to us. They probably feel like they've learned what they needed to know."

"Are you saying that someone else from our team survived?"

I nodded. Old Tang and his soldiers were still lying dead in that passageway, but I hadn't seen Old Cat or Pei Qing among their number. Pei Qing's skill as a prospector was well known and Old Cat seemed to have some special status. If they were still alive, our superiors would probably have asked for their report before one of ours. "You're right about getting out of here," I said, "but you've got to calm down. You see how secretive they are about everything. It won't be up to us when we leave."

"That may have been true before, but now that you're here we can handle this no problem. Have you said anything about the film yet?"

I shook my head. No one had brought it up. "You held onto it though, didn't you?"

"Sure I did. It was still strapped to my back when the search party came bursting into the room. I continued holding onto it until Ma Zaihai handed it over when he gave his report. Before he left I specifically told him not to say anything about watching the film unless he had to, but who knows whether he was able to keep his mouth shut? You remember how soft that kid was." Wang Sichuan sighed. "He probably spilled everything as soon as he got in there. He started feeling sick that same day, and only a few hours later he was gone. I never got the chance to ask him about it. It's bad enough that when they found us we were in the goddamn projection room. Pretty much with our hands in the mother-fucking cookie jar, you know?"

"Yeah, I get it. Neither of us knows what he said in his report, so we have no idea how much to reveal in ours. And if they're different, the jig is up."

Wang Sichuan nodded. "You see what I'm talking about. First Ma Zaihai gives his report, then he dies mysteriously. That's what saying the wrong thing could mean. Here's what we do. One of us sticks to the script we devised back in the projection room, while the other says what really happened. This way, no matter what he said, one of our stories will fit and the other will sound like a total lie. The liar will be accused of perjury, the innocent man will be the witness, and both of us will be escorted to the surface so they can investigate the crime. But so what? At least then we'll be safe."

I thought about it for a moment. Back then the punishment for such crimes was severe. If we messed this up, we'd be accused of being rightists or worse, but I knew we had no other choice. Soon it was settled: I'd tell the truth and Wang Sichuan would lie. We took a few minutes to get our stories straight, then Wang Sichuan told me to go back to my tent. "For now," he said, "we're just going to have to play it by ear."

We shook hands before I left. Countless thoughts bustled through my mind, but neither of us said another word.

Walking back to my tent, I became increasingly certain we were in deep trouble. Watching that film had been a mistake far more serious than any I'd made before. We'd surely be brought before a military tribunal. And to make matters worse, I knew that if we'd just minded our own business and returned to the surface, Ma Zaihai would probably still be alive. But then those nights alone with Yuan Xile would never have happened. Given the choice, I couldn't say which alternative was preferable.

I couldn't stop thinking about my report. What would I include, what would I leave out, and how would I account for the gaps? Those nights I spent with Yuan Xile were too many to be simply glossed over. How was I going to explain them?

When I reached my tent the head doctor and one of the nurses were standing outside, engaged in deep discussion. As soon as the doctor saw me he hurried over. "Where on earth did you run off to?" he asked. "Command has been looking for you."

I froze in astonishment. Before I could manage a reply he let out a high-pitched whistle. Four soldiers instantly appeared.

"Sir," one said as they all saluted me without expression, "you are requested at headquarters."

As I saluted them back my heart skipped a beat. I'd never expected it to be this soon.

23 THE REPORT

This was my first time out of the medical camp since the rescue. On my way over I watched sparks fly as equipment was welded together and structures were speedily rebuilt. Headquarters was in a small cement building at the base of the dam. When I arrived it was in the process of being thoroughly reinforced.

As soon as I entered, the officers stopped talking and turned to look at me, their faces not giving anything away. Commander Cheng was among them. Had this been any other time, I wouldn't have been worried. I'd always been skilled at dealing with my superiors. Though I never failed to get the job done, I didn't automatically do what I was told. The higher-ups probably figured it's not worth their time to make me fall in line, but I was well aware I'd never be up for a promotion. This time, however, was different. I'd never seen most of the men present before. I had no idea how to handle them. And the atmosphere was stifling. With my palms sweaty and my stomach doing flips, I was afraid I'd collapse before my report even began. Concealing my nervousness was already out of the question, so why bother? Let them think I was simply weak-kneed at having to appear before command.

The report lasted two hours. I spoke without thinking, my mind in a daze. I don't know how I made it through. Most of my experiences I recounted only vaguely, but I made sure to emphasize that we had watched the film. Yet the officers appeared indifferent, as if this were no problem at all.

After finishing my story I waited apprehensively for their verdict. This was the moment of truth. After reviewing their notes, they merely asked a few minor questions, told me to make a written report, and said I was free to go.

A cold wind blew from the underground river as I exited the tent, freezing the sweat on my back. Shivering, I thought of the way the officers had watched me as I spoke. Were they always this serious? Perhaps my report had upset them and they'd been unable to hide their displeasure. Over and over I analyzed it, becoming increasingly agitated and getting nowhere. A hundred explanations occurred to me, all useless. I almost wished I could lose my mind like Yuan Xile. At least then the thoughts would stop.

Wang Sichuan came looking for me two days later. He'd just given his report and was similarly perplexed. He'd skipped right over the part about the film, and done a rather sloppy job of it, too, but they'd said nothing, and at the end he was breezily dismissed. Had we been overthinking the matter? Were the officers being deliberately mystifying? Perhaps they truly didn't care about the film or what we'd experienced. Had they simply been going through the motions? These men were too high-level to do something just for show. They were the leaders of this operation and constantly busy. If they really didn't give a damn about our reports, why take the time to listen? They could easily get junior officers to do it for them. What if everything that had happened up until this point had been just a prelude, and only now was the real mission about to begin? Were they just double-checking before proceeding as they'd already planned?

***

We remained in the medical camp for another week. Our restrictions were loosened and we were allowed to receive visitors. At first Wang Sichuan and I were extremely careful not to give the spy easy access to our respective jugulars, but we soon discovered that even though guards were no longer posted outside our tents, the medical camp's overall level of security had increased tenfold. Entry to Yuan Xile's tent, however, was still prohibited. Though I often went to see her and asked everyone I could if they'd heard anything, I made no progress. Slowly I become numb to it all.

The engineering corps had occupied the entire cave system. Other encampments had been established on all of the underground river's tributaries. Four months had passed since we had gathered at Jiamusi to start our journey. I already knew I would always remember the vast, pitch-black abyss and the terrifying shape I'd seen towering within it on the film. And I would never forget the four days and nights I spent alone with Yuan Xile. I'd always wanted to experience the fearful thrill of life on the battlefield. Although this wasn't quite the same, the mystery and strangeness of it all were nearly as satisfying. This had been a dark and dangerous time, I told myself, and there would never be another like it.

But I was wrong. A few days later I discovered that my suspicions had been correct: our mission had only just begun.

24 TRANSFERRED

Our written reports disappeared like stones in the ocean. Neither of us ever heard one word of feedback. Wang Sichuan was right; we'd been through the shit to get us here and they still wouldn't tell us a damn thing about what was really going on. Now that our mission was over, we figured we'd be sent topside. Instead we were ordered to stay at camp until further notice. This made no sense. I couldn't help but feel that something big was waiting for us just around the bend. Our superiors made no attempt to explain themselves. I didn't argue. I'd already screwed up once and didn't want to make things any worse.

We were transferred to a unit barracked at the edge of the iron platform, far from any of the geological teams. Command dispatched a colonel to meet with us about the confidentiality of the operation. He told us what we were doing was top-secret. No one was to ever discuss it. None of the other soldiers ever asked Wang Sichuan or I about what we'd experienced. I assumed they'd been ordered not to. Still, I saw the way they looked at us. They had to know almost all of our team had died. Rumors spread like wildfire. Some said we'd nearly gone mad, others that we'd been investigated as enemy spies. I can't say whether their looks were of fear or pity, but I found it all pretty ridiculous.

It was around this time that I ran into Pei Qing. He'd also been assigned to our unit. Although he and the young corpsmen who'd stayed in the warehouse had experienced nothing compared to us, his hair had turned even whiter than before. We spoke for a while. It was just as I'd suspected: he'd given the first report. He told me, in an utterly indifferent tone, that four others had survived along with him. I asked him about Old Cat. He hadn't seen him either, but I remained certain the old scoundrel was still alive. He was much too clever to have died in a place like this. Perhaps he was already topside. Then again, he'd been the first to get lost. Who could say for sure where he'd ended up?

Over the next month, we did our best to do as we were told. Wang Sichuan knew a few of the guys on the geological teams. Little by little he began to ask them what was going on. We learned nothing important. Day by day we muddled along, watching far-off sparks fill the dark air. Things were constantly being built, worked-on, reconfigured. I couldn't forget the high-tech Soviet machinery I'd seen near the medical camp. If we were going to be here for the long term, then there was no need to overhaul our equipment at such a furious pace. And how much gear could really be required for an investigation of the abyss? I knew something was going on, something big, and I didn't like it. Trapped in the dark, wet environs of the cave, I started to grow uneasy.

Half a month later, the geological teams began to depart one by one for the surface. Suddenly, our rations improved. For the first time in my life, a whole chicken leg appeared in my mess tin at dinnertime. In those years, a chicken leg was as rare and valuable as a bear paw. Until then, the greatest feast I'd ever enjoyed had been at a celebratory conference in Yan'an. The event was held in honor of our recent success in Karamay. I'd been selected to represent the younger generation and was there to give a report. At dinner we were served tofu and salted pork, more than three pieces of each. For someone who'd always survived on meager portions of dry wheat flour and rice, three pieces of pork and tofu were more delicious than dragon flesh. People never failed to be jealous when I told them about that night; it was so different from what we usually ate. My little brother was sent to the northeastern countryside a few years ago to join a production brigade. He told me each person was given only one pound of dry wheat flour and rice per month. Nothing else. One has to wonder how that could ever have been enough.

So you can imagine my surprise when I saw this chicken leg laid before me. I doubted my own eyes and worried I'd finally gone soft in the head, but after that deliciously oily, fatty flavor exploded in my mouth, I began to tremble with pleasure. I spent an hour eating that chicken leg, licking the bone clean, and when I was done, my first thought was how jealous the guys on my regular prospecting team would be when they heard this. The chicken leg meant little to Wang Sichuan. A skilled hunter who'd grown up in the mountains, he'd been bagging wild birds since he was young.

Although that was the last time we were given chicken legs, the quality of our meals never dipped. Night after night we were served rare delicacies like shrimp or shiitake mushrooms. The shrimp overwhelmed me with thoughts of time gone by. When I first left home to work, I sent back as much of my salary and grain vouchers as I could. Seeing the hardships I was enduring for our family, my little brother would catch shrimp in a stream near our home, dry them and ship them to me. As soon as I saw the shrimp on my dinner tray now I thought of home. All at once I missed my family and the carefree days of my youth. I've never been the sentimental type. Something about this place was getting to me.

***

I spent my days waiting uneasily for the next bit of news and sneaking over to the medical camp, hoping to catch a glimpse of Yuan Xile. She remained shut inside her tent, but it was enough for me to simply stand outside and feel our closeness. I would think of those nights we'd lain together and, with my heart calm once more, I'd smile. Although I knew I could ask Wang Sichuan's friends if they'd heard anything about her, I never did. I was shy and worried what I might learn. More than that, though, I feared what they might ask me.

One week later I arrived at her tent to discover that not only had the guard disappeared, but that the tent flap was also wide open. I initially assumed I was at the wrong tent, but a shiver ran through me as I realized I wasn't mistaken. What could this mean? Had she been cured? Or was she dead?

I frantically shook my head, trying to rid it of such inauspicious thoughts, then stared at the wide-open tent. Suddenly I had no idea what to do. All along my greatest hope had been to go inside. Now here was my chance, and I didn't move. What was I supposed to say to her? How should I look when I walked inside? I stood there for what felt like forever. Finally, I forced myself to calm down and stepped through the opening, a lepidopterist's daydream of butterflies fluttering in my stomach.

She wasn't there. No one was. All that remained was an IV stand and her bed, the covers lifted halfway off. Running my hands over the covers, I imagined her lying there. Slowly, my worries disappeared. She was probably getting some kind of evaluation or just some fresh air.

My reverie was interrupted by a sharp voice from behind. "What are you doing here?"

I turned to see a middle-aged nurse glaring at me. I recognized the woman. She'd taken care of me during my recovery. "I was just looking for Comrade Yuan Xile," I responded. "Is she all right?"

"She's in another tent for her physical. She won't be back until tonight. This is a woman's tent. If you want to visit her, you'll need to schedule a time and have your commanding officer accompany you."

"I'm sorry. Her guard was gone. I assumed it was okay to come inside."

"Well it isn't. If everyone behaved like you, how would she ever rest?" Then she picked up a steel food tray and headed for the exit, presumably to go fetch Yuan Xile's dinner. "Don't wait up for her either. I'm not going to let you see her when she comes back. Go on, head back to your unit, and don't forget to close the flap behind you. If you're still here when I come back, I won't be so polite." She bustled out of the tent.

I sighed, disappointed. I'd been sure that at long last I'd see Yuan Xile. And since no one was allowed in or out of the medical camp at night, it would be a mistake to wait for her. Mournfully, I straightened her bed and turned to go. Before I made it outside, I realized I had to leave something for her, something to let her know I'd been here. I checked my pockets. All I had was my cigarette case. Seeing it, I sighed, remembering how we'd smoked together in the safe room. I took out a cigarette and stuffed the case inside her pillow. As I strolled out of the medical camp smoking my cigarette, I began to feel a little less wound-up. I wondered whether Yuan Xile would know who'd left her the cigarettes. I found myself daydreaming that I, rather than my case, was now lying beneath her pillow, quietly awaiting her return.

Over the next few days I had no time to look for her again. The project's ideological instructor had—apparently on a whim—assigned us a slate of political quotations to memorize. This "work" kept us busy from morning 'til night. I made no progress. This, plus my inability to see Yuan Xile, meant I was soon in a foul mood. We passed a week engaged in mind-numbing study. When it was finally over, we were told the first informational meeting was going to be held. We couldn't imagine what they were going to tell us.

25 THE MEETING

In retrospect, going into this meeting knowing nothing was good training. It was hardly the last time we would be going in blind.

The meeting was the first time I'd seen Old Tian on this mission. Wang Sichuan and I exchanged a surprised glance. We recognized him from classes we'd taken at the Party school in college. He was sitting beneath a blackboard at one end of the tent, wearing his trademark thick glasses and busily organizing his materials. From the looks of things, he was just as insufferable as ever. He was only seven or eight years my senior, but he gave the impression of having been born into the wrong decade. I'd heard the Party had introduced him to a wife, but marriage didn't seem to have changed him. He was the same stuffed shirt I'd known back in school. There were more than a few true believers in those days, but I wasn't one of them.

We all took out the leather-bound notebooks and ballpoint pens we'd been given earlier that day and prepared to take notes. Writing supplies like these were expensive and hard to find, usually obtained only as awards or morale boosters so we all began writing on the upper left-hand corner of the inside cover. No one wanted to waste any space.

After taking attendance, Old Tian began his lecture. He drew several lines in the shape of a staircase. He was in his element. "Today," he said, "we will be covering various aspects of the structure and geology of the abyss."

Wang Sichuan yawned. Old Tian's northern accent wasn't always easy to understand, but I did my best to pay attention. I wanted to learn everything I could about the abyss.

Old Tian's lecture was divided into several segments covering widely varying topics. He lectured with all the feeling and expression of a robot. It was as if he was on an island practicing his speech in front of the sea. He moved from one topic to the next at the pace he'd predetermined, regardless of how confused or bored we might be.

They'd recently started to remotely survey the abyss, he began. The first ledge was 300 feet below the dam. That ledge went on for 2,000 feet or so, then fell abruptly to a depth of almost 800 feet.

"It was just like a flight of stairs," he said. They'd established this by firing mortars at different angles into the abyss and listening for the blast when they hit bottom.

Three hundred feet was not that deep. You could probably drop all the way in with no more than a rope and pulley.

Old Tian said the Japanese had presumably built a second base at the bottom, and from there had transmitted the telegram. The next step was to dispatch a group to this first step so they could conduct a preliminary exploration. They would travel to the first step's edge, determine what they could about the second, and whether there was a third beyond. The engineering corps would then decide if it was worth it to descend farther.

"Assuming the abyss formed at the same time as the surrounding rock," said Old Tian, "then in its earliest stages it was far smaller than it is today." Eventually the rock around it had begun to collapse, enlarging the cavity, with rock walls falling off faster and faster until, at last, the abyss reached a stable size. But not for long—geologically speaking. Once more the area around the abyss began to erode, beginning a new stage of expansion until it once more stabilized and stopped. This process repeated again and again, forming the enormous staircase-like abyss that presently existed.

The mist had its own explanation. Much of the rock within the cave was full of mercury. When the river water fell into the abyss, a mercury-filled mist rose on the air currents, creating a deadly weapon. Mercury is a serious poison that can cause severe dizziness, vomiting, memory loss, mental disorders, and even death. When the devils constructed their base here, these mercury-filled rocks were their primary building material. They mixed them with cement when they were putting up the dam. This meant that when the wall-hung light bulbs got hot, mercury was volatilized from the walls around them and released into the air. That's what killed the men in the tomb-like barracks off the main tunnel and caused the "ghosts in the shadows."

Later, the Japanese started hanging lights from the ceiling or surrounding them with sheets of iron. The main tunnel and its complex of passageways were already too polluted, though. They simply sealed them up. The underground river water, on the other hand, was filled with sulfur. The sulfur neutralized mercury and, to a certain extent, relieved the effects of mercury poisoning.

"But if the river water is sulfuric," asked one man, "should we really be drinking it? Isn't it too acidic?"

Old Tian shook his head. "Drinking sulfuric water for one or two months won't cause you any harm. It's only over the long term that problems arise. What the river has done, however, is seriously corrode the buildings here." The river level rose only after a heavy rain. Nonetheless, the combined effect of the damp and acidic environment had worked its corrosive effect. "We were lucky to find the place now," he said. "In ten years the base of the dam will probably have collapsed."

It was impressive how much Old Tian knew. Every iron surface around us was severely rusted. I'd assumed this was merely from the passage of time. He, on the other hand, had pinpointed the exact cause.

We applauded politely when Old Tian finished. At last we can leave, I said to myself, but Old Tian stepped outside and called someone over. An officer entered the tent, carrying a rolled-up screen. Then came a projector. The officer asked us to raise our right hands and prepare to take an oath.

My heart skipped a beat. I'd been right. This thing was far from over.

We were shown a film, the very film we'd watched in the projection room. My eyes went wide as soon as I realized what it was. If I watch this I'm screwed, I knew. For an instant I almost stood up and walked right out of there. I knew that by watching it I was effectively signing up to descend into the abyss. There would be no turning back. But it wasn't like I had a choice in the matter. Even if I closed my eyes it wouldn't make a difference. Wang Sichuan and I glanced at one another. His face was pale. I'm sure mine was as well. This was why command hadn't cared whether we'd watched the film. They were going to show it to us sooner or later. Why punish us for having already seen it?

I didn't notice anything new the second time through. I waited restlessly for the film to be over. All the blood drained from the faces of the guys seeing it for the first time. The officer switched off the projector and began to tell us what was coming next. Command had already dispatched a team to survey the entire dam. After reaching the icehouse, they'd confirmed that the frozen bombs were filled with mercury.

Mercury bombs are terrifying weapons. They released a cloud of mercury killing, everything within a certain distance almost immediately. Nothing would grow there for a very long time. The devils had probably planned to use them to break their stalemate with the Soviet Union, but the Soviets' mechanized troops were much quicker than expected.

The search team had also located a mercury refinery within the dam. It was determined that, at first, the Japanese were here only to mine mercury. It was only later that they became interested in the abyss. The Japanese first built the simple iron platform that bridged the river. Then they built twin cement complexes on either side. Last of all came the dam and the Shinzan's takeoff structure rising over it. All the documents and data we'd seized had also been translated. Much of it was confidential, but the officer did tell us the coded transmission from the abyss meant "Safely arrived." No one had been down into the abyss, though.

That's where we came in.

My heart dropped out of my chest. I wanted nothing to do with this. I could tell Wang Sichuan was thinking the same thing. We'd barely escaped with our lives once and now we were being ordered to risk them again. All we could say for sure about the abyss was that it was filled with poisonous mist—not a good start. Who the hell knew what else was waiting for us down there? But I knew we had no choice. We were the only ones fit for the job. And now that we'd watched the film, we'd never be allowed to walk away. That road had vanished.

I continued to scour my mind for a way out. Then another thought occurred to me. Supposing I was lucky enough to somehow complete the mission? My future would be set. I might even be able to use this success to become section chief back home. No longer would I be forced to endure the hot sun and brave the wind and rain to earn a living.

And had everything gone as planned, no doubt that's what would have happened. But neither I nor anyone else could have anticipated the chaos of the Cultural Revolution right around the corner.

Naturally, Wang Sichuan and I were selected for top positions on the exploratory team. I was to be squad leader and Wang Sichuan my deputy. Old Tian would be our accompanying specialist and three engineering soldiers would tag along as well. The soldiers were no older than nineteen. Seeing them, I instantly thought of Ma Zaihai. He was celebrated as a hero after his death and posthumously awarded the rank of squad leader, but it was all too late. If only he could have experienced just a second of that long-sought honor while he was still alive. Now it meant nothing to him.

I was satisfied with our team but for one thing: Old Tian. I had a feeling this guy would be a burden. Our assignment just wasn't fit for an intellectual, but I knew he had to come. He would have to personally survey the abyss and select the necessary samples. I was sure he'd never back out. He knew exactly how he'd reached his current position and what it would take to rise even higher. Once we were actually down there, though, I figured he'd regret his decision.

Old Tian reentered the tent and began to lecture on some more basic information. My eyelids grew heavy, but I stopped myself from drifting off. I was a leader now. No longer could I be so lax. When the meeting was over, I was requested for a short chat with Old Tian and the officer. By the time I left the tent it was already late. I thought of Yuan Xile. The medical camp would still be open for a little while.

Almost without meaning to I'd already walked to the boundary between our two camps. Yuan Xile's tent was visible in the distance. I could see the middle-aged nurse and several of her friends. They were probably off to get something to eat. I had to admit that the nurse was right; visiting Yuan Xile alone would not look good. It would be best to bring along a few others and perhaps a gift or two, make it seem like I was really just visiting an injured comrade.

Feeling defeated, I turned to head back, but just then I heard someone shout from behind me. I looked back. It was one of the nurses. I continued to walk away, but I heard her call for me to wait. I turned around. It was Yuan Xile's nurse. She hurried over to me. The nurses behind her had all stopped and were staring at me curiously. I almost considered running away, but I always preferred to meet things head-on.

"What are you doing hanging around here all the time?" she asked. Her expression was as imposing as before.

Stuttering, I pointed at the tent behind me. "I-I just got out of a meeting. The tent was filled with cigarette smoke and I needed to get some fresh air."

She regarded me skeptically. "Well, in any case I'm saved the trouble of looking for you. You left this behind last time." She pulled my cigarette case from her pocket and handed it to me.

I didn't know what to say, but she just turned and walked back to her friends. I just stood there and watched her go.

This auntie acted like a head nurse. I wondered if Yuan Xile ever even saw the cigarettes before the nurse realized what I was up to and took the case away. I stared gloomily at the nurse's receding figure. How stupid I had been. All the thoughts that had consoled me over the past few days had been nothing but fantasies. Well, I told myself, I was out of cigarettes anyway. At least this saved me a trip. I flipped open the case to pull out a cigarette. It felt heavier than usual. Beneath the cigarettes was a delicate wristwatch—Yuan Xile's. A strip of paper lay underneath. I unrolled it in the light of a nearby gas lamp. "I miss you so much. Xile."

She'd actually written to me! My heart beat fast. Standing there, buffeted by the cold wind but ignorant of its chill, I suddenly felt short of breath. Time seemed to stop. In that moment I so badly wanted to see her and take her in my arms and never let her go again.

26 LONGING

Previously, my desire for Yuan Xile had been like a white candle, burning quietly. Sooner or later the candle would have melted and the flame died. Now it was as if that candle had been thrown into a forest of dry leaves, starting a raging inferno that was impossible to extinguish. I could no longer just return to my tent and act as if nothing had happened. I had to see her, and would risk anything to do so.

In those days, it was madness to think such things. At first, I myself was frightened at the strength of my feelings. I tried to control myself, but it was no use. I wanted what I wanted. The potential consequences of my actions flashed through my mind in countless tragic variations, but things I would normally avoid at all costs meant nothing to me now. Not that I didn't fear the punishments to which I might be subjected; rather I simply refused to believe they would happen. I didn't think this was impulsive, as I did not feel agitated; I knew only that I had to see her and could wait no longer.

I looked at her tent and the guard standing out front. Sneaking over there should not prove too difficult. I could drop into the river beneath the iron platform and swim the whole way.

I returned to my tent, carefully wrapped Yuan Xile's wristwatch in my handkerchief, and placed it beneath my pillow. Then I snuck back along the edge of the medical camp until I found a good place to slip into the river. Our base had been set up in and around the structures on either side of the river where it met the dam. On one side was the medical camp, our camp and our canteen. On the other side was headquarters, the engineering corps and their canteen. The medical camp was its own independent area, with over 20 tents of all sizes and more than 100 nurses living within. Between my tent and Yuan Xile's was the canteen. Like the rest of our base, it sat atop a sprawling network of iron platforms and walkways that had been built by the Japanese and expanded by us. I could count on the walkways overhead concealing me for most of my swim. The only issue was getting out of the water once I'd reached her tent, but I could figure that out when I was in the water.

I took a swig of strong baijiu, limbered up, and slipped into the river. Holding onto the platform overhead, I began to make my way forward. Wooden planks had been laid across the platforms then covered with a layer of waterproof tarps. I sloshed along beneath a constant hubbub of conversation and argument, laughter and clanging footsteps. The water was so cold my teeth chattered, but my heart was burning hot. I had swum 50 feet past the canteen when the iron platform abruptly disappeared. I dove underwater and continued on. When I resurfaced everything was silent. I nearly sneezed as I looked for a way out of the river. Up ahead a bright beam of light pierced the platform and shone onto the surface of the water. Slipping back underwater, I swam closer. The light was emanating from a circular hole in the platform overhead. It was just big enough for a man. I climbed through. The hole was surrounded by buckets of water. It was a well. The cold wind blew through me, raising goosebumps all down my body. I tore off my clothing and wrung out the water. Then, my dripping clothes under my arm and wearing only a pair of shorts, I crept towards Yuan Xile's tent.

A soldier stood guard at the entrance. The tent was staked into the plywood covering the platform and the corners secured with heavy wooden boards. The tent was sealed off. I snuck around to the back and put my ear up to the side of it. Nothing. The tent was silent, not even a whisper. Taking a deep breath, I found my pocket knife and sliced a small hole along the bottom edge of the canvas and then wriggled through. The air was much warmer inside. Within seconds my whole body was tingling from the change. A single lamp dimly lit the small space. My breath caught in my throat. There she was—sitting up on her bed and staring at me. I didn't dare say a word.

Yuan Xile's hair had grown longer and her face was even lovelier than before. The cold and capable aura of the woman once known as the Soviet Witch had disappeared. We stared at one another, neither of us knowing how to react. Suddenly I felt awkward just standing there, wearing only shorts, my body blue from the cold. Had I ruined the image she had of me? Before I could finish the thought she pounced on me and buried her face in my chest. Red-hot desire blazed through my ice-cold body and I hugged her close.

***

For the next few hours we couldn't even speak for fear of being found out. Yuan Xile immediately shut off the light and we snuggled close in her bed, enjoying the heat of each other's bodies. I thought of how things had been between us in the safe room. This was so similar, and yet also so different. I don't know if what I felt was happiness or contentment or something else; only that, at that moment, I didn't want to be anywhere else.

We communicated in the dark by tracing out words on each other's hands. Although this was limited and occasionally confusing, I was still elated. I asked her question after question, but to most of them she just shook her head, as if she didn't understand. This had to be the aftereffects of the mercury poisoning, I realized. My heart was filled with pain, but I knew I couldn't remain too long. The nurses would be coming to check on her at midnight. Yuan Xile knew this, too, and didn't press me to stay. I rose reluctantly and crawled out of the tent. Then I crept carefully back to the water and retraced my route.

Upon reaching my tent I was nearly frozen to death, and yet my heart was content. I told my startled comrades I was just returning from a cold wash in the river. I found Yuan Xile's watch underneath my pillow and discreetly looked the timepiece over. It was an exquisitely crafted man's wristwatch, a Soviet Kirovskie, small and thin. Soviet goods are famously sturdy. Back then Kirovskies were as rare as they were well known. You couldn't buy them anywhere. They were given only as diplomatic gifts.

Flipping the watch over, I saw a sentence scratched into its metallic underside: "You must pity me, no matter what I become." It sounded like a line from some famous opera. Perhaps it was one of her favorite quotes. The words were barely legible, roughly cut with some makeshift tool. My heartbeat quickened. There had to be some deep meaning behind the origin of this watch. Placing it in my palm, I kissed its face. As I did so I felt a sudden presence, as if Yuan Xile were standing beside me. I could even smell the delicate fragrance of her hair.

I knew by now that I was already lost. In middle school I had a crush on one of my classmates. She was a fair-skinned girl who was not easily approached. Later I learned her father was a regiment commander in the PLA. I became determined to join the army and become a Party cadre. Nothing ever happened between us, but I still remembered how she would look at me and how I would feel inside. That, too, was love, but it was nothing like this. Then, even with the infatuation, I could control what I thought about, but now there was only the image of Yuan Xile, pressed against my chest. Nothing else mattered anymore. There was no turning back. Still, I couldn't help worrying. In those days you paid a huge price for falling in love, especially with a woman like her. Who knew whether she would ever fully regain her wits? And how much could I really expect to accomplish in a place like this? I harbored no great hopes. I only wanted to see her again.

Wang Sichuan brought in some friends to play cards. I had no interest but also no excuse, so I played apathetically and lost royally. My face was soon plastered with strips of paper, each the penalty for a lost game. After a while the others became bored and went outside to smoke and brag.

As I lay in bed thinking of everything that had happened, a flurry of emotions filled my heart. Certain scenes flashed through my mind and I felt my face go hot. What a vile fellow you are, I said to myself, but I couldn't help smiling. Consumed with these thoughts, I gradually fell asleep.

I dreamed that the regiment commander's daughter had come looking for me. As I watched, her face turned into Yuan Xile's and then back again.

"What is this, some kind of face-changing Sichuan Opera?" I asked impatiently. As soon as the words left my mouth, I realized I was surrounded by people, all of them staring at me. I rubbed my face. It was covered with strips of paper, each bearing the same sentence: "Wu has a girlfriend."

Turning pale, I began frantically trying to tear them off. They were stuck tight. Even though my skin stretched and ripped from my face, the strips held fast. At last I awoke, gasping for breath.

As I opened my eyes, I realized that my face was still covered with the paper strips from the game the night before. In my sleepy reverie I'd forgotten to remove them. Wang Sichuan pulled on my cheek, trying to get me up. He was excited about something. A wild din sounded from outside the tent. Through the open flap I saw a great crowd of people running past. Shaking off my tiredness, I asked him what was going on.

"Hurry up," he said. "It's finally happening."

27 THE STEEL CABLE

Wang Sichuan yanked away my covers and dragged me out of bed. Shivering from the cold, I kicked him off of me and pulled on my clothes. Outside the tent I saw everyone was running toward the dam. We hustled after them.

By the time we reached the top of the dam it was so crowded we could barely move. Before long an officer appeared and ushered most of the people back down, but, being technical personnel, we were allowed to stay. A group of engineering soldiers were weaving together a couple massive coils of steel cable. Transporting these must have been a nightmare as each coil surely weighed over a ton. The two lengths were woven into a single strand, then secured within an iron sheath. This cable was fed into a windlass. The other end of the strand was attached to a great hunk of black iron. Several soldiers were levering the iron hunk into the mouth of a flying thunder cannon—one of those makeshift cannons made from a sawed-off oil drum that were common during the War of Liberation.

The flying thunder cannon had initially been designed for use against elevated enemy positions. Later, during the bandit suppression campaigns, they were filled with stones and it became a kind of minesweeper. The bandits were foolish enough to bury their mines right next to each other. When one mine was hit it would blow all those around it. The thunder cannon could fill the sky with stones and when these crashed down the whole minefield would explode. Now I understood: they were going to shoot one end of the steel cable into the abyss and pull it taut as a zip line. Realizing this, I unconsciously took a step back. Everyone around me did the same. Some even covered their ears.

Just as I was thinking about how amusing this looked, I noticed a strange man through a newly opened space within the crowd. He was some distance away, standing at the edge of the abyss and staring off into the blackness as if he didn't give a damn about what was taking place. When I say he was strange, I don't mean his appearance was somehow irregular. He was probably a perfectly ordinary-looking fellow where he came from, but that was just it—he wasn't Chinese. This man was a Soviet.

What was a Soviet doing here? I couldn't understand it. Given the secrecy of this project, it seemed impossible that a foreigner would be allowed down here. The Soviet was tall and robust with a close-trimmed beard and pale skin. He gave the impression of being capable of explosive force. A cigarette dangled from his lips as he stared blankly ahead. The black abyss was inches from his feet and a fierce wind blew from out of the void yet he was utterly indifferent to it all.

I asked one of the soldiers beside me about the man, but discovered that he'd only just arrived and was supposedly an elite specialist of some sort. I was about to ask another question when the cannon suddenly roared. The ground shook and then the iron hunk was flying through the darkness, steel cable trailing behind it. Before long its forward momentum was exhausted and it dropped towards the bottom of the abyss. The steel cable continued to uncoil from the windlass, twisting back and forth all along its length and emitting a piercing sound as it cut through the air, threatening to slice in half anything in its path. The cable continued to uncoil for a long time. Only when the line stopped moving did I get closer. Piercing the darkness below the dam at a 45 degree angle, it ran into the blackness of the abyss.

"Will it hold?" asked Wang Sichuan.

Several of the engineering soldiers grabbed the line and pulled down as hard as they could. "This is the kind of steel cable they use for pile drivers," said one of the soldiers. "You tell me if it'll hold."

"All right," said Wang Sichuan, imitating the soldier's accent. "I believe you. But if I fall, you're paying for my head."

"No problem," said the soldier. "You could have a head the size of an elephant's and I wouldn't be worried."

I was glad to hear the confidence in his voice. Sooner or later we were going to be sliding down that cable. Wang Sichuan laughed and handed the soldier a cigarette. I reached up and tugged hard on the cable. It didn't move a millimeter. That was a relief. After securing the windlass to the side of the dam, the soldiers cranked it until the cable was so straight and tight that no amount of wind could make it sway, or so they said. As I stood at the edge of the abyss I could hear a powerful wind whistling over the line, making it vibrate all along its length. Wang Sichuan was soon on good terms with several of the soldiers and he began asking them about the project. I continued to stare at the spot where the cable disappeared into the depths, wondering how I would to be able to make out anything down there. I thought again of the tall Soviet and his earlier nonchalance. By now he had long since left the dam, so I walked over and stood at the edge of the abyss, just as he had. The wind was so strong I was nearly blown over the side. Overcome with fear, I backed up.

After that morning I didn't see the Soviet again for some time. Although my curiosity about him remained, it didn't consume me. I did manage to learn a little more while chatting with some soldiers after dinner. The Soviet's name was Ivan. He'd arrived only recently and he was known to haunt command headquarters. No one knew exactly what he did, but all the leaders showed him a great deal of respect.

Thinking aloud, Wang Sichuan asked whether he might have been sent to develop our leftist spirit.

"No way," I replied. "The Soviets lost their influence over us a long time ago. That's what makes his appearance here so strange."

One week later everything was ready. A short mobilization meeting was held, then we strapped on our packs and prepared to move out. A pair of engineering soldiers would be the first to descend. The cable was strong enough to hold 100 of us at a time, but just to be safe we were going to descend in groups of two. Once each group made it down safely, they would fire a signal flare to alert those up top.

The two soldiers strapped on their gas masks and were off. Their speed of descent was astounding. They disappeared into the darkness faster than the eye could follow. Only from the vibrating cable did we know that they were still attached. I was way more than nervous, smoking one cigarette after another as I waited to go next, but after three hours there was no sign of a signal flare. We waited a little longer, but at last there was no denying it. They were gone.

Wang Sichuan and I glanced at one another, then over at the on-site commander. His face had gone pale.

***

The operation was postponed at once. Old Tian was summoned to a meeting and I was given my own assignment: reassuring the troops and raising morale. But with the two other soldiers swallowed by the abyss, Old Tian in a meeting, and neither Wang Sichuan nor I in need of much reassurance, the "troops" consisted of only a single engineering soldier. This remaining soldier was clearly in need of something.

As he sat before me his legs shook uncontrollably. Day in and day out, engineering soldiers like him braved countless dangers, taking in stride anything that came at them. If there was a river, they built a bridge. If there was a forest, they blazed a road. Even a wild tiger wouldn't have scared him this badly. Such soldiers are often most scared of what they cannot see. To be honest, the void frightened me, too, but I was more realistic. Why be afraid of one's fate, especially when it cannot be changed? In those years, no thought was ever given to aborting the mission. If difficulties appeared, then those difficulties were overcome. No victory came easily. Only through sacrifice and untold effort were the Chinese of my generation ever able to succeed. I was sure that we would soon be forced to descend.

"How do you know it's not some paradise down there?" Wang Sichuan asked the soldier. "They've probably got nurses with long, thick hair and girls from the military academy. I'll bet those two were so happy they forgot all about firing the signal flare."

No one laughed. It was a lousy joke. And so the morale-boosting meeting ended in failure. Thankfully none of the higher-ups ever asked me about it.

Old Tian returned from his meeting later that night. He said nothing about it, just sat and looked over his notes. I figured he'd been unable to think of a solution. The way I saw it, though, the situation was simple; neither mathematical analysis nor deep discussion was going to yield a solution. In the end, we'd just have to go for it.

My suspicions were borne out the following day. This time no one bothered to tell us there would be another test-descent. Luckily Wang Sichuan got wind of what was going on and, after I demanded that we be allowed to attend, command finally relented. We arrived atop the dam to see two more engineering soldiers wearing full-body protective suits. Long ropes were tied to their waists. I asked the on-site commander what they were doing.

"This time we're making sure we find out what the hell is going on down there," he said. "The moment something seems wrong, we're pulling them back up."

This didn't seem like it was going to turn out any better, but I knew there was no point in saying anything.

The two soldiers were battle-hardened veterans—you could see it in the way they carried themselves. That didn't make them any less nervous. After all, some things take more than a gun to handle. Still, they loaded their machine guns, strapped them on, and holstered their flare guns. They began to descend, moving much slower than the previous pair. The searchlight stayed on them as they dropped bit by bit into the darkness, until at last they were out of sight. No one said a word.

Please let nothing happen to them, I thought, listening to the fierce wind blow through the abyss. Seconds passed as we waited for the flare, then minutes, and I slowly realized that something was wrong but, with everyone else silent, I said nothing. After half an hour, I was positive.

"Pull them up!" yelled the on-site commander.

At once the soldiers began cranking the small winch, but when they pulled the rope in, the soldiers were gone. The rope had snapped and the end of it danced in midair, blown by the abyssal wind.

As I stood there, stunned, the on-site commander angrily threw his hat to the ground. His eyes were bloodshot. He checked the bullets in his gun, then clipped himself to the cable, put on a gas mask, and prepared to descend. Wang Sichuan tried to stop him, but the commander just waved him away.

"Deputy Squad Leader Wang," said one of the young soldiers, his voice wavering, "please ask command for their orders."

"You can ask them if I don't make it back out," said the on-site commander. "Now who's coming with me?"

All the young soldiers promptly stepped forward. I knew this was a bad idea, but before I could say anything Wang Sichuan's voice rose above the hubbub. "Out of the way," he said. "I'll go."

No way was Wang Sichuan going down there himself. There were only a limited number of us technical personnel and our safety had to be ensured. Command was not going to be happy if one of us got dragged into this. As expected, the on-site commander refused to take him, leaving us deadlocked. Fear gripped my heart. What kind of world was hidden within the abyss? Why did it swallow all who entered?

Holding onto the cable, I walked to the edge, trying to figure out what to do next. Suddenly, I felt the cable trembling. I brought my ear up to it. I could hear vibrating.

Something was climbing out of the abyss.

28 INCOMPREHENSIBLE

I whistled for quiet and called the others over. As they listened to the vibrations their faces turned pale.

"What the hell is on the cable?" asked Wang Sichuan.

"I don't know," I said, my forehead damp with cold sweat. Either it was one of the soldiers, somehow still alive, or it was whatever had killed them. "Hand me a gun," I said. If it was one of the men, then he was in great danger. The distance was too far and the wind too strong to climb the cable alone. Someone would need to go help.

Someone passed me a pistol. I very nearly clipped myself to the cable and slid down to investigate, but after all we'd been through, whatever bravado I had in me was practically gone. It was the on-site commander and one of the young soldiers who went instead, one after the other, while the rest of us kept our guns trained on the cable. If it really was a monster climbing up the cable, several machine guns would be more than enough to send it back where it came from.

After 20 minutes, the on-site commander shined his flashlight into the darkness overhead, signaling us to send the next man. Two hours later he and the young soldier reappeared, carrying someone with them. As soon as they were close, the on-site commander yelled for us to find the head doctor as fast as possible. The man they carried appeared barely human. His skin was burned black as night. We laid him flat and waited for the doctor to come. No one present recognized him. His body gave off a strange odor and his face had melted away. His eyes were clouded and he seemed unable to see or speak. Every now and then his mouth would open, as if he wanted to say something, but no sound escaped.

Tears fell from the on-site commander's eyes as he cleaned the man's wounds. "Where the hell is the doctor?" he yelled. "Tell them if they're not here in one minute I'm putting this man out of his misery!"

It took Wang Sichuan and I a moment to get over our shock. Then we ran over to help. "Comrade," I cried, ripping open the wounded man's clothes, "hold on!"

His whole body shook when I said this. He turned his melted face towards me, suddenly reaching out and seizing my collar. As he pulled me close, his terrifying features twisted and his clouded eyes seemed to go wide with surprise. Then he began to scream, again and again, his voice incomprehensible and filled with unimaginable anguish.

Ignoring the pain in my ears, I listened closely. It sounded almost as if he was saying, "How can it be you again?"

But sometimes it didn't sound like that at all. What could it mean? Moments later the doctors and nurses arrived. They loaded the man onto a stretcher and carried him away. The rest of the soldiers followed behind them. Soon Wang Sichuan and I were the only ones left atop the dam.

Wang Sichuan looked off into the abyss and then back at me. His expression was stricken. "Old Wu," he said, "what did he say to you?"

I shook my head and gazed out into the abyss. I'd been so scared I could barely think straight. Who knows what I heard? My hands were still shaking too much to light a cigarette. I reached up and grabbed the cable overhead. It was still vibrating slightly, wet with whatever had been on the man. We'd all been thinking the same thing: Thank Heaven I didn't have to go down there.

Suddenly we heard shouts from the receding crowd. "There's something in his hand!" someone cried.

Wang Sichuan and I looked at one another, then hurried over to the crowd. The on-site commander was still prying open the soldier's fingers. From them he pulled out a single stone the size of an ink bottle. It was covered with small holes, like a sponge. When held in the light it gave off a strange luster.

***

The doctors later found an ID card in the clothing of the burned man identifying him as He Ruping, leader of the third company's fourth squadron. He'd just turned 26-years-old. Although he managed to survive, he soon fell into such a deep coma with no hope of reviving him. A verdict had yet to be reached on his full-body burns. There was no acidic residue, nor did his body bear signs of having roasted in flames. It was almost as if he'd been cooked from the inside out.

The rock in his hand was black cloud stone, an extremely common variety, especially for where we were. Much of the rock surrounding the underground river was of this type. Old Tian believed that after He Ruping lost his mind from the pain, he'd grabbed the stone without really intending to and just never let it go. I disagreed. It made no sense for someone undergoing that level of suffering to pointlessly haul a stone inch by tortured inch back up the cable. It had to be some kind of clue, a window to the hell He Ruping had seen, one which he'd given his cognizant life to show us.

The only truly curious thing about the stone was the tiny holes covering every bit of its surface. Black cloud stones were formed by eons of pressure bearing down on sediment. These holes wouldn't have appeared while the stone was forming. I guessed some corrosive element in the air—the mist, most likely—had eaten out the little holes. Old Tian split the stone open. Its interior and exterior were identical. We didn't understand this theoretical stuff, so Wang Sichuan and I left the examination to Old Tian and waited in our tent for the result.

After three hours with no updates, we grew impatient. Several of us took turns strolling over to Old Tian's tent and attempting to learn what we could. At first, only Old Tian and his students were inside inspecting the stone. Later Pei Qing joined them. Pei Qing had been spending most of his time convening with the higher-ups. Whatever they were working on was not for us to know. He was a smart guy with an encyclopedic mind— by all rights he should have been invited to examine the stone from the start—but Old Tian couldn't stand him. For Old Tian to call him meant Old Tian and his students had become utterly stuck. Still, there was no news. I began to give up hope.

Sure enough, we received a message that night: the mission was postponed indefinitely.

29 THE SECRET OF THE STONE

While eating dinner that night, I thought again of He Ruping and shivered involuntarily. I was sure some kind of hell awaited us in the abyss and that sooner or later we'd be ordered to face it. The project might be suspended, but I knew this was only temporary. No one was going to escape this unscathed. For a moment I considered quitting the mission, but I didn't have the guts. Desertion was always an option, but the consequences would haunt us forever. Regular soldiers looked at cowardice as something that everyone must face and overcome, but I knew that sometimes there was reason to feel afraid. What could I do, though?

Supposing I really did refuse to go on, endured the excoriation of the battalion commander, then the brigade commander, and finally the division commander—well, they couldn't make me do it. But my life would be ruined. Who knows what label would be waiting for me on the surface, what hardships I would be made to suffer?

"There's a bit of a problem with this comrade." This sentence could be used as an excuse to mess with anything from my housing allotments to work salary. And if a deserter ever received something "extra," there would be the inevitable complaints, someone always wondering, "Why does the deserter get this and I don't?"

I didn't give a damn about what other people might say, but I didn't want to be pushed around because of it. A man needed to approach a decision like this as if his life depended on it. I thought about what my dad would say. Actually, the old man probably wouldn't care too much. He'd endured more than his share of suffering in his lifetime. Whether I deserted would be trivial. My little brother, however, would be furious. I'd always been his hero and I knew how sensitive people his age could be. In the end, though, I was sure he'd understand.

Wang Sichuan was standing by the center tent pole, feeding wood to the stove while he spoke his thoughts aloud. "What if there's just a field of lava down there and the moment we land we're dead?"

"Molten lava is bright enough that we would be able to see it from up here," said a voice behind me. "And the hot air rising off it would roil the mist. Right now it's much too calm." It was Pei Qing. He must have just returned from Old Tian's tent.

We asked what he'd discovered, but he just sighed and shook his head.

"Nothing yet," he said. "I only came back to get something to eat." He paused for a moment, as if considering something, then continued. "Actually, it's not unlikely that there are significant geothermal heat sources down there. When the underground river water hits bottom, it's turned into super-hot blasts of steam that'll sear your skin like a piece of meat as soon as it touches you."

"But why did He Ruping bring back the stone?" asked Wang Sichuan, shaking his head in befuddlement.

"He probably didn't even know himself," said Pei Qing. "If you ask me, the only way the Japanese were able to send out their message was by airdropping the transmitter into the abyss. Whatever methods of entry they attempted prior to that all ended in failure. We're wasting our time."

We shook our heads gloomily. At first glance he seemed to have a point. Perhaps He Ruping was trying to warn us that the bottom of the abyss was certain death. Yet, this argument was untenable. The telegraph transmitter would require a stable power source to remain in operation these past 20 years. Given the technology available at the time, the only suitable mechanism would have been a small-scale water-powered generator. Nothing else could keep working over the long haul without any maintenance. Equipment like this couldn't just be dropped-in and expected to function on impact. It would need to be set up. It was possible to survive at the bottom of the abyss; we just hadn't figured out how. Our only clue was the stone He Ruping had brought back.

"Perhaps we should check whether the stone is missing something," said Pei Qing. "Too often we look only for surplus, when we should also be paying attention to deficiency."

"He Ruping was an engineering soldier," I said. "I think that's where we need to start. Engineering was what he knew about. I doubt he understood much, if anything, about geology."

"You've got a point," said Wang Sichuan. At once he flung open the tent flap and called for the soldier standing watch to come inside.

The soldier trembled with terror as he entered the tent. He probably thought we were about to send him into the abyss. "Name, age, and company?" I asked.

"My name is Pang Tiesong," said the young soldier. "I'm eighteen years old and a member of Third Company."

This was nothing like the movies. The soldier's fearless revolutionary spirit must have deserted him. He seemed to suddenly realize this and, afraid we'd notice his fear, feigned calm. It was an amusing sight, but I had no desire to toy with him.

"What kind of engineering soldier are you?" asked Wang Sichuan. "The same as He Ruping?"

Pang Tiesong's face turned even paler, but he managed to salute Wang Sichuan as he barked out, "The same, sir!"

Wang Sichuan motioned for him to sit down and handed him a cigarette. "I'm going to ask you a question," he said. "When you engineering soldiers see a rock, what do you think of?"

"Indomitability! Steadfastness! Eternal perseverance!" The young soldier was totally serious.

If He Ruping had brought back that stone only to tell us that we must show eternal perseverance, steadfastness, and indomitability in our mission, then he was truly an uncommon individual. That was more than a little farfetched. No one being burned alive at the bottom of a black abyss would think of such things.

"Bullshit!" swore Wang Sichuan. "Enough slogans. This isn't political class. I'm talking about all of this." He motioned at the floor, walls, and ceiling of cave rock that surrounded the tent. "And I want a good answer. What do you think of when you see this kind of rock?"

Pang Tiesong thought for a little while, but was clearly too frightened to answer. Realizing that he'd scared the young soldier, Wang Sichuan changed his tactic. Adopting the countenance of a kindly superior, he closed the tent flap and, in as friendly a voice as he could muster, said, "It's okay, you can speak freely. This is a private meeting known only to us. Anything you say here will remain our secret."

Pang Tiesong straightened his back and, as if searching for the right answer, began. "Sir, when I see the rocks here I think of the cave we dug in the Kunlun Mountains. And since this cave is so much bigger than that one, I start to wonder why we even dug it in the first place."

Wang Sichuan and I glanced at each other in dismay. Pei Qing was right. Engineering soldiers really did think differently than us. Attempting to be more specific, Wang Sichuan asked, "So, if you saw a rock that had broken off the cave wall, what would you think?"

"A single rock?" asked the soldier, confused. Wang Sichuan nodded and traced the approximate size of such a rock with his hands. "I would think of quarrying," said the soldier, "of the broken rocks that surround us when we cut through mountains. This cave is very stable, though. Any broken rocks here probably fell when the Jap devils were building their dam."

I sighed to myself. If this was what He Ruping had been thinking, then the stone was meaningless. And if it wasn't, then we were getting nowhere.

"Is that what all engineering soldiers would think?" asked Wang Sichuan.

Pang Tiesong shook his head. He didn't know. If we wanted, he said he would ask around.

Wang Sichuan was about to respond when Pei Qing stopped him and motioned to Pang Tiesong. "You can leave now," he said. "And not a word about this to anyone."

Pang Tiesong left at once, looking as if a great burden had been lifted off his shoulders. Pei Qing turned back to us. "What that kid just told us was not entirely worthless," he said. "Think about it. Given the low visibility at the bottom of the abyss, it's unlikely He Ruping would have noticed a rock that small. Instead, he probably saw a whole field of broken rocks, and since he was an engineering soldier, we now know what his first thought would have been, 'I'll bet these came from the dam.' However, it was his next thought that really mattered, for it was this that convinced him, already on the brink of death, to pick up one of those rocks and carry it all the way back here."

"Maybe so," I said, "but we'll never be able to guess what it was. We need to ask an engineering soldier."

"But it can't be the kid who asks the others," said Pei Qing. "Too much information would get out. We need to be precise about this if we want to learn the truth. I'll prepare a few questions and have command call in the rest of He Ruping's company to answer them."

This was obviously a much better method than just guessing blindly. We all agreed to it at once.

After Pei Qing left to make the necessary arrangements, Wang Sichuan looked over at me. "When this guy's not out of his mind, he's actually pretty damn smart."

I smiled bitterly. There were times when I found myself shamed by Pei Qing's intelligence and hard-working nature, though it was tough to say which was preferable: my life of quick-witted indolence or his of focused ambition. I knew only that a comfortable existence was enough for me, but perhaps my comforts were nothing compared to his. Turning to Wang Sichuan, I asked, "What do you think about all this? Since when do you not have an opinion?"

"This kind of stuff is not my strong point," he said, "and talking just to talk can mess with other people's thinking, but I agree there was something to what Pang Tiesong said. I've been curious about that dam from the start. It's just strange as hell."

"What do you mean?" I asked.

"I mean, why build the dam at all? Clearly they had to, otherwise why bother? Can you imagine how much effort must have gone into that thing? No way did they build it solely to generate power. They could've just strung electrical cables down here from the surface and saved a ton of trouble."

Goddamn, I thought, as my pulse began to race. Not once had this ever occurred to me, yet Wang Sichuan had tossed it off like it was no big deal. My spirits sank. I'd admit to being dumber than Pei Qing, but Wang Sichuan? No way.

"I think the reason the Japanese built this dam was to control how much water flowed into the abyss," he continued. "Figure out what happens when the river water hits the black cloud stone and you'll have your answer to what's going on down there. It's a shame we don't have the authority to participate in the investigation. With that bookworm Old Tian in charge, it'll be weeks before they learn a goddamn thing. That's why it's good we have Pei Qing there to nudge the higher-ups along. At least that guy knows what he's doing."

I nodded. I wanted to say Old Tian wasn't that bad, but I kept quiet. I had a feeling Wang Sichuan would hear none of it. I couldn't say why exactly, but between Old Tian and Pei Qing, I preferred Old Tian. After receiving that note warning me to "Beware of Pei Qing" and witnessing his erratic behavior, I felt that he was somehow different than the rest of us.

It was still early when I finished dinner that night. The medical camp was still open. I decided it would be a good time to give Yuan Xile a proper visit. If denied, I could always sneak back later. If her condition improved much more, they'd be sending her topside soon. Although I'd be sad to see her leave, I knew it was for the best, especially with everything that was happening. Sooner or later we, too, would be entering the abyss, and I needed to focus on the mission. But I was also aware that once she was gone my chances of seeing her again were next to nothing.

I arrived at her tent to find a crowd of nurses standing outside. They regarded me rather oddly as I walked up, intermittently glancing back inside the tent. I wondered if Wang Sichuan and the rumors had already started to spread. Peering inside, I saw the tent was filled with people, several doctors among them. Most surprising of all was that Ivan, the mysterious Soviet from atop the dam, was there as well.

30 IVAN

The people in the tent were all speaking in Russian when I entered. Seeing me, they went silent, as if stunned. One of the doctors took a long look at me, then walked over and waved me out of the tent, telling me to wait 'til they were finished. The Soviet raised his head and looked at me. When it came to foreigners, I can't tell a happy expression from pure rage, but I stepped quickly outside, feeling rather annoyed.

The Soviet Union had been sending specialists to China since the 1950s. Their efforts had been of great help in the early days after the war, but there was also a clear political and strategic element to this assistance and the men and women sent were not always of the highest quality. Many persisted in old-fashioned ways of thinking and showed not the slightest inclination to change or listen to reason. As leaders they were often excessively domineering. Add to this the differences in custom and the later rift between China and the Soviet Union, and it was no wonder that most of us grew to resent these Soviet specialists.

I didn't like them from the start, though. A Soviet specialist was sent to an area where I had once been stationed. Knowing little about the local environment, he forced the use of alkaline-heavy fertilizer in soil where the salinity was already very high. Over 300 acres of crops were ruined for the next three years as a result. In the end it was the local production leader who was punished. I think he was even sent to jail. The specialist was merely transferred back to the Soviet Union.

Before long all the doctors exited the tent. I stood up and was about to go inside when the head doctor pulled me back. "Let them be alone for a while," he said to me. "You'd better just head back to your camp."

"Let them be alone for a while?" I asked, an uneasy feeling rising in my stomach. "Why? I just want to see how she's doing." I wriggled past him, but again the doctor yanked me back.

"Be sensible for a moment. Don't you realize who that is in there?"

"No," I said, smiling coldly, "but why should I care? He's just some Soviet. So what? You have no reason to prevent a member of the proletariat like me from visiting his old comrade-in-arms."

"Who cares if you're a member of the proletariat or anything else?" said the doctor, still tightly gripping my shoulder. "This has nothing to do with that. Have you honestly lost your mind? What business do you have disturbing an engaged couple from their reunion?"

I went stock still at his words. "What did you just say? They're engaged?"

"Comrade Ivan is Yuan Xile's fiancé. He has braved untold hardships to journey here from the Soviet Union. The two of them have not seen each other in three years. Can you not show a little restraint?"

As he was saying this, he dragged me away from the tent. I no longer resisted. "Her fiancé?"

Seeing the expression on my face, the doctor seemed to understand what was going on. "Proletarian comrades, eh?" He laughed, shaking his head. "You're punching way above your weight class, kid. Next time you pursue a girl you better make sure she's not already taken first. Try and be a little more realistic. You can't just do whatever you want and think there will be no consequences. It's time you returned to your tent."

He and the rest of the group dispersed. I continued to stand there, dazed, my heart in turmoil. Before long I began to feel mad as hell, so I left.

To be honest, even I didn't know what I was mad about. Probably I was just mad at myself for being such a fool. Images of Yuan Xile and I together flashed through my mind. I'd believed that her affections were directed at me, that in her eyes I was somehow special. Now I could see that whatever longing she felt for me had been just a product of her terror. It was random and coincidental and there was nothing special about it. She had a goddamn fiancé. What else needed to be said? There had never been a place for me in her heart. It had all been in my head. But what about those four days and nights we spent together in the dark? Did they mean nothing? In the midst of all my anger, I was overcome by a feeling of calm. If that's how it is, I thought, then everything is just back to normal. I'd been living in a dream and now there was no longer anything to long for, no longer anything to worry about. I'd woken up, and not a moment too soon.

Whenever I'd read novels, I'd always found the protagonist's feelings too numerous, too exaggerated. Now, however, I understood. My mind may have gone still, but I could feel that behind that stillness whirled countless indescribable emotions. Even the sight of her tent became distasteful to me. Simply spotting it out of the corner of my eye made my heartbeat quicken. Unfortunately, it was the tallest tent around.

I walked aimlessly through camp and finally made my way to the top of the dam. No one else was there. A fierce wind swept across the empty expanse. Staring off into the vast darkness before me, I gradually began to calm down. Step by step, I made my way to the very edge, sat down, and let my legs hang over the side. The vast darkness made my head spin. I felt as if all my mixed-up thoughts and feelings were being sucked into the void. Compared to the immensity of nature, the affairs of men were nothing. I would discover what was down there, I thought, for now there was no longer anything to fear. A wise man once said that love gives men courage, but the opposite is also true. Heartbreak brings courage, too. It's difficult to say whether I made my decision because I once had love, or because I lost it. Probably a little of both.

At this point, however, none of this mattered anymore. I was changed, yet everything around me stayed the same. When I returned to my tent Wang Sichuan and the others could tell something was different. When they asked me, though, I told them I was just stumped from mulling over the meaning of the stone.

From then on Yuan Xile's name became taboo. The moment I heard it my heart was in my throat. I made sure to engage only in things that had absolutely nothing to do with her. I didn't visit her again and all those feelings I couldn't fully suppress I at least did my best to control. As for Ivan, the few times I chanced to see him I found him even more despicable than before. I cared little about the activity happening around me. Anyone who'd gone through what I was going through should have been able to see it in my face, yet no one said anything. Everything just meandered along until Pei Qing and Old Tian had made enough progress to hold another meeting. With great reluctance, I managed to rouse myself and attend.

31 BATTLE OF WITS

Old Tian and Pei Qing had arrived at different conclusions on what was hidden within the abyss and how best to proceed. From the beginning they'd never seen eye to eye. The only option remaining was to vote on the two choices by a show of hands. The winner would determine our next move. I asked Wang Sichuan whom he favored.

"I don't really understand Old Tian's theory," he said, a sheepish look on his face. "So, for now at least, I'm going with Pei Qing, though I still think his plan is much too bold."

The meeting was small and tightly packed. Old Tian went first. Honestly, I had a tough time understanding Old Tian's presentation, too. My knowledge of theory was slightly better than Wang Sichuan's, but this was still way over my head. Old Tian and his students first determined that the black cloud stone had been ripped with great force from the cave wall, though whether this event was natural or manmade they couldn't say. Wang Sichuan nudged me and rolled his eyes. Of course the stone fell from the cave wall; it's not like it appeared out of thin air. The holes continued all the way through the stone, Old Tian continued. This was an effect of acidic corrosion. Old Tian believed this was not a manmade phenomenon, but was rather caused by acidic warm water pouring into the abyss and over the stone.

He'd touched upon one of the knottiest of geological questions: Was this stone's porous exterior formed by the water at the spot where it was found, or was it shaped somewhere else and carried into the abyss? We could labor for months on this issue alone. Just hearing it raised made my head hurt. Acid runoff from the dam might have drained into the abyss and soaked it porous, but it was equally likely the acid had washed over the stone before it got swept down into the abyss. The problem hinged on He Ruping's reason for picking it up. Was he trying to tell us the bottom of the abyss was covered in strong acid? But the edges of the stone's many holes were worn smooth. Clearly no acid had touched it for a long time. The man had been burning alive in a pitch-black hell. How could he have managed to identify this stone as an exemplar of acidic corrosion?

And He Ruping's wounds were from scalding, not acid. The only thing that really made sense was Old Tian's notion of the significance of where the stone was found. First, he conjectured that the abyssal end of the steel cable was anchored near a geothermal hotspot. Next he pointed out that anywhere the underground flowed would most likely maintain a relatively low temperature. So, he concluded, He Ruping's reason for picking up this water-washed stone was to tell us that the abyssal course of the underground river was safe and that the only reason he survived was because he'd dropped from the cable directly into the water.

Pei Qing's position was entirely opposite. "Given our depth underground," he said, "there are probably open cracks at the bottom of the abyss revealing lakes of liquid hot magma. When the underground river water rushes over these cracks it becomes superheated and puts off a layer of steam hot enough to sear human flesh on contact. The higher the steam rises, the cooler it becomes, eventually turning into mist. The lowest levels never even begin to cool off. Blanketed by this dense layer of mist, they just grow hotter and hotter."

Here Pei Qing noted that He Ruping had previously been an iron and steel worker and so was accustomed to laboring in high-temperature environments. Not only would he be more resistant to heat, he would also know a few things about how to survive in such situations. The burns on He Ruping's right palm were much less severe than those on the rest of his body, meaning the stone must have remained cool, or at least cooler than much of the abyssal bottom. This, Pei Qing argued, was the very reason the stone was brought back. In the midst of this hellish environment, He Ruping had happened upon a comparative cool spot. He had grabbed the stone to alert us of its existence.

"Then how do you explain He Ruping's full body burns?" asked one of Old Tian's students.

"Those didn't happen until after he left the safe zone and headed back up the cable," came Old Tian's reply. "Some of the others are probably still alive down there, trapped wherever he found the stone. That's why he came back, to tell us that survival is possible, and that the others need our help."

Old Tian's student was undaunted. "But why didn't they fire a signal flare?"

A man who appeared to be one of the head engineering soldiers spoke up in response. "If Engineer Pei is right, then with all the humidity down there a flare would never fire."

I had to admire Pei Qing. His victory seemed practically assured. In school I loved refuting my professors' opinions and I'd never lost the fighting spirit. Pei Quing's deductions were all highly logical and they made Old Tian's half-formed guesses seem all the more implausible in comparison.

Now Pei Qing turned to the officers overseeing the meeting. "I recommend that as soon as the river level drops, we immediately close the dam's sluice gates. Once all the water has drained from the abyss, the mist will quickly thin out. This is why the Japanese built the dam. The only way to enter the abyss is to stop the flow of water. And to demonstrate how confident I am in my proposal, I am willing to personally lead a team into the abyss."

"No doubt," scoffed Old Tian, standing off to the side. "Young people are always willing to rashly throw their lives away. But since we remain unclear on what is actually happening down there, I advise that we wait and discuss the matter further."

"People are probably still alive down there," said Pei Qing. "We don't have time to wait. I'm confident in my opinion and willing to pay with my life if I'm wrong. But you, Old Tian, your problem is simple: you're scared."

"I'm a scientist," said Old Tian, his face turning red, "not a daredevil who's going to gamble on some hunch!"

The officers chairing the meeting glanced at each other. Then one of them adjourned the meeting, saying they had matters to discuss. Old Tian was finished. They'd ended the meeting to give him a way out. Pei Qing knew this as well. As he left the tent his face broke into a rare smile.

I had half a mind to go congratulate him. These graybeards had been pushing us around from the start, dictating everything and telling us nothing. Although I wouldn't normally approve of the insulting way Pei Qing had spoken to Old Tian, in this instance it seemed well deserved. But I knew that showing my support right now would be looking for trouble.

165

It would be like sticking another knife in Old Tian's wound. Sooner or later he'd find a way to return the favor. So upon leaving the tent, we all dropped our heads and walked off in separate directions.

Before I'd gone 10 steps Pei Qing called after me. I looked back to see him striding towards me. Off to the side, Old Tian and his underlings were already gazing darkly in my direction. My heart sank. I was still wondering whether I should just keep walking when Pei Qing threw his arm around me and began leading me toward an empty part of camp. His hand was covered in chalk, leaving a white five-fingered print on my sleeve. His grip was immensely strong. I had no idea what he wanted with me.

"What the hell are you up to?" I asked him.

"How'd you think I did just now? Who'd you believe, me or Old Tian?"

After looking behind us to make sure no one could hear, I pointed at him and, in a low voice, said, "You."

"Good." He didn't seem surprised at all. "Then would you be willing to do me a favor?"

"What kind of favor?" I asked, frowning.

"I need someone to accompany me into the abyss, and you're my top choice."

"What about the engineering soldiers?" I asked. "Wouldn't you rather take one of them? I'm sure that's who they're going to send with you."

"Then I will refuse. They don't need to risk their lives on my behalf. Enough of them have died already. We prospectors might seem more valuable, but in reality they're worth a lot more."

The nerve of this guy. This was some favor. "Why should I go risking my life?" I said, laughing. "What the hell do I owe you?"

Pei Qing smiled. "That's not what I meant. Actually, I'm almost positive my deduction is correct, but the unforeseen can always occur and the descent will be dangerous no matter what. I need someone I can trust."

"Then why not ask Wang Sichuan?"

"You know he doesn't like me, and anyway he's too impulsive. By now you must have realized that I don't normally get along well with other people. Well, out of everyone here you're the only one I admire. There are some things you do even better than me."

"That's nice of you," I said, knowing I was still going to refuse, "but it's not yet time for me to get involved. I'm sorry. As for those things you're referring to, they were probably just luck."

Pei Qing's expression didn't change. He didn't seem at all put off by my refusal. "Why don't you think about it?" he suggested.

I laughed and shook my head. Not now and not ever, I said to myself. I can still complete this mission without putting my life on the line. I knew that once the situation down below was clearer our task would no longer be so dangerous. This wasn't cowardice speaking; I just didn't think I had to be the one to take this risk, especially when it was only to prove Pei Qing's theory.

I hadn't walked more than a few steps before he was back. This time no one else was around, so I no longer had to be so careful about my choice of words. "I will go into the abyss," I said, "just not this time. But if you're so certain your theory is correct, why not just go by yourself? Or I'm sure the on-site commander would accompany you if you wanted."

"I wasn't coming back to press you. I understand why you don't want to go, and from the start I didn't think I'd be able to convince you. I just wanted to give it a try." He handed me a cigarette. Something fishy was going on. He wasn't behaving like himself today. After lighting our cigarettes, he continued speaking. "I wanted to give you some advice before my descent. Yuan Xile is a high-ranking woman—in the military and in society. At this point you two are not well-matched and you won't have many opportunities to win her over."

The son of a bitch knew. I felt my face go hot with anger. How the hell had he found out? It wasn't like he normally paid me much attention. "I already said I'd be joining you down there sooner or later. As for Yuan Xile and I, that's none of your business."

"If I die down there," he said, "then the mission could very well be canceled and everyone will go their separate ways. I'll let you decide what's best." Before I could say anything in response, he began walking away, saying, "She'll be married soon, but you already knew that, didn't you?"

I was too stunned to reply. Was this a threat, or was he still trying to persuade me? The moment he'd spoken her name my heart had seized up in pain, but she was no longer my business. I found Pei Qing's excitement to enter the abyss more than a little strange, but it wasn't just posturing. I could tell he'd made up his mind. Now all he had to do was find the right partner.

What was he thinking? For an instant I considered chasing down Pei Qing and telling him I'd do it, but I held myself back.

32 FACE TO FACE

While playing cards after dinner that night, Wang Sichuan asked me what Pei Qing had wanted, so I told him the whole story. As soon as I finished he became indignant. I knew he was angry Pei Qing had chosen me over him. Wang Sichuan had always felt that, when it came to self-defense and skill with one's hands, he was clearly my superior. For the most part he was right, but Pei Qing wasn't looking for a bodyguard. What he needed was someone with good judgment, someone who could adapt to the unexpected.

I realized now that Pei Qing had been figuring all this out since the moment we were saved. He was like a deer in the headlights when a situation was at its most dangerous. His instinctive reaction was to sit and think. But when faced with a speeding car, the crux of the matter is not whether diving one way is better than diving the other. It is, in that instant, are you able to stop thinking and move? Wang Sichuan, despite how he might appear, was actually a very smart and attentive man, but his emotions too often got the better of him.

Pei Qing was right to choose me. I'd always had my own way of doing things and had never needed a textbook to guide me. This was more than could be said for most of my comrades. Although I made the golden mean my rule—remaining moderate in all things—as soon as a situation called for it, I could toss all that out the window. I was just the kind of person China needed in those years—someone who, at the critical moment, could drop all pretense of doing things the accepted way and do them the way they needed to be done.

Yuan Xile's impending marriage continued to linger in my mind. I wondered if she would be impressed if I descended into the abyss. At the very least, I hoped it would leave a deep enough impression that she would never forget me, that she might even feel indebted to me. This is the kind of thinking that makes men behave like fools. What was the difference if Yuan Xile remembered me or not? Her future was fixed. She wasn't going to choose me no matter what I did. At this very moment she was probably pressed close to her fiancé's chest, completely unaware of all of my ridiculous ideas. And I knew that in a few years I would probably fall in love with someone else. Why not give myself a little time?

I paid no attention to my cards and soon my face was covered in strips of paper. For some reason this only increased Wang Sichuan's anger. By now the guy was really pissing me off, so I tossed my cards to the table. "I need to go get some air," I said. "You guys keep playing."

A crowd of people had been waiting to join since the beginning. As soon as I got up someone had already taken my place. Wang Sichuan glared at me and cursed, but the tent was too full of noise for me to hear him. I found a quiet place beside the underground river and sat down on a wooden crate to smoke. Every now and then I would absentmindedly flick my ash into the water. After a little while I heard movement from the river beside me. Startled, I leapt to my feet. A white shape rose out of the river. It was a man, pale as a ghost and completely naked. He glared at me. It was Ivan.

"You flicked your cigarette ash onto my head," he said.

His Chinese wasn't bad. He had a thick Russian accent, but he spoke clearly and was easy to understand. I relaxed. "I didn't see you," I said, happy to stop searching my brain for the few words of Russian I still knew. "What were you doing down there?"

"Bathing. Can't you tell?" He plucked a wash cloth from the water and wiped the ash from his head.

The river was so cold that even from here I wanted to shiver, but the Soviet just stood there, pink with chill and seeming not to care at all. "You're not scared of getting sick?" I asked.

He didn't reply, just wrung out his towel, draped it around his neck, grabbed the iron handrail nearby and pulled himself out of the water. He was totally unaffected by the cold. I doubted he'd even call it cold at all. "I've heard you Chinese take only two showers in a lifetime," he said.

"That's the Mongolians," I replied. Wang Sichuan was giving us all a bad name.

He laughed. "I was kidding, though it does seem like you prefer hot water."

I nodded. I hated this guy. For a second I almost turned around and walked off. We passed the next few moments in silence. He retrieved his clothing from a nearby wooden crate and got dressed. Then a sudden thought made him pause. He looked up at me. "I know you," he said. I'd wanted to leave as soon as I was done with my cigarette, but now he was walking over to me, an excited look in his eyes. "That's right," he said.

"You're the one who saved Xile." He reached out and shook my hand. "I'd been hoping for a more formal occasion to express my gratitude."

You disgusting hairy beast, I said to myself, to hell with your gratitude. Had I known you were up here, Yuan Xile and I would have stayed down there and let you die of worry.

Even fresh from the cold river his hand was burning hot. This guy was obviously in peak condition. "I apologize for not thanking you outside Xile's tent," he said. "No one told me you were the one who saved her."

"Don't worry about it. I was just doing what I could for my comrade."

"I understand, but to me she's more important than anything in the world, so trust that my gratitude is sincere. My name is Ivan."

"So I've heard," I said and, slurring my pronunciation a little, added, "Ivan Shit-for-Brains." He said something in Russian, his expression telling me he hadn't understood. So I did it again. "Ivan Bowl-of-Shit." But there was a limit to how much fun I could have just toying with him and it made me feel rather petty, so I changed the subject. "How did you end up here?" I asked.

"I'm not too sure myself. This place..." He looked around. "There's something almost marvelous about it. I thought I was just coming here to see Xile, but now they want me to stay."

"What did you do in the Soviet Union? Were you some kind of

researcher?" I tried handing him a cigarette, but he declined.

"I was in the military, a soldier." He produced a pack of foreign-made cigarettes from his jacket pocket. "Men should smoke these," he said.

"Says who?"

Either he didn't hear the edge to my voice or he didn't care. "Says Xile," he said.

I looked at the pack. Only once before had I smoked a Soviet cigarette. It was extremely strong, something to be enjoyed by those who spend much of their lives in the bitter cold. Unadulterated pick-me-ups are what people like that need most. He handed me a cigarette and I lit up. That's when it hit me; this was my chance to find out what was happening with Yuan Xile. My heart clenched. I felt separated from my body, no longer in control, but I took this as a challenge. I was face-to-face with my rival for Yuan Xile's love. I would not retreat. This was war and my enemy was my own sense of inferiority. I knew that if I could discuss Yuan Xile with her Soviet fiancé, then I clearly did not fear him. "How is Yuan Xile doing now?" I asked.

He took a deep breath and smiled at me. "She is doing perfectly well," he said. "She's just as lovely as ever, and so to me nothing is the matter. Time, illness, recovery—all these concerns can be brushed aside."

This was not the response I'd expected. Before I could say anything, he'd stubbed out his cigarette, put on his hat, and grasped my hand once more, saying, "I'm so happy I ran into you. I was lucky to sneak away from my guards long enough to take this bath, but I must be getting back soon. I'm not supposed to be speaking with other people."

"Why?" I asked.

"I don't know," he replied, shaking his head. "You Chinese are always so secretive, though, of course, there are Soviets who are the same way. I hope to see you again soon." Then, pointing to my cigarette, he continued. "Don't waste that. Xile always said that a good man does not waste his tobacco."

We strolled back toward camp as he continued to speak. "Right now I am doing my utmost to convince them to let Xile return to the surface," he said. "As soon as this is over, she and I will be married in China. I'm sure you mean a great deal to her. I hope that you can attend."

My heart plummeted. A million thoughts swirled through my mind. "I...um...I..."

"No matter what," he continued, "when the time comes, I hope that you will not refuse. Goodnight." Saying this, he turned on his heel and continued off in another direction.

I remained fixed to the spot, surprised at how abruptly our conversation had concluded. All the courage I'd filled myself with fell away. I felt like an empty shell. I stood there for a long time, depressed and humiliated. Suddenly, I knew what to do. It was a foolish idea, but the moment I thought of it I began to feel better.

33 INTO THE ABYSS

Our fireproof asbestos suits were extremely cumbersome. We looked like members of the Soviet Red Army, ready to defend our country from the Germans in wintertime. I've definitely seen too many movies. Just from looking at our heavy gas masks I could tell they'd be uncomfortable. When I thought about the environment we were soon to enter, though, I made no objection. The thicker the better, I figured. Pei Qing was so skinny our gear was almost too heavy for him. His face became pale and his breathing ragged, but his expression was no less determined than before. He seemed able to ignore these annoyances. Seeing this, I began to feel calmer myself. There was no way I was being put to shame by some bookworm.

The dam's sluice gates had been shut for three days and the mist had thinned out considerably. The time had come. Command had wanted to send some engineering soldiers with us as well, but Pei Qing had refused. We were moments away from descending.

Just before shutting his mask, Pei Qing glanced over at me. His eyes were filled with a steely resolve. "I hope you won't regret this," he said.

"Why?" I asked. "Worried I'll blame you?"

"No," he said, "you won't have the chance. By then your goose will be cooked. But don't worry. I'm confident we'll make it out of this alive. Just prepare yourself. We don't know what we're going to find down there."

Save your breath, I said to myself. Even death doesn't scare me now. I waited as Wang Sichuan made a final few adjustments to my suit. He patted me on the shoulder. "You be careful down there," he said.

I nodded and signaled that I was ready. Without another word, one of the soldiers gave me a push. A moment later my feet were free of the dam and treading circles in the air. By the time I steadied myself we were already flying over the dark abyss. A fierce wind shrieked out of nowhere, rocking us back and forth, but we were locked into the cable overhead and could not be blown free. The dam's searchlights tracked our course, their four beams illuminating the darkness around us. For an instant I could still see the people on the dam and hear their cries. Then they were gone.

By now I thoroughly regretted my decision. My heart was practically beating out of my chest. As I looked at my feet swaying in the wind and the mist below, I couldn't understand how I ever thought Yuan Xile could be so important. My recriminations lasted no more than half a minute. We dropped into the mist. It was no longer dense at all. I could hear Pei Qing breathing nervously, but the wind stole my words as soon as they left my mouth. I signaled to him that it was all right, hoping to calm him down. He looked at his thermometer. The temperature had not risen. The searchlight beams reached us only dimly. Before long they had vanished altogether.

Turning on our flashlights, we scanned our surroundings. The darkness pressed in on us. We could see nothing but the light of our twin beams. So long as I survived, I knew I'd never forget this experience for the rest of my life. We were dropping into an impenetrable blackness, with neither ground below nor sky above, with a wild wind blasting us from every direction. It was like nothing in this world. For an instant I asked myself, where am I? It was as if I'd died without realizing it and was already in the dark-land beyond.

As we continued to fall, the wind died down and all was quiet. Our beams now lit upon the surrounding mist. We were sinking into a vast cloud of cotton. Gradually Pei Qing and I became aware of the heat. We'd been dripping sweat from the start in our heavy asbestos suits, but now the temperature was clearly rising fast.

"Careful," he said. "If we see steam you need to hit the brakes immediately."

I nodded, keeping one eye on the pressure gauge as I reached for my flare gun. It was already covered in drops of water.

"If the mist becomes too thick it will be difficult to breathe," said Pei Qing. "And at this depth the flare won't fire—or if it does, it won't light up. You're wasting your time."

The temperature was now at 158 degrees Fahrenheit. I wanted to tear off the suit, but I knew that without it I would be far hotter. And once I took it off I'd never be able to get it back on. Pei Qing pulled the brake. If the temperature continued to rise it might be wisest to stop here and turn around. As he studied the thermometer, I noticed something clinging to the cable ahead of us. Shining my flashlight across it, I realized at once what it was.

A man.

He'd been cooked into a congealed mass. His flesh had melded with the cable and liquid fat dripped from him like wax. I wanted to vomit. Pei Qing was silent, but I'm sure he was feeling the same.

"You see that?" he asked me.

"Yeah. This shows it used to be far hotter than it is now. One hundred fifty-eight degrees or not, the temperature has dropped way down. You were right."

He ignored my compliment. "What I meant was, this thing's blocking our way. We need to get it off."

Such talk about a dead comrade was a little callous for my liking, but there was no use in criticizing Pei Qing. The only thing he cared about was confirming his theory and triumphing over Old Tian. And he was right after all; this was no time to get sentimental.

I shined my flashlight across the body. We weren't going to be able to just pull him free. He was too wrapped around the line. We had to sever the man's limbs one by one, then cut loose what remained. I knew Pei Qing wasn't going to be able to do it. I told him to stay put, then swung my legs up and hooked them around the cable. I unclipped my safety harness and wrestled my body up atop the line. It rocked with my movements, swinging us back and forth.

"Be careful!" Pei Qing yelled up to me.

The melted man became even more horrifying as I crawled closer. His face had sunk into the upper part of the cable, his mouth wide open as if in unimaginable pain. His features had melted together like a shrunken candle. His singed hair was fused to his face, strangely motionless in the wind. I closed my eyes.

"Forgive me," I said. I hoisted my machine gun, took aim, and carefully fired three short bursts into his right arm, severing it. As the arm dropped soundlessly into the abyss, I took aim at the other. It too cleanly fell away. When I tried the same thing on his legs, though, they held fast, each remaining tightly coiled around the cable. And his upper body was glued in place. Slinging my gun over my shoulder, I pulled out my dagger and crawled closer.

Even through my mask the stink was overpowering. Forcing back the urge to vomit, I held my breath and began cutting into the corpse where it met the cable, trying to scrape the flesh free. Our faces were pressed so close that they almost touched. I did my best not to think about him, all the while cutting deeper and deeper. Eventually the weight of his body gradually dragged his torso from the cable, until from waist to head he was hanging in mid-air. Where his body slid from the cable, all that remained was viscous fat. Proceeding slowly to keep from slipping, I crawled forward and began cutting his lower half free. With each cut more of his body weighed against him. Soon those sections still stuck to the cable began to tear. Before long he was hanging on by only a thread of skin. I gave him a push and watched as he tumbled into the abyss.

That's when I noticed something black wrapped around the cable where the corpse had been. It took no more than a glance to recognize a bandoleer of hand grenades. A string looped through the firing pins of each grenade and trailed down into the abyss. The other end, I realized with horror, must be attached to the corpse. I froze, my heart hammering in my chest, my body straight as a board.

Then I watched in dumb animal terror as, all at once, each of the firing pins flew free and the grenades began belching smoke.

34 FALLING

I was only an arm's length away from the bundle of grenades about to be blown into scattered heaps of smoking flesh. I couldn't say how much time remained. Wood-handled grenades like these were unlikely to have more than a five-second fuse. What was I supposed to do up here, sitting atop this narrow cable? Even on level ground, five seconds was barely enough time to respond. I kicked hard against the grenades, then kicked again with both feet. The grenades just slid a little farther down the cable, where they wedged against one of the soldier's still-stuck severed legs. Now I was really done for.

I scrambled up the cable toward Pei Qing. Adrenaline pumping through my veins, I managed to climb almost nine feet before the boom resounded behind me and the whole cable twisted like a snake with the force of a steel whip.

My body shook. A pile driver slammed into my legs and back. The next moment I felt something smack viciously against me. There was barely time to feel any pain. I'd already been blasted off the cable and was sailing through the air. Falling, I suddenly realized something was rushing up towards me. It was the ground. Knocking into it practically headfirst, my brain buzzed from the impact. A wave of dizziness rushed over me. I managed a single, astonished thought.

How had the ground come up so fast?

Minutes passed before I realized I was still conscious. At last I became aware of the pain. It was excruciating, covering every inch of my body. I struggled to sit up. All around me was darkness. The drop had shattered my headlamp. Still I could barely believe my luck. I had been only a few feet from the grenades when they exploded. Not only did I avoid being blown to bits, I'd also survived the fall into the abyss. Or maybe not. Maybe I really had died this time and was now in hell. No, that couldn't be. I was still wearing the same asbestos suit, its exterior shredded.

Pain shot through my body with my every movement. Gritting my teeth, I pulled out my flashlight and switched it on. Cracks striated the lenses of my gas mask. I found myself in a field of shattered stones. Each was black and covered in small holes like the one He Ruping had retrieved. A dense mist shrouded everything. I shined the light across my body. The suit was in pieces and blood had begun to seep through, much of it from my legs. When I touched them the pain was so severe I almost fainted. I coughed violently, feeling like blood was in my throat. I had no idea how serious my injuries were. I needed to think of something quick. Thankfully, Pei Qing's theory had been correct. Hot as it was down here, the temperature had nonetheless fallen dramatically.

I immediately wondered where he was. Had the cable snapped and rocketed him into the darkness? Forcing myself to endure the pain, I rose to my feet. A light was shining up ahead. I staggered closer. It was Pei Qing's cable harness. His helmet was lying on the ground, its light still shining. He was nowhere to be seen. I gasped for breath as I called out his name, stumbling on the rocks underfoot. He was sprawled on the ground behind a large boulder. His gas mask had fallen off and his face was covered in blood. I covered his nose and mouth with a piece of cloth and put his gas mask back on. He'd been higher up on the cable and had clearly fallen hard. I had to shake him a few times before he woke up. He blinked open his eyes, wrinkled his forehead in pain and glared at me.

"What the hell did you do?" he asked. "Why did that guy suddenly explode?"

When I told him what happened, he cursed in disbelief.

"That soldier must have wanted to sever the line so no one else could descend," he said. "He died before he could finish, but you managed to complete the job for him."

Looking into the darkness overhead, I smiled wryly to myself. Command was surely going nuts this time. Not only had we disappeared, but the cable itself had also snapped. Pei Qing pulled out his flashlight. The iron mound that had anchored the cable sat less than 30 feet away from us. Now I understood. We'd been almost at the bottom. If we'd simply unclipped and jumped down we'd probably be in much better shape. I looked around. No survivors, no corpses, no sign of human presence at all. If the other soldiers were still alive then I had no idea where they had gone.

I asked Pei Qing what we should do next. Looking around, he said he didn't know. Then he laughed. "How about that," he said. "I was right after all. This is exactly the environment I theorized."

"You're fucking amazing," I said, "and I really mean that, but this isn't the time to celebrate. Command has no idea we're still alive. If we don't tell them soon, they're going to think you were wrong and reopen the floodgates. And that would be an unjust death."

Pei Qing grimaced. "You're right."

I helped him to his feet. Once he was standing, it was clear his injuries were much less severe than my own. Composing myself, I pulled out my flare gun, flipped open the barrel, and let the loaded flare slide into my hand. At a glance I could tell that it wouldn't fire. The flare looked like it had been soaked in water, the gunpowder sodden. I checked my extra flares, as well as Pei Qing's. They were all useless. It was just as we'd feared—this place was far too damp. I didn't want to give up. I loaded one of the flares, aimed my gun at the sky and pulled the trigger. Nothing. Not even a spark. Cursing beneath my breath, I shook the flare from the chamber and replaced it with another. This too failed to fire. I tried several more, all duds. The PLA had better start making some better equipment, I thought, my heart sinking. Pei Qing didn't seem worried in the least. Picking up his flashlight, he began walking into the depths of the mist. I did my best to hobble after him.

"What are we supposed to do now?" I asked.

"Don't worry," he said, "we have time. There will be several days of meetings before command decides to do anything. All we need to do is find somewhere free of moisture to dry these flares. Look, there have clearly been people here before." He swept his flashlight across the broken rocks underfoot. They were all different sizes, some as big as a dining room table. "These rocks are leftovers from the construction of the base up top," Pei Qing continued. "Look how level they are. After dumping them into the abyss, the Japanese smoothed them into a road. I'll bet we'll find something ahead."

By now my leg was hurting so bad I could barely stand upright. Pei Qing didn't seem to care. His callousness frustrated me, but it wasn't like I could say anything. We walked for several more minutes. A vague shape appeared in the mist ahead. We drew closer.

It was a three-story cement tower, so corroded it was nearly unrecognizable.

35 ON THE EDGE

I gasped. All along I'd been unwilling to believe the devils actually had a base down here, but this crumbling tower was proof. It also appeared to be all that was left. Cement structures fall apart easily in an environment this damp. We walked closer. The tower was tilted to one side, its exterior riven with cracks. It probably wouldn't even hold the two of us. We shined our flashlights inside. The first floor was empty save for a ladder leading upwards.

I glanced over at Pei Qing. Perhaps we'd better not enter, I was thinking. The tower was narrow, nothing appeared to be inside, and exploring it would be very dangerous. But Pei Qing's flashlight revealed scattered footprints across the floor and they appeared fresh. Before I could respond, he'd already stepped inside and begun climbing toward the second floor. I followed after him.

The second floor was cramped and windowless, about the size of a small attic. Three men were huddled together in the corner. I sighed. They were our comrades, their bodies covered in terrible burns and their eyes now closed. Kneeling beside them, Pei Qing prodded the men one by one. He looked back at me and shook his head.

"Had Old Tian listened to me sooner we probably could have saved these men," he said.

I was staring at the three young soldiers in silence when Pei Qing turned around and motioned for me to follow him back outside. We walked around the tower and kept going, but there was nothing else to see. The makeshift road stopped there, the rocks becoming as jagged as sharp teeth and terribly uneven. These rocks must have fallen from the ceiling during a cave-in, as the gaps between them were dark and deep. We could go no farther. This ruined tower was likely the devils' only achievement down here. Pei Qing refused to give up. He continued on, crossing one gap after another. Gritting my teeth, I followed after him, but the pain in my leg soon made walking too difficult. I called out for him to wait. He glanced back at me, annoyed. Then he grudgingly made his way over, helped me up, and supported me as we continued on.

"Old Tian said that this plateau extends for three thousand feet at most before reaching the cliffs," I said. "The Japs would never have been able to build on this terrain. We're not going to find anything over here."

"Wrong," he replied. "We already have." He shined his flashlight beam into the gaps between the rocks, revealing an electrical cable that ran from the tower and snaked through the crevices ahead. "The devils would never have built that tower if this place was worthless. Something very important is up ahead, something that could not have been built anywhere else."

The way he said this made it seem like he already knew what he was looking for. "What do you think it is?" I asked.

"I think it's a signal tower."

I didn't understand. "Why a signal tower?"

"It's obvious," he said, breathing hard. "It has to be that, and we'll find it as long as we keep following this cable. Once we're there I'll explain everything."

Between breaths Pei Qing urged me to go faster, but it was no use. He barely had strength enough to bear the weight of his own gear. Supporting me quickly wore him out. We continued along haltingly, frequently stopping to rest. Suddenly the mist thinned out and a fierce wind blew through us. We were approaching the edge of the plateau. Around us everything was black, the twin cones of our flashlights nearly worthless. Then, all of a sudden, I saw a dim reflection in the darkness ahead. It was an immense iron structure at least 10 stories tall—a signal tower.

Pei Qing laughed triumphantly. "You see that? Was I right or what?"

"How did you know?" I asked, my surprise outweighing my terror. "You've been here before?"

"Of course not," he said, staring at the dark structure. "Like I told you, there had to be a tower here. It even looks just as I'd imagined."

Pei Qing scanned his flashlight over our surroundings. There appeared to be nothing but the signal tower. Regaining his composure, he turned back to me. "You still remember the telegram that was transmitted from the abyss?" he asked. "Old Tian said that it originated here, but not only is this place close to the dam, it even has electricity. So, if they were transmitting from here, why didn't they just make a phone call?" Gesturing at the mist behind us, he continued. "Much of this first plateau is shrouded year-round by a mist thick with heavy metals, and the dam itself is located at the narrow mouth of the underground river. If you wanted to build a station for receiving and transferring signals sent from the abyss, neither of those places would have fit the bill. Right here, however, where the mist thins out near the cliff's edge, this would have been perfect."

If he was right, this meant the devils had descended even deeper into the abyss. At the meeting Old Tian had denied this possibility, saying it was too unrealistic. Pei Qing had said nothing. I cursed under my breath. I had believed Old Tian, but now I couldn't deny that Pei Qing's explanation made a lot more sense.

"Not only did they keep descending," said Pei Qing, "they survived. That message was definitely sent from somewhere down below."

As Pei Qing said this, I noticed a slight tremble in his voice. This was strange, but I didn't have time to give it much thought. We continued on until we reached the base of the tower. Pei Qing immediately craned his neck and stared upwards. Something didn't seem right. Ever since entering the abyss, Pei Qing had been almost gleeful. Where had this stark change in personality come from? Was he merely happy to have thoroughly defeated Old Tian?

The signal tower was made of iron, the frame covered in cement. Many other layers of stuff, probably rust-proofing, could be seen beneath the disintegrating exterior. Compared to the buildings you see today, this tower was by no means tall, but for us it was a magnificent sight. The electrical cable entered the tower through a small hole in the side. An iron ladder scaled the wall all the way to the top, much too rickety to climb. We walked around to the back of the tower. There, not 30 feet on, the ground dropped away, plummeting to the next level of the abyss. Sharp, fang-like stones pointed into the darkness beyond, like spiked parapets on a castle wall. The darkness itself was vast and silent. Somehow, when compared to the void beyond the dam, this one seemed even darker, even deeper.

We laid our flares along the edge, hoping the wind would blow the gunpowder dry. By now Pei Qing had calmed down. Staring off into the abyss, he seemed to have turned back into his old self. The wind slowly dried my asbestos suit and it rested lighter on my body. My bleeding also seemed to have stopped, but the bloodstain was discomfortingly large. Sitting down beside Pei Qing, I too fell into a daze. There was no way to make the gunpowder dry any faster. We could only sit and wait.

After gazing blankly into the darkness for several minutes, Pei Qing turned to me. "You ever heard the Legend of the Fox Spirit?" he asked. When I shook my head, he continued. "I think it comes from the Strange Tales from a Chinese Studio. A scholar is taking shelter from the rain inside a cave. There he meets a beautiful young woman who leads him deeper underground. The cave seems to go on forever, until at last they arrive at a fairy world. The scholar eats, drinks, and makes merry. He is wonderfully happy. The next day the young woman pleads with him not to go, but the scholar misses the hustle and bustle of life in the outside world. And so he leaves. When he finally makes it back to the surface, though, he finds the world has changed. The scholar wanders the earth for many years. Eventually he returns to the cave, hoping to find the fairy world waiting for him once more, but this time there's nothing inside but ugly stone."

"What are you trying to say?" I asked.

"I'm saying, what would've happened if that scholar never left the cave?"

"The young woman in the story was a fox spirit. If the scholar remained underground, the two of them would probably have fallen in love, like in the Legend of the White Snake. Inevitably, however, he would have missed the surface. He would have worried about his parents and his place in society. Sooner or later, he would have left."

"What if someone entered a cave like this, one they knew to be perfectly ordinary, and promised to never come out? You think they would succeed?"

"Not unless their faith in what they were doing was extremely strong." I had no idea what he was driving at.

"What kind of world do you think is down there?" he asked, pointing at the abyss.

I thought back to the towering figure in the flight recording. Given my limited imagination, I couldn't even begin to speculate. I shook my head.

"If someone made you live out your entire life in a place like this, would you do it?"

"What are you talking about?" I was becoming annoyed.

"What I'm getting at is this: Do you think any Japanese people are still alive down there? Their faith is extremely strong."

I looked out at the darkness. It was tough to say. Twenty years had passed.

But if the abyss was somehow habitable, then anything was possible.

Climbing to his feet, Pei Qing picked up a flare and loaded it into his gun. He looked up. From here the signal tower would block the trajectory of his shot. He walked a short distance away, aimed at the sky and fired. An orange tracer flew through the dark air. Swept up by the wind, it arced toward the top of the dam. It had worked. Immediately I felt much more at ease. Pei Qing fired a second flare. This one was green. The light of the two flares overlapped, creating a strange color and illuminating our surroundings.

All around us flat iron platforms were balanced atop the broken rocks. On some were tents, on others tarp-covered pieces of machinery. I was astonished. I called Pei Qing over and we lifted up one of the tarps. Numerous components, their names unknown to me, lay underneath—all scrap, long since rusted together and unusable. We continued on past the first few platforms, discovering dozens more behind them. Pei Qing climbed atop a relatively tall rock and looked around.

"Interesting," he said and motioned for me to aim the flashlight beam in a certain direction.

"What is it?" I asked.

"I'll tell you in a moment. Keep aiming your light over there." Pei Qing aimed his flashlight in the same direction. When the two beams were parallel he began walking in the direction they were pointing. I didn't know in the least what Pei Qing was doing. He stopped, shined his flashlight around and called back to me. "Not only did we wipe the floor with Old Tian, we've also made a truly remarkable discovery."

I didn't want to look stupid by asking more questions, so I nursed my ignorance silently.

Pei Qing jumped back down. "The Japanese hid one of their biggest secrets here, and I've just discovered it."

36 THE BIG SECRET

My heart thumped in my chest. "What is it?" I asked. I looked where he was pointing.

Under the light of our beams I could see the platforms positioned in a long, straight line—a line you couldn't see except when looking from the right angle. They were covered with all manner of equipment, stretching farther than the eye could see. I looked back at the other platforms we'd seen. They ran in a neat line parallel to this one, but there were also several other platforms that seemed to have been scattered without rhyme or reason.

"What's the purpose of all this?" I asked.

"It's an airplane runway," said Pei Qing.

"Maybe if the pilot wanted to commit suicide," I said, looking at the jagged rocks between the two rows.

"They just never finished building it." He shined his flashlight across the equipment stacked on the platforms. "These things here would've been high-powered signal lights. And you see how the whole runway slopes down? That's because this place isn't long enough for a full-scale one. They had to slope it to create enough surface area."

"What are those?" I asked, pointing at the other platforms placed outside of the two lines.

"Have you never taken a night flight on a military plane?" he asked. "Those are auxiliary signal lights. I've seen them flying into Karamay."

Pei Qing was often grouped with other specialists and flown all across the country to work on top-secret projects. The oilfields at Karamay were a national priority and so Pei Qing was often sent to the deserts of Northwestern China to make firsthand examinations. It might have sounded like he was just showing off, but I knew this wasn't the case.

"The space behind the dam is too small," he continued, "so this is where they planned to build their main runway."

"That's the big secret?" At most this was just a regular discovery.

Pei Qing shook his head. "Just listen, all right? The Japs would've required a huge amount of power to get these signal lights to shine through the mist." He squatted down, reached behind one of the iron platforms and hauled out a black length of electrical cable. The cable was pockmarked by corrosion. "This contradicts my original theory." He seemed puzzled.

I motioned impatiently for him to just spit it out.

"If what I initially said was correct," he continued, "then after the dam's sluice gates are opened, floodwater and super-hot steam will cover this whole area. So the only way the Japs could have built a long-term airport here would be by ceasing to operate the dam. Otherwise the planes would all be underwater, not to mention that during the rainy season this flooding problem surely becomes much worse. So I doubt the Japanese intended this runway for regular use. And the wrecked bomber behind the dam makes it clear that not only did the plane take off, it also flew back. But construction on this landing strip had barely begun. Did they plan to finish the job while the plane was still in flight? I find that extremely unlikely. In an environment like this, even a huge team of troops would be unable to complete an entire runway in such a short amount of time. The buffer bags lining the underground river make it clear the first flight was always intended to make a crash landing, but to fly only once and then crash would be a waste of all that preparation. To fully explore the abyss they would have needed to fly again. This runway was stage two of the Japs' engineering project. And since there was a stage two, there must also be another plane."

Going through this logic made me dizzy, but now that he'd reached his conclusion, I could see how rational it all was. I looked over the iron platforms. To see these things and immediately think of all that was something no regular bookworm could have pulled off.

"This other plane should still be in pieces inside the dam's warehouse," said Pei Qing. "Now wouldn't you agree that that qualifies as one of the devils' biggest secrets?"

"I guess so, but it doesn't really seem all that groundbreaking." Of course it would have been impressive had Wang Sichuan or I been the one to figure this out, but Pei Qing was already among the country's top oil prospectors and his fame was well earned. Compared to his previous discoveries, a hidden plane didn't amount to much.

"When the time comes, you'll see how important this is," said Pei Qing as he adjusted his gas mask and motioned that it was time to go. "At the right moment, many things that normally appear insignificant can become more valuable than anything else. If my suspicion is proven true, this project's largest and most vexing problem will be instantly solved. And I will be good to my word; a portion of the credit will go to you."

"Don't start bragging just yet."

Pei Qing laughed. "Bragging's never been my specialty. Now let's head back and see what method they've cooked up to get us out of here."

37 THE EXTRA MAN

We walked back to the bottom of the cliff. Thin streams of water dripped down its face, the immensity of it humbling. We wandered about for two hours before finding a thick rope hanging down. First we collected the corpses of our fallen comrades and fastened them to the rope, then we hooked ourselves in and were raised slowly upwards. When we reached the top of the dam, I saw nearly all of the head officers were waiting for us. We'd been taking our time down in the abyss, but up here they must have been nervous as ants dropped in a frying pan.

Everyone applauded as we were helped onto solid ground. Wang Sichuan gave me a bear hug so tight I nearly fainted. The fallen soldiers were laid in a row on a raised part of the dam. Seeing these mangled men, the officers took off their hats and many soldiers began to cry. Others began confirming the corpses' identities.

Suddenly, one of the young soldiers performing the inspection cried out in surprise. "Commander, something's not right here!"

The commander looked to him. "What is it?"

"The number of men is incorrect."

"Incorrect? What do you mean?"

"There's one man too many. Four people were sent into the abyss. Engineer Pei said that one man was dead on the cable and another managed to make it back up here. That should've left two down in the abyss, but instead we have three."

Another man beside him called out. Squatting next to one of the corpses, he yelled, "Commander, there's something wrong with this corpse!"

We all walked over to see the soldier peering at the teeth of one of the corpses, its face unrecognizable. "What's the problem?"

"This is He Ruping," said the soldier.

"He Ruping?"

Wasn't He Ruping lying comatose in the medical camp?

"How is that possible?" asked Wang Sichuan.

"I don't know," said the soldier, "but this is him all right. He's missing the same three teeth."

The soldier who'd first spoken up walked over and looked. After a moment he nodded. "He's right. He Ruping was missing those three teeth. This has to be him."

Cold sweat began to drip down my back. I turned to look in the direction of the medical camp. "If this is He Ruping, then who was the man we saved?

"It was the spy!" cried the Pei Qing. "We saved the spy! The dead man on the cable must've been trying to stop that son of a bitch from reaching the top. He must have snuck through camp while we were all asleep and descended the cable."

One of the officers gave Pei Qing a look. Pei Qing shut up. Then the officer turned to the bodyguard at his side and spoke a quick command. At once the bodyguard went tearing off towards camp. Later I learned that the fake He Ruping was immediately put into custody, but he came out of his coma. The knowledge that he was the spy proved useless. At the time I couldn't understand it. Why had the spy risked his life to descend into the abyss? Nothing of value appeared to be hidden down there. Had we missed something?

Several mid-level cadres escorted me to the medical camp while Pei Qing went immediately to give his report. I didn't notice Old Tian anywhere. I'd really wanted to see the look on his face. That very day I went through an endless surgery in which 24 pieces of shrapnel were removed from my body. The main reason I was still alive was that wood-handled grenades direct most of their explosive power out to the sides. Luckily, I'd been directly in front of the bundle. Even so, my left foot had been severely damaged and they told me it might have to be amputated.

I remained in the medical tent for many days, but unlike my previous stay, this time I had numerous visitors. Yet one thing remained the same: whenever the tent was quiet and no one was around, I would always think of Yuan Xile, still laying in a tent only a few steps away from my own. This closeness couldn't help but throw my heart into confusion. Many times I wanted to go see her, but a strange feeling always stopped me. Although I tried to forget her, there was something in me that wouldn't let her go. It was like when you don't know whether a fire has gone out and so you wait and you wait, and after some time you really think it's finally been extinguished, but if you pour oil on the embers, the fire will blaze hotter than it ever did before.

When I finally left the medical camp two weeks later, everything had changed. Many tents had disappeared. The entire dam was now covered by a great curtain. Guards had been stationed out front and all but the top brass were barred from approaching.

That night Wang Sichuan and some others held a welcome back party for me. I hadn't been able to relax and chat with my friends for a long time, so the evening was a lot of fun. While we were playing cards, I asked them what had been going on recently and why a curtain had been draped over the dam. As soon as I said this their expressions changed. I saw something flash through their eyes. Had something happened while I was incapacitated?

When I asked them further, Wang Sichuan glanced outside the tent, and then in a low voice said, "Weird things have been happening ever since you two came back up."

First of all, everyone continued to receive only top-quality food at mealtimes. Of course they all enjoyed this, but it also made them increasingly suspicious. Then the giant curtain was draped across the dam. Loud mechanical noises would sound periodically from behind the curtain. Equipment that had previously been covered by the waterproof tarpaulins began to disappear. Now they were sending people back to the surface in droves. Of course I wanted to be sent home, too, but I knew a part of me would remain unfulfilled if I never found out how it all turned out. On the other hand, if we remained there, who knew what was in store for us.

While most managed to stifle their suspicions, Wang Sichuan couldn't bear the secrecy. What had Pei Qing told the higher-ups? No one had seen him since he gave his report. A few days before, while pretending to head to the bathroom, Wang Sichuan had attempted to slip behind the curtain. He was discovered by a patrolling soldier, locked up for three days and made to write a self-criticism. I asked him if he'd seen anything. Clapping a hand on his thigh and scratching his head, he said that he'd glimpsed only massive pieces of equipment. A whole bunch of them, in fact. After thinking about it, I said that, based on the situation, we were probably building some large-scale, Soviet-style radar.

Wang Sichuan shook his head. "I doubt that," he said. "If you ask me, it's obvious what's going on back there: We're building another plane."

38 BEHIND THE CURTAIN

Although Wang Sichuan's suspicion made the hair stand up on the back of my neck, inside I remained skeptical. Anything involving aircraft fell under the supervision of the Chinese Air Force, a very mysterious entity. At the founding of the People's Republic in 1949, our military possessed only several planes, all of them captured from the Kuomintang. From then on, the development of China's aircraft industry was kept strictly confidential.

Not that there was much to tell. China's only means of acquiring aircraft technology was through the Soviet Union. For a long time our lack of an industrial foundation made aircraft construction a near impossibility. Many of our engineering soldiers had never even seen a precision-operated crane. This became a big problem in the Korean War, during which the majority of our army's losses came from the sky. While stationed in North Korea, helplessly watching the slaughter of their men at the hands of enemy fighter pilots, Peng Dehuai, the Commander of the Chinese forces, turned to Mao Zedong and asked, "But what about our planes?"

Four days after I returned to my unit, we were notified that our presence was required at a special meeting. The meeting was small. In fact, it was the smallest I'd attended since arriving there. It was held in a little tent with only 11 men present and no film projector. Each man facing us at the front of the room was a top officer, the kind accustomed to eating chicken legs for dinner every night. Commander Cheng was there, but he was not chairing the meeting. That honor fell to a 60-year-old man in a dark Mao suit. His eyes radiated energy in all directions. This was no ordinary officer.

One by one Commander Cheng introduced the men in attendance and we stood to shake one another's hands. The man in the Mao suit was introduced last, and only then did I understand his true importance. I cannot reveal who he was, but he was high-ranking in both the military and the Chinese Academy of Sciences. In fact, I was not at all surprised to see him there; given the size of the project and its strict confidentiality, it made perfect sense that someone from the very highest echelon of government would be sent to make sure everything went according to plan.

When we'd taken our seats, this senior cadre began the meeting by once more swearing us to secrecy. This was my third time taking an oath over the course of this story. It was also the last. And if what has happened up until now has seemed unbelievable to you, then prepare yourself, because you ain't seen nothing yet. I decided from the start to tell my story in a simple and straightforward way so that, upon reaching this point, readers would be able to accept what happened next.

Of the 11 people present, six were senior officers, while the other five were Wang Sichuan, Old Tian, Zhu Qiang, Abdullah Mohammed, and I. Wang Sichuan and I were grassroots prospectors, while Old Tian and Zhu Qiang were both academics. Old Tian had studied under Li Siguang and was already a director at the Party school. I now learned that his full name was Tian Little Trick, but in fact he was a good deal older than us. I didn't know what Abdullah Mohammed's role would be. From the looks of things I guessed he worked in the base command center. Zhu Qiang was a cameraman. He told us it was he who'd set up the projector at the post-rescue meeting.

The meeting was very brief. They simply explained what was to come next and nothing more. First of all, they were sending more troops back into the abyss, but this time we wouldn't be sliding down a cable—we'd be flying in.

Wang Sichuan glanced over at me, as if to say, 'What did I tell you?' There was nothing self-satisfied about his expression, though. He looked solemn and uneasy.

Commander Cheng said they'd been planning to do this ever since Old Cat survived the first mission and told them what was hidden inside the cave. They had considered bringing a plane into the cave in pieces and had already brought in the crane lifts required, but it would be quite some time before the airplane parts arrived. Then Pei Qing discovered that all the components required to build a Japanese bomber were stored in the warehouse. This made things much simpler. We could build another takeoff structure according to the designs left by the Japanese, as opposed to designing a new one based on the specifications of our aircraft. Now, thanks to the tireless, round-the-clock work of the engineering team, the second Shinzan would soon be complete. Since no Chinese pilot was capable of flying a bomber this big, they'd found a Soviet pilot, one who was already staying in China. His copilot would be a surrendered Kuomintang airman. I realized immediately that they were talking about Ivan, but he was not at the meeting. Clearly there were things that even our pilot didn't need to know.

I cannot describe how I felt at the time. For the rest of the meeting I barely took anything in. Still, by then I had already accepted my fate. After the meeting was over, we underwent a comprehensive physical examination. Then we continued to wait.

It was Zhu Qiang who filled us in on Ivan's true background. He was a flight instructor for the Soviet Union and one of its top pilots. He was nicknamed Crazy Ivan because of his penchant for stunts. Supposedly, as part of his marriage proposal to Yuan Xile, he'd attempted an extremely difficult aerial flip. The maneuver had previously been considered impossible, but Ivan managed to complete it by sheer luck. Two things happened because of this: first, Yuan Xile decided to marry him, and second, he was arrested and brought before a military tribunal. To avoid punishment, he agreed to be part of the final group of Soviet specialists sent to China. Not long after his arrival, Chinese-Soviet relations turned hostile, but he decided to remain in China for Yuan Xile. In other words, at that moment in time there was only one man in all of China whose skills were up to the task ahead, and that man was Ivan.

I listened in silence, thinking that my quest for Yuan Xile's heart was looking increasingly hopeless. There was no comparison between Ivan and me. I was an undistinguished slacker from the geological team. He was a decorated ace pilot. Plus, he and Yuan Xile had already gone through so much together. By then, however, she'd already left camp. My chances of seeing her again were almost nil. Whatever her thoughts were on the matter, they no longer included anything for me.

As the days passed, we continued to wait. Our minds filled with worry, yet never once did we discuss the mission. First of all, we weren't allowed to, and second of all, none of us wanted to. Honestly, who wants to discuss how one is probably going to die?

Since Zhu Qiang was responsible for recording the mission, he was first to be allowed behind the curtain. He wouldn't say what was back there; just that he'd filmed some footage that needed to be delivered to the surface. They'd covered up the rising sun decal on the side of the Shinzan. Should the mission be a success and the footage released, the higher-ups didn't want the public knowing the bomber was Japanese. For them to be capable of filming the plane's facade meant it must have been essentially complete. I felt even more nervous than before.

Had we met under different circumstances, Wang Sichuan and I never would have been friends. Our personalities were simply much too different. But during those anxious days we discussed everything; the past and the future, dreams and reality. We had the same doubts and fears about what was going on around us and so were apt to trust one another. Wang Sichuan called many of my opinions into question, to the point where I began to wonder about the very foundation of my value system. In some ways his thinking was more open-minded than my own—just as that of his ancestors had likely been. No matter how you put it, the two of us formed an alliance, and it is entirely thanks to this that I am able to tell my story today.

***

At last we were led behind the curtain. Although we already knew what was back there, seeing it with our own eyes was another matter entirely. Gas lamps brightly lit the enclosed space. A giant bomber perched atop a sloping railway, the whole contraption aimed like an anti-aircraft gun at the silent void beyond the dam. It was the first time I'd seen an entire bomber—or at least one that was still whole—with my own eyes. Staring at the long, flowing dark green fuselage, I was practically awestruck. First of all, it was gigantic. The wrecked Shinzan at the bottom of the river had been shocking, but newly-made and still intact, it was, well, rather terrifying. The plane looked to me just like an enormous demon about to take flight.

An eager technician gave us a tour of the plane's cabin, each of us stepping over the round, steel frames jutting along the length of its body like a man's ribs. Inside it smelled of soldered metal and kerosene. As we walked, the technician related a wealth of basic information to us—where we would sit and how things would be different in the air. I absorbed almost none of what he told us.

That night, I had a strange dream. I was in the cockpit of the Shinzan, facing an endless darkness, and yet utterly calm.

39 TAKE OFF

Little by little our flight date approached. Two days after we went behind the curtain, Wang Sichuan asked a guard for an envelope so he could write a letter to his family in case he didn't return. He did not want to die without having said a few things. I wrote a short note, too. When I took it to the organization department all the female soldiers looked at me with a strange light in their eyes. I wouldn't necessarily call it worshipful, but there was some strong emotion behind it. I thought of the uncertain road ahead and countless sensations flooded my heart. Day after day I continued imagining the most outrageous scenarios despite all my efforts to the contrary. We spent our days training, our nights holding meetings. Again and again our superiors would tell us to uphold the "Courage of the proletariat," though in fact, we were no longer particularly afraid. Soon enough, the big day arrived.

Much to my surprise, I slept well my final night at base. The next morning I arrived long before the operation was to begin. A number of engineering soldiers were already there. They'd been practicing all through the night. I waited for the rest of the team, and then we lined up and walked inside the plane. Seeing Ivan at the front of the line, I frowned. I was not looking forward to having to work with him. We were each wearing Jap flight suits given to us by command. They fit most of us well, but Wang Sichuan and Ivan were both tall and solidly built. The suits and helmets appeared to be several sizes too small for them. We walked immediately to our seats and strapped on our seatbelts. Then we sat stock still, listening to the crackle of the flight cabin intercom and the shouts and mechanical noises reverberating from outside. We no longer felt nervousness; just

210

resignation, numb resignation.

The searchlights were all aimed straight ahead. The direction of the wind was extremely important. If it started blowing straight down, the plane would be forced downward as soon as it left the takeoff structure. We'd crash before we could gain any speed. The plane began to rock from side to side. They were removing the huge clamps that secured us to the track. Amid the swaying, Wang Sichuan handed out cigarettes. He then asked the three soldiers performing our final inspection where they were from. One was from Gansu, one from Shanxi, and one from Harbin.

"You guys are really all over the place," said Wang Sichuan, making small talk.

The eldest of the three replied that they'd all joined the revolution when they were little and were doing odd jobs in the Communist camps before they were in their teens. They'd served on the battlefields of the War of Liberation under the command of He Long, but then, just a few years later, the war was over. All three had been born into poverty and now army barracks were the only places they called home.

One of them was from the same small region as me. I spoke a few sentences of local slang to him and his eyes lit up, but I could tell that behind his smile he was nervous. I smiled grimly. What reason did he have to be nervous? We were the ones about to fly. After finishing their inspection, they turned to us and saluted. It was as if they were saying goodbye to a group of dead men, I thought, suddenly feeling a lot worse.

Pei Qing had said nothing this whole time. He hadn't even smoked. Instead he'd fiddled with his cigarette until it was bent out of shape.

"Don't look so glum," Wang Sichuan said, patting him on the back. "This thing's not even that dangerous. When the Japs crashed their plane only the pilot died. Us back here have nothing to worry about."

Pei Qing gave him a condescending look. "I'm not scared of death," he said. "Unlike you people, I've got no family."

"Good," said Wang Sichuan. "Then since you're so enlightened, if we ever need to lose some weight, we can toss you off first."

I could tell the remark stung, but Pei Qing didn't reply. Instead, he turned to the rest of us.

"Any of you realized yet that an airplane is far from the best way to explore the abyss?" he asked.

"How are we supposed to get in if we don't fly?" asked Wang Sichuan.

"He's right," said Zhu Qiang. "For a space like this, a dirigible would actually be the ideal mode of transport. Command considered using one, but they lacked the technology to build it."

"Technology isn't the issue," said Pei Qing. "If we weren't able to fly, the engineering corps would just build a cliff-side road running into the abyss. So the question is: Why do we have to use a plane?"

"A cliff-side road might work," said Old Tian. "With enough people, anything is possible."

I knew there was no use asking Pei Qing what he was hinting at. Just when I was about to change the subject, a voice sounded over the intercom. "Ground preparations are complete. Prepare for takeoff."

A hush fell over the cabin. After a moment, Wang Sichuan spoke up. Placing a cigarette behind his ear, he said, "Where I come from, we do this for good luck."

We glanced at each other, then one by one we followed suit. The only person who didn't was Pei Qing. He stuck his cigarette in his mouth, leaned against the side of the plane and said no more.

We passed the next 10 minutes in silence. I could hear the engine start up. The plane began to vibrate. It rocked violently as we rolled along the track. It got so bad I thought we might topple off before we even made it into the air. As we rapidly accelerated all of our cigarettes dropped from behind our ears. Pei Qing smiled coldly at us. There was no time to be angry. An instant later my head was spinning and I was so dizzy I could barely think. Old Tian began to cry out. With my stomach in my throat and my teeth clenched, I pressed myself tight against the bulkhead and tried as hard as I could not to vomit. As we picked up speed my throat tightened. I don't care if we fly or crash, I thought, but, goddamnit, just let one of them happen soon.

Just as it seemed I might pass out, the shaking stopped and all that was left were the sounds of the engine and the airflow passing over the fuselage. I was about to take a deep breath when, suddenly, the entire plane tipped forward and dropped. With our nose aiming downwards, we screamed into the abyss. The feeling of weightlessness hit and Old Tian finally began to vomit. My mind emptied of all thoughts, crying only, Hold on!

Gradually everything returned to normal. Covered in cold sweat, I looked over at Wang Sichuan and Pei Qing. They didn't know whether we'd succeeded either. Ivan's voice echoed over the intercom. "We are now flying levelly," he said. "You can undo your seatbelts and begin working."

I didn't even have the strength to breathe a sigh of relief. When I finally got my seatbelt off, Wang Sichuan and I locked eyes. Then I glanced back at Old Tian. He was comatose. Wang Sichuan, I noticed, had thrown up as well. I laughed bitterly to myself. Flying on a plane was nothing like riding a horse. Looking up, I noticed Pei Qing had already walked over to one of the windows and was gazing out. He seemed impatient to get started. Outside the window everything was pitch-black. I yelled for Ivan to switch on the wing-mounted lights. A moment later we could see folds of granite wrinkling the walls of the cave. For some reason, under the bright white lights of the plane, this sight appeared especially strange.

Hello void, I said to myself. I'm here.

40 FLIGHT RECORD

We spent the first hour in a mixture of terror, amazement, and exhaustion. It took more than 15 minutes for Old Tian to regain consciousness. Zhu Qiang had also vomited, but he still managed start up the camera attached to the exterior of the plane. We all watched the monitor to see what was being recorded. Outside the plane all was dark and silent. I'll never forget that sight. Even now, when I'm flying somewhere at night, I'll look out the window into the pitch-black sky beyond and be suddenly struck with the feeling that I'm back underground, soaring across the abyss.

"The rock around us is all biotite granite," said Old Tian, back on his feet and cleaning his vomit-soaked face mask. Walking up behind us, he coughed intensely, then continued. "It was formed during the Tertiary Period. I really wish I could take a sample of it."

The small portion of rock illuminated by the plane's floodlights was black and extraordinarily uneven. Old Tian stared at it, pointing out the lines formed in the cliff face by millennia of pressure and lecturing endlessly on geological theory. None of us had seen anything like this before.

Gradually the walls began to recede as the cave widened. It was like flying out the mouth of a horn into a vast open space. Darkness descended and the floodlights ceased to illuminate anything. The rush of airflow softened

215

as the plane slowed down. Soon only the hum of the motor was left. We walked to the middle cabin and lifted the top hatch, revealing the roof of the cave. In this limitless void, the only end in sight was up.

Unexpectedly, the plane began to climb. The higher we flew, the more overwhelming the sight became. I imagined this must have been what the Monkey King had seen after the Tathagata Buddha trapped him beneath Wuxing Mountain. Above us sharp cones of jutting rock had formed from splits in the stone and hung like huge thorns. The ceiling resembled a jagged mountain range seen upside-down. As the plane leveled out, I fantasized that I had reached through the hatch and grabbed onto one of the stones overhead. In my mind I saw the plane flying away; then I was falling through layers of mist down into the abyss until at last I hit bottom.

Our initial excitement soon subsided. The danger had passed. Plus there was nothing really to see. After a moment, Pei Qing rose to his feet and walked to the machine gunner's cabin. Wang Sichuan and I glanced at one another.

"What the hell is that guy up to?" he asked. "Why does he always have to act like such a miserable loner?"

Laughing sadly, I said I'd met people like this before. Working with them was never easy. I figured Pei Qing was just too smart for his own good. It made it hard for him to get along with other people. Think about it; what if you were grouped with others who were both happier and less intelligent than you? You probably wouldn't want to associate with them either.

Over the next several hours we took turns recording our observations, all of them essentially worthless. At this point there was almost nothing to see. Then, three hours later, we began to descend toward the bottom of the abyss.

Each of us crowded against the windows to record our observations. I was standing next to Zhu Qiang and looking down. The mist below was indistinct, resembling a dense layer of cottony clouds. From this far away I almost imagined we could land directly on it, but as we drew closer we could see its surface rippling. I remembered it was filled with mercury. My throat tightened. Wang Sichuan and Pei Qing fired a round of tracers. The light revealed not even the hint of form within the mist. It appeared that the bottom was still far below us, but with our radar jammed by all the heavy metals, the only way to find out was to fly down and see for ourselves.

"Oxygen masks on, everyone," said Ivan, his voice sounding through our earphones. "We're about to descend into the mist."

As a red warning light flashed overhead, we unfortunates all strapped on our masks. The plane rumbled. As our altitude dropped so did visibility. Before long there was nothing outside the window but a dense gray haze.

"How are we supposed to discover anything like this?" asked Wang Sichuan.

During one of our meetings, Old Tian had made a bold hypothesis. He theorized that, like clouds on the surface, the mist down here split the darkness into two parts, higher and lower. The problem was that we had no idea how far down the mist actually went. This was very dangerous. If the mist was too thick, we could easily lose our way and smash into one of the cave walls. Or if Old Tian's hypothesis was incorrect, and the mist continued all the way to the bottom, then we might fly right into the abyssal floor.

Wang Sichuan and Pei Qing continued to fire bright tracers into the haze. We strained to see out of our respective windows, making sure none of the tracers ran into hidden obstacles. No one spoke a word. There had been not one indication that the mist would end.

At last Wang Sichuan spoke up. "Old Tian, you sure you didn't make a mistake? If we descend any farther we're gonna hit bottom. No cloud is this thick."

"You've forgotten that this is a mercury mist," replied Old Tian. "It's not a regular cloud. There's no way for us to estimate how deep this place goes. Our only choice is to risk it." He no longer sounded as confident as he had at the meeting.

Switching on his microphone, Wang Sichuan asked Ivan, "What is our current depth?"

"Ninety-three thousand feet," said Ivan. "Old Tian, if we continue like this we're going to crash."

This figure seemed to surprise Pei Qing. "How far have we descended?" he asked.

"Almost two miles," I answered.

As he looked at the thermometer, a puzzled expression came over his face. "Strange," he said. "The temperature keeps falling."

"What's strange about that?" asked Wang Sichuan. "Of course hell is cold[1]. " But then his face suddenly changed. "Wait a second. That's not right at all."

Zhu Qiang still didn't understand. "What are you guys talking about?"

Wang Sichuan explained that the bottom ought to be burning with geothermal heat.

Zhu Qiang's expression grew worried. "Then why would the temperature keep falling?" he asked. "Could the science be wrong?"

"No," replied Old Tian, "the science is correct. The reason the temperature keeps falling is because this extremely dense mist is acting as a natural heat insulator. The air outside of it is surely much hotter."

"So then what are all of you so worried about?" asked Zhu Qiang, baffled.

"The temperature is dropping because the mist is growing thicker the farther we descend," said Old Tian. "However, because mercury requires heat to evaporate, the temperature should be relatively high wherever this process is occurring. Previously we had believed that the bottom of the abyss was covered with pools or deposits of mercury. This became the

1 In the East, hell is often imagined as being ice-cold.

219

basis of much of our reasoning. But since the temperature continues to fall, there appears to be a third alternative: perhaps the mercury and the geothermal heat are buried much deeper underground. Thus the mercury is heated up below the ground and rises through cracks to form mist in the cooler air. If that's the case, then there might only be a very small space between the bottom of the mist and the floor of the abyss."

"In short," said Pei Qing, "the falling temperature means we're already very close to the bottom."

"Pei Qing, you know that's just a guess," said Old Tian.

"No," replied Pei Qing, "it's not. The falling temperature proves it. By now, I'd say we're only three thousand feet up. If the bottom is mountainous, we're screwed."

Wang Sichuan immediately switched on his mic and warned Ivan. Just as the words left his mouth, Zhu Qiang cried for us to come quick. I hurried over. The dark shape of a mountain peak loomed out of the mist. The plane practically scraped its rocky face as we flew past.

I glanced over at Wang Sichuan. "Pull up!" he cried into his mic. "We're going to crash!"

Ivan made no response. Maybe he still hadn't understood. Wanting to get a closer look at the mountain, I climbed swiftly into the gun turret. A moment later, numberless black, jagged peaks appeared where before there had been only mist—a mountain range made entirely of enormous stone. These were remnants of the cones we'd seen hanging from the ceiling, fallen over thousands of years and piling up on the abyssal floor. Wang Sichuan rushed into the cockpit, although by now Ivan must have been long since aware of the terrifying scene before us. He pulled back on the control column.

I watched as we coasted just over the dark mountains. Cold sweat dripped down my forehead as I turned to look back. We were so close to being rubble. Before I could begin to catch my breath, a loud curse sounded from the cockpit. I look forward. A towering form—shaped like a horse's head and absolutely enormous—had suddenly emerged out of the mist before us.

Ivan reacted instinctively, yanking the plane over, tilting it 70 degrees to the side. The force of the turn threw me against the side of the turret. Pressed against the window, I gazed on as we cut sideways, arcing alongside the dark shape. At last it burst from the mist no more than 30 feet from the belly of our plane. In a daze, I watched with perfect clarity as a wall of dark rock swept past. My heartbeat was no longer quickening. It had simply stopped. I imagine my blood had probably frozen in my veins. I distinctly remember every detail of those moments. It could not have taken longer than 13 seconds, but to me it felt endless. By the end of it the plane was on its side, one wing straight up and the other straight down. Bombers cannot barrel roll. Like turtles, once they flip over they cannot flip back. Ivan immediately attempted to right the plane. I could hear him roaring up front. I knew he was no longer thinking, just acting purely on instinct. Unable to help myself, I, too, began to yell.

When I opened my eyes a moment later, I saw something suddenly sweep past overhead. Before I could register my surprise, a sharp cliff appeared from out of the mist, smashing into the gun turret and shattering the windows around me. Amid the thundering crash and flying glass I shielded my neck. Gale-force winds rushed in through the opening, nearly blowing me out of the plane. I grabbed onto the safety handle.

The scene was breathtaking. With the glass gone, it was as if I was standing exposed atop the plane. My field of vision was incredibly vast. Braving the wind, I stood and took in my surroundings. Then I looked down.

I gasped.

There, deep within the dark shapes rising from the bottom of the abyss, I saw a faint light.

41 THE BOTTOM OF THE ABYSS

A moment later the plane righted itself and my view of the light was gone. At first I doubted what I'd seen. Perhaps amid all the tossing and turning I'd mistaken the light of the tracers for something else.

But the more I thought about it, the more convinced I became. The light had been far away, hidden between the dark shapes on the abyssal floor. The plane made several more tight turns, banking from side to side. I stuck my head through the broken window to get a better view, but the light never reappeared. I undid my harness and scurried back down to the passenger cabin so fast I almost fell.

The cabin was in total disarray. Zhu Qiang was bleeding from the forehead and our things were scattered everywhere. As I stepped from the ladder, a loose flashlight suddenly dropped and knocked me on the head, the pain so bad that tears came to my eyes. An instant later Wang Sichuan appeared.

"Are you all right?" he asked. "What was that noise up there?"

I was too agitated to respond. Like a madman, I rushed headlong toward one of the windows and looked out. Darkness greeted my eyes. I could see nothing. As the plane made another steep turn I grabbed for the safety bar, nearly toppling over.

"Put on your seatbelt!" Wang Sichuan shouted to me.

Fumbling wildly, I managed to clip myself in.

"What are you looking for?" he asked.

"Lights! I saw lights down there."

His eyes went wide. "Are you sure?"

"Of course I'm sure!" I yelled.

At once he, too, ran to the window. The others quickly followed suit. "Where is it?" he cried.

"You can't see them anymore," I said. "The angle's not right."

Wang Sichuan checked one window, then another, but still couldn't see anything. He looked quizzically back at me. I knew there was no use trying to convince him. With all the tracers that had been fired, even I couldn't be completely certain. As the plane leveled out, the shapes below receded even farther into the darkness. Looking down at them, I wondered about the light. Suddenly Pei Qing clapped his hands and motioned for us to come quick. We rushed over and looked out. As the plane passed over a dark mountain, a huge swath of lights expanded into view. No way could this be tracers. We stared in slack-jawed disbelief. Gradually the lights disappeared as the mist once more enveloped the plane. Soon the dark mountains were gone as well.

"We made it!" shouted Ivan, his voice sounding in our earphones as the plane began to ascend.

A moment later, his copilot climbed back into the cabin and up to the gun turret to inspect the damage. One after another we drew back from the windows and slumped to the floor. Our initial fear and astonishment had become a chaos of competing emotions.

"Could those goddamned things really have been manmade?" asked Zhu Qiang, his face ashen. "Who's down there?"

"Is it really the Japs?" asked Wang Sichuan, banging his head against the bulkhead. "Did they really make it all the way to the bottom?"

"Maybe it's some natural phenomenon," continued Zhu Qiang. "Phosphorescence? Electrical energy?"

We all shook our heads. First of all, I had never witnessed an instance of that much natural light in my whole life, and more importantly, it was much too steady, never even flickering. No, I said to myself, that was definitely lamplight. It made me think of the Legend of the Fox Spirit, the story Pei Qing had told about a ghost world concealed deep within the cave. Could there really be some unearthly paradise beneath the mist and mountains? I thought of all the equipment and supplies we'd seen in the warehouse, of the continuously repeating message sent back from the abyss. Had we underestimated the Japanese? Rather than just airdropping in a few men, had they established an entire outpost?

We held a brief meeting to discuss what we'd seen, although Wang Sichuan, Pei Qing and I knew it was pointless. We were well aware that intellectualizing would solve nothing. Afterwards, Pei Qing took the microphone and told Ivan to note our coordinates and pay attention to the route on the way back.

Suddenly, the copilot called out from inside the gun turret. "To the left! We have a situation off to the left!"

Old Tian and the others rushed to the windows and looked out. They weren't going to see anything from that vantage. I climbed back into the turret. "Where is it?" I asked the copilot. "What kind of situation?"

"Those lights!" he said. "Those lights are following us!"

I looked to where he was pointing. Sure enough, several lights shone dimly through the mist to the left of the plane. They were no more than 1,000 feet away. At first I thought they must be lights from the ground somehow visible up here, but they were different. There were only three or four of them and they were blinking steadily. We continued to climb, the lights following our movements so closely it seemed almost as if they weren't moving at all. Several times Ivan sped up or slowed down and each time the lights followed suit. As we readied ourselves for combat, my heart filled with dread. Whatever this thing was, it had come from the abyss. We had drawn it out.

But it was definitely not alive. Looking at the flickering lights, I became convinced it was some kind of machine, though it was impossible to tell what it looked like.

The copilot turned to me and whispered, "It's a plane."

Had the Japs built an airport in the abyss and sent a fighter plane to follow us? The pilot would already be an old man. The only way to know for sure was to fly out of the mist and see if it followed.

Ivan ascended very slowly, ready to react if something popped out of the mist. In silence we watched and waited. Finally the mist began to thin out. We broke through to the other side, the thing still right on our tail. My stomach was in my throat as the lights became clearer and clearer. Then the mist trembled and, a moment later, a gigantic plane came soaring out. The plane was obviously Japanese and incredibly immense. It was a bomber, just like ours.

"Prepare for battle!" I roared from the gun turret.

Everyone was thrown into a panic. Nothing is too strange for this world, I thought, gritting my teeth. As the others switched out the tracers for live ammunition, Ivan began flashing light signals to the other plane, hoping to communicate. A moment later the other plane's lights began to flicker. It was responding. I asked the copilot what it was saying.

After thinking for a moment, he frowned. "That's not a response. They just repeated our question back to us word for word."

"What was the question?"

"We asked them their nationality and unit number," said the copilot as our plane's signal lights once more began to flash. After a few moments, the other flashed its response. I looked back at the copilot. His face was puzzled. "Again it was the same as ours. How could they not understand what we're saying?"

"What year was this system invented?"

"That I don't know."

"Could it be new enough that the Japs never learned it?"

"That's impossible," said Ivan, his half-cooked Chinese sounding over our earphones. He'd used these very signals all the way back in Germany during the war.

Just as I was considering what all this could mean, Wang Sichuan called out, "What are you worrying about all this for? Let's shoot them down and figure the rest out later."

"You know there's a truce between China and Japan," said Ivan. "We need to respect it. We should not be first to open fire."

"Yeah, well, where was their respect at Nanjing?" asked Wang Sichuan. "There's no point in trying to reason with the Japs."

"We won't learn a thing by attacking them," I said. "And who's to know if we'd even win?" I kept my eyes on the other plane. Something about it didn't feel quite right.

The signals continued. First our plane would flash a message, then, moments later, theirs would flash an identical response. By now I was growing increasingly uneasy. Why did everything about their plane so closely resemble ours? I called down to the cabin for some binoculars. Wang Sichuan handed them up. I looked out at the plane. My eyes went wide. I rubbed them once, then looked again.

There was no mistaking it: the glass case surrounding the other plane's turret was also shattered.

As I scanned the rest of the plane, a terrifying realization swept over me. This was another Shinzan, identical in every way to our own.

"Could this be us?" I asked. "Are we looking at ourselves?"

42 SEEING DOUBLE

Climbing back down into the cabin, I told everyone what I'd seen.

Wang Sichuan immediately disagreed. "Be a little more realistic," he said.

"What do you want me to say?" I replied. "I'm just telling you what I saw."

Old Tian cut in, telling me not to panic. "There's actually nothing strange about this," he said. "It's probably just a result of light refraction. When light passes through air of different densities at a certain angle, it sometimes creates a kind of mirror image, like a mirage in the desert."

Old Tian's authoritative assurances had nearly gotten us killed just now. It seemed wise to be careful before trusting everything he said. "Can mirages be this clear?" asked Wang Sichuan.

"If a cave this big can exist beneath the earth," said Old Tian, "then what's so strange about a mirage being a little clearer than normal? We need to believe what our eyes are telling us."

"No, that's not possible," said Wang Sichuan. "If it's really a mirage, then how come there's a delay in its response? As soon as we flash our lights it should respond simultaneously, like a mirror."

To test this theory, Ivan flashed another signal and we timed the response. It took 20 seconds for it to appear, though it was still identical to our own.

"Comrade Tian, please explain this to us!" cried Wang Sichuan.

Old Tian's face had turned pale. "This means...um," he mumbled.

"Actually," said Pei Qing, "there's a very simple way to find out whether that's really us. We just need to fire a few tracers. It is highly unlikely they will be carrying this type of ammunition, and, if they are, it is even more unlikely that the colors will be identical." He glanced over at Wang Sichuan, who switched in the tracers, aimed into the emptiness, and fired several dozen rounds.

One after another they flew into the darkness, tailing trails of light. Holding my breath, I watched the strange plane below us. Twenty seconds later, it also fired a cluster of identical tracers.

"Same color, same rate of fire," said Old Tian. "You see? You see? I was right after all. This must be some undiscovered natural phenomenon, most likely related to the mercury mist. After all, everyone knows mercury is used to make mirrors..."

I breathed a sigh of relief. At least now we knew it wasn't the Japanese.

"There's something really goddamn wrong with this place," said Wang Sichuan, his face red with anger. Looking at him, though, I could tell he was really just frustrated with Old Tian.

As I gazed back at the plane one last time, I still had a vague sensation something about it was amiss. Soon I would discover that my fears had not been misplaced. Unfortunately, by the time we figured this out it was already too late. For the moment, however, the phantom plane appeared to be nothing more than a false alarm. Gradually, everyone managed to calm down.

I looked at my watch. Five hours had already passed since takeoff. Wanting to talk to Ivan about the rest of our itinerary, I climbed into the cockpit.

He turned around as I entered. "Perfect. I was just about to go look for you," he said. Something about his expression was a little off. Checking that no one was behind me, he turned off the cabin mic and motioned for me to sit in the copilot's chair. Curious, I climbed into the seat.

Ivan pointed at several gauges on the instrument panel in front of us. "First of all," he said, "we used far too much fuel flying out of the mist just now."

"What do you mean we used too much?"

"I mean we'll probably only be able to cruise for another three or four hours before we drop."

"Are you saying we don't have enough fuel to get back?"

"Not necessarily. I'm going to turn off two of the engines and fly back at a crawl. If our luck is good, we should be able to glide in for the landing. I'm confident in my abilities. We should be fine. But I don't think we've flown as far as the Japanese. We're not going to be able to see what they saw and complete the mission."

Even if we did complete it, I thought to myself, it wouldn't matter unless we brought something back. "Just now you said, 'first of all.' What's second? What else is going on?"

"Look to the left," he said.

Through the windshield I could see a rock wall illuminated by the floodlights. "Are you intentionally flying along the wall?" I asked.

"No. I was surprised to see this myself. The terrain here is not at all like we predicted. While flying through the mist just now we made several turns. I think it's probable that, without realizing it, we somehow flew into a whole different cave. And the problem is the space here is so narrow that I doubt we can turn around."

I asked him if he could be a little clearer. The guy's Chinese was still pretty lacking.

After thinking for a moment, he said, "You still remember the last part of that secret Japanese footage?" I nodded. "When the cameraman was filming that..." He paused for a moment, searching for the right word to describe the enormous humanoid shape.

"Thing," I said. "You can call it a thing."

"Okay. When the cameraman was filming that thing…" Licking his lips, Ivan used one of his hands to pantomime a plane and angled that plane steeply. "The reason the cameraman was able to film the thing from so many angles was because the plane was circling it very tightly. I think you'll agree that the angle my little plane here is turning at is roughly the same as that of the plane in the recording. Herein lays the problem: our plane is too big to execute a maneuver like that in this cave. If we tried it here, we'd smash right into the rock wall."

"Then how were the Japanese able to do it?"

"That's what I was wondering. Possibly the cameraman was filming from a much smaller aircraft."

"Impossible," I said, shaking my head. We had all seen the wreckage of the Shinzan, had even found a camera mount attached to its exterior.

"In that case, there's a second possibility. Namely, this section of cave is not where they filmed. We've gone the wrong way."

43 THE IMMELMAN TURN

To be honest, I still only partially understood what he was saying. How could we have gone the wrong way? Had we flown into some branching cave? I knew, however, that none of these questions mattered. We had a very big problem that needed to be solved. "So what are you thinking?" I asked. "You're an ace pilot. No way would you be saying this to me if you didn't have a plan."

"Actually," he said, his voice perfectly composed, "it is a pilot's responsibility to alert his comrades if death is certain. That said, there is one more thing we can try. I will warn you, however, that our chance of success is exceedingly small."

"Say it!" I cried, slapping him on the back.

"Well, even though there's not a lot of room on either side of us, there's enough space above and below for me to flip us in the opposite direction."

"Can a bomber do that?"

"Have you forgotten what got me kicked out of the Soviet military? It's an extremely tough move, but this plane is actually a good bit smaller than the one I used."

"How the hell are you gonna flip this thing?" I asked. "What do you need us to do? Pray?"

Ivan evidently did not understand my joke. He went right on explaining, using his hands to demonstrate. "After we flip upside-down and the belly of the plane is on top, I will momentarily lose control, causing us to drop. Assuming that I have angled the plane correctly, then at this point I should be able to use some inertia to roll us right side up while cranking the engine to pull us out of the dive. The reason we're doing a backwards somersault as opposed to a forward flip is because the latter would give us no time to right ourselves before we crashed. But in order to get enough space above us to pull this off, we have to drop back down into the mist. I need all of you to keep a close eye on our surroundings."

I nodded. "When will we begin?"

He looked at the fuel gauge. "At most, I'd say you have ten minutes to talk it over and get ready."

I silently cursed this slow-acting Soviet. Why the hell hadn't he said anything sooner? Then, without another word, I rose to my feet, clapped him on the back and rushed into the rear cabin.

Interrupting the ongoing argument, I roared, "Everyone! Get back to your seats, put on your fucking seatbelts, and grab hold of anything you can. We're dropping back into the mist. Every man is responsible for a window.

Let's go!"

Everyone began yelling at once.

"Have you lost your mind?" cried Wang Sichuan.

"There's no time to explain. If you don't listen to me, we're gonna be walking back."

After hustling them into their seats, I climbed into the gun turret and told the copilot to head back down the ladder. "You need to return to the cockpit," I said. "I'll handle things here."

Ivan switched on the mic. "No matter what," he said, "if you see something, you need to call it out. When the plane is upside-down I won't be able to see a thing."

"Upside-down?" said Wang Sichuan. "What does he mean upside-down?"

Before the words even left his mouth, the plane began dropping swiftly toward the abyss. I was almost tossed from the turret. Holding myself steady, I gritted my teeth against the fierce wind. It felt like my head was about to be blown clean off my body.

"Engineer Wu!" shouted Wang Sichuan from below. "If you don't tell us what the hell is going on, I'm going to report you to our superiors!"

Idiot, I thought, report me all you want. So long as we survive, you can tell them I'm a counterrevolutionary for all I care.

The plane dropped savagely through the mist. We could see nothing. Ivan's voice sounded through our earphones, calling out the altitude. Up in the machine gun tower, the world was open to me. It was an experience I'll never forget. I began to see dark shapes in the mist below us. "Is this deep enough?" I asked.

"We still need to drop a little farther. Don't worry; we're not as deep as last time." Ivan's voice was extremely calm.

I could see the shapes become clearer and clearer until it felt like we were about to crash right into them. Then, at the last possible second, the nose of the plane suddenly rose and we began to climb. Through our earphones we could hear Ivan reciting something in Russian, his voice quiet.

"What's that supposed mean?" I asked.

"It's what I said to Xile when I asked her to marry me, and it's what I was saying to myself when I pulled off this maneuver for her. Perhaps it'll bring us luck this time, too." He paused for a moment. "I hope Xile can hear me."

As he said this, the plane finished its ascent and began to roll backwards. Our speed dropped and the space around me spun. We burst out of the mist at a 90 degree angle. I gripped the safety bar beside me. We began to topple over backwards. I couldn't help myself—as my head dropped back, I began to yell. Ivan maintained tight control over the plane, dropping it slightly to one side, giving us the angle that should roll us back over.

This kind of flip was called an Immelman Turn. It's a stunt generally performed only by fighter planes. Ivan's voice remained extremely calm. Was this due to the Soviet flight instructor's extreme skill and daring, or had he perhaps already given up hope? Either way, compared to the Wang Sichuan shouting curses and Old Tian forcefully vomiting, Ivan sounded like a mere spectator, not the man controlling this lunatic maneuver.

As the plane teetered towards falling completely out of control, I, too, somehow became very calm. I knew then that whether or not Ivan regained control of this plummeting colossus no longer had anything to do with us. In a situation like that you understand what people mean when they say things like Fate, God, belief—whatever you want to call that stuff. Only then do you truly see their marks on the world.

As the plane gradually began to roll over, we dropped once more into the mist. We were almost right side up when Pei Qing's voice suddenly rang out over the earphones. "Stone mountain!"

Then a moment later I saw it: a jagged rise hidden in the mist not far below us. We were still dropping straight down, the plane totally out of Ivan's control. I watched as the shape drew closer and closer. I closed my eyes, fully aware of why Ivan had mouthed those words. Though the men and women of my generation would often sigh at our fate, few could say what the word actually meant. In those seconds, however, I understood it precisely.

Opening my eyes, I saw the mountain sweeping by only inches away from me. A moment later Ivan was back in control and we were zooming ahead.

As my mind went blank, I heard Wang Sichuan yell, "Look out! There's something to the left!"

A row of craggy peaks shot out just beside us. Our wing grazed one of them, aggressively shaking the plane and sending sparks in all directions. Lucky it wasn't a direct hit, I said to myself, but then, not far in front of us, a brutal expanse of rock jutted through the mist. We'd never be able to avoid it. I knew what to do.

"Blow these things to kingdom come!" I yelled. I loaded the machine gun and began to fire.

The gun's power was immense. Rocks danced away with each shot. Bullet trails flew from every window of the plane. In an instant the first barrier crumbled. Before I could catch my breath, I saw another jagged row rise up behind it.

"We're fucked!" Wang Sichuan roared over the earphones.

"Don't stop!" I yelled with all my might.

At that moment our fear didn't matter. Even whether we survived didn't matter. The stone mountains before us were our most ferocious enemy and all we could do was keep firing, our bullets like deadly waterfalls rushing through the darkness. As the rocks flew apart we sped through them, not knowing how many were left. We smacked into one of the remaining peaks, the force knocking me to the floor. I heard something scrape against the belly of the plane, but we kept going. Moments later we were through, the plane only slightly off-kilter from the crash.

Leaving the stone mountains behind, we began our ascent. I climbed to my feet and looked back. The rocks had been mostly cleared out. The big chunk we'd smashed into was tumbling into the darkness. Our gunfire had done the trick. Had that big piece of granite not been riddled with bullets, no way would it have toppled so easily. The wreckage of our plane, not the rock, would now be rolling down the mountain.

The sound of Ivan's wild laughter echoed over the earphones. "I love you all!" he cried.

Near collapse, I grabbed the safety strap to keep myself from falling. Suddenly I thought of Yuan Xile. After she said yes to Ivan's proposal, the damn Soviet must have laughed to shake the heavens. This man belonged to the sky. How could Yuan Xile have ever refused him?

"All right, Old Wu," said Wang Sichuan, an edge to his voice, "it's time you came down here and explained a few things. Just what the hell were you two plotting up there?"

"I'll tell you in a moment," I said. Then, with no strength left, I closed my eyes.

44 THE FIGURE

I remained sitting in the gun turret, lost in thought and gazing at the darkness surrounding me. Never in my life had I so badly wanted a cigarette. I tried to think about what had just happened. Instead I found myself remembering when we'd first assembled in Jiamusi. Could I ever have imagined at the time that something like this would happen? In fact, if someone told me now it was all just a dream, I wouldn't have necessarily doubted them. Still, as I looked around, I couldn't deny that everything seemed real as could be.

Again Wang Sichuan's voice sounded over the earphones, saying that if I didn't come this instant, he was going to climb up and drag me down himself. I rose lazily, descended the ladder and told them what had happened. His face red and vomit-smeared, Old Tian reminded me that he was partially in charge of this mission. Why had I not discussed this with him beforehand? This was a serious error, he said, and if he chose to report me, I would find myself in big trouble.

Why the hell couldn't this guy have just choked on his own vomit? I thought. I'd always figured Old Tian wasn't that bad of a guy, just an old-fashioned intellectual who'd been raised within the Party. Of course he was accustomed to doing everything by the books and always respecting the established hierarchy. Back then all the puffed-up members of the intelligentsia acted this way. It didn't necessarily mean they believed what they were saying. At this moment I had no desire to argue with him. I just turned and walked away.

Old Tian was no good at dealing with people like me. All he could do was mumble inaudibly to himself. When he saw no one was coming to his assistance, he quickly stopped talking. I could never have known that ignoring Old Tian like this would one day come back to haunt me, but that occurred later. It has nothing to do with our current story.

At last we began heading back. To save fuel, Ivan turned off some of the plane's searchlights. It was during these calm hours that I first conceived of writing down our experiences. The idea came upon me suddenly, as if someone had planted it in my brain. It surprised me. I'd never been particularly interested in literature.

By this point we'd spent seven hours in this flying heap of metal, neither eating nor drinking. I needed to piss badly, but more than anything we all craved tobacco. The feeling clawed at us, until every moment was torment. Eventually, Wang Sichuan figured out a way to smoke behind his facemask. Pei Qing and I just closed our eyes and relaxed.

The stillness was broken three hours later by a strange noise and the cabin lights blacking out. At first we were all very nervous, but the copilot appeared and told us it was merely a problem with an electrical circuit and that he would go check it out. We sat in the darkness listening to the roar of the engine. I walked back into the cockpit. Old Tian made sure to follow close behind. A pitch-black expanse stretched out in front of us, the cockpit itself lit only by the green glow of the instrument panel. Ivan's face was pale within the gloom.

"Is something wrong?" I asked.

"No, not for the moment, at least," he said. "I can control how much fuel we use. The rest is up to Fate."

"Flying like this doesn't frighten you?" I asked, pointing at the darkness ahead.

"Planes are different than cars. When flying at night we generally rely entirely on guided navigation. In any case, repairing the light circuit should be a simple matter."

As soon as he said this, the plane's headlights flashed on and off, as if they were almost fixed. I relaxed and was about to leave when something hit me. Just now, when the lights had briefly turned on, I'd seen something outside the plane. I looked for it again, but everything was shrouded in darkness. My initial inclination was to forget about it, but the more I thought, the stranger it seemed. We could afford no more mistakes.

I ran back into the cabin and yelled for Wang Sichuan to fire a string of tracers into the darkness. Wang Sichuan was still badly shaken and now assumed something else had gone wrong. Swearing, he ran to the window and began to fire. Back in the cockpit, I moved to the window to get a closer look. There really was something out there. Straining my eyes, I could see it in the star-like light of the tracers. My knees went weak. Staring out of the darkness were two gigantic, sunken eyes, gazing at us as we flew past.

The eyes were unimaginably huge, their sockets so deep that my blood froze as I looked at them. I was too shocked to speak. I could hear Wang Sichuan mumbling to himself over the earphones.

"My God," he said, "what is that?"

We flew closer and closer. Before long I saw an enormous face, dark and grotesque and at least five stories tall. By now we were flying very steadily. The face almost appeared to be moving out of the darkness towards us.

"Looks like this was the figure in the film," said Ivan, his voice almost indifferent. "I never expected it to be this big."

"Light it up with more tracers!" I yelled toward the cabin. A moment later another of the aircraft guns began to fire. As the brightness increased, the thing's body was revealed, standing amid dense clouds of mist. No one spoke. The only sounds were the blasts of gunfire. Everyone's attention was completely focused on the figure. As we drew closer I could see its massive body was pockmarked with countless dark holes. They were pressed close together, as if eaten through by worms. I looked on in silence, my body ice-cold, as I remembered the rotted corpses in the boarded-up room. But this was stone, not flesh, the luster of its body identical to the rocks surrounding it. Someone had carved this thing.

I stared at the strange stone face. This wasn't an image of the Buddha, nor could I think of any other ancient figure it might be depicting. The face was rough and crudely carved. I couldn't figure out how this thing had been made. Had some ancient people really entered the abyss? Had they really carved a massive figure amid the mountains of stone jutting from the void? Who were they?

Even with our modern technology we were unable to plumb the depths of the abyss; not only had someone explored its very bottom, but they'd left behind a structure of awe-inspiring proportions.

45 PEI QING

We were silent for a moment. "This is an ancient statue," Old Tian mumbled over the earphones. "What is it doing down here?"

"It probably fell through during a cave-in," said Pei Qing. "After being carved on the surface, this Kua Fu[2] must have dropped underground during an earthquake."

"Is that possible?" asked Old Tian.

"I think it's a lot more possible than the ancients entering the abyss and carving the statue down here," said Pei Qing.

Was that really what had happened? I sensed the abyss was hiding many other secrets, ones that we could never even begin to imagine.

The plane continued to approach the colossus, until we were only 50 feet away. From here we could clearly make out the holes dotting its body, each

---

2 Kua Fu was a mythical Chinese giant who died of exhaustion after chasing, and failing to catch, the sun.

of them big enough to fit a person. Looking at them, I couldn't help but feel that something was hidden inside. Unfortunately, after only a moment we'd flown past. Before we could take a closer look at the figure, it was already behind us, receding into the darkness.

"It's a shame we couldn't pause for a few minutes and look," said Wang Sichuan. "I'd give a prize to the man who invents a plane that can stop in place."

"Stopping may not have been necessary," said Pei Qing.

"That's right," said Old Tian. "Zhu Qiang, did you film it?"

"Yeah," he said. "I got it."

"Good," Old Tian sighed. "Then our mission is complete." It looked like a huge weight had been lifted from his shoulders.

Just then there was a buzzing sound from outside. A moment later, the plane's surface lights and searchlights all turned back on.

"You all right?" asked Ivan.

Slapping myself, I tried to get my brain working again. In my whole life I'd never seen anything so strange, yet I actually felt very tranquil, so tranquil I was momentarily unable to think. Looking at me, Ivan shook his head and laughed.

"You didn't find that at all incredible?" I asked him.

"What I find most incredible is that we're still alive," he said. After pausing for a moment, he continued. "That's right. We need to get rid of some weight to save fuel. Tell the others to go through our supplies. Anything we can get rid of needs to go, the sooner, the better. I'll open the bomb bay doors."

The first thing I thought of was Wang Sichuan. Laughing to myself, I walked back into the cabin and told the others what was going on. Most of them were still in a state of shock. I clapped them each on the back and they gradually got moving, albeit very slowly; thus it remained up to me to get rid of most of the stuff. The bullets and aircraft guns were the heaviest of the lot. We started to dismantle them. Wang Sichuan was loath to part with the weapons. Having hunted with old iron rifles since a young age, his feelings toward guns were difficult for outsiders to understand.

With the bomb bay doors open, a cold wind swirled through the air. I moved the dismantled guns onto the track and pushed them through the opening. In an instant they'd dropped away into the void. Next I wrapped up the ammunition belts and some other supplies and pushed them through as well.

Not even the mist was visible through the open hatch. The giant figure had vanished in the darkness. For a moment I was lost in thought. Then I heard something behind me. It was Pei Qing. He was clutching a canvas bag. After shutting the door, he walked over and lit a cigarette. There was something strange in his expression. I asked him what was going on

He smiled at me. "There's something I need to say to you."

I looked him over. What was this guy scheming about now?

"I've heard about your background," he said. "You, too, were also born a member of the Five Black Classes. You must know the effort it took for your father to finally shed this stigma. I never knew my mother and father. I was raised by foster parents. They didn't mistreat me, but they didn't truly care about me either. When I was growing up, nobody in my village ever told me anything about my mother. They wouldn't even say her name. But they never let me forget that my mother's identity made her child a second-class citizen."

I knew what he was talking about. This was the disease of those years, but why was he suddenly bringing it up now?

"For a long time I had no idea what my mother had done," he continued. "Only later did I learn that my parents were Japanese. Can you imagine what it must have felt like for me, after receiving all those years of anti-Japanese education, to learn that I was in fact Japanese?" Although I didn't answer Pei Qing's question, I suddenly felt a measure of compassion for him. "If I am Japanese, then why was I left in China? And if I am Chinese, then why do they say I have Japanese blood?"

As he spoke, I could detect no anger in his words. He must have asked himself this question countless times. He was merely saying aloud something that had been hardening his heart ever since he was young.

"Once I became an adult, I began searching for my parents' whereabouts. I needed an answer. Either I would find them or I would learn they were dead. I examined endless archives and searched all across the country. I finally located my parents' names in some old record books. They were Japanese geological engineers and, after joining a project in Inner Mongolia, they both disappeared. In my parents' absence, I was entrusted to the care of their friends, but when I was three years old they returned to Japan and left me behind. It was only after learning this that I decided to join this assignment."

I stared into the darkness beneath the bomb bay door. "You mean, your parents were...?"

Pei Qing smiled and gazed out the window, the look in his eyes vacant, yet burning with fervent hope. The pieces suddenly came together. I remembered the woman approaching the Japanese officer in the secret footage. At the time she'd felt familiar, but I couldn't figure out how. Could she have been Pei Qing's...?

Before I could finish this thought, I saw him slip the canvas bag he was carrying onto his back. It was a parachute.

"In the end," he said, "I am certain that they entered the abyss." He turned to face me. "You'll find my bag in the cabin. Inside are all the national grain coupons I've saved. Give them to my foster parents for me. Once I'm gone, do your best to get all the wages coming to me as a fallen soldier. My little brother should be able to use this money to attend university."

"Have you lost your mind? Too many years have passed since then. Even if they did go down there they'd have to be dead by now."

"What does it matter to me whether they're dead or alive?"

"You're not bringing enough food. The abyss is much too big. You'll starve to death before you even find them."

"I have seventy hours," he said. "You remember that expanse of lights? I think it's over there."

I could say nothing in reply.

"No one else is going to know what happened to me after I jump. I'm sure you're aware that if you tell them what I just told you, they're going to place you under investigation. Just say I went crazy from the poison. That way no one else will be implicated."

Shaking my head firmly, I started towards him. He pulled a pistol from his waistband. I flung myself at him but it was too late. He fired and in a burst of pain I fell to the ground. In the same instant I looked up only to see him leap through the hatch into the blackness. A moment later he disappeared into the void. It was too dark to even see his parachute open.

After lying there dazed for a moment, I got back to my feet and returned to the cabin. The others immediately crowded around me, but the pain in my chest made speaking impossible. I pushed them away, all except Wang Sichuan, who examined the wound. It wasn't life threatening, but I was afraid the poison might enter it. Pei Qing hadn't been aiming to kill. Had he wanted to, he could have shot me point-blank in the head. Still, having never been shot before, I was surprised at the severity of the pain. It was way worse than anything you see in the movies.

Wang Sichuan asked me what happened. I told him Pei Qing had gone mad. It worked like a charm, just as he'd expected. More than anything else, I was just shocked. Even the fact that Pei Qing had shot me seemed insignificant. Where was he now? That was all I could think. He had only 70 hours to find a possibly illusive outpost amid the deep valleys and stone peaks of the abyssal floor, and there was no way for him to get back.

I couldn't pass judgment on Pei Qing's decision. I knew all about the misfortunes of the Black Generation. Throughout time, those hurt by war had always taken out their anger on such children who, through no fault of their own were born members of the "enemy." For Pei Qing the words "your mother is Japanese" must have taken on the weight of a terrible curse, invading his dreams and waking him from sleep every night. Leaving the house in the morning, he was probably greeted with stones and spit. He both longed for his mother's love and hated her for what he had to go through. I'm not sure whether readers still remember how Pei Qing cried after we excavated the frozen corpse of the female soldier. Seeing her, he must have thought of the similar fate that probably befell his own mother. And hearing the dirty insults laid upon her, he must have recalled the things often said to him as a child.

But none of that mattered anymore. Pei Qing was gone. He'd left this story to begin his own. We, on the other hand, had to continue on—flying home through the darkness.

46 SILENT WELCOME

We waited three hours, cruising through the darkness. Finally, Ivan announced we were approaching the dam. I couldn't see the lights of our base, but I recognized the black granite cliffs around us. It was just in time, too. The fuel gauge was at zero. Wang Sichuan helped me into my seat and strapped on my seatbelt. Everyone else did the same. I wasn't worried at all. I'd seen Ivan make our bomber do a backflip. Landing on an underground river runway shouldn't pose much of a problem. I shut my eyes and imagined the earth beneath my feet. Most of us were just simple country folk. We never felt comfortable unless we were on solid ground.

Suddenly Ivan's voice sounded over the microphone. "Something's not right."

"What is it?" I asked.

"According to the navigation system, we're already very close to base, but I still can't see the searchlights that are supposed to guide me in."

I undid my seatbelt and stumbled into the cockpit. We were flying into total darkness. "How far away are we?" I asked.

"Less than two miles at most. We should be able to see the lights from here."

"Are you positive you're flying in the right direction? It would be awfully tragic to fly all this way just to end up in the wrong place."

"There wasn't much to lead us astray, and there's no way the guided navigation could be mistaken."

Just then the shape of the dam appeared before us, the cement pale in the plane's searchlights. All the dam's lights were extinguished. A silent, dark expanse was all that greeted us. I could barely believe my eyes. No way could all the lights have malfunctioned. At takeoff our camp had been lit up like some war-ready battalion. Now it appeared utterly abandoned. It was almost as if our superiors had simply packed up and left.

"Lights or no lights, we still have to land," said Ivan. He patted me on the back and motioned for me to return to my seat.

As soon as I sat back down the plane began to descend. Wang Sichuan and Old Tian both asked me what was going on, but I had no desire to explain.

Ivan's voice sounded in our ears. "Everyone remain seated, we're about to land. Unfortunately, it seems no one will be there to greet us."

I looked out the window. The rock walls surrounding the mouth of the river drew closer and closer. I held my breath. A moment later the dam flashed past. We made it, I said to myself.

Suddenly Ivan gave a startled cry. "Fuck! Where the hell is the runway?"

"What do you mean?"

He didn't reply, only shouted, "Hold on!"

With a ferocious crash we struck the river, our angle so steep the plane was practically nose-down. At once the entire cabin twisted upwards from the impact. I nearly snapped my restraints and flew into the air. My head smashed into the wall beside me and my vision went black and I lost consciousness.

Luckily, I quickly came to, vomiting from the pain in my skull. It felt like I'd been out for a long time, but the whole plane was still shaking from the crash. The cabin was silent. It seemed everyone else was still unconscious. Sparks splashed around the dark plane. All the lights had gone out. It took several minutes for me to undo my seatbelt and stagger to my feet. Wang Sichuan and Old Tian had fallen to the floor, their faces covered with blood. I shook them, but they didn't respond. I climbed out of the plane, turned and looked back. Despite the icy chill of the river water, I was momentarily transfixed by the sight of the wreckage. The plane had split in half, the front end now facing heavenward. Blood ran down my leg, but I ignored it. I felt my body begin to go numb.

Forcing myself to stay conscious, I dragged one man after another out of the submerged cabin. Miraculously, the plane had not exploded. It had to have been the river and buffer bags that saved us. With the men laid out like corpses on a nearby iron walkway, I paused, exhausted, and tried to catch my breath. Some dark liquid covered my hands. At first glance I thought it was blood, but it was only rusty water.

And then I heard a crash from the cockpit. Someone was trying to shatter the windshield. Gritting my teeth, I rose to my feet and walked toward the front of the plane. I smashed out the rest of the glass and helped the copilot climb out. His face was covered in tiny cuts and his mouth was filled with blood. His left ear hung down beside his neck, attached only by a thin piece of skin.

I helped him over to the walkway. "Ivan," he said to me. "You need to go help Ivan."

I quickly climbed back onto the plane and jumped into the cockpit. Ivan was still sitting in the pilot's seat. He'd taken off his oxygen mask. Blood covered his face and ran from his mouth, so thick it seemed he would choke. I climbed closer, wanting to help him up, but he waved me away. His chest was red and heaving.

He spoke haltingly. "The cabin took the brunt of the impact. I tried to pull up just before we hit, but it was no use. Damn Japanese technology. You can't trust it."

I couldn't keep from laughing. "Trying to find an excuse for the crash?"

"No one shot us down and I made no mistakes in the landing. The real problem was the runway disappeared. You Chinese can't be trusted either. Just because you say something'll be there doesn't mean it will."

I looked out at the water surrounding the plane. The dam was empty and silent. All the cranes and equipment were gone. The place appeared deserted. "All right," I said, "no need to waste your breath. In a moment I'll go see what the hell's going on here. Can you climb out yourself or do you need my help?"

Ivan ignored my question. "If you ever find out who took apart the runway, do me a favor and beat the crap out of them. Now go. I need to be alone for a while." Seeing how pale his face was, I felt uneasy just leaving him, but he continued to wave me away. "It's all right. Go handle your business while the Soviet sits by himself. He has things to think about."

Although I knew what this meant, I just nodded and climbed back through the window. As I jumped from the plane, he called out a final sentence, but I couldn't make it out.

Half an hour later, Wang Sichuan went to check on Ivan, but he was already off to that big airfield in the sky. He died surrounded by the dials and instruments he loved most, in the cockpit, his most familiar place in the world. His chest wound had been fatal. One of his ribs had broken and pierced his heart. "Crazy" Ivan Ivanovitch, 37, was killed in a black abyss unknown to man. He'd come here for no reason other than love, and had pursued it to the very end. Not once had he lost his trademark cool. Even in the moments before death, the Soviet had accepted his fate. If I succeed, then I will hold her again. If I fail, then she will never forget me. This was his code, his promise to himself and to Yuan Xile. He never broke it. Who could ever forget a man able to backflip a bomber in the moment of truth?

Yuan Xile wasn't alone. I would never forget Ivan, either. We left him in his cabin and did not mourn. I don't believe men like Ivan wish for such sympathy.

His life was also not the only one lost. Zhu Qiang and the copilot both died soon after. Zhu Qiang was probably dead when I pulled him from the wreckage. While his body bore no obvious wounds, his internal injuries must have been severe. The copilot also had internal injuries. He was initially full of energy, but by the time I'd finished resuscitating Old Tian, his body had turned ice-cold.

For a long time after that we just sat there, waiting to be rescued, but no one came. Once Wang Sichuan had regained some of his strength, he went off to scout the area. When he returned his face was pale. "All the equipment, all our stuff—it's gone. There's nothing left."

I greatly admired Wang Sichuan's calm under pressure. I'd just about reached my limit and felt neither the strength nor the inclination to move, but Wang Sichuan kept pushing at me. I finally climbed to my feet and followed him.

The changes were far greater than I'd imagined. If the issue had just been that no one was left at camp, I could have conjured up all sorts of reasons for their departure. Maybe these conjectures would've been wrong, but at least they might provide us some consolation. Instead, not a single piece of equipment or machinery remained.

All evidence that we'd ever been there had vanished, even down to the welding marks we'd made on the rock walls and preexisting buildings. It was as if we'd never been there at all.

47 NIGHTMARE

Everything was covered in a thick layer of rust. The place was more than just abandoned; it was wiped clean. This was impossible. The army would never have been able to eliminate all signs of their presence, especially not over an area this large.

"Well, what do you think?" asked Wang Sichuan, lighting a cigarette. "What the hell happened here?"

There seemed to be only one realistic explanation, but I found it difficult to believe. "It looks to me like we've landed in the wrong place. The Japanese must have built more than one dam on the abyss."

"Are you being serious?"

"Can you think of any other explanation?"

"Follow me." Wang Sichuan tossed away his cigarette and strode over to a nearby cement tower.

"What are you doing?"

"After that incident with the curtain, they locked me in here for three days as punishment. To kill time I carved a few things into the wall in an out of the way spot. No way could they have found it."

We rushed up the tower into the cell. The space was tiny. Kneeling down, Wang Sichuan removed a brick from the wall.

His face went pale. "Nothing! There's nothing here! Then this place really isn't... But this room, it's exactly the same as the one they locked me in!"

Japanese slogans and spots of mold covered the bricks. A barred window was on the wall opposite. Through it I could see the river below and the wreckage of our plane. Only by the light of the still burning flames could I make out the whole scene. I gasped.

From up here, the flaming carcass of the Shinzan looked extremely familiar. I looked closer. At once I realized what I was seeing. The appearance and position of the plane were more than just familiar.

They were identical to the Shinzan that had crashed here over 20 years ago.

I couldn't believe my eyes. This must be a mistake, I told myself. I must be dreaming. After calming down, I gave the plane another look. It really was the same, all of it—the height of the wing rising above the water, the angle of the nose, the charred metal of the fuselage. Even the location of the crash. It was like looking into the past. What was going on?

Leaving the tower at once, I hurried back down to the plane. I hoped it was all just an illusion, but up close the feeling grew even stronger. The only thing different were the strips of plaster covering up the Japanese characters and flag. Sections of the stuff had already burned away, revealing a round sun underneath, like a great red eye staring out at me. Another piece had only melted halfway off. I couldn't read the symbol underneath. I walked closer. It was a seven. I froze. My eyes locked on the number. It felt like someone's hands were wrapped around my throat. The breath wouldn't come.

"What's wrong?" asked Wang Sichuan.

"Is this the plane we were just on?" I knew how irrational this sounded.

"Are you crazy? Of course it is."

"Then what about the wrecked bomber that was here before, the Japanese Shinzan?"

"That rusted hunk of metal? It must still be somewhere nearby. No way could they have moved a whole plane out of here."

"You sure about that?" I muttered.

Wang Sichuan walked off to look for it. It didn't take long for him to return. All the color had drained from his face.

"Strange," he said. "Where the hell could it have gone? I looked and looked, but couldn't find it anywhere. You don't think they took it with them, do you? Or could we have flattened it in the crash?"

Shaking my head, I pointed at the flaming wreckage before us. "No," I said. "It's right here."

***

I couldn't even begin to understand how it had happened, but I was certain the wrecked Shinzan we'd found and the bomber we'd just crashed were the very same plane. How could we have found the remains of our plane before we had even taken flight? The problem, I felt, had to be with us. We must have inhaled too much mercury and consequently gone mad. The hair on the back of my neck stood up as I considered what this meant. If we really were crazy, there was no telling what we'd see next.

I told Wang Sichuan what I was thinking. He didn't seem particularly concerned.

"If that's true, then there's nothing to worry about," he said. "By now I bet we've already been saved and are lying in one of the medical tents. Ivan's probably still alive."

"Perhaps we haven't even landed yet," I said coldly. "Perhaps Pei Qing hasn't even jumped."

"We probably just need some sleep," said Old Tian. "When we wake up everything should be back to normal."

"If it's really all in our heads, then we've got a lot more to think about," I said. "There's no way to know when we first began to lose it. Perhaps we were already crazy when we ran into Yuan Xile. Perhaps it started the moment we arrived. And everyone else here might be crazy, too. Sleeping isn't going to help a thing.

"Think about it," I added. "How can you be sure you weren't crazy all along? Hell, you might just be some old lunatic strapped to a bed somewhere, with this cave and all of us no more than a product of your diseased mind. We need to be careful where we take this. If we start believing everything we're seeing is just a hallucination, that's where the real madness begins."

"So then how would you explain it?" asked Wang Sichuan.

"If something seems unexplainable, then we shouldn't try to force it. That's what my father always told me. When things don't make sense, don't worry about them. Just do what needs to be done. I say we calm down and think. Given the situation, what should our next move be?"

We all looked upriver.

"I want to see the sky," said Wang Sichuan. "How long has it been since we've seen it? I refuse to die in this goddamn place."

"Then let's go," I said. "They're probably waiting for us at the entrance to the cave, ready to pull us to safety like last time."

"And then will they give us an explanation?"

Unlikely, I thought, though I said nothing more.

The three of us scavenged the plane. There was little food to be found. Not much had been onboard to begin with and we'd tossed some to save fuel. We then set off, each of us carrying only a light pack. We followed the iron platforms back up the river. The water was so low it did not rise above our knees.

"This isn't the way we came," said Wang Sichuan. "I was swept down here by River One. It would be best to take the high route back."

"If we take that route, we'll have to climb that three-hundred-foot cliff at the cave mouth. We should just follow River Zero the whole way," I told him. "Some of the others told me it's a much easier walk. In the end you just step through a little hole in the rock and you're outside."

We followed River Zero up and up. Two days later, feeling cold and hungry, I saw a strange light up ahead. At first I didn't know what it was, but then Wang Sichuan roared with joy and I understood.

It was the sun.

By then I was already running, fighting waves of dizziness as the blinding light hit my eyes.

48 THE HUMAN WORLD

The exit was an inconspicuous slit in the rock. A net covered in green vines had been placed over the hole, but the webbing was already rotted and torn. The sun shone through from outside, so beautiful I could barely breathe. One after another we climbed out.

In an instant, my eyes were greeted by all the colors of the world, a vast expanse of forest and mountains. After living in a sunless world for many months where the only colors were black darkness, gray cement, and pale white electric light, I cannot describe how dazzling, how full, were the colors of nature. The golden sunlight, the endless blue sky, the deep-green forest. I nearly fainted on the spot.

Wang Sichuan bellowed at the top of his lungs then, prostrated himself before the heavens. Old Tian and I fell down beside him, letting the sun's rays cook our skin, cook away the gloom and damp of all the time we'd spent underground. Never before had I realized how pleasurable it was to roast in the sun.

After we'd rested a spell my eyes grew accustomed to the light of the world. The forest and sky I'd once found so dull were now an endless delight. Climbing to my feet, I took a look around. We were halfway up the sunny side of a mountain, overlooking a green valley. River Zero was the largest of the underground rivers, the trunk of the system, but by the time we reached the cave mouth it was merely a small stream. This I never would have guessed. I couldn't be sure of our distance from the original entrance, but based on how long we'd walked, I doubted it was far. The surface headquarters should also be nearby.

Wang Sichuan was first to speak. Pointing to a nearby cliff face, he called for us to follow him. A small waterfall was running down the rock. Just below it a gentle slope led into the valley. After washing our faces, we descended the mountain.

After walking for half an hour we found a suitable lookout point. Exhausted, Old Tian collapsed on the ground while I climbed to the edge and took in the view. The mountain we were on was not especially tall, but I was still able to see a long way. There were no camps in the distance and no sign of smoke, only trees, stretching endlessly to the horizon. The trees before me were massive, unusually so, their ranks stern and impregnable. The strength I'd felt only moments before began to fade. If we were planning to make our way back out on foot, I doubted the journey would be any less difficult or dangerous than our time in the cave.

Ordinarily one shouldn't smoke in forests, but right now I didn't care. I took two deep puffs of a cigarette. Immediately I felt a newfound energy rising from my lungs and filling my body. I sighed. No matter what worries I might have, standing beneath the blue sky was incredibly refreshing. I stared at the vastness of it, understanding why Wang Sichuan believed the sky was king of the gods. I truly felt as if I'd escaped hell and returned to the human world.

We set up camping on the mountainside. That first night we had only a soup of wild herbs to eat, the food just enough to allay our hunger. Then we crowded round the fire and, with our eyes on the starry sky overhead, gradually fell asleep. The next morning Wang Sichuan whittled several tree limbs into makeshift bulus and went hunting. He returned that night with several pheasants. We roasted the birds and ate well. After the third day, we began looking for the way out. To avoid getting lost, we had Old Tian stay behind and keep the campfire smoking. Each day we'd tromp through the forest and each night we'd follow the smoke back. After two days of searching, we found the old Japanese military outpost.

Waist-high weeds covered the ground. Long vines climbed the chain-link fences. The barrack roofs were so piled with leaves that they seemed about to collapse. There was not a soul in sight. Incredulous, I waded through the tall weeds and looked around. When our troops were stationed there the grass had been cut and the leaves swept from the rooftops. How had it gotten to this state? The camp could never have become this overgrown in only a few months' time. In fact, from the looks of things, no one had been here for 20 or so years. For an instant I wondered whether we'd arrived at the wrong camp.

"Why does it seem as if every sign of our presence has disappeared?" asked Wang Sichuan.

Unable to reply, I walked into one of the cabins. Everything was covered in a thick layer of dust. Insects filled the cracks in the walls. This level of disuse was impossible to fake. It was like a dream. Or rather, it was like the moment after a dream, the moment you awake and discover that none of it was real. Had I been alone, I really would have believed I was dreaming. But Wang Sichuan and Old Tian were there and seeing the very same things. What the hell was going on? Had we truly all gone mad?

No one said a word. Quietly, Old Tian began to sob. Refusing to give up, Wang Sichuan dragged us along to inspect the rest of camp.

"The grass here probably just grows quicker than normal," he said.

But the more we looked, the stranger it all seemed. Not only was the camp in complete disrepair, even the plank road the engineering corps had built was gone. The trees they'd cut down all seemed to have grown back. At last we returned to the barracks. Wang Sichuan and I attempted to rest.

Old Tian just huddled in the corner, muttering to himself. "We've gone crazy, we've all gone crazy." Suddenly he laughed. "You two don't realize you've gone mad. You're incurable. But I know I have, so I can still be saved."

I sighed. Old Tian was a rigid thinker with a one-track mind. It was difficult for him to adapt. I wasn't sure what to do with him. He continued to laugh wildly and the atmosphere in the cabin grew even more uncomfortable. If things keep going like this, I said to myself, he won't be the only one losing his mind.

That was it. I wasn't thinking about this strangeness anymore. What we should really worry about was what we were supposed to do next. If we just couldn't find the rest of the troops, we'd still be able to locate their tire tracks and make our way out of the forest. But now, without any hint of where to go, we were stuck there, forced to figure everything out for ourselves. The route leading there had been kept secret from us. We had no idea where we were. If we were somewhere outside of China's borders, straying too far in the wrong direction could be dangerous.

No doubt about it. The situation was beginning to look grim.

49 STRANGE HAPPENINGS

No matter what, our first order of business was to figure out where we were.

"Supposing we're somewhere in Mongolia," said Wang Sichuan, "then we need to be extremely careful not to wander into Soviet territory. But no matter what direction we walk in, it's going to be a very long way to any kind of civilization. And given how easy it is to get lost out here, I'd say our best bet is to hole up and think of a plan."

"We've all spent months in the wilderness," I said, thinking a long walk beneath the blue sky hardly seemed so bad. "If we keep walking south we're bound to get out of here. Time's not an issue."

"The issue," he replied, "is that you've been shot. We have no medication and the wound isn't going to get better on its own. Before long, the skin around the bullet will start to rot. We could dig it out, but if we're not careful the wound will become inflamed and things will only get worse. We also have nothing to eat. We're not going to get very far on empty stomachs."

"Then what are you thinking?" To me, he didn't appear all that worried.

"This camp is a long way from everywhere," said Wang Sichuan. "Look how tall and dense the trees are here. It's the same as far as the eye can see. That means it's been decades since any have been chopped down. We both know how long it took us to drive out here. Now, with you injured and Old Tian acting the way he is, we'd better just stay and recuperate for a while; no reason to rush things. We can burn damp logs while we wait. If any hunters or rangers are nearby, they'll see the smoke, assume there's a forest fire, and come running. At the same time we can hunt, dry fruit and stock up enough supplies for the journey."

I could see his point. Even though we'd all trekked through the wilderness for months at a time, we'd never been more than a three or four day's walk from the nearest supply point. We'd also had donkeys and mules to help carry our supplies. This time was completely different. Without a gun, we'd be forced to rely on Wang Sichuan to catch enough pheasants, rabbits and other game to keep us going. Hunting and walking was out of the question. We'd have to stop and wait for at least a half day whenever we needed food. And if Wang Sichuan got sick or injured, we'd be done for. When I first arrived at the 723 Project Headquarters, it had already been late fall. We'd waited at the lower camp for more than a month, by which time the weather had already turned cold. We then endured another couple of months in the depths of the cave. I figured it was now the spring of 1963. We still had time before it got cold again.

So we moved all our things from the mountainside into one of the cabins. That night Wang Sichuan burnt some plants and coated my wound with the ash. He attempted to swiftly extract the bullet from my chest. It didn't work. He spent almost half an hour digging it out with his belt prong. This hurt far worse than getting shot. It was a pain impossible to put into words.

The next day Wang Sichuan went hunting alone, but once my wound healed he started taking me along. Hunting with Wang Sichuan proved very interesting. While I didn't have a prayer of learning how to throw the bulu—a skill that required both natural talent and years of practice beginning at a young age—I was able to learn how to set a variety of traps. When we returned each night, we'd select some of our catch for dinner and smoked the rest. At that time of year, the northern woods were full of wild animals. Nearly every day we managed to come home with something. Before long our cabin rafters were packed with dried meat.

Old Tian remained at camp, pondering our predicament as he wandered the premises in search of clues. No matter how much he thought or how long he searched, he could make neither hide nor hair of what was going on. Frequently he would leap to his feet in the middle of the night, desperate to relate to us the most absurd theories. As time passed, he became more jumpy, more upset, and before long was spending his days drifting between confusion and relative sanity. Since he was unsuited to any job that required real thought, keeping watch over camp was the only productive thing he could do.

On several of our hunts, we passed an area that looked a lot like the place where we'd first dropped into the cave. Leaves covered the ground, far more than seemed possible in such a short time. We'd been told the entrance to the cave had been discovered under a pile of leaves, but we were unable to find the mouth of that so-called Pit of Heaven. Even stranger was the marked change in temperature. It was beginning to grow very hot. Based on my calculations, we should still be in the midst of spring, but the blazing sun that rose each morning told me this was not the case. Wang Sichuan was just as confused.

The northern regions were not normally visited by four distinct seasons. Winter and spring are more or less the same and summer is often pleasantly cool. Then fall quickly turns chilly. By October the snow is already coming down. With the temperatures we were experiencing it seemed obvious that it was already the heart of summer; either that or the north was being visited by an unusually warm spring. Wang Sichuan started to believe we were somewhere near the Pacific and warm sea breezes were influencing the weather. And he was sure we'd miscalculated how much time had passed. A spring this warm was very rare in the north, he said. According to him it was already summer. Once the weather really turned hot, the vegetation would flourish and, given where we were, wolves would arrive. As we had no weapons, this would mean trouble.

After taking stock, we concluded our dried meat would last us more than a month on the road. Initially we'd hoped to save enough for two months, but we figured it was better to depart ahead of schedule, while the wolves were still in the grasslands. Then, two days before we planned to leave, a cold rain began to fall.

Once it started, the rain wouldn't stop. Day in and day out we could do nothing but sit in the cabin, waiting for the sky to clear while the ground outside turned to mud. Before long the cold, damp weather made me ill. Several times in my feverish state I imagined I was still trapped within the cave.

As the days passed our agitation gradually began to ease. The situation would have to improve, we told ourselves. Old Tian even managed to say a few wise words while in his right mind. The northern climate was generally dry, he told us. So once this rain was over (something he said would happen soon), there would be a long period of clear skies. Why brave the foul weather when we could wait it out indoors? Still, comfortable as we were, we prayed for the rain to stop. Everyday Wang Sichuan would stick his head out of the cabin to look at the color of the clouds, and every day he would say that in another week it would clear up. A week passed, and then another, while the rain kept right on falling. It seemed almost as if it were waiting for something.

Around midnight on the second day of the third week of rain, I was awoken by a strange noise. Something was knocking against the outside of the cabin. I froze, telling myself it had to be the wind, but as I listened closer I realized it was the sound of someone knocking at the door. I looked over.

Wang Sichuan and Old Tian were lying beside me. Cold sweat trickled down my back. We were deep in the forest. How could anyone be knocking at our door?

50 GUESTS OF THE FOREST

I waited in silence, sitting in the dark and listening to the sound. A moment later Wang Sichuan woke with a start.

"Who the hell went outside in the middle of the night?" he whispered.

"No one," I said, looking over at Old Tian. "All three of us are right here."

We both looked back at the door. At almost the same instant, three more knocks suddenly sounded. We looked at one another in disbelief.

"You think it's a black bear?" asked Wang Sichuan.

"Black bears are never so polite," I replied.

The knocks were low and gloomy and came in brief bursts, followed by short, almost hesitant, pauses. Wang Sichuan glanced over at me, then grabbed a still-burning log from the fire to use as a torch. Together we stepped to the door. Wang Sichuan cracked it open. The torchlight illuminated the darkness beyond. There was nothing. Looking closer, however, I saw two huge footprints in the mud. My heart skipped a beat. I was about to say something when Wang Sichuan stopped me. Holding his torch before him, he stepped outside. At once I saw them—mounds of mud standing in the pouring rain at the edge of the torchlight. There were over a dozen of them under a rain tarp.

I walked closer. The mounds were actually people covered head-to-toe in mud. One of the mounds suddenly called out, "Useless Wu, is that you?"

I froze. "Useless" was, unfortunately, one of my nicknames. I suspect that everyone surnamed Wu, no matter how dignified or imposing their given name, runs into this trouble sooner or later. (Translator's note: Wu, Old Wu's surname, has many homophones. Among the most common is a wu that means "without." By adding the word for "use" (yong) to the end of Wu's name, it becomes nearly indistinguishable from the Chinese for "useless.") If only Outlaws of the Marsh had been more popular in those years... (Translator's note: Outlaws of the Marsh is one of the four great classical Chinese novels and features a story in which a man, surnamed Wu, defeats a tiger with his bare hands.)

Since my most recent promotion very few people had called me this nickname. I didn't know anyone in my new unit very well and my superiors were so busy they probably didn't even remember my real name. At once, all the rest of the mounds began to move, stepping out from beneath their rain tarp and quickly taking it apart. Their faces were caked with mud and nearly unrecognizable. Then I turned to the person who'd called my name. As I looked at her face, I felt all my thoughts come tumbling from my mind. It was Yuan Xile.

Although her face was covered with mud, I immediately noticed her bright eyes shining through. She wasn't crazy anymore, not at all. Smiling happily, she walked towards me. I was dumbfounded. Wang Sichuan's eyes went wide as he mouthed, "What the hell is going on?"

The rest of her troop approached as well, several of them leveling assault rifles at us. "It's okay," said Yuan Xile, "they're on our side."

Seeing the cabin behind us, her men were overjoyed. "Thank God," said one of them. "Finally someplace dry."

In a daze, I led the mud-caked soldiers inside, my eyes fixed on Yuan Xile the whole time. I could tell from the soldiers' equipment they were all part of the geological division. Although none of them looked familiar to me, when they saw Old Tian they were shocked. It was obvious he recognized them as well. This was all too much to handle.

After removing their outer garments, the soldiers huddled around the fire. Wang Sichuan gave me a quick glance while he fetched dried meat for our guests. He was obviously just as confused as I.

"What exactly are you three doing here?" asked one of the men.

My eyes went wide. It was Su Zhenhua, the special emissary we'd found raving mad, scurrying on all fours through the warehouse. He seemed to be in his right mind now, though. How had Yuan Xile and he recovered so thoroughly? What were they doing here now? Instead of responding, I pinched myself, hard, trying to see whether this was really all just a dream. I scanned the rest of their group. There was another man, the oldest in the group, now coughing discreetly. Yuan Xile handed him a towel. He wiped the mud from his face. I couldn't believe my eyes. He was an old expert, extremely famous and supposedly living in the Soviet Union, but I'd seen his corpse tangled in wire at the bottom of the sinkhole. And there was Old Cat inconspicuously smoking a cigarette, that familiar worldly expression on his weathered face.

"Mao Wuyue," I said Old Cat, unable to contain myself.

Surprised, he looked at me. "Who are you? Have we met before?"

Frowning, I studied his expression. I couldn't tell whether his confusion was real or fake, but at this point it no longer mattered. Had we run into only Yuan Xile and the special emissary, I could have come up with some other explanation, but now that I'd seen the old expert, I could no longer deny what was really going on. Sitting before me was the first prospecting team of the 723 Project.

***

Another team had explored the cave prior to our arrival. Yuan Xile had been its leader, Su Zhenhua its special emissary, and the old expert its skilled advisor. They and the rest of their nine-person team had encountered danger after danger within the cave, until all but three were dead. Old Cat alone had made it to the surface. Yuan Xile and Su Zhenhua had remained below, both having lost their minds to mercury poisoning. But now every single member of this team was alive and well and sitting before us. Not only that, there were also far more of them than we'd been told. Had Old Cat lied to us?

From the looks of their equipment, they seemed ready to begin prospecting work in the area. They were probably searching for the cave.

How was it possible for us to run into them here? We were this team's reinforcements. How were we meeting them now? I could think of only one explanation. Had we somehow traveled back in time to when this whole thing was just getting started?

I thought back on everything that had happened, how when we'd landed the plane—our runway gone, camp empty, and all our equipment vanished—there remained not a single sign of our presence at the abandoned Japanese camp. Had something happened to us while we were flying through the abyss? Was this even possible? If it was, then how had we done it? I had no idea. I knew only that at this point, if our two choices were having either lost our minds or traveled back in time, then I was sticking with Old Tian. Madness remained much easier to swallow.

I remembered a long ago conversation with one of my old teachers. He'd told me about a strange story he'd heard while prospecting for oil in the Taklamaklan Desert. A local had told him that somewhere in the desert was a mysterious region from which people would often vanish, only to reappear the next night, sometimes over a hundred miles away. The strangest part was that those who survived never had any idea of what had occurred. Each could say only that they'd lost their way in the endless desert and had walked several days and nights before they were found, but none were gone more than 24 hours. The doctors all said it was an illusion caused by dehydration. My teacher disagreed. While he was prospecting in the area, a member of his own team disappeared. Only later did they find his corpse over a hundred miles from camp. There was no way he could have wandered so far, unless he'd intended to kill himself.

I couldn't help but wonder: Had we experienced something similar while flying through the abyss?

51 SMALL TALK

Cold sweat trickled down my back as I thought this through. Something still seemed amiss, as if I was lacking a piece of the puzzle. I looked at the faces of the men sitting before me. None of them revealed a thing.

If I was right, then Yuan Xile's team had been dispatched not long after we arrived at this place. The main camp had to be somewhere relatively nearby. But I couldn't just ask them about it, for strange as it was for us to see them, it must have been equally unsettling for them to run into us out here, asleep in this cabin in the middle of nowhere. And it wasn't like I could tell them we'd traveled back in time. So we found ourselves in a very awkward situation. They were on a top-secret assignment and we had appeared, unannounced and without explanation, smack in the middle of the very place they were supposed to be exploring. If we messed this one up, we might soon be in a whole heap of trouble. I had no idea what to say or do, nor did I know whether Wang Sichuan had thought of anything himself. The best we could hope for was to keep them in the dark long enough to think of a plan.

Wang Sichuan was decidedly unflustered. As he met my eyes, I could tell he had a plan. I sighed with relief. Now all I had to worry about was making sure Old Tian didn't say anything too strange. Old Tian appeared more than willing to keep our secret. His previous semi-consciousness had given way to a state of full confusion. He was seated at the very edge of the circle, his knees to his chest, his glazed eyes staring out at our guests.

His head bobbed incessantly.

The special emissary's unanswered question hung in the air. Seeing I was unable to reply, a brief, curious look flashed across his face. Then he turned to Wang Sichuan and asked again, "What are you three doing here?"

Wang Sichuan was as cool as a cucumber. "We were part of a large brigade on temporary assignment, but we got lost. Because the assignment itself was classified, I naturally cannot reveal what we were doing."

The special emissary gave all three of us a strange look, as if deliberating something. He was much more uptight than the others. For her part, Yuan Xile hardly seemed concerned. After washing the mud from her face and rinsing her hair, she turned. "When we first came upon your cabin and saw the firelight inside, I thought for a second there was some demon of the forest. Who would believe we'd run into fellow prospectors this far from civilization?"

"We've been following your smoke for the past few days," said a young soldier. "That's how we found you."

Wang Sichuan said we'd already been stranded for some time and that all of our equipment was gone. "But now that you've arrived," he continued, "we have nothing to worry about. Just how far is it to the nearest town from here?"

Yuan Xile's face took an awkward expression. No one replied.

"I don't believe it," I said, feigning ignorance. "You're all lost, too?"

"I'm afraid not," said Yuan Xile, her expression serious. "The issue is that the location of this area is highly classified. Having arrived here accidentally, you three are not in any trouble; however, we cannot give you any specifics." As she spoke, Yuan Xile kept one eye on the special emissary. The strictness of this secrecy obviously came from him.

"At the very least, don't we need to think of some kind of plan?" asked Old Tian, speaking up at last. "The three of us need help. We've all gone crazy."

Everyone laughed. "With all this goddamn rain, who wouldn't go crazy?" said one of the young soldiers. "I've just about lost it myself."

I looked over at the special emissary, trying to gauge his reaction. "Unfortunately, I have no say in the matter," he said. "Once the weather clears up, we'll send a cable to headquarters so they can decide what's best. Don't worry; we'll probably just end up having Little Einstein here lead you guys out." He motioned toward a kid with a boyish face and a fire in his eyes.

You could tell he was different than the others. Seeing that I was looking at the telegraph transmitter sticking out of his pack, he smiled at me.

"Exactly how long have you been stuck here?" asked the special emissary.

"From the time we realized we were lost up until now," said Wang Sichuan, "it has to have been about a month."

"In that case," continued the special emissary, handing Wang Sichuan a cigarette, "have you had a chance to explore much of the surrounding area?" His voice and expression were perfectly relaxed as he said this, as if he were merely making conversation.

Yuan Xile and her team had been trekking through the rain for days on end. Now they'd finally found a place that was warm and dry, where there was food to eat and comfort to be had. It was an easy-going, cordial atmosphere. Old Tian was once more treated with respect and our hope of getting out of here was rekindled. There was nothing strange at all about the special emissary offering us cigarettes. But as for his question, even a fool could see what he was after.

"We've traveled a fair bit to the east and west," said Wang Sichuan, watching his words carefully. "Elsewhere there are only cliffs. What direction are you coming from?"

"I've got no idea," replied the special emissary. "All I know is we've been walking all over the place, and it's been a long time since I had any clue what direction we were headed." He paused to smile at us. "But back to my original question. You three have explored the area around here, at least to some extent. Have you encountered anything that was at all, well, strange?"

Wang Sichuan laughed. "What could be strange about a place like this? The only things you'll find around here are trees and more trees. We were damn lucky to happen upon this cabin. Believe it or not, the Japs built several more nearby. There are even a few warehouses off to the right. The devils must have been planning something big, though who knows what."

Seeing the natural way Wang Sichuan responded—evasive, but not overly so, neither saying too much nor too little—I relaxed. This guy is truly talented, I said to myself. It would be a real shame if he doesn't make officer one day. With all the people present, conversation flowed freely. Knowing I had none of Wang Sichuan's talent for deception, I rose and began preparing our guests' sleeping arrangements. From the look of things, Wang Sichuan was going to be able to handle this first challenge all by himself. Besides our reason for being here, everything he'd said was true, making it easy for us to stick to the same script. I wasn't at all worried Old Tian would give away our secret. I knew he'd rather die than break a rule. Given all the oaths of confidentiality we'd sworn, his silence was assured. I was now our biggest problem. I was certain my earlier actions had been very suspicious. The special emissary kept glancing over at me, wanting to see my reaction while he talked with Wang Sichuan. For now at least, I needed to avoid his eyes and think of an explanation for my unusual behavior.

What I didn't realize at the time was that my actions weren't the problem. The real issue was that this place was almost definitely within some hotly contested border region—outside of China, in other words—so it was impossible that there could be other prospecting teams there. How could Su Zhenhua not be suspicious? As for the rest of the team, they were probably like us, left totally in the dark about the place's true coordinates and thus blithely unconcerned about finding us there. Still, the events that were to happen soon made the cause of Su Zhenhua's suspicion irrelevant.

Yuan Xile and her men were exhausted. As the chatter subsided, they each took to their beds for a much-deserved rest. Usually I slept well in our cabin, but with all the excitement tonight I found myself staring at the ceiling for hours. Not until dawn light filtered in through the windows did

I finally fall asleep. There was something specific about our guests that I failed to notice. What I did see, however, was Yuan Xile's sleeping face, past Wang Sichuan's smelly feet, illuminated by the firelight. Her hair was not yet as long as when I found her in the cave. My mind was filled with a thousand thoughts, but as I watched her peaceful expression, I was gradually overcome by a sense of calm. No matter what happened, no matter what was going on, so long as she was here it couldn't be that bad.

And yet, I couldn't shake the feeling that this was all just a dream.

52 THE BEST POSSIBLE PAST

I woke to find the rain had finally stopped. The beds around me were filled with people. Last night had been real after all. Some of the others had already gotten up, including Wang Sichuan and Yuan Xile. I walked outside. The sun greeted me like a long-lost friend. I stretched in its warmth, then went looking for Wang Sichuan. He didn't usually wake this early. I assumed he was looking for an opportunity to talk with me alone.

The ground was still muddy, but I found a relatively clean pool amid the muck and washed my face. Someone was in the woods nearby, shaking leaves from a tree. These would be much easier to dry and use as kindling than the sodden specimens littering the ground. I hoped it was Yuan Xile. I found myself nervous at the thought of it, but I still very much wanted to speak with her alone. As I drew closer, I saw it was only Little Einstein. Although he appeared to be no more than 15-years-old, he was skillfully carrying a huge stack of firewood on his back. It was obvious this kid knew what he was doing. More voices sounded from deeper in the woods—Old Cat's and someone else's—but the trees blocked my view.

"You a Northeasterner?" I asked the kid. No way could a Southerner handle a tree like that; Southerners burn rice straw for warmth. Little Einstein just smiled and kept going. I motioned that I would help him carry some of the firewood, but he shook his head and continued toward the cabins, the huge stack on his back dwarfing his small frame.

"Don't worry about him," said a voice from behind me. "He may look young, but he's stubborn as a mule."

I turned around to see Yuan Xile emerging from a patch of trees. She was brushing her hair. Drops of water covered her face. Her hair was still wet. While a female prospector cannot be choosy about the godforsaken places to which she is sent, she won't just stick her head in a mud puddle when it's time to get clean.

Seeing my face up close, she began to laugh. "There's a fairly large pool of water in the woods back there," she said. "Why don't you go and give yourself a good wash? From the looks of things, you haven't scrubbed your face since I last saw you."

I laughed. "We both know I don't have a chance of finding a wife in this lifetime, so why take the trouble?"

"It takes effort to find a wife," she said. "They're not going to just come to you. But why lose heart so easily? There are more than a few female prospectors around. Come on, time to wash up. I'll show you where the pool is."

I followed her into the woods. We soon arrived at a clear pool of water. Kneeling at its edge, I gave my face a thorough scrubbing. Once I was finished, she looked me over and nodded. "Doesn't that feel a lot better? I've always thought men should have a look of vigor about them."

I smiled. "I could wash my face three times a day and still have nowhere near the vigor of a certain Soviet aviator. It's not fair to compare me to your fiancé. I can't measure up." I would never have been comfortable speaking to her like this before, but she no longer seemed unapproachable.

Wiping her face with a handkerchief, she stared at me in amazement. "How did you know about that? I've barely told anyone. Who told you?"

I laughed. "There's not a wall on earth that doesn't let some wind through."

She smiled. Her cheeks were bright red. "That was all in the past. He'll never be able to leave the Soviet Union. Our relationship ended when I returned home."

"How can you be so sure he's not coming for you? Perhaps he's just been held up along the way."

"Even if he did come, we could never be together. Our countries might both be communist, but they're entirely different. No matter what, I would have to refuse him."

"But isn't that a shame? Refusing a man that exceptional?"

She looked at me as if I were being ridiculous. "How do you know he's so exceptional?"

Believe me, I know, I said to myself. If he wasn't, then my charred corpse would be lying at the bottom of a black abyss.

"Perhaps at the time he truly did seem special to me," said Yuan Xile with a look of resignation, "but the hotter the relationship, the more likely it will end when the passion cools." She sighed. "Sometimes even I don't know what really went wrong, but so what? It's over, and I don't want to talk about it anymore." She turned and sped off towards the cabins, leaving me behind.

I wanted to follow her, but I hesitated. Before she'd gone too far, she spun on her heels and marched back. Staring straight at me, she said, "Don't tell anyone what we talked about today. I don't care who you heard that stuff from." I nodded. Then, after glancing back at the distant cabins, she continued. "Our assignment here is very unusual, and trust me, you don't want any part of it. Mind your own business and I'll do my best to convince Su Zhenhua to allow you three to return home."

"What if he says no?" I asked.

"Then you'll probably be forced to join our team. But I don't see why you three should have to take the risk." She put a finger to her lips. "Be careful what you say. I might know you, but no one else here does. Some of them are bound to be suspicious." She gave me a final glance, then turned and left for good.

I knew she was right. Having seen how all this would end, I could say with absolute certainty it was going to be one hell of a dangerous mission indeed.

I watched her figure recede all the way until she entered our cabin. Then I went to find Wang Sichuan. He was in the rear courtyard, stacking firewood. When he saw me, he waved for me to come help. While the two of us kept up the appearance of being hard at work, I told him my theory. He told me he'd originally been thinking the same thing, but he'd decided it was too fantastic. It was much more realistic that all these people were actually mountain spirits, come down here just to toy with us, he said. Spirits? Now that was even more ridiculous. Eventually Wang Sichuan agreed. Unfortunately, neither of us could think of another explanation. In the end we had no choice but to believe that we'd really traveled half a year back in time.

Yuan Xile's team was obviously searching for the entrance to the cave. At this point I would have rather died than be forced to join their ranks and go back in that cave. We needed to think of a way out, a way to convince Su Zhenhua to allow us to return home. No matter what, the most important thing was to survive. Yuan Xile and Su Zhenhua were certain to be discussing this today. Since Little Einstein was the telegraph operator, we assumed he'd be privy to their conclusion. Wang Sichuan decided to get on good terms with the kid, hoping he might pick up some information. If they weren't going to let us leave, then we needed to think of a way to escape as soon as possible.

This sort of subterfuge was hardly my specialty, so I let Wang Sichuan have at it. He went off to invite Little Einstein hunting. I returned to the cabin. There I did my utmost to act normally, hoping the special emissary would forget my behavior from last night.

Wang Sichuan and Little Einstein returned to camp around midday, dragging an impressively large buck. Even after everyone had eaten their fill, a lot of meat remained. I helped Wang Sichuan smoke the leftovers and hang them to dry. Yuan Xile and her crew were too hungry to keep subsisting on their own dwindling supplies. We had no choice but to help them. Wang Sichuan's hunting had served two purposes—he'd curried favor with Little Einstein and helped preserve our provisions for the long walk home. My admiration for the big man was growing by the day. He was quick-witted, able-bodied, and full of energy. Other than a slight tendency towards impulsiveness, he didn't have any major shortcomings. One couldn't help but respect the Mongolian people—excellence was in their blood.

That afternoon the prospecting team began exploring the area, leaving behind only those few not yet recovered from the journey. Wang Sichuan and I sat outside our cabin, chatting as he stripped meat from the deer carcass. Seeing no one was around, he turned to me and said that, from what he'd heard, Little Einstein was going to be asked to lead us back to civilization, a journey that would take several months. According to Wang Sichuan, however, no way had Yuan Xile and her team traveled that long to get here. He was certain there was a large military outpost somewhere nearby. We weren't supposed to know about it, so Little Einstein was going to take us the long way back to avoid the troops. We were supposed to believe Yuan Xile's unit was merely another prospecting team exploring the area, not the vanguard of a much larger undertaking.

"This is just what I was hoping for," said Wang Sichuan. "Once we're out of here, we can find a little village to lie low in and wait for our future selves to be dispatched to the cave. Until they leave, we cannot return home. Otherwise we'd never be able to explain ourselves."

Yuan Xile must have convinced the special emissary to let us go. I thanked my lucky stars for ever meeting Xile. Then I suddenly remembered what she'd looked like when we first found her in the cave. "Wait a second," I said, "we can't just leave them like this. If we do nothing, most of these people will die."

"To you and me, they're already dead." Wang Sichuan's voice was solemn. He'd clearly already thought this through.

"What if we just warn them a little bit? Perhaps things won't go nearly so bad."

Wang Sichuan immediately shook his head. "Absolutely not. If we really have traveled back in time, then I cannot even begin to imagine the consequences of us giving them any kind of warning. Their future is our past. Their fate has already been decided. Anything that changes this fate will affect our present. I don't know what might happen, but I doubt it will be something either of us is willing to accept. As it stands, Yuan Xile, Su Zhenhua, and Old Cat will be the only survivors of this mission. But if we warn them, then maybe these three will die and someone else will survive."

He was right. If the majority of Yuan Xile's team did survive, then it would be them, not us, aboard that underground flight. And there was no telling whether Yuan Xile would survive the crash. We'd already experienced the best possible past, or at least as good of one as I could hope for. I thought again of Yuan Xile, lost and alone in that pitch-black cave. Her future was fated to be a nightmare, but for her sake, I had no choice but to sit back and watch it happen.

I took a deep breath, telling myself that the fate of man is decided by Heaven alone. I might be able to see into the future, but if I was wise, I would do nothing.

53 THE PLAN

The venison dried all afternoon. Evening fell. Yuan Xile still hadn't announced the news Wang Sichuan had hoped for. This was no surprise. Such matters always required some time for discussion.

Before falling asleep, I mentally organized everything that had happened—the past, the present and the future. The more I thought things through, the easier it was to accept our situation. This was real. We'd traveled back in time and were now several months in the past. If we did as Wang Sichuan advised and avoided warning the others, then they'd be picked off one by one in the cave until only three remained. And I would still be working with my regular prospecting team, blissfully unaware of the order I was about to receive.

There was still time before all this happened. When our team discovered the Shinzan, it was already so rusted I'd assumed it had been there for at least 20 years. The toxic subterranean environment would corrode the plane rapidly, but I figured it still needed at least four months. We'd entered the cave in mid-November of 1962. So, to give the plane time enough to thoroughly rust, we must have crashed it in the summer of 1962—early July, most likely. This was the reason for the high temperatures. Summer had already arrived. We'd been here for about a month. It would still be another three months before the future me arrived. If Yuan Xile and her men entered the cave one month before us, then they still had another two months to go. What did they do in all that time? Had it really taken them two months to find the entrance?

The cave was covered by a thick layer of leaves. Wang Sichuan and I had been hunting very close to the hidden entrance and we hadn't found it. Still, they didn't lack for people. They could painstakingly search the entire region inch by inch and still find the cave within a month. Had something kept them from entering the cave sooner? Was it the rain? The rainy season had already begun. The underground river was probably so high that even if Yuan Xile and her team found the cave, it would be too dangerous to go inside. They'd have to wait until the water level dropped before continuing their exploration.

Suddenly, I had an idea. Rather than just warning them, what if I went ahead and did something that put a stop to their entire expedition— something like blowing up the entrance to the cave? I could even use the frozen bombs from the dam's icehouse to do it. But even though this seemed like it would save Yuan Xile and her team, it would also cause a series of unpredictable changes. The other me would be unable to join a project that had already ended. None of what I'd experienced would occur. This was a paradox. If I was never involved in this project in the first place, how could I now be here to stop it from proceeding? No matter what, they were going to enter the cave and meet with disaster, after which I would be trucked out here to continue the investigation.

The whole thing was one big loop, with neither beginning nor end and no way out. I knew only that I'd better not do anything rash. Who knew what might result? And yet whenever I thought of the danger Yuan Xile was soon to face, my heart shivered. When the time came, could I really just sit back and do nothing?

With all these thoughts swirling in my head it was difficult to sleep that night. I truly hoped Old Tian was right, that I was crazy and this was all a dream. Even if I were to open my eyes and find myself strapped to a hospital bed, I would breathe easier. I spent the night in semi-consciousness, drifting in and out of numberless dreams, their portent impossible to fathom.

The next morning I awoke to the sound of Wang Sichuan loudly arguing with someone. Climbing out of bed, I found him just outside the cabin hurling invective after coarse invective at the special emissary. No one was going to intervene until the fists started flying. Back then things needed to get physical for something to be considered a fight. Otherwise it was just a "heated verbal exchange" and most bystanders weren't willing to get involved. I couldn't stay out of this, though.

I walked between them and waved for Wang Sichuan to stop. "What's going on?" I asked.

"This son of a bitch is making us stay here!" snapped Wang Sichuan. "He's not letting Little Einstein take us back."

"Is that true?" I asked, turning to the special emissary. "How can you find us stranded out here and do nothing to help? Aren't we all comrades?"

"Unfortunately we have been unable to reach headquarters," replied the special emissary, his voice perfectly even. "This decision is not one we can make on our own. Our assignment is quite urgent and cannot be delayed any longer. We have no choice but to ask you to stay here. Once our work is complete we will come get you."

"We've already been stuck here for nearly a month," said Wang Sichuan, his face red with anger. "We, too, have an assignment to take care of."

"Then it's too bad for you that we showed up," said the special emissary.

He wasn't fighting with Wang Sichuan, just watching him react. Something subtle must have changed behind the scenes. Perhaps they had reached the higher-ups and this was what our superiors had decreed. In any case, although I was upset, I understood their decision. They could never know the location of every prospecting team at all times, but for us to appear here unannounced was not a matter to be taken lightly.

"All right then," said Wang Sichuan, "get on with your goddamn mission already. I'll just walk out of here on my own."

"I'm afraid not," said the special emissary. "This forest is a very dangerous place. The three of you must remain at camp to await our return. It would be wise of you not to wander too far afield. For your safety, we will leave a few people behind to wait with you." Without saying anything further, he turned and walked back inside the cabin.

Shaking with anger, Wang Sichuan roared after him. "Wait with us? Don't you mean monitor us? What the hell do you think we've done?" He was on the verge of losing his mind.

The special emissary ignored him. I glanced over at Wang Sichuan, signaled for him to cool it.

Then I lit a cigarette and followed the special emissary inside with Wang Sichuan behind me. "When do you expect to return?" I asked him.

"Hard to say, but it won't be too long. As long as you three wait here calmly, everything will be fine." The special emissary didn't even look at me as he spoke.

"If it's just a normal prospecting job then perhaps we can help. That way you can keep all your men and we won't have to wait so long. We've all worked with Yuan Xile before. She can vouch that we know what we're doing." I glanced over at Yuan Xile, but she gave no response.

"She doesn't need to," said the special emissary. "Our confidence in your ability is not the problem."

He didn't doubt our skills; he doubted us. I was about to respond when Old Cat walked over and patted me on the shoulder. "It's not that we don't need your help. While we're gone you can catch us some more food, make sure we have enough for the trip back." He looked at me and laughed. Everyone else began to laugh, too. I knew Old Cat was just trying to give both parties a way out of the conversation, but I was still annoyed.

No matter. The decision had already been made. Anyway, they were still behaving politely, which meant they hadn't had time to investigate our backstory. If we kept arguing, we might make them more suspicious. Better to appear resigned to our fate while we thought of a plan. Nodding silently, I sat down on one of the beds and pulled Wang Sichuan down beside me. Old Cat looked over at us, his eyes hinting at something, though whether it was sympathy or something else, I don't know. He turned and sat on one of the beds at the other end of the room.

After that the first team began to explore the area in earnest, leaving behind only Little Einstein and a few other men to look after us. We never knew where they went, but they always came marching back every three to five days. While at camp they made sure not to discuss any of their work in front of us.

While the main force was off exploring, Wang Sichuan and I would go hunting. Little Einstein didn't accompany us, but he always made us leave our packs behind. He figured that without our equipment and a considerable amount of food, we weren't going anywhere. Wang Sichuan thought otherwise. He began skinning our catches in the field and hiding the meat in the trees to dry. It always went bad in a few days. Escape wasn't really an option. We didn't have enough food and the soldiers wouldn't hesitate to shoot us dead.

As the days passed I felt increasingly apprehensive. It wasn't us that I was worried about—it was them. I knew Yuan Xile and her team would inevitably find the cave and the water level would inevitably fall. And once they dropped below the earth, the hour of their death would be at hand.

54 THINGS FALL APART

It was already early September. The weather had grown much cooler. Yuan Xile and her men had been away for some time. Days passed and still they did not return, nor was any message sent back. Little Einstein was obviously uneasy. He tried to pretend otherwise, but it was no use. Our own behavior began to change as well. Wang Sichuan became increasingly calm. I grew more and more nervous. My premonition was finally coming true.

Things soon became extremely awkward. No matter how difficult it was to find the cave, we all knew they should have long since returned. Having heard nothing to the contrary, we could more or less assume they'd already suffered some accident, gotten lost or trapped somewhere. Little Einstein, Wang Sichuan, and I went on several searches for them, but because we weren't allowed to bring any supplies, these had to remain relatively small in scope. The kid was too goddamn stubborn. Even in a situation this serious he still refused to trust us. This continued for another week. There was no longer any denying it—something had gone wrong. Their food would have lasted them two weeks at most. By now a month had already passed.

Two of our three guards prepared to set out. I immediately asked Little Einstein if we, too, could join the search party. This would allow us to form two groups. People's lives are on the line, I told him. If we don't act fast it will be too late. Still Little Einstein hesitated. After thinking for a while, he finally responded, "You three need to stay here. That's what the special emissary ordered."

"You honestly think Su Zhenhua would rather you look after us than save his life?" I asked. "By waiting here, all we're doing is giving them time to bury their dead. This is no time to tiptoe around the issue. If you really don't trust us, then take a gun and stay with our group the whole time. You afraid we'd still try and make a break for it?"

And yet his ambivalence continued. The kid was obviously impervious to reason. To hell with it, I thought. I grabbed a bag and began stuffing food and equipment inside. It was time to get to work. Wang Sichuan began organizing two bags as well (one of them filled to the brim, albeit covertly, with smoked meat). Once Little Einstein saw the two of us were packed and ready to go, it was as if something suddenly clicked for him. Stamping his foot, he yelled for the two other men to come quick. Once everything was set we were divided into two groups: Old Tian, Wang Sichuan, Little Einstein, and I in one, the two soldiers in the other. And with that we headed into the woods.

I soon realized the situation was much more serious than I'd thought. The newly-dense vegetation made everything look the same. All the paths we'd walked before seemed to have disappeared. To keep us from getting lost, Wang Sichuan used a hatchet to carve the character 王 (Wang) onto some of the trees we passed. Yuan Xile and the others always came back every three to five days to resupply. The area they were searching couldn't be more than one to two days' travel from camp. But seeing how easy it was to get lost out there, I realized they might have taken a wrong turn and accidentally traveled a very long way. If so, their fate would not be pretty. Or they might have already entered the cave, though this seemed unlikely. Why would they go hungry when they could return to camp, restock, and then continue their exploration?

At first we headed northeast into the mountains, calling out their names. Before long we found a lookout point. The vast forest spread out below us, an endless sea of green. We sent up a smoke signal, hoping they would respond. No such luck. Five days passed with no sign of them. We were hemmed in on all sides by thick foliage and tall trees. I knew that if we kept searching like this—haphazardly, with no plan—our chances of finding them were extremely slim. Losing people from a prospecting expedition was hardly rare. Locals would be asked to bring torches and join the hunt, but it was never any use. In this case, however, I was convinced Yuan Xile and the others were still alive.

As we marched through the forest, Wang Sichuan kept signaling to me that we should make our escape. We were already carrying enough food to survive. All we needed to do was subdue Little Einstein. Yuan Xile's team was not fated to die in the forest, he said. It was possible they'd already been found by the other search party or even returned to camp on their own. We didn't need to worry about them. He had a point, but I still refused to go along.

The reason, which I didn't say aloud, was the vague recollection of the corpse we'd found under the canvas sheet in the warehouse. I had realized it was Little Einstein. If I was right, then Little Einstein would eventually enter the cave himself. He would not be kidnapped by us and led south. If we tried anything, we'd likely be the losers, shot dead by Little Einstein's gun. Wang Sichuan's impatience was getting on my nerves. Only when we began angling our search south did he calm down.

"Don't worry," I told him. "If we don't find them, we can just continue on in this direction out of here."

Traveling south, we made our way deeper and deeper into the forest. Seven days passed. On the afternoon of the eighth day Wang Sichuan suddenly cried out. We looked in the direction he was pointing. A plume of smoke was rising from a distant mountainside. Wild with joy, Little Einstein took off running. We followed close behind. The smoke was rising slowly, sheltered from the wind by the mountain. It took seven hours to reach our destination. There was an encampment of six or seven tents. Even though I'd known that our comrades were all right, it was still no small relief to have finally found them. The three of us sprinted towards the tents, Little Einstein calling out his teammates' names. But when we arrived and I saw where we were, a cold sweat ran down my back. I knew this place.

This was where they'd found the Pit of Heaven, the vertical shaft through which we'd first entered the cave. The place looked the same as before, except every inch of ground was covered by a thick layer of leaves. As far as I could remember, though, this entrance hadn't been that far from the old Japanese camp, nor had it been in this direction. Had we gotten turned around along the way? Had we made one gigantic circle?

Little Einstein began to call out, "Special Emissary Su Zhenhua! Special Emissary Su Zhenhua!"

No one replied. We entered one tent after another, but they were all empty.

"What, were they all carried off by wolves?" asked Wang Sichuan, having not yet realized where we were. "Where could they have gone?"

I knew the answer. I turned and hurried up the mountain slope. I burst into a clearing. There, surrounded by leaves and black earth, was the cave. Little Einstein followed close behind. Seeing the cave, he immediately ran to its very edge. He stood there for only a split second before the ground beneath his feet gave way. If I hadn't grabbed his arm, he would have tumbled into the darkness. I pulled him up and brushed away the leaves around the cave. An old net covered half the opening. The net was made of extremely thick rope, but had rotted through. Several new lengths of rope dropped into the darkness beyond the net, their other ends tied around a nearby tree.

I gulped. A considerable amount of time had passed since they'd first set out, more than long enough for their rations to have been entirely depleted. So why hadn't they come back? Had something already gone wrong?

55 THE HAND OF FATE

Everything was happening much too quickly. It was still early fall. There were another two months to go before Wang Sichuan, the rest of the second team and I entered the cave in November. I'd assumed Yuan Xile and her men had been trapped underground for a month prior to our arrival, but if they'd already run into trouble, then perhaps twice as much time had actually passed. This didn't add up. While trapped in the safe room, I'd seen only a few dozen empty cans of food. No way could these have been enough to sustain them for two months. Nor had I ever heard Old Cat mention that they'd been underground for that long.

As I was mulling over these questions, Little Einstein suddenly turned towards me, raised his rifle and aimed it at my heart. I instinctively dodged out of the way. "What the hell are you doing?"

"I saw you sprint up here just now," he said, turning the gun on Wang Sichuan and motioning for him to stand beside me. "Tell me you didn't know the cave was here."

My heart skipped a beat. Shit. I hadn't known this little son of a gun was paying such close attention. "That's not it at all," I replied. "I just wanted to find a lookout point."

He pulled back the bolt on his rifle. "Your behavior was extremely suspicious and I don't believe you for an instant, but right now you two need to follow me down into this cave so we can save the others."

Little Einstein raised the barrel so it was pointing right at our heads. Just perfect, I thought, glancing over at Wang Sichuan. Before we'd been the ones trying to catch the spy; now we were accused of being spies ourselves. "I think we'd better talk this over," I said. "None of us knows what's going on down there. If we rush into things, we're likely to meet with disaster."

"Stop stalling," said Little Einstein. "If they die, you'll pay with your lives."

"They won't die," I said, my voice calm and steady. "I promise you."

Stepping another foot closer, Little Einstein pointed his gun at my heart. "Engineer Wu, the special emissary ordered me to watch you three at all times. Right now I need to go save my comrades. I don't know whether you really are spies, but if you decide to remain up here, out of my sight, then I will have no choice but to kill you."

I was so stunned I was unable to respond. What kind of absurd logic was this?

"As you can see," he continued, "it would be best for everyone if you would simply go down with me."

"Are the special emissary's orders really so important that you would be willing to kill three innocent men?"

"If I am wrong then I will pay for my mistake with my life!"

Little Einstein's eyes twitched. He'd lost all sense of reason. I motioned for Wang Sichuan to stand down. He swore once, clearly unhappy with this turn of events, but quickly complied. I looked at the entrance to the cave. It appeared even gloomier and more frightening than it had before. But there was no turning back. With Little Einstein yelling at me to hurry up, I steeled myself and we climbed down into the darkness. Little Einstein followed close behind, his gun still trained in our direction.

We soon reached the bottom. The underground river was much higher than before, its current far stronger. While this couldn't be considered an outright flood, it would make navigating the river on foot very difficult, not to mention the water was bone-chillingly cold. Little Einstein yelled at us to hurry up. As much as I wanted to resist, I forced myself to do as I was told. Suddenly Wang Sichuan grabbed my arm and pulled me back.

"What are you doing?" I asked him.

"Listen," he said, pointing upriver.

Holding my breath, I listened closely. Sure enough, I could hear voices, the sound almost hidden beneath the roar of the river. Little Einstein immediately began charging toward the voices. After wading against the current for nearly 300 yards, a long slab of rock appeared, rising above the water ahead. On it a campfire blazed, surrounded by standing and sitting shadows.

"Special emissary!" cried Little Einstein as he scrambled up the rock. They all turned in our direction. At a glance I could see things were bad. Nearly everyone seemed to be injured. Some that were lying on the ground weren't moving at all. Then I spotted Yuan Xile. She was kneeling by the fire, changing an injured man's bandages. Seeing me, she swooned. I rushed over and held her up. She threw her arms around me and began to cry.

Astonished, I took in the whole scene. I absolutely could not fathom what had happened to them. Everyone was injured, some on the verge of death. The special emissary was nowhere to be seen. Little Einstein had already begun to search for him. The poor kid was practically out of his mind with shock and anguish. I quickly counted up the people present. Without Little Einstein and the two other soldiers left to watch us, Yuan Xile's team should have numbered 17 in total. Now I saw only seven. I asked Yuan Xile what had happened.

She paused for a moment to collect herself, then told me everything. They'd discovered the cave, climbed inside and begun exploring the upper reaches of the underground river. After they'd traveled some time, the river suddenly began to flood. It was already much too late to make it back to safety. Nine men were instantly swept downriver. Others were slammed violently into the rock walls. They'd suffered the most serious injuries.

Wang Sichuan, Old Tian, and I immediately began checking the wounded. Two were already past the point of help. The responsibility for caring for the wounded had fallen entirely on the shoulders of Yuan Xile and two of her more lightly injured men. The three of them were so exhausted they'd nearly given up hope. They'd eaten practically nothing for the last six days. Yuan Xile had sent a man to the surface to get help, but he had never returned. I doubted things had gone well for him. In fact, I much preferred to imagine that he had simply deserted. Most of the injured had fractured one bone or another. It wasn't possible to haul everyone to the surface. They'd found themselves in truly dire straits—able to do little more than keep the fire going and tend to the wounded. Periodically, though, they'd sent someone up to maintain a smoke signal. Lucky they did, too, as that was what had led us here.

My head spun as I listened to Yuan Xile's story. Their experience had been nearly identical to our own. The main difference was that Old Cat had arrived just in time to rescue us. Had he not, I imagine we would have met a similar fate. This was probably why Old Cat had reacted so quickly upon hearing that a heavy rain was falling on the upper reaches the river. He'd already gone through this very sort of disaster. It was then that I noticed Old Cat wasn't here. He must have been swept downriver.

We boiled several slabs of dried meat. Our comrades devoured them like wild animals. Once they were finished, I told them to get some rest, saying we'd look after the injured. Not five minutes later they were all fast asleep. Little Einstein, however, never took his eyes off of us. This kind of person always makes me shudder. Who are they living for anyway? Themselves or their superiors?

Not until midnight did I finally permit myself to get some rest. It was a far colder sleep than any I'd had on the surface. Waking the next morning, I found myself mulling over memories of the cave, ones I'd long since tried to forget. My heart felt stopped-up, filled with old emotions that had failed to cool.

Climbing to my feet, I saw several of the men with more minor wounds were organizing their equipment. It looked like they were about to set out somewhere.

I hurried closer and asked what they were doing. Little Einstein appeared to be their leader. He responded that they were heading off to search for the men who'd been swept away. This kid is getting much too big for his britches, I said to myself angrily. I told them that since they had no idea what the situation was like downriver, I refused to allow them to proceed. Only when they brusquely ignored my order did I remember I actually had no say around here.

"I thought you needed to keep watch over us?" I asked derisively.

Little Einstein pointed behind me. Turning, I saw an injured soldier watching us from where he laid, his gun placed on the ground beside his pillow. He looked no older than 20. My face went red. Go off and die for all I care, I thought. But as I considered it some more, I realized if some accident should befall them, it would be up to us to come to the rescue. This could turn into a very big hassle indeed. I asked Yuan Xile to back me up and not let them go.

Yuan Xile also seemed to have lost her mind. Not only did she agree with them, she indicated that she would be heading out as well. "Now that you can accompany us, we've got enough manpower to start the search," she said. "Most likely the people downriver are in bad shape. We need to go find them."

Do you have any idea how many people will die if you go ahead with this? I thought. Unfortunately I could only stamp my foot in frustration. Yuan Xile must have thought I was just being a coward.

"Trust me," she said. "I'm certain this is the right decision. In situations like this, it's sometimes necessary to take a few risks. Useless, in all the times we've worked together, haven't you always been able to count on me?"

In that instant I nearly let it all spill out. Only when Wang Sichuan gave me a truly ferocious glare did I decide to keep quiet. He was right though, and in any case this was not the time to tell them. They'd probably just think it was some angry outburst and wouldn't believe a word I said. Helpless to do anything else, I told Yuan Xile that she and her injured men had better just stay there and let Wang Sichuan, Little Einstein and I head downriver ourselves. Only healthy individuals would do for this mission, I told her, otherwise how would they actually rescue the missing men once they found them?

Thanking me for the suggestion, she said that she and her teammates would figure out the best way to handle the matter. From the tone in her voice, I could tell my advice wasn't much appreciated. Little Einstein was now regarding me with near open dislike. I sighed. I never so truly understood the meaning of "casting pearls before swine." The real tragedy for the man who knows everything is that no one will believe him.

What I didn't know at the time was that fate was already governing my every action. In arguing with Yuan Xile and Little Einstein, I had forgotten the most important point: logic and reason would very soon cease to matter. When I think back on all that occurred, I find that Ivan was right after all. When fate decides to show its hand, there's nothing one can do to resist.

56 THE RESCUE

There were no novices among Yuan Xile's men. The standards for placement on the first team were undoubtedly much more stringent than they had been for our second team. Many had probably served with Yuan Xile since they were students. In any case, they clearly didn't think much of us. And now Yuan Xile was acting like the Soviet Witch. She didn't even resemble my Xile.

While we were getting ready I listened to Yuan Xile and some of her injured comrades discuss the probable structure of the cave ahead and how we should proceed. I tried to stay out of it. Their analysis was exhaustive, never-ending, and worthless. None of their conjectures about the geology of this place were going to be of any use when it came to rescuing those men. The times when I did interrupt they ignored me. The last time I tried, Yuan Xile frowned at me, a look of disgust in her eyes. She seemed to think I was being very unprofessional. I was so mad I could barely breathe. Before I could respond, Wang Sichuan took me aside.

"Right now these people aren't going to listen to us," he said. "Let them make a few mistakes and suffer the consequences. Then they'll see who really knows what they're talking about."

When our preparations were complete we set off downriver. At first the water rose no higher than our thighs, but the farther we went, the deeper it became. Soon it was over our heads. The current was moving dangerously fast. Yuan Xile ordered us to rope ourselves together and carry on. The woman was hell-bent on finding those men. Unfortunately, she had no idea of what was in store. I did. This cave was shaped like a water hyacinth, with a reservoir-like water cavity at the back where we'd found the giant iron door. The river would continue to rise until it reached a positively terrifying depth and that cavity was full. Those nine men had most likely been swept all the way to the water dungeon. There, thanks to the area's great height and many rocks, they should have been able to escape the current. I was sure we'd find them there—so long as they hadn't already drowned. Thus, given the current height of the river, we'd never be able to reach them on foot. Right now we were just wasting our time.

After we'd traveled another 50 or so feet downriver, the current really picked up. It was moving so fast we had to hold onto the rock walls. Yuan Xile had always been a stubborn woman and she kept pushing on. After only a few feet, the current picked her up, rushing her deeper into the cave. We dragged her back by the rope around her waist.

"We'd better turn back," I said. "It's too dangerous to keep going right now."

Just when she seemed about to listen, Little Einstein hauled himself out of the water and began climbing the rock wall, a look of crazed determination in his eyes. Glancing back, he waved for us to follow.

"This is no time to show off!" I yelled up to him. "You won't be able to make it!"

Wiping the water from his face, he waved again for us to follow. He was upset and acting irrationally.

"Forget it, Little Einstein!" cried Yuan Xile. "We need to head back and think of a new plan."

The kid just untied the rope around his waist and continued climbing deeper into the cave. Gritting my teeth, I cursed the poor bastard. Then I undid my rope and begin scaling the cave wall.

"What are you doing?" asked Yuan Xile.

"I'm going to bring him back."

"It's too dangerous!" shouted Wang Sichuan. "You're still not completely healed! Let him go. If he wants to die there's nothing we can do."

I disagreed. The kid might be a punk, but his life was still worth saving. Also, this wasn't where he was meant to die.

"Useless, are you sure you're all right?" called Yuan Xile, her voice hesitant, her hands tightly gripping the rock.

"What if I'm not? Who's gonna go get him? You?"

Her eyes went wide. This one must have really ticked her off. I'll bet she never imagined I could be this impudent.

"You start hauling them up the river!" I called to Wang Sichuan. "Once they're safe and sound, come back here and wait for me."

One of Yuan Xile's men yelled at me. "Useless, since when are you the one giving orders around here? This is still Yuan Xile's mission!"

Idiot, I thought, do you want to save Little Einstein are not? Rather than respond, I merely wiped the water from my face, signaled to Wang Sichuan and then continued scaling the wall.

The man's voice grew sterner. "Useless!" he yelled as Wang Sichuan began dragging him and the others upriver. "You are in serious violation of military code! Headquarters will be hearing about this! I'm going to make sure you are demoted!"

But I could tell from the man's face he'd long since fallen apart.

After climbing some distance along the wall, I came upon Little Einstein. He was 10 feet below me, his lower half submerged in the river, his fingers curled around a crack in the rock. He must have slipped. Seeing me, his face went red and he desperately tried to scramble up the wall. He immediately slid back down. I could tell he hated for me to see him like this. For an instant I was seized with the desire to kick this fool into the river, then head back and tell them I'd been too late. But I saw how young he looked, clinging stubbornly to the wall. I, too, had once been young and believed that nothing could hurt me.

I climbed onto a solid-looking ledge jutting several feet above him and reached out my arm. For a moment he hesitated, but then he grabbed on. Once I'd pulled him onto the ledge, I motioned upriver, yelling, "Go back now!"

He turned and began climbing deeper into the cave.

I'd known more than a few headstrong people in my day, but I'd never met anyone like this. I tried to pull him back, but he swatted my hand away and with that my patience reached its limit. Grabbing him with both arms, I refused to let go. He glared at me, his eyes blood-red, and made to push me off the ledge. I was too fast for him. I smacked him across the face, grabbed his hair and slammed his head against the rock wall behind us. In my anger, I used a little more force than perhaps was necessary. Little Einstein was immediately knocked out and toppled forward into the water below. I reached out and grabbed onto him, but the current wouldn't let go. Shit, I thought. That was reckless and now I'm going to pay for it. Then, from behind me, I heard Wang Sichuan's voice.

"Nice one!" he yelled. "I've wanted to smack that little bastard forever!"

I looked back. Yuan Xile and her men were all there. They were staring at me, their eyes wide and their mouths open. "My hand slipped!" I cried. "Come on! Don't just stand there. He's about to be swept away!"

Wang Sichuan tossed me the rope. I fastened it around Little Einstein's body then tied it round my own. Then I hopped into the water and yelled for them to start moving. We all pulled ourselves along the wall, fighting the freezing current for every inch. After no more than a dozen paces, I heard an odd noise upriver. The sound was barely audible above the roar of the water, but I could tell it was coming terrifyingly fast. Suddenly, it dawned on me.

"Everyone look out!" I cried.

With a crash, an enormous tree trunk came into view, rocketing down the river. It sailed towards us, ricocheting from one side of the cave to the other. Then, in the blink of an eye, we were all knocked from the wall and rushed uncontrollably into the darkness.

By the time I got my head above the surface, I was already 30 yards downriver. I coughed water. The rope dragged me under. I unclipped it and floated back up. Wang Sichuan and several others were even farther downriver, holding onto the tree as it rushed along. Wang Sichuan waved for me to swim closer. I ignored him and turned to look for Yuan Xile. She was above water, albeit some distance downriver.

"What do we do now?" she called out to me.

Panting heavily, I spat out a lung-full of water. "Swim for the sides!" I knew there was wire netting hidden on the bottom of the river. The water was high enough that we probably wouldn't get stuck, but if we did, the consequences could be deadly.

Every second we were being washed deeper into the cave. Soon we'd reach the rock-strewn rapids. That was not something I was looking forward to. The experience, I imagined, would feel something like being run through a cheese grater. Maybe the water was high enough and some of us might escape with only slight injuries. Not everyone would be so lucky, though. I thought about climbing atop the tree trunk. We might be able to ride over some of these underwater dangers. And should the thing itself become stuck, we could wait on top for the flood to be over. But there was simply not enough room for all of us. Our weight would sink the tree. Even more than all this, though, I worried about the 30-foot waterfall somewhere up ahead. I had seen the iron wire strung all the way down its length. Get caught on that and the results would not be pretty. Even if we were lucky enough to get by, we'd still have a long drop ahead of us.

No matter what, we needed to stop ourselves before we hit the falls.

57 FUTILITY

You can never understand what we were up against. Our strength was no match for the current. We had to just save our energy and remain calm. I did my best to float toward the side of the cave and shone my flashlight downriver. Up ahead the river was turning, and at the turn the current seemed to slow, albeit slightly.

"Get to the wall!" I cried. "When we hit this turn everyone needs to be holding on!"

Everyone immediately began swimming hard for the side. I could see at once there were too many of them.

"All of you need to spread out!" I yelled. "Make sure you don't knock into the person in front of you!"

Yuan Xile suddenly cried out in alarm. Spinning around, I watched as she paused for a moment then all of a sudden disappeared beneath the water. She resurfaced a second later, still in the very spot she'd been before while I'd already been rushed past her. I cursed beneath my breath. She'd gotten herself caught on the iron wire.

I swam to the side at once, grabbed onto the rocks and, with all my strength, attempted to hold on. The wall was too slick. In a flash I was swept nearly 20 feet downriver, fingernails scraping rock the whole way. By the time I finally found a handhold, my nails were bloody and torn. The river kept rushing by, pulling my body horizontal. Pressing myself closer to the wall, I looked up to see Yuan Xile struggling vainly against the iron trap.

"Don't fight it!" I yelled to her. If she kept moving, she'd only become more tangled. I jammed the flashlight in my mouth and crawled towards her along the wall, my legs trailing uselessly behind me. By the time I reached her I was completely exhausted. She was pressed against the wall, her legs so tangled she could barely keep her head above the surface. The river was rising fast.

Panting heavily, I took the flashlight from my mouth. "I'm going to dive underwater and untangle you," I said. "While I'm doing that, you need to hold on tight. If you let go of the wall, you're going to be pulled under. Do you understand?"

She nodded, her face white with fear. I took a deep breath and dove, my arms wrapped tightly around her waist. Little by little, I climbed down her body. Her clothes were blown open in the current. As I felt her slender waist and smooth skin, memories of days gone by flooded my mind. Smiling grimly, I continued downward until I reached her calves. The iron wire was wound tightly around her pant leg. I tried to pull it loose, but army pants were damn strong. Reaching for her waist belt, I unsheathed her dagger and slashed open the fabric. The cut wasn't particularly large, but the force of the water immediately ripped it wide open. In the blink of an eye she was free and the two of us were being rushed downriver.

We held one another as the current swept us along, Yuan Xile in a panic and I doing everything in my power to keep us level and our heads above water. With one arm wrapped around her waist, I tossed away the dagger and tried to remain calm. The turn was just ahead and coming up fast. My heart skipped a beat. We needed to get to the side immediately, but Yuan Xile still hadn't come to her senses.

Suddenly, several flashlight beams hit us from downriver. I heard someone call out, "Over here!"

"Little Einstein!" I yelled. I raised Yuan Xile out of the water and pushed her as hard as I could toward the side.

In a flash, Little Einstein leapt off the rock and grabbed her arm, his other hand gripping a leather strap held by the men on the wall behind him. With a roar, he pulled her towards him as the current tried to force them both downriver. The strap held, and a moment later they were dragged back to the wall.

That little son of a gun proved useful after all, I thought. Before I could catch my breath, I was swept abruptly around the turn. Using my final bit of strength, I reached frantically for the wall, managing at last to grab a protruding rock with the tips of my fingers. The current blasted against me, threatening to tear my arm from my body and hurl me into the darkness. I howled and held fast. The pressure decreased and I was able to steady myself, both hands on the wall and my legs once more beneath me.

Nice work, I thought, panting heavily. Suddenly I heard a strange sound coming from upriver. In an instant our flashlights all swiveled to the sound. I could hear my heart heaving in my chest.

"Everyone! Get underwater and hold on tight!" Wang Sichuan yelled.

A 12-foot high wall of water tumbled toward us, huge and inescapable, filling the narrow channel. There must have been a collapse somewhere upriver. I plastered myself to the wall and dove underwater. Even then I knew nothing I did would be of any use. In a flash the wave was on top of me, tearing me from the wall and hurtling me downriver. It felt like getting hit with a fire hose blast at close range. The last thing I saw was Wang Sichuan and Yuan Xile being ripped from the wall and flung into the wild, white-capped current.

***

When I finally staggered from the water onto relatively dry land, I found that I had run aground on a rocky shoal. Although my flashlight was long gone, I saw a beam nearby, illuminating a small patch of ground. Wiping the water from my face, I walked over. Wang Sichuan was laying face down, his flashlight tightly in hand. I rolled him over. His skin was pale and he wasn't breathing. I immediately began pumping hard on his belly, trying to force the water from his lungs. Then I rolled him over so there was a rock beneath his stomach and clapped him several times on the back. In a fit of coughing he came to. I went to look for other survivors, but there was no one else.

Just downriver was the water dungeon. My earlier prediction had been pretty spot-on, but the river was much higher than I'd imagined. The shoal was now mostly covered by churning rapids. We sat on an island-like strip in the middle of the river. Yuan Xile and her men must have been swept much deeper into the cave.

I pulled Wang Sichuan all the way out of the water. Then I sat and considered our predicament. We didn't have many choices left. Large, jagged rocks awaited us if we headed deeper into the cave. Our missing comrades probably wouldn't be able to stop until they reached the cement platform where we'd found the sinkhole. Not only was it built high enough to avoid the flood, it was also where we, as the second team, would later find the first team's tents and equipment. There seemed no way for us to get there. Still, I couldn't help but wonder whether the river just might be navigable. I strolled to the edge and tested the current.

Just as I placed my foot in the water, I heard Wang Sichuan call out behind me, "Give it up, man!"

I turned.

He climbed to his feet, coughed several times, then continued. "You won't be able to change anything! Their fate has already been decided. There's nothing you can do."

I was well aware that if I continued I was essentially signing my own death warrant. I just didn't want to believe it. "We must be able to do something," I persisted.

"These people are already history—our history. If you change a part of that, then something with us has to change as well. But nothing has changed. If you jump in the river, you'll just die here. You'll disappear without having accomplished a thing."

"But—!"

"To us they're already dead!" he cried. "If we are to arrive here later, then all of this must happen. There's nothing we can do."

As I stared at the dark and rushing river, I couldn't deny that he was right.

"If you leave things as they are, then Yuan Xile will not die here and you may see her again someday. But if you jump into that river, then you will never have another chance."

I sat down beside the water and stared off into the darkness, feeling utterly dejected. Gradually, listening to the roar of the river, I lost consciousness.

58 WHAT WILL BE WILL BE

Wang Sichuan was right. Yuan Xile and her men had gone to meet their fate. Although for them the future was a mystery, we knew exactly what was going to happen, and knew, moreover, that it had to happen this way. Yet my heart still couldn't bear the thought of Yuan Xile stumbling alone through that pitch-black cave. Going after her would be an all-or-nothing gamble. We'd won the first round. If we continued to play, we might win far more, but we could just as easily lose it all.

By the time the water level finally began to drop, 24 hours had passed. Anguished and not knowing what else to do, I walked a short ways downriver. There was nothing to see—no corpses, no people, not even the smallest sign of anyone having passed through. The water cavity emptied rapidly. Before long the river was so low we'd need to scale the walls if we wanted to continue on. Taking my arm, Wang Sichuan motioned that it was time for us to go. At last I relented. Even if I was able to climb to the next cave, who knew what would be waiting for me on the other side?

Old Tian had been among those swept away. I wasn't concerned that his past and future selves might accidentally meet. It hadn't happened before, so it shouldn't happen this time through either. Most likely he had simply drowned and would never be discovered. There was nothing left for us to do. So Wang Sichuan and I locked arms and slowly made our way back to the surface. I had been utterly defeated.

***

When at last we were topside once more, Wang Sichuan quickly organized our food and water. He said we needed to get a move on. I stared into the silent mouth of the cave, my mind on Yuan Xile. I knew that to leave here was equivalent to leaving her, and that once I was gone I would most likely never see her again. It was unbearable. I decided then that I had to stay and help her, even if it meant my death. My head kept trying to talk me out of this, but my heart was a weight pulling my body into the cave and I could not hold it back.

Wang Sichuan did all he could to change my mind, but finally, his preparations complete, he strapped on his bag and stood before me. I knew this was my last chance. He was fundamentally opposed to staying here and dying alongside me. If I wanted us to remain together, I had but one choice.

Seeing that I was beginning to waver, Wang Sichuan let out a deep breath. "What will be will be," he said. "You cannot change fate."

Sighing, I nodded my head. Then I suddenly realized something was amiss. "What did you just say?" I asked him.

"What will be will be," he said, looking at me strangely.

A chill ran down my spine.

"What is it?" he asked.

"How did you know this sentence? Where did you see it?"

"I never saw it anywhere. I just made it up. Why? What's wrong?"

What will be will be. I remembered the safe room, how Yuan Xile had shown me a single sentence carved on one of the walls within. An impossible idea occurred to me. Why had she needed to show me that strange sentence? For what reason had it been carved there? Who had done the carving? I remembered what the fake He Ruping had said when he heard my voice: "How can it be you again?" He had fairly screamed it at me, his face frozen in pain. At the time his reaction felt extremely strange, but then what if...?

It all suddenly made sense. By the time I was able to respond my whole body was soaked with sweat and my hands were shaking.

"What the hell is going on?" asked Wang Sichuan.

Taking a deep breath, I replied, "I have to go back into the cave."

I was a part of Yuan Xile's history. I knew that now. My fate had been decreed. The reason the fake He Ruping was so frightened of me was because we'd met before. And Yuan Xile had undoubtedly shown the mysterious sentence to me as a kind of clue, a clue that I myself had planted so that as soon as I heard Wang Sichuan speak those five words, I would instantly understand what I had to do. This was my way of telling myself that this thing was not over for me, that I needed to go back underground and find Yuan Xile.

From the moment we'd first entered the cave, it had seemed as if some force was pushing us along, making sure things happened a certain way. More than a few times I'd found myself gazing off into the darkness, convinced someone was looking back at me. Someone had placed those two notes in my pocket. Someone had lowered the caisson when we were all inside. Someone had even loosened the air vent in the projection room, allowing us to escape to the sealed tunnel where the grate had also been loosened. What if Yuan Xile wasn't really crazy? What if, knowing everything that was going to happen, she'd merely acted that way? Could this be why she'd behaved so affectionately towards me, why she'd curled up on my chest?

I could wait no longer. Enough time had been wasted. I needed to get going now. It might already be too late. I told Wang Sichuan what I was thinking.

He shook his head. "That's impossible," he said. "It's probably just a coincidence."

No way, I thought, my mind flashing back to the five words carved into the wall. "It's all right," I said, "you should go. This is just something I have to do. Some risks you have no choice but to take." If my theory was right and I didn't go, then I couldn't even begin to imagine what might happen to Wang Sichuan and I. It was truly ironic. The very reason that had stopped me from interfering now compelled me to involve myself. I couldn't help but laugh.

"It's too dangerous for you to head down there alone," said Wang Sichuan.

"I'll go with you. It's clear Tengri has destined that we do this thing together."

I thought about it for a moment, but then shook my head. "There's no reason for you to go back inside. And I never saw any sign that you did." If Yuan Xile and I had planned this whole thing out, we must have done it in private. "No, this is my thing."

He didn't argue. I didn't blame him. Were it not for Yuan Xile, I wouldn't have even wanted to stand near that black hole. As soon as I was out I would have kept on going and never looked back. "All of this was already decided," I said to him, strapping on my pack. "What will be will be. There's nothing else I can do."

Our eyes met for a moment, then Wang Sichuan sighed and patted me on the shoulder. "Take care of yourself in there," he said.

My heart filled and trembled. Over the past few months I'd learned Wang Sichuan was truly a man you could trust. If I somehow lived to see him again, I knew we'd be friends for life. Then Wang Sichuan turned and headed south. I reentered the cave. My mind was unusually calm. When you know what you must do, there's really nothing else to think about.

I carefully navigated the steep descent and dropped to the cave floor. The water level was already at its lowest point. I thought back on the previous two times I'd been here and how I was now all alone. Each time I'd left the cave I'd sworn never to return, and yet I was always forced back under increasingly dangerous circumstances. This was fate. As I walked through the blackness, I remembered how Ivan had said Fate sometimes felt so near you could almost reach out and touch it.

Had he lived to see this day, I'm sure he would have found that not only could Fate be touched, in certain situations it could slap you right back.

59 THE FINAL JOURNEY

With a grim smile I organized my belongings, braced myself for the dangers ahead, then began following the river, its waters now shallow and calm, into the depths of the cave. Journeying along the underground river alone was a terrifying experience. Many times I imagined indistinct figures were menacing me from the blackness. I followed the river, going where it went, avoiding where it did not.

Two days later I reached the water cavity. The last time I was here we'd found an iron door buried beneath the rocky ground. The water had risen and we'd fled for our lives, only to be rescued by Old Cat and taken down a branching channel located at the top of the cavern. The cavity itself was just as I remembered it—a giant, underground pit. Before long I found the rock we'd climbed to escape the water. I scaled it, lit a fire and rested for the first time since I'd reentered the cave.

Even though I hadn't slept in two days, I found myself unable to do so now. I worried about catching up with the others. By this time anything could have happened. Memories of what we'd experienced here flashed through my mind, one vivid scene after another. I wondered whether Yuan Xile really had been feigning madness the whole time. Having never met a crazy person before, I couldn't say for sure. Classical Chinese novels were filled with characters biding their time, pretending to be mad, only to drop the charade when the moment was right. That sentence carved on the wall was definitely a clue, one someone had told her to show me. But if she wasn't mad, then why, once we were alone in the safe room, hadn't she stopped pretending and told me the whole story? Maybe she'd been afraid I wouldn't believe her. Indeed I can well imagine what I would have thought of all this at the time: utter nonsense, no different than "ghosts in the shadows."

Then again, maybe she really had been crazy, and it was luck alone that made her remember to pass along this piece of information. Either way, there was no goddamn point in mulling over this stuff now. For me it was all in the past, or should I say the future. I would have to wait and discover the truth for myself.

All the same, though, I did hope she hadn't been crazy. So saying a silent prayer, I fell into a fitful sleep.

Upon waking, I climbed the rock wall until I reached the high channel and then continued on. The water level had dropped below my knees. Many things once hidden were now revealed. There was the wrecked fighter plane we'd found at the bottom of the river. Its rusted exterior and the track upon which it sat were both clearly visible, but I did not pause to inspect them.

Soon after I reached the cement platform where we'd found the generator hidden in the sinkhole. Tents had been set up on the platform and a campfire was burning.

I kept my distance. This really was where the survivors from Yuan Xile's team had washed up. I considered how best to make my appearance. Should I watch them covertly from afar or step right up and say hello? If I was to convince Yuan Xile to dispense that clue for me, I needed to gain her trust. But thinking of the corpses of her men scattered throughout these caves and the gunshot wounds in the young soldier, I feared whatever came next would not be so simple. There was still the matter of the spy. Until I discovered his identity, revealing myself didn't seem wise.

I had no choice but to lie in wait and see what happened. It didn't take long for me to realize that no one was at the camp. The area illuminated by the firelight seemed deserted. In fact the fire itself had mostly died down. Something was definitely wrong there.

Cautiously, I slipped underwater, then swam for the base of the platform. There I waited, listening for movement, but heard not a sound. Even if they were all asleep, it still shouldn't be so quiet. I crept into camp and looked around. The place was completely empty. No one was sleeping inside the tents, no one was standing guard outside. They were all gone. The fire was still warm, so I sat down beside it, lit a cigarette and began to think. After spending a night there to regain their strength, Yuan Xile and her team must have continued deeper into the cave. Their camp looked just as it had when we found it before. Once they'd left this place, they never returned.

Finishing my cigarette, I tossed it in the fire. Then I stood and went to investigate the sinkhole. That's where I discovered their ropes, anchored securely and dropping away into the darkness. Heading this direction, the distance to the dam was extremely short. Things were coming to a head. No longer could I simply react to what was going on around me. Instead, I needed to take a moment and carefully consider my next move. Sitting back down beside the fire, I found myself unconsciously reaching inside my pocket. This time, however, no secret note awaited me. Laughing bitterly to myself, I pulled out some of the meat Wang Sichuan had given me and boiled a pot of water to soften it.

What should I do once I found them? By then, who knew what would be happening? Maybe I would need to save them again.

First of all, I needed to do everything I could to make contact with Yuan Xile while no one else was around. If I was discovered by the rest of the team, I'd once more be required to obey the special emissary. I might even be placed under supervision again. Given the size of the dam, I knew they'd be extremely difficult to locate once inside. I tried to think of somewhere they'd be sure to go, somewhere I could delay them long enough to speak with Yuan Xile alone. Only one place came to mind: the poisoned passageways.

Before long I'd come up with a rough plan, as well as several places I'd need to visit. Then I organized my belongings, rolled up my pants, and climbed down into the sinkhole. My progress was quick. We'd had some trouble here before, but this time I found the tunnels easy to navigate, the leeches eminently avoidable. Once I made it to the cliff at the tunnel's end, I leapt into the mighty River Zero below. The current had slowed considerably and I smoothly made my way to the chain-link barriers. Standing there, taking in that old familiar darkness around me, I knew for certain that I was back.

I switched on my flashlight and used a strip of clothing to dim the beam. The Shinzan looked nothing like it had three months ago. The acidity of the underground river had already heavily corroded the plane's exterior. My surroundings were still pitch-black. The power was still off. No matter. I was already much too familiar with the place; I didn't need lights to show me the way. I could see no hint of a campfire. They had to be inside already. I mentally rehearsed my route into the dam's interior. I needed to get to the ready room outside the iron chamber and take one of the hanging hazmat suits.

I climbed the rickety ladder to the top of the dam. None of the searchlights were on. The place was blanketed in darkness. I couldn't see the abyss, but that somehow made it even more frightening. I gazed into the emptiness and couldn't help but wonder: Just what sort of force was hidden inside that void?

Walking along the dam's edge, I quickly found the ladder we'd descended before. Last time one of the rungs had broken beneath the deputy squad leader. I couldn't remember which rung it had been, nor could I tell if any were weak. I steeled myself against the fierce wind and carefully climbed down. This descent was without incident and I soon made it to the ready room. Hazmat suits hung on one of the walls, just as I remembered, but two of the hooks were empty. Someone had arrived before me.

The spy.

He must have snuck inside and taken a suit for himself. Could there be two spies? I wondered. That was impossible. Besides Old Cat, every member of the first prospecting team had either died or gone mad. The spy must have simply taken an extra one for himself, just in case.

I stuffed a suit in my bag and headed for the door. As soon as I crossed the threshold I suddenly felt uneasy. Who knew what was going to happen? I turned back and grabbed another. As I was strapping on my pack, a low, ominous sound abruptly emerged from the depths of the dam. Before long it had spread throughout the entire structure, now emanating from the very walls around me. The lights began to flicker. For a moment I was stunned. Someone must have switched on the power. As the sound grew louder, I watched one searchlight after another light up, their beams shooting into the abyss. Some of them flashed on for only an instant before going out. Others flickered momentarily and then stabilized. At first I felt only relief. Having the lights on couldn't help but make my job easier.

A moment later I grasped what was really going on. Shit, I thought, the prospecting team would never have known how to find the central generator, nor would they have risked searching for it.

This was the work of the spy. He was about to strike.

I hurriedly climbed back atop the dam. Nearly all the lights were now on. The place had returned to life, but I knew behind this facade lay a deadly trap. There was no time to waste.

I pulled out my pistol, an old TT-33. I quickly checked the ammunition, then began sprinting toward the projection room.

60 GHOSTS OF THE PAST

Where was the master switch that controlled the dam's electricity? I remembered a long, rectangular room about the size of a basketball court, filled with all manner of machinery—the control room. Last time we were there, we discovered evidence that someone had arrived before us and had operated the equipment. Everything was falling into place. Seeing that the spy had grabbed a pair of hazmat suits and switched on the power, it was clear he'd already trapped Yuan Xile and the others within the poisoned passageways. All the spy had to do now was turn on the lights and wait until they dropped, one by one. Any that did not succumb to the gas could be easily mopped up in person.

There was no time to waste. In fact, time might already be up.

Running as fast as I could, I soon reached the electrical canal. I took several deep breaths to slow my racing heartbeat, then cautiously crawled forward. At last I was above the control room. I could see the beam of a flashlight below, but its user was hidden by the darkness. All I could hear were his footsteps. I hesitated. Should I take him out right now? What would happen if I killed him? The spy was not meant to die here—that I knew.

And yet, if I only did what I was "meant" to do, then there was nothing I could do. Or, if everything was predetermined, then no matter what I did, were my actions not predetermined as well?

I took a deep breath and slid out of the ventilation shaft. For an instant I was blinded by the flashlight. Then I saw a hazmat suit. I raised my pistol and I fired. Three rounds burst from the barrel of my gun. A moment later the man crumpled to the floor. He fell on his flashlight and the room went black.

Although I'd undergone extensive weapons training, this was the first time I'd ever used a gun in the field. I found myself unable to fire another shot. Switching on my flashlight, I stepped to the fallen figure. He was splayed out on the floor, his chest red with blood and his breathing ragged. One of his hands was reaching for the strap to his assault rifle. For an instant I paused at the sight of the blood, but I summoned my courage and walked closer. Kicking away his hand, I grabbed the assault rifle and slung it over my shoulder.

Shining my light in his eyes, I tore off his face mask and yelled, "Now let's see who you really are!"

It was the special emissary. Holding his wounds, he looked at me in disbelief.

"So it was you," I said, smiling coldly.

"Useless!" Su Zhenhua cried. "What the hell are you doing here? How did you know about this place?"

"Heaven sent me," I said. But then I heard a sudden rush of air and something slammed into the back of my skull. My vision immediately went black. For an instant I lost consciousness.

When I came back in seconds, I was falling forward onto the special emissary. I tried to stand, but he held me down. I was struck again across the back of the head. In a daze, I felt someone pull me off the special emissary and toss me to the side. A moment later my gun was gone, snatched from my hands. Doing my best to keep from fainting, I slowly raised myself off the floor. My vision returned and I found myself looking down the barrel of a gun. The special emissary was still off to the side, holding his wounds and staggering to his feet. What the hell? There were two of them? Cursing beneath my breath, I looked up at the second person. My mouth dropped open.

It was Yuan Xile. She was aiming a gun right at my head.

"You?" I was so surprised I could say nothing else. The whole world seemed to come crashing down around me.

Yuan Xile regarded me coldly, then turned to the special emissary. "You all right?" she asked.

The special emissary nodded and walked over to her. Then, looking straight at me, he said, "Kill him."

Yuan Xile shook her head. "Not yet. First I need to ask him a few questions. This guy knows far too much about us and I'm going to find out how." She passed him the assault rifle. "Go do what needs to be done."

The special emissary gave me a murderous look, but I could tell he agreed with Yuan Xile. He removed his hazmat suit. Only one of my shots had hit, and only in his shoulder. It seemed I hadn't been as accurate as I'd imagined. Gritting his teeth, the special emissary tore off a strip of clothing and placed it over his wound. Then he took one of the hazmat suits from my bag, put it on and headed for the door, gun slung over his shoulder.

Just before crossing the threshold, he paused and looked back at Yuan Xile. "You'd better be quick about this."

Yuan Xile nodded and watched him leave. She turned back to me. "All right. Out with it. Who the hell are you? How do you know so much about me?"

I looked at her, wondering what I was supposed to do now. I knew I needed to escape, but I found it impossible to think of a plan. I found that I didn't even want to try. I simply could not understand what I was seeing. What was going on? This was clearly wrong. This was not how things were supposed to be. I had returned to save Yuan Xile. That had been the plan. I was going to sabotage the spy and protect the girl and make sure she survived all this so one day we'd meet again. I refused to believe Yuan Xile was a spy.

How was this even possible? I thought back on everything that had happened. Had all of this been a trap? Scene after scene flashed through my mind like sparks of electricity. Though I didn't want to believe it, I knew that what I was seeing was far from impossible. Only two members of the first team had survived down here: Yuan Xile and the special emissary. Could this really have been just a coincidence? No. By the time we found Yuan Xile in the cave, she already knew I was going to travel back in time. So she set a trap, one that would make this idiot think he was some "hero of love" ready to sacrifice his life so she'd have the opportunity to use me all over again. Everything she'd done—staying with me in the safe room, sleeping on my chest, saving me from our so-called enemy, even giving herself to me—all of it had been a lie, perpetrated for her own benefit, to make sure I'd protect her in the cave after I went back in time.

Was this what had really happened? I had to admit she'd done a damn good job of escaping suspicion. By the time we'd taken off, she'd already been transported to the surface and, as far as I knew, had never been investigated in the least. No one had ever doubted her madness.

What a fool I'd been. How could I have ever believed a woman like Yuan Xile could fall for a guy like me? It was just as that doctor had said; there was nothing about me that could have drawn her in. And it wasn't as if I could ask her about it now, for the person standing before me was not the Yuan Xile I'd once known, but a merciless enemy agent, through and through.

All my hope was gone. All I could do was stare at her in silence.

Her eyes narrowed. "Don't think you can just play dumb and everything will be all right. You know who we are, so you must know what we're willing to do. My time is limited. If you don't want to suffer, you'd better speak up."

I took a deep breath and continued to stare at her. What was I supposed to say now? That I was a man from the future? That you had seduced me into returning here only to help fulfill your plans? Even in my head it sounded ridiculous. So I just stared at her, saying nothing.

Yuan Xile seemed to grow a little uncomfortable. Frowning, she sat down on the floor and studied me. "I've dealt with more than a few people like you in my time," she said. "Usually, the silent treatment means either the person is trying to look like a hero or thinking of a way to kill me. But with you it's different. It's like you can't even be bothered. This I've never seen before." She abruptly lowered her gun and pointed at the door. "Get out of here."

It was obvious what she was doing. She wanted me to think I had a chance to survive. I knew as soon as I made a break for it, she'd raise her weapon and yell for me to stop. When a man knows his death is imminent, he abandons all hope and all threats are useless against him. She hoped to rekindle my instinct for survival, break my calm and pull my weaknesses into the light.

Yuan Xile looked at me, then looked back at the open door. Still I did not move. Sure, I saw through her little trap, but that wasn't why I remained seated. There was simply nowhere I wanted to go. I sat back and leaned the back of my head against the wall, consumed by the blackest despair. What should I do? What did I want to do? It had all been a farce. My actions meant nothing. I was a fool, and had been utterly, utterly duped.

Finally, Yuan Xile could take the silence no longer. "My friend will be back soon. If you don't leave now you'll never get another chance."

I looked up at her. "Do me a favor and keep your opinions to yourself. If I want to stay somewhere I'll stay there."

She raised her eyebrows at me. I was gripped by a sudden impulse. I climbed to my feet and began to walk towards her. Her eyes went wide. As she raised her gun and stepped backwards, I ran at her. Although surprised, Yuan Xile was obviously well trained. Her bullet caught me on the left shoulder. I staggered, but felt no pain, and then I was on her. Grabbing her gun hand, I forced it to the side. I pressed her up against the wall and kissed her.

It was several seconds before she could react. She shoved me off. The look on her face was somewhere between fear and amazement. She continued backing away, her hair wild and the barrel of her gun pointing at my chest. Her finger trembled. By now my shoulder was really beginning to hurt, but though I winced with pain, I kept my eyes fixed squarely on her. I thought of the kiss, of the familiar fragrance of her body. I wanted her to shoot me in the heart and be done with it. At last I slumped to the floor, trying to catch my breath. Never for a moment did my eyes leave her face. I want you to remember me, I thought, as our eyes met. I want you to remember how I was different from all of the others.

She looked down at me in disbelief, her chest heaving. "You goddamned lunatic!" she panted. "I'll kill you! I'll fucking kill you!"

I closed my eyes. I heard her cock the pistol. My breathing slowed and I went quiet as I awaited that final moment. Come on, I thought, just do it. Don't make me wait too long. In my mind's eye I reentered the cave as if for the first time, undergoing all of its dangers—the rising water, the poisoned passageways, the iron chamber. I remembered our flight into the abyss, our crash landing and my miraculous survival. Finally, I recalled those days and nights Yuan Xile and I had spent together, alone in the dark, but this I could not take. This, at last, was too much for me, and I wished to hear that telltale crack and leave this world behind.

I waited for a long time. In the end, I heard nothing. I raised my head and opened my eyes. She was still looking at me, still pointing her gun at my heart, but her expression was strange. She walked to the corner, grabbed a large wooden club and struck me over the head as hard as she could. I crumpled to the floor.

Lights out.

61 FORCED CONFESSION

The cold brought me back. I was tied to the leg of an iron desk. Water dripped from my face. I was still in the control room. Yuan Xile was standing nearby. The special emissary was standing over me, splashing me with water from his canteen. I had no desire to look at him. I ignored the spray and glanced over at Yuan Xile. She'd fixed her hair and her face was once more coldly professional. It seemed I'd been out for a long time. I wondered whether the special emissary had managed to complete his bloody business. I cursed beneath my breath. Not only had I failed to change the past, I'd gotten myself caught up in it as well.

"How could you have made such a mistake?" asked Yuan Xile angrily.

"There wasn't enough time," the special emissary replied. "I did turn the lights on a bit too early, but I was early only because they were moving much slower than planned. They were no farther than the outskirts when they realized what was going on, so they were able to escape back through the projection room before the worst of it began. So yes, they got out, but it doesn't matter and you don't need to worry. They've already inhaled too much of that stuff to survive much longer. And anyway, we have bigger concerns at the moment. Something isn't right here." He took my face in his hands. "So then," he said, looking right at me. "How many of you are there?" He slapped me so hard I saw stars. "Answer me! How many of you fuckers are there?"

In fact, his question caught me by surprise. I didn't quite understand what he was getting at. But if I wasn't going to answer Yuan Xile, then I definitely wasn't going to answer him. I just stared straight ahead, my eyes coldly meeting his gaze.

"You're wasting your time," said Yuan Xile. "This guy's out of his mind."

Keeping his cool, the special emissary turned to her. "You're positive he's not a Chinese agent?"

"Yes. We often worked together in the past. I can assure you he's received no kind of special training. He is simply not the sort of man who is tapped to do espionage work. Just now he had a chance to escape, but he..." She trailed off and looked at the door. "Suffice it to say that if he were really an agent, he'd already be long gone."

The special emissary smiled mirthlessly. "I think it's all an act." He grabbed his bag and dug something out.

"If it is, then why didn't he escape? The point of acting crazy is to get away, not to get oneself killed." She crossed her arms and looked at me. "This guy gives me a very strange feeling. He clearly knows far more than he should, but no way is he an agent."

"Then how'd he know about our plans?" The special emissary let the bag drop. I saw the gleam of a dagger in his hand. "You were there when he nearly killed me just now. This guy's a specialist and he's not alone. As for why he let you live, I think that's obvious. The poor bastard's fallen in love with you."

Yuan Xile turned away. "What kind of specialist would fall in love?"

There was a hint of embarrassment in her voice, but that was the least of my concerns. He's not alone? What's he talking about?

The special emissary sat down on a chair in front of me and cleaned his dagger with a bottle of baijiu. Then, without preamble, he dug the blade into his shoulder and pried out a bullet. The look on his face never changed. He didn't even blink. One got the impression he hadn't felt the slightest bit of pain. The special emissary raised his head and smiled at me. "I wanted you to get a good look at my methods." He tossed the bloody bullet away, poured baijiu on the wound, wiped it clean, and covered it with a piece of fabric.

Then he walked towards me, slowly waving the dagger back and forth. "It's time for you to start talking. If you don't, I'm going to do things to you that will make even Yuan Xile turn away. You might think you're pretty tough now, but I guarantee that in three minutes your resolve will be gone. In five, I'll have your intestines hanging from your stomach and dripping blood on the floor. Then I'll make you watch as I cut them apart, piece by piece by piece. But that won't be the end of you. No, your suffering's going to continue for as long as I want it to. I can tell you're not afraid of death, but you should know that there are two ways to go: the easy way and the very, very hard way."

Whatever rashness or apathy or heroism I'd felt before was gone. I was afraid. I knew the man wasn't joking. And he was right. I didn't fear death, but I didn't wish to die like that. My eyes wandered from the special emissary to Yuan Xile, my mind replaying torture scenes from various movies I'd seen.

A visible change must have come over me, for the special emissary smiled. "So then, what'll it be?" he said. "I've got a point, haven't I?"

I took deep breath. I couldn't help but give a grim laugh. I wasn't laughing at myself. I was laughing at the man standing in front of me. As scared as I'd been, in this moment I realized things were actually very simple. Either way I was going to die. Now all that mattered was saving face. After all, Yuan Xile was here. I couldn't give in too easily. Suddenly, I had an idea. Just the thought of it was terrifying, but pulling it off would be a thrill. With a smile, I said, "You still don't understand the situation, do you?"

"What do you mean?"

"I'm not afraid of death. There's no use in threatening me." I looked over at Yuan Xile. "That said, we might be able to make a deal."

With a smug look, the special emissary turned and glanced back at Yuan Xile. Then he once more met my eyes. "What kind of deal?"

"I'll tell you what you want to know, but I want it to be Yuan Xile who cuts me open. If you agree, then give her the knife."

For a moment the two of them just stared at me. Then the special emissary spoke. "If you think that because she's a woman she won't be able to do this, then you're wrong. Yuan Xile is far more ruthless than I."

"That's not the point. You wouldn't understand anyway. Just do as I say and you'll get what you want." I glanced back at Yuan Xile. She was watching me closely, probably looking for cracks in my façade. I smiled at her. Revenge was delicious. I knew she'd never find the least bit of cowardice in my expression.

The special emissary's eyes flashed with anger. He rushed at me and sliced open my shirt. "My apologies, but I'm the one who makes the rules here. In a moment, the contents of your stomach will be staining the concrete— and I will be doing the cutting. Then we'll see just what exactly I wouldn't understand."

"Fine," I said, "but I will tell you nothing. Try it if you don't believe me."

The special emissary pressed the tip of the dagger against my stomach, not so hard as to draw blood, but almost. He looked at me. I took a deep breath, held it in then calmly met his gaze. I nodded for him to go ahead.

His face contorted into a mask of rage. Just as he was about to strike, Yuan Xile suddenly called out, "Wait!" She walked over and plucked the dagger from his hand. The special emissary sighed and turned away.

I was elated. This was exactly what I'd been hoping for. Yuan Xile squatted down in front of me. Her slender fingers gripped the dagger. She brought its blade to rest against my neck. "Useless, it doesn't need to end like this. We can still give you a way out."

I listened to the sound of her voice. Her tone was warm and encouraging. I'd often heard her speak like this during her days as squad leader. I just shook my head. Tears began to run down my face. "There's no point," I said, looking into her eyes. "It's too late now. You saying this won't change anything. So just do it. There are things I need to say to you that I can only say just before I die."

She stared at me, shocked and uncomprehending. It took her a long time to respond. "You're...not crying for yourself, are you? No, I can tell. You're crying for me. Who are you? And why is it that when I look into your eyes, all I see is pity?"

62 PITY

Yuan Xile's question hung in the air. For a moment I really did want to respond and say, Yes, you're right. It is pity, but not pity for you. Pity for the future that you and I will experience together. But as soon as that word crossed my mind, something inside my head sparked.

Pity?

My thoughts stopped in their tracks. Suddenly, it was as if I was seeing double, as if the Yuan Xile standing before me had split into two identical women: one a steely-eyed spy, the other my Xile, a woman from a different time and place. I remembered the sentence etched on the bottom of the watch, the delicate Kirovskie, that Yuan Xile had given me: "You must always pity me, no matter what I become."

I gave a start. "Wait!" I cried, and not a moment too soon. Although hesitant, Yuan Xile had already drawn back the blade and was about to strike. At the sound of my voice, she froze and looked at me, even more perplexed than before. "Please," I said, "I still need a few minutes to think."

A river of information flooded my brain. I considered one strange thought after another, but none seemed to offer any clues. Finally, with the suddenness of revelation, I hit upon the crux of the matter. "What will be will be."

To ensnare me with this sentence, Yuan Xile had to know of its existence in the first place. Given our current situation, it seemed highly unlikely that I would ever tell her about it. Who could have told her? Was there really anyone else besides me who knew about it? No, there clearly was not.

It was then that I once more recalled the moment we first ran into Yuan Xile. She'd been wandering the underground river, entirely alone. Yuan Xile and the special emissary were a team. They'd come here together, would search for the frozen film together, and should eventually leave in kind, but that didn't seem to be what had happened. We found the special emissary still in the warehouse, obviously looking for the film. Something must have come between them. These two were hardened professionals. The split wasn't some personal problem. Whatever caused the rupture must have been something much more serious, something like betrayal. Two things were apparent. First, it must have been me who told Yuan Xile about "What will be will be", which meant I wasn't going to die here. And second, the relationship between these two spies was about to turn ugly.

But with the way things were going, five minutes from now I'd be staring at my intestines as my life passed before my eyes. What could I do to stop this from happening? It wasn't as if Yuan Xile was going to suddenly turn around, knock the special emissary unconscious and untie my hands, saying, "Comrade, you've no idea how long I've wanted to do that."

I watched Yuan Xile's dagger, thinking of those five words carved on the wall of the safe room, and of that sentence—"You must always pity me, no matter what I become"—etched on the underside of Yuan Xile's watch. Regardless of whether Yuan Xile had planted these clues for me or if I'd left them myself, the intent was the same: to convince me to involve myself in this history. The first sentence had persuaded me to return underground. The second had just informed me that the situation was about to change drastically. But if all of this was inevitably going to occur, why did I need that watch clue? With the first clue, it was important that I not only find it, but also understand its significance and act accordingly. So what if this assumedly imminent, supposedly drastic change was not some automatic occurrence? What if, having properly understood the second clue, I was meant to somehow make it happen? But what did I need to do to bring it about?

I had no idea and, at this point, I could only do my best to survive. This is crunch time, I thought. I looked up and saw Yuan Xile staring at me, baffled. I smiled. "All right. I'll talk. I've thought things through. Whatever you want to hear, I'll say it." Yuan Xile just kept looking at me, her expression unchanged. I waited a few seconds. "Like I said, I've come around. So long as you don't kill me, I'll tell you everything."

Still she was silent. She turned and looked back at the special emissary. He appeared just as confused. Suddenly, her eyes red with fury, she lunged at me and pressed her dagger hard against my neck. "Useless! Are you messing with me?"

I shook my head. "I'm serious," I said. Yuan Xile glared at me, her normally pretty features now cold and hard as a sheet of ice. I was afraid she might slice my windpipe out of sheer temper, so I quickly spoke up. "You two are looking for a film canister, right?"

The special emissary's face lit up. He pulled Yuan Xile off of me, grabbed the dagger from her hand and placed it on the table. He pointed at me. "You," he said, "are quite a character. So much for what you said about this guy being untrained. If you ask me, even you're no match for him."

With an audible smack, Yuan Xile slapped me across the face. The blow stung, but I just looked at her and laughed.

Su Zhenhua was undeterred. "How did you learn this information?" he asked.

"This I cannot tell you, but it wouldn't matter to you anyway. What I can say is where the object is located."

"I'm listening," he said, his eyes fixed on me.

"I'm assuming you looked at a blueprint of the dam before arriving here, which means you should also know that at the bottom of this place is an extremely large icehouse." I watched as they glanced at one another. "After the Japanese troops parachuted into the abyss, the rest of those on the plane returned to base with a film of their journey. That film is now in the icehouse. The only problem is that it's frozen beneath the ice."

The special emissary looked at me for a long time, lost in thought. "Even the airdrop you knew about. Just who are you?"

"You wouldn't believe me even if I told you. Anyway, that's hardly the extent of my knowledge. I also know, for example, that in a little while you're going to kill Yuan Xile to cover your tracks." I fixed my eyes on the special emissary. There was only the dim light of the flashlight beam, and I may have imagined it, but I thought I saw him twitch. I still remembered how Yuan Xile viciously attacked the spy in the poisoned passageways. It was obvious there'd been a split and right now Yuan Xile about to strike. I also figured that simply saying this prophecy aloud should be enough to get things started. After all, women are naturally distrustful.

Silence descended upon the room. For some time neither of the spies spoke. It seemed I'd hit upon a sore spot. At last the special emissary responded. "Nonsense. If you're trying to sow discord, you can save your breath. Yuan Xile and I are in this together. We need one another to survive."

"You don't have to hide it," I said. But when I glanced over at Yuan Xile, she merely gave me a cold smile.

"You really think I'll believe you?" she asked.

My heart fell, but it was too late to stop now. "I have proof. If you come over here, I'll whisper it to you."

The special emissary shook his head. "Don't listen to him. The guy's got a silver tongue."

I gazed at Yuan Xile, praying for her to believe me. If she came closer it meant I still had a chance. For a moment she hesitated. Then, just when she seemed about to walk over, the special emissary stepped in front of her.

"What's the matter?" she asked him. "You got a guilty conscience or something?" She pushed him out of the way, turned to the side and lit a cigarette. She took several deep puffs, then fixed me with a sinister glare. She strode over and whispered, "Speak!"

As the scent of her body flooded my nostrils, I began softly. "First, you need to believe me, otherwise you don't have a chance of getting out of here alive. You don't know it, but only one person is meant to survive your mission—and it isn't you. I know a lot of information about you, information from a source very close to you. I was sent here to help." She tried to move away, but I just kept right on talking. "I know about the moles on your back," I said, quick as I could. "I know you have three and where they're located."

Yuan Xile paused, shivered, then reared back and slapped me across the face. "Bullshit!"

My cheek instantly went numb.

The special emissary looked as surprised as me. "I told you not to listen to him," he said.

Yuan Xile turned to face him. "Go investigate the icehouse and see if this guy's telling the truth. If he's not, we're killing him when you get back."

The special emissary nodded. "All right, but you be careful. There's no way he's the only one here."

Yuan Xile watched him go. Then she untied my hands, lifted me from the floor and slammed me against the table. "How the hell did you know about all of this?"

The pain in my shoulder was so bad I nearly fainted. I gritted my teeth. "Do you believe me or not?"

"Answer my question and I might."

"There's no time. Now that I've said something he's going to act sooner than planned. He's probably right outside this room, waiting for his opportunity. If you want to live you need to trust me."

She shook her head, about to say something, but a figure suddenly appeared in the doorway. Without thinking, I grabbed Yuan Xile and rolled both of us off the iron desk. At the same instant I heard the rapid-fire roar of a machine gun. Sparks flew in all directions as bullets struck iron.

"Turn off the flashlight!" I yelled.

Yuan Xile pulled out her pistol, popped up and shot the flashlight from where it sat atop the table. The light spun across the room. I saw someone rush through the doorway and into the dark chamber. I grabbed Yuan Xile and pulled her back down. A fusillade of bullets sprayed the area where she'd just been standing. The shooting stopped. Silence once more descended upon the room. It was short-lived. Yuan Xile seemed to notice something amid the blackness. Without pausing to think, she fired shot after shot in its direction. From my hiding spot behind the desk, I heard our attacker sprint out of the room.

Cursing, Yuan Xile fired a final bullet and yelled in the direction of the doorway, "You son of a bitch! You really were plotting this all along."

"What could I do?" he called back. "These were my orders. Otherwise you'd be much too pretty to kill."

My left shoulder was hurting so much I could barely move my arm. I grabbed Yuan Xile with my right and pulled her down beside me.

"All right," she whispered, "you told me to trust you. Now what's our next move?"

I pointed at a nearby air vent. "We need to get out of here. Your half-empty pistol's no match for his machine gun."

In the darkness her expression was impossible to make out, but I assumed she agreed. I pulled the pistol from her fingers, pushed a chair beneath the vent, and watched her shimmy inside. I turned back towards the door, let off two quick shots and hit the deck as another burst of machine gun fire rattled the front of the desk. When at last the shooting stopped, I quickly shoved the pistol down the back of my pants and followed Yuan Xile into the vent.

The two of us crawled for a long time. At last we reached the electrical canal. Once we were back on our feet, it was obvious Yuan Xile had no idea where to go. I grabbed her hand and led her in the direction of the warehouse. I recognized our surroundings and before long we arrived at the trap door where the spy had once sealed us in. This time, thankfully it was unlocked, but as I climbed out a terrifyingly familiar sound reached my ears—the air raid siren. It was echoing throughout the dam, so loud I could barely think. Not that I needed to, though.

I knew exactly what this meant. I took a deep breath. Things were getting interesting.

63 180-DEGREE TURNAROUND

Yuan Xile's face turned pale. "What's going on?"

"The dam's discharging excess water," I said, cursing beneath my breath. The recent heavy rains had been too much for the dam to bear. As soon as the floodwater hit the floor of the abyss, a toxic mist would rise and enshroud the dam. We were trapped and I only had one hazmat suit left. But I knew exactly where we had to go. I grabbed Yuan Xile's hand and hurried her onwards.

Immediately she pushed me off. "Where are you trying to take me now?"

"We need to hide and I know the perfect place."

"Hide?" Her expression was incredulous. "What are you talking about? The only thing we need to do now is find that son of a bitch and take him out."

"It's too late," I said. I explained to her about the mist. "Also," I continued, "you should know that before long a very large contingent of troops will be arriving here—more than one hundred men in total. When they see you and Su Zhenhua are the only survivors, what are they going to think? How are you going to explain yourself? Who are they really going to believe—you, a woman just returned from the Soviet Union, or their own special emissary?"

Yuan Xile stared at me, not saying a word. She obviously wanted to ask how I knew all of this, but she restrained herself.

"Only the warehouse and the three areas connected to it are safe from the poison. The ventilation system here is specially equipped to filter out the bad stuff, but that bastard is too close and we've got nowhere to hide. There is, however, one other place..." The poisoned passageways, I thought. He'd never look for us there. But when I told her the plan, she frowned.

"What about the poison?" she asked.

"I know a place that's safe. You need to trust me. I have no reason to trick you."

She hesitated for a moment. Then, for the very first time, she firmly gripped my hand. My cheeks went hot. I led her upstairs to the second floor of the warehouse, where we found the iron door leading to the atmospheric purification room. It was unlocked. Once inside, I located the correct airshaft. Then we crawled all the way back to the poisoned passageways—that place of love and nightmares.

All the lights were off, but just to be safe I had Yuan Xile wear the hazmat suit while I covered my face with a piece of clothing. We followed the winding corridors through the darkness. At last we arrived at the flooded hallway. I waded through the water and we climbed into the room. It was like reentering an old dream. Turning a slow circle, I scanned my surroundings. Ah yes, I thought, I'm really here. I sat down on the bed and glanced over at Yuan Xile.

After taking in the unfamiliar surroundings, she turned to look at me. "All right," she said, "now that we're here, why don't you tell me who you really are?"

"If you insist," I said. "Though allow me to make another prediction. You are not going to believe what I'm about to tell you." I removed my shirt and looked at the wound. It was crusted over with blood, but the bullet was gone, having entered just above the armpit and exited the other side. Breathing a sigh of relief, I dipped my shirt in the stagnant water and wiped my shoulder clean. I looked back up at her. "If you're really ready to listen, I'll tell you what you have to do. I can get you out of this, out of the life you've been living, but it won't be easy." I told her the whole story, from its very beginning up till right now. Nothing was omitted.

The expression she wore when I reached the end matched my expectations exactly. It was more than simple disbelief. It was the look one wears when faced with a mental patient.

"You really think I'll fall in love with you?" She gave a short, humorless laugh. "In your dreams. But you were right about one thing: I don't believe a word of what you've just said."

Reaching into my pocket, I pulled out the watch she'd given me.

Her eyes went wide. Snatching it from my hand, she compared it to the one on her wrist. "I've never seen a watch like this in stores," I said. "I doubt they're available to just anyone." Keeping her eyes fixed on the watch, she slumped onto the bed. "Ivan gave me this."

I looked at her. "Doubt me all you want, but how else could I know this many secrets about you?"

She thought about it, but still she shook her head. "I don't believe you," she said, burying her face in her hands. "This is impossible."

Squatting down in front of her, I looked into her eyes. My heart ached. To Yuan Xile, everything we'd experienced together was no more than some baseless fantasy. "In the end you don't have to believe me," I said, "but for your own sake you'd better do what I tell you. Once this thing gets started, you'll see everything I said was true."

At first she was silent. Then she sighed and nodded her head. "Okay. What do you want me to do?"

"First I want you to tell me what your objectives were, all of them. Your superiors have already betrayed you. Even if you don't trust me, there's no reason to hide this stuff. I need to get an idea of what the special emissary's next moves will be."

Staring straight at me, she began. "We came here for two reasons. The first was to find that film you mentioned, but the second, the more important one, was to send a message."

A message?

Yuan Xile then told me how she'd been a member of the final Japanese contingent sent to the Northeast as part of the 53 Plan. At the time she'd been no more than a child. Before she could even begin her training, the Japanese were defeated. She was left in a Chinese orphanage, where she lived until the day she joined the PLA's Geological Division. It was the special emissary who'd recruited her for this assignment. This was her first mission for her homeland. I knew she'd had no other choice. Her identity had determined her fate. Now it seemed her first mission would also be her last.

As for the message, she had no idea what information it was meant to contain. The special emissary had handled that part. She had, however, been privy to the maps and blueprints provided by their contacts in Japan. They'd studied these intensely. When their plan was finally set, they joined up with the 723 Project and entered the wilderness. Never once had she expected things would turn out like this.

I recalled how the fake He Ruping had snuck through camp in the middle of the night and descended into the abyss. Had he been trying to send a message? The special emissary's body had never been found. Was the fake He Ruping actually the special emissary? And what the hell was in that message, and to whom was he sending it? My God, I thought, could this mean that people really were living down there? Had Pei Qing been right all along?

"What is it?" asked Yuan Xile, giving me a curious look.

I brought myself back to reality. "Okay, I'm going to tell you the plan. For your sake you'd better not forget a single word."

***

I spelled it out for her, everything we were going to have to do, while at the same time piecing the details together in my head. I realized now that things were not quite as predetermined as I had imagined. The clues I had left for myself could merely point me in the right direction. They could not force my hand. Had I not returned here to convince Yuan Xile of the special emissary's deceit, she'd already be dead. My actions had changed her fate. I could not simply allow things to happen on their own. I could no longer tiptoe around the action, dispensing veiled pieces of advice while trying not to get over-involved. I needed to take heart and act.

I then thought back on everything that had happened since I first entered the cave. At each critical juncture in my journey, someone had pushed me onto the right path. First there was the sinkhole, which we'd entered for no reason other than for a strange note I'd found in my pocket. Who'd planted it there, I wondered, and when? Then, after we were trapped in the caisson, who'd started it up and dropped us into the icehouse? And what about our escape from the projection room? Who'd loosened the screws on the vents that led us to safety? Who'd made the marks on the walls of the poisoned passageways that guided Yuan Xile and me to the exit? Every single time our fate was about to be sealed, someone had prepared us a way out.

That someone was me. It had to be; it could be no one else.

As I told Yuan Xile about the road ahead, I realized we'd have our work cut out for us. If I wanted my future self to survive, there were a great many things I'd need to take care of. None, however, were particularly difficult. All I needed to do was follow the instructions already written into my memories.

When I was finished speaking, I realized Yuan Xile had not understood everything I'd said. This was only natural. It was impossible for someone to digest all that information at once. She didn't need to know the whole plan. So long as she was clear on certain key situations, that would be enough. First, when she encountered the second team in the upper reaches of the cave, she needed to feign madness. Then, after the rest of us left Ma Zaihai, Chen Luohu, and her behind, she needed to lead them back down to the dam to escape the floodwaters. Once they arrived, she'd have to get them to the caisson as fast as possible to avoid the rising mist. Next, after I lowered the caisson into the icehouse, she would need to think of a way to slip out of the iron chamber while the lights were off. I still didn't know how she'd managed to silently escape, but I was sure she would come up with something. Once she was out, she'd need to head to the poisoned passageways and enter the safe room. There she would wait. When at last she heard Wang Sichuan, Ma Zaihai, and I arrive at the great tunnel, she'd return to the room where we found her and begin making noise to draw our attention.

Yuan Xile nodded as I told her what to do, but still she appeared doubtful. "Useless," she said, "what if none of what you said happens? What am I supposed to do then?"

"Trust me. From my perspective, all this stuff has already occurred. It won't change, nor would I want it to."

She stared at me in silence. Suddenly she blurted out, "How do you know this isn't all just a dream?"

I thought for a moment before responding. "Even if it is a dream, for you, at least, it won't be a nightmare." Then, seeing as we were already there, I figured I might as well get to work etching Wang Sichuan's "What will be will be" onto the wall.

Just as I began to walk away, Yuan Xile called out, "Will we really fall in love?"

I glanced back at her, my heart in turmoil. I had once been positive that the answer was a resounding yes. Now I wasn't so sure. Not in my wildest dreams could I have guessed our story would begin like this. "If I am to defeat a man who can reverse a bomber in midair," I said, "my only hope is to reverse the course of Fate. I can't predict your feelings, but I am absolutely certain that I, at least, will fall in love with you."

She studied me in silence, as if mulling over something. I waited, but she said nothing. So I took the dagger from her waistband and waded through the water to the bed against the wall. Splashing through the darkness, I thought of the future that awaited me. Much of it was in my control, but Yuan Xile's feelings were not. Still, I was confident that as each of my prophecies came true, her trust in me would deepen. At the very least she'd follow my instructions well enough to get out of here safely.

I moved the bed out of the way and shined my flashlight along the concrete wall, trying to determine where the words had been before. Suddenly I saw something that stopped me in my tracks. Someone had already carved a line of words onto the wall. I looked closer. "What will be will be."

I nearly fainted. Not only were the shapes of the characters identical, the sentence had even been carved in the exact same place. I looked down at the dagger in my hand. For a moment, I even imagined that I had etched these words myself. What in the hell was going on? Was I really not the one who wrote this sentence?

I ran my fingers over the words, cold sweat trickling down my back. This was wrong. This was wrong. Oh, heaven, it was wrong!

64 ME, MYSELF, AND I

I should have been the one to write these words as a reminder to my future self, but the words I was supposed to write were already there. And they appeared to have been written some time ago. I had no idea what this could mean, couldn't even begin to fathom it. I just stood there, staring at the roughhewn characters and feeling as if my head was about to split open.

The situation had always been complex, but I thought I'd gotten a handle on its ins and outs. Now that I'd discovered these five words, I realized everything I'd been thinking was wrong. From the moment we'd traveled 10 months into the past—something I still believed to be true—everything had fit as it should have. Why was this irregularity appearing now?

Yuan Xile could tell something was wrong. "What is it? Is there a problem?"

I glanced back at her, lost as to how to explain this one. "It's nothing," I replied, but my hands were already beginning to shake.

I took several deep breaths and made myself calm down. Who could have done the carving? Only two people even knew about the sentence: myself and Wang Sichuan. I obviously hadn't written it, had he? Impossible. I hadn't told Wang Sichuan my plans, nor did he know how significant this sentence was to Yuan Xile and me. Even if he had been able to slip into the safe room before me and carve out these words, why would he have wanted to? That would have been far stranger than my discovery of the sentence. Unfortunately, I could think of no other explanation.

I looked back down at my dagger, feeling awkward and unsure. Should I cross out the sentence and write my own? Or simply add an "x2" at the end? What if I did add an "x2?" Would this somehow change the course of events still to come? I figured not, though it would certainly cause my future self to feel a bit puzzled.

I shined my flashlight around the section of concrete surrounding the words. Something caught my eye. I pulled the bed farther into the room. There, near the foot of the wall, several inches below the sentence, was a line of marks; it seemed someone had scraped something off the concrete. As I ran my fingers over the scratches, I realized these had once been words, eight of them in total. Could it also have been some kind of message? If so, then who had written it and who scratched it out?

At last I began to understand that nothing was as simple as I'd thought. All my experiences were just the tip of an iceberg floating in a circular river of time. "What will be will be." Only one person could have written it: me. But I hadn't written it just now. In finding this sentence, had I encountered traces of the true beginning of this entire affair? Did this mean that after my work here was done, I'd once more return to the cave and travel even farther back in time? This was truly a terrifying prospect.

I put the dagger away and sighed to myself. From the looks of things, I didn't yet have what it took to change my fate, but there was no point in worrying about these matters now. Still, I couldn't help but wonder. If a man was meant to change his fate, was this change not merely a part of his fate to begin with? In any case, I could no longer be certain of what would happen next. I was in the same boat as Yuan Xile, able to do no more than proceed one step at a time.

***

I wondered what the special emissary was doing now. He'd said that Little Einstein and the others had managed to escape his trap before the poison fully set in. I remembered finding the old expert's corpse in the sinkhole, his gums black, most likely from mercury poisoning. I remembered Little Einstein in the warehouse and still more of the team in the telegraph room. At this point these people were probably still alive, but severely poisoned. Still, so long as they lived, the special emissary could not ignore them. And this gave us some room to maneuver.

Could I save those who still lived? I knew they'd escaped from this area, but how had the special emissary tricked them into coming inside in the first place? Could he have smoked them out of the projection room, much as he'd done with us? At the time of our escape, the vent covers had already been loosened. If the projection room was merely a ploy to lure the first and second teams into the poisoned passageways, then perhaps the special emissary had loosened the covers himself.

It was the first team's numbers that made the trap necessary. Had the special emissary not tricked them into entering the poisoned passageways to escape the smoke, they probably could have forced open the door to the projection room door. They were never warned of the "ghosts in the shadows." It would have taken them longer to notice the poison, but the special emissary had turned on the lights too early, before they'd traveled too deeply into the poisoned passageways. As a result, the first team was able to survive long enough to climb back into the ventilation shaft, where they were safe within the darkness. When they could assume the special emissary had taken them for dead, they must have escaped back through the projection room.

By the time that the first team escaped, though, they must have already begun suffering the effects of the poison. As their nervous systems went haywire, the remaining men and women would have parted ways. Little Einstein would never be willing to turn tail and run. He'd most likely believed the special emissary had taken Yuan Xile prisoner. He'd then set out to save her and do away with his former superior. He was killed in the warehouse before he could accomplish either task. The old expert, on the other hand, had dearly wanted to live—he was high ranking and had a lot to lose. He'd attempted to escape, but succumbed to the poison in the sinkhole. Then there was the group Old Tang had found in the telegraph room. They'd placed the mission above all personal concerns and, with the little time remaining to them, had attempted to contact the outside world.

I didn't know how these three had managed to find the telegraph room. Perhaps they'd happened upon it before and remembered its location. I was sure, however, that their original message was not what we heard when we picked up the ringing phone in the cement tower. That latter telegram had to have been written by the special emissary himself. He must have found the three prospectors in the telegraph room, killed them and altered their message. His motives remained unclear, but this at least explained why he chose to allow the telegram even after he'd discovered it.

So this was how it had all went down, I was almost sure of it. As a result I knew I didn't have a chance of saving the others. It was already too late to save the old expert and I didn't know where the telegraph room was located. I might have a chance of saving Little Einstein, but since he'd died and the special emissary survived, I knew I'd fail. Of course, I couldn't deny that this was just justification for using my comrades as distractions to keep the special emissary's attention scattered. And because he'd never expect us to hide here, I had more than enough time to take care of a few matters.

First, I marked the walls of the corridors leading both to the great tunnel and to the exit. Because the lights were off, I had to shimmy up the walls and inspect the filament of each bulb to determine whether it would switch on. It was slow going, but eventually I cut a pair of trails that each avoided as many working lights as possible.

Once I was finished, I returned to the safe room and waited. I was delighted that even after all this time, the special emissary had yet to make an appearance. He probably assumed I'd long since departed. I probably would have, too, if it weren't for Yuan Xile and the role she would play in the survival of my second team. Without her interference, we'd likely have died just as swiftly as the ones who came before us. I couldn't just take her and leave. She needed to be coached in what to do.

I waited with Yuan Xile in the darkness for nearly a month. Early on I located a number of bags left in the surrounding corridors. Upon discovering the gas, Little Einstein and company must have dropped their heaviest belongings and run for it. Their cans of food and my bag full of jerky meant we were able to get by rather comfortably.

All traces of our previous intimacy were gone, though. Yuan Xile kept a close watch on me, especially at first, though as the days passed she became accustomed to my presence. When we spoke, which we did often, I told her about Ivan and all he had done, as well as many other things. Most of the time she just listened quietly and I could tell that her attitude toward me was beginning to soften.

From a distance, she seemed no different than my Xile, the woman I'd loved and lain with. Yet as soon as I approached, she instantly became a stranger. Eventually I gave up and we passed our time in the darkness without incident, counting down the days. When at last I decided that the second team would be entering the cave within the week, Yuan Xile and I slipped out of the safe room and started making our way to the surface. We saw no sign of the special emissary. Although I was certain he was somewhere nearby, this place was so big that even if we abandoned all caution, we were unlikely to run into him.

***

After that, everything pretty much went according to plan. I prepared two handwritten notes. One said "beware of Pei Qing," the other "enter the sinkhole." While I was certain of the second note's purpose, the reason for the first remained vague. Why did I need to beware of Pei Qing? All he did was shoot me once and that was just for show. Had I really been the one to write both of these notes? I couldn't say for sure, but I scrawled them on strips of a labor insurance form anyway. Even though I didn't totally understand the warning about Pei Qing, I knew I nonetheless had to slip it into my pocket.

A strange feeling came over me after I finished writing out the note. It seemed to be meant as a subtle nudge, meant not to cause a specific action, but affect the way I approached events. The note's motive was indiscernible. Had I not received the note myself, I never would have conceived to leave one behind. Which was the chicken and which was the egg?

I thought again of the scratched-out words I'd seen on the wall behind the bed. I may have written the notes, but that didn't mean I was the one to get them to their target. Someone was controlling all this, but it wasn't necessarily me. Had someone else really guided all of these events? Perhaps this person had been unhappy with the way things were turning out down here and decided to interfere. He'd involved himself in ways both critical—"enter the sinkhole"—and abstract—"beware of Pei Qing." Who was he? The caution admonished by this second note alone had changed my whole attitude, setting off a chain reaction whose purpose I couldn't begin to grasp.

Such thinking was only making me crazy. So long as I was the one to hand off the notes, things would be much simpler. If the notes had been left by someone else, then I knew that everything I'd experienced was merely part of a much larger plan, one I would be powerless to resist. I preferred to believe the former. Even though I'd begun to believe that the latter was actually occurring, this prospect too terrifying to fully accept. There was no way for me to determine what was really going on. The possibilities were simply too many. Perhaps it really had been Chen Luohu who'd slipped me the first note. I had no choice but to play it by ear.

After passing through a fork in the cave, we found ourselves back beside the tributary upon which my team had first traveled. We marched along it, heading upriver. Hours passed. Suddenly, the sound of rifle fire split the dark air. It was coming from somewhere in front of us. I had found myself.

Sprinting ahead, I soon reached a towering rock wall. A waterfall tumbled down its face. At its bottom lay Big Beard. Pei Qing was atop the cliff, desperately firing his rifle into the sky. I kept my distance. The fallen soldier was wedged amid a pile of rocks. He wasn't moving. I told Yuan Xile to hide behind the waterfall Then I carefully scaled the cliff. By now my future self had already heard the gunshots and was making his way over here as fast as he could. I crept past Pei Qing. I made sure to stick to the shadows, but it didn't much matter. He was far too agitated to pay me any attention. Once I was some distance away, I scurried behind some rocks and watched as the deputy squad leader and his soldiers came running past, followed by Wang Sichuan and me. When the coast was clear, I hurried back to the camp.

I had left my jacket to dry beside the fire. I grasped the "beware of Pei Qing" note and slipped it into the pocket. Just as I was about to leave, I suddenly heard footsteps behind me.

"What's going on?" a voice asked.

It was Chen Luohu. He was on all fours. He'd crawled back after being unable to keep up with the others. Holding his ankle, he climbed to his feet. Although far from a weakling, the guy was not particularly coordinated. For a moment I just stared at him, unable to respond. He didn't seem to notice.

"What's going on?" he asked again. "Why did Old Pei fire his gun?"

I looked off into the darkness, listening to the distant gunshots. "I think someone fell," I said, "but I couldn't keep up with them. When I noticed you were gone, I came back here to look for you."

He pointed at his leg. "I just twisted it little. Don't worry about me. I'm fine."

"Good to hear it." I faked a concerned expression. "I'm going to head back and see what's going on. You wait here." I turned and rushed into the darkness.

After running some distance, I looked back. Chen Luohu was sitting on the ground by the fire, not paying me any attention at all. He hadn't noticed a thing. I stroked my chin in thought. The darkness had certainly been a factor, but it seemed I still looked more or less the same. This would allow me to do far more than I had imagined.

I returned to the edge of the cliff. I hid behind a rock and watched as they retrieved the corpse and carried it back through the darkness. Once they were gone, I climbed down the rock wall, found Yuan Xile, and the two of us climbed back up. We crept towards their camp, making sure not to get too close. We observed from our perch in the darkness. The fire was high and bright. Wang Sichuan and I were relaxing beside it. Yuan Xile grabbed my arm, her fingernails digging into my flesh. I was also staring at the other me. The feeling was indescribable. If only he knew who was gazing at him from out of the darkness. If only he knew all that would soon happen to him.

I glanced back at Yuan Xile. Her moment had arrived. Putting my hand on her shoulder, I signaled for her to remember all I'd told her. Yuan Xile nodded, looking serious. For the first time she finally seemed to trust me. For a moment our eyes met. Then she took a deep breath and turned to go. I couldn't stand it anymore. At the very last moment, I grabbed her arm and pulled her back. Before she could react, I kissed her. Unexpectedly, she made almost no resistance. As our lips parted, I could see a strange glimmer in her eyes, lit by the distant campfire. She gave me a long look, then turned and walked towards camp. She did not glance back once.

I crouched behind a rock and listened to the commotion that followed, knowing exactly what was happening. I felt both nervous and calm at the same time.

After that things were simple. I tailed the second team to the water dungeon and pulled Pei Qing down into the river. Then, when I jumped in to save him, I floated a corpse towards myself headfirst. As my future self began to panic, I slipped the second note into his pocket. I followed myself until I reached the dam. When at last all parties had entered the caisson, I started it up and dropped them into the icehouse.

After that, the rest was up to me.

65 THE WANDERING YEARS

With my tasks completed, I returned to the surface. The old Japanese outpost was now bustling with activity. Trucks ran along the newly-built plank road that encircled the log cabins and wound through the forest. Construction projects were underway and everywhere people were hurrying about. I snuck past camp and began traveling south down the plank road.

I walked for days. About halfway along I ran into Wang Sichuan. He was waiting for me by the side of the road. I was surprised to see him, but had our roles been reversed I would have done the same thing; for not only were we friends, we were now unlike everyone else in the whole world.

"Were you successful?" he asked. I nodded, but said nothing.

After we'd walked for two weeks, a heavy snow began to fall. Luckily, we soon found a tree farm where a small train was loaded up with lumber. We snuck aboard and, when the train reached a wood station, we got off, already so cold we could barely speak. We pretended to be construction soldiers from another tree farm who'd lost their way. The station staff gave us overcoats and some rations and we boarded a larger train to Jiamusi.

There was no such thing as a national surveillance network in those days. Our ID cards and military credentials enabled us to travel wherever we wanted and eat at dining halls in every town and city. Wang Sichuan asked me what I was planning on doing. I said I wanted to return to my hometown in the South, but I knew this was unrealistic. Our best bet was to hide out in a remote village for a while. I suggested we head for the mountain communities near the Daqing oilfields. Geological surveys were still taking place there, so we should have no problem lying low, pretending to be part of the troops.

We checked a map and found a village that could only be reached on foot. Then we exchanged all our belongings for grain coupons and set out. We discovered a wonderfully peaceful little hamlet awaiting us. The people there barely even knew about the war against Japan. Their village was surrounded on all sides by mountains and so remote that none of its men had been conscripted into the army. At the local administrative office we traded some of our grain coupons for various necessities and a room in town. There we waited out the winter. By the time our grain coupons ran out, summer had nearly arrived. A man from the distribution collective arrived in town to take census. We convinced him to sell us a radio and broadcasted dramatic programs for the locals in exchange for food. We headed out of town when the weather grew hot.

Unable to report back to my regular unit, I finally returned home. I told my parents I'd deserted the army after nearly perishing at the hands of the Soviets. My superiors all thought I was dead. Most villagers wouldn't know any better if I made up a war with the USSR. My father was surprised I'd deserted, but I was still his son, so he allowed me to stay for a while and hide out. Back then this sort of thing was actually fairly common. When a war was over, if a soldier was unable to find the rest of the troops, he had no choice but to return to his home village while the army took him for dead. Eventually he had to reapply for ID under someone else's name. My father asked a friend in the military to find an unused identity for me, but there was nothing.

At last, unable to bear the torment any longer, I decided to go find Yuan Xile. I'd already been home for some time, so it wasn't difficult finding a pretext to leave. Although I was heading out onto the open road, I wasn't particularly worried about being discovered. I'd grown a thick beard. No one was going to recognize me. And my military ID meant that as long as nobody checked my credentials too closely, I could eat and ride for free. Given the level of secrecy surrounding the 723 Project, it wasn't going to be easy to find Yuan Xile, but if she was still alive, then I'd find her sooner or later.

Yuan Xile was a Northeasterner, so I went there first. I traveled from city to town to village, visiting nearly every hospital in the region. Even when I wasn't searching I was thinking about her and about those four days and nights we'd spent in the safe room, hiding out from the poison. Our time together had been short, but I remembered each moment perfectly. When I closed my eyes, I could still see her standing before me, clear as day. But when I opened them, she was nowhere to be seen. It was as if she'd vanished from the face of the Earth. No matter where I searched, I couldn't find the slightest trace of her. Eventually I grew frustrated and then finally numb to it all. By the time I ran into Wang Sichuan, after many months on the road, I was certain I'd never see Yuan Xile again.

He too had returned to his hometown, where he once more found work in his father's mine. At this point he was no longer interested in self-advancement. He only wanted to stay in this out-of-the-way place and live peacefully for a time. His father was a powerful man and had no trouble finding his son a new identity. Wang Sichuan guaranteed he could do the same for me, but I politely refused. By then the events that would come to be known as the Cultural Revolution had already begun to unfold. As a tidal wave of activity swept across China, it was difficult to say just what the future held in store. At a time like that, it seemed better not to try anything.

I told Wang Sichuan of my fruitless search for Yuan Xile. He suggested she'd most likely ended up in a military hospital, after which her family must have come and taken her home. But Yuan Xile was an orphan. It was up to her military unit to look after her, which meant they'd probably placed her in a local psychiatric hospital.

Yuan Xile's unit was headquartered in the South. There I traveled from hospital to hospital, asking if they had a patient named Yuan Xile and stalking the corridors to see for myself. She was nowhere to be found. In fact, the name Yuan Xile was so unusual I never came across another like it. By the end, I began to feel as if fate was toying with me. Still I continued on, numb from my failure, yet unwilling to give up.

At last, I arrived at the Shuangliu Psychiatric Hospital on the outskirts of Chengdu. By then it was winter. I had already been searching for two years. This was my final stop in Sichuan and I was anxious to keep going. Winter in Chengdu was notoriously freezing and that day an icy rain was falling from the sky.

I had just presented Wang Sichuan's father's letter of introduction and had started down the hall towards the patients' quarters when I saw a woman standing beside a window with her back to me. She was watching the rain. Even from a distance I could see her face dimly reflected in the glass. I walked over and tapped her on the shoulder. She turned.

Our eyes met. I wanted to speak, but in that moment, I found I couldn't say a word.

EPILOGUE

That was my story. Specifically, it was the story of my youth. Over the last few turbulent decades, these memories of fear and love and adventure burrowed deep into my subconscious. All along I expected that, sooner or later, they would be worn away and forgotten. However, in writing this tale, I found that once I located them and blew the dust from their surface, it felt as if the events took place only yesterday. I'm sure this story is difficult to believe. Many people have asked me whether it's really true, whether there really was a 723 Project and an enormous void beneath the forests of Inner Mongolia. Although I want to give a simple answer, I cannot. Now that you've finished reading, though, I feel the question should no longer matter.

At the beginning of this tale I warned you to take what follows as mere fabrication. In this I had no choice. When events are barred from the history books, who would dare say they are real? So I must ask you not to investigate anything I've said here. You will find nothing but trouble.

Of course, mine is not the only book that purports to tell the truth through a veil of fiction. This is fine. I did not write this story to be unique or to make others believe. I did so because, for me, this is far more than just a story. It is a memory of the best years of my life and the greatest people I have ever known.

Perhaps some of you will want to know what happened with me and Yuan Xile, but I feel that is also unimportant. For in that final moment, as I stood before the window with the rain falling outside, I realized a truth about the world. There's no reason for so much of what happens in a lifetime. Events don't occur because of some past action or to precipitate a future one. They just occur. And if anything matters, it is the moments themselves, not what comes next. If you and another person have ever shared a moment like this, you will understand what I mean.

***

Four years later, I obtained a new identity and once more passed the test to become a prospector. Two years after that, I was transferred to a local school to lead their training course for future prospectors. The Cultural Revolution was already in full swing and China was a dangerous place. Wang Sichuan and I no longer even communicated for fear of being found out. Still, fate wasn't quite done with me yet.

For a long time I tried to learn what happened to the 723 Project, but all I found was that it had ended in 1965. Yet I was certain that the story wasn't over, that some sign would eventually appear and force me to return to the cave. But although I waited, nothing came.

Then, in my second semester as a teacher, a new student joined my class. He said he was here for a final assessment before going to the Northeast to join something called the 347 Project. Prospecting work up there had begun winding down and, though I'd heard 347 was supposed to be enormous, it was meant to be the final wrap-up for the region.

The student took his seat. I glanced down at my attendance sheet. There was his name, all the way at the bottom: Mao Wuyue, 28-years-old.

I rubbed my eyes and looked at it again. Could someone else really have the exact same name? For some reason, no matter how crazy it sounded, I knew it had to be him. That afternoon I made a point of sitting near him in the dining hall. His face was familiar, although much younger. He didn't recognize me at all.

When he saw I was watching him, he gave me a curious look and asked, "Teacher, is there something you wanted to tell me?"

I studied him for a long moment before replying. "Yes. More than you can possibly imagine."

That was my story.

POSTSCRIPT

Hello everyone, I am Nanpai Sanshu (Xu Lei).

Please accept my apologies for taking so long to finish this series. These two novels were supposed to be no more than a single novella, but the more I wrote, the more I liked the material, until at last it became the story you just read. In fact, now that I think about it, this series is my first complete work. I finally "filled the pit," as they say[3]. Since I've never finished a series before, I've never had the opportunity to write a postscript. Now that I'm finally done, there are a few things I want to say.

Dark Prospects was an odd series to write. My ideas about where it was going were different at the beginning, middle and end. As time passed, the things I wanted to express changed as well. At first, it was merely a very strange adventure novel. Later on, I discovered I could transform it into a story unlike anything I had anticipated.

---

3 In Chinese Internet parlance, long web novels, such as the Dark Prospects series, are known as "pits." When an author begins writing a web novel, he has started "digging the pit." When a reader begins reading a web novel that has not yet been completed, he has "fallen into the pit." When the author posts a new chapter, he has begun "filling the pit" or "shoveling dirt." When the novel is complete, the pit is now "level." And if the author heartlessly decides to betray his readers and cease updating his story, he has "abandoned the pit."

When I finished writing Dark Prospects: Search for the Buried Bomber, I considered what direction I should take the series. Should its structure be open-ended, with strange event following strange event, or deliberately sealed, with a definitive conclusion? I chose the latter because I wanted to try writing a story in which every detail ties together. Normally this technique is only attempted from the third person. Trying it from the first, in which the "I" is doing the writing, surely amounts to a kind of self-torture. Still, I hope this experiment turned out well and you enjoyed reading it.

I have always felt that, with fiction, it is better to drop a few clues than to spell everything out for the reader. A novel isn't a textbook, after all. I have found, though, that many people are accustomed to having the author himself dispel all mysteries, and won't be satisfied otherwise. Therefore, I have decided to list a few of the official possibilities concerning the events of the book:

Yuan Xile and the special emissary were enemy agents. Their mission was to transmit a telegram into the abyss. After sabotaging both prospecting teams, the special emissary entered the abyss and made his way to the signal tower. Because he knew about the superheated atmosphere at the bottom of the abyss, he was wearing a special heat-resistant suit. He was stealing the ID card and supplies from one of the near-dead soldiers in the tower when he was discovered and chased back to the cable. A fight broke out and the special emissary's suit was torn, exposing him to the hot steam. The other soldier, who was already severely burned, died atop the cable. In his final moments he tried to destroy the cable, but perished before he could finish the job. All parties involved in this incident died or fell comatose, so the narrator could never have known what happened.

As for that enormous statue, it was created by an ancient civilization. Just as Pei Qing said, it eventually fell underground during an earthquake. (Initially I wanted them to discover Megatron!)

What force was hidden within that vast abyss? In the area beyond the statue there existed an asymmetrical relationship between space and time, causing the latter to flow backwards and an entire Shinzan to be transported many months into the past.

What were the Japanese after? At first they were in the cave only to mine mercury, but once they discovered the abyss, they became curious as to what was inside. They built a fighter plane and flew in to find out. The plane passed through the time vortex and when it returned the Japanese may not have even completed construction of the dam. Perhaps, just as they had finished hauling the parts for the plane underground, the thing itself came flying out of the abyss. From this it wouldn't have been hard for them to figure out what happened. That's why they lined the river with buffer bags: because they knew that, at any time, another plane could emerge from the darkness. This put them in a difficult—and rather absurd—situation. Say the Japanese officers held a meeting to plan for an upcoming flight. Who was to say that, halfway through the meeting, the plane they were preparing to fly wouldn't come soaring back out of the abyss?

Before the Japanese could fully explore the abyss, their nation surrendered. Undaunted, they still managed to parachute a group from a bomber into the abyss, research supplies in tow. They also set to building a runway on the first level of the abyss, but before they could complete it, something unexpected happened and they left. The base still had not been discovered, so whatever caused them to clear out must have occurred underground. I leave it up to you to determine what this was, for I have left more than enough hints throughout the books. I could never come right out and say what happened. That would entail the narrator deducing this information himself, which I find highly unlikely. I could also tell you the answer now, but that would be much too easy.

There is, however, no need to investigate the source of the lights in the abyss, or the question of whether the Japanese survived down there. The thing that makes this underground world interesting is that anything is possible. That said, if you find this response unsatisfying, if you insist on being logical, then only one thing could really be down there: rocks. That's right, nothing but rocks. What answer could be more logical than that?

I'm sure you have many other questions, for example: To save Yuan Xile, how many times did the narrator have to travel back in time? What ended up happening to the 723 Project? How many other things were going on behind the scenes of this simple yet complex story? And what was the meaning of those scraped-off marks on the wall of the safe room? If you've read carefully, you should be able to guess the answers to these questions, though I haven't left things black and white. I'm sure by now you've realized I could have eliminated all this suspense by making things clearer in the story itself, but had I done so, the series would have lost that air of mystery that makes you ponder what happened even after the book is over. In this style I'm not alone. There's a recent movie in which it is left unclear whether a top will finally stop spinning—and everyone ends up with different opinions. My intent isn't to leave you unfulfilled, but to give you something to chew on.

On another note, I imagine there are some who will feel the love story in this book isn't a "real" love story. To this I say that, for the majority of men, their first time falling in love was probably a good deal as I described it. Given how unrealistic most fictional romances are these days, I'd say getting to read a fairly authentic one is actually a pretty good deal.

Thank you everyone. I hope my explanations were neither too complex nor too simple.

Nanpai Sanshu(Xu Lei)

12/10/2010

ABOUT THE AUTHOR

With over a million subscribers to his microblog and five million books sold, Xu Lei is one of China's most popular and highest grossing novelists. Born in 1982, he was inspired by his parents' travel stories to write fanciful tales about tomb raiders, which he then posted online. The series became Secrets of a Grave Robber, which now boasts eight volumes in print, three of which have been published in English. Search for the Buried Bomber, the first book in the Dark Prospects series, was hailed as China's most spectacular suspense novel of 2010. Xu Lei currently lives in Hangzhou, China.

Made in the USA
Monee, IL
05 February 2022

90651444R00223